"BRILLIANT."
San Francisco Examiner & Chronicle

Please turn the page for more reviews. . . .

"OUTSTANDING."
Booklist

"[A] stunning tale of a serial killer loose in the city's self-help groups. In her incisive characterizations of Policewoman Skip Langdon and of New Orleans itself, Julie Smith proves herself to be a wise and wonderful novelist."

SHARYN McCRUMB

"Great premise. Great promise. Solid follow-through. Nobody gets inside her characters like Julie Smith.

LINDA BARNES

"THE AXEMAN'S JAZZ is a socially acute, powerfully character-driven entertainment. And in Skip Langdon, Smith has one tough, sharp-tongued cookie."
The Oxford Reviews

"[A] very smart and appealing story . . . A fast-moving plot . . . with a powerful emotional ending."
San Jose Mercury News

Also by Julie Smith:

NEW ORLEANS MOURNING*
HUCKLEBERRY FIEND
TRUE-LIFE ADVENTURE
TOURIST TRAP
THE SOURDOUGH WARS
DEATH TURNS A TRICK*
DEAD IN THE WATER*

*Published by Ivy Books

THE
AXEMAN'S
JAZZ

Julie Smith

IVY BOOKS • NEW YORK

Ivy Books
Published by Ballantine Books
Copyright © 1991 by Julie Smith

Library of Congress Catalog Card Number: 91-19064

ISBN 0-8041-0954-0

This edition published by arrangement with St. Martin's Press, Inc.
Manufactured in the United States of America

First Ballantine Books Edition: September 1992

FOR VICKY BIJUR AND CHARLOTTE SHEEDY

Acknowledgments

Thanks, as usual, to Betsy Petersen and this time to William Petersen as well; also to Rhoda Faust, Becky Alexander, Chris O'Rourke, Carolyn Shaffer, Jon Carroll, Diane Angelico, and the knowledgeable staff in the accident room at Charity Hospital, especially Scott Slayden, Dr. Paul Brunik, and Dr. Eric Lucas. More thanks to John Taylor at Atascadero State Hospital, Bob Bunn and Belinda Maples of the FBI, Luisah Teish, author of *Jambalaya*, which I enjoyed and relied on, and to numbers of helpful if necessarily anonymous folk in various twelve-step programs. Special, extra thanks to Captain Linda Buczek of the New Orleans Police Department, who is exceedingly patient and prodigiously generous with her time and expertise. If I got things wrong, it certainly isn't the fault of anyone whose name appears here.

One

NEW ORLEANS COULD wreck your liver and poison your blood. It could destroy you financially. It could shun you or embrace you, teach you tricks of the heart you thought Tennessee Williams was just kidding about. And in August it could break your spirit.

It was the steady diet of cholesterol and alcohol that got your body, the oil glut that had hit the economy. The weather did the rest. If you could tolerate the heat and the damp, the lightning changes in the atmosphere, indeed, if you took to them, you could get addicted. If you didn't, you didn't belong.

If you were one of those who did belong, you could know the fragile sweetness of love on a rainy morning, the feral taste of lust on a stormy afternoon, the randy restlessness that travels through the air with the scent of ozone.

But sometimes in August, when the city had been a sauna for months, when the unmoving air seemed as toxic as that of Pluto, everything seemed to stink and so did everyone. And you couldn't move.

You couldn't make a phone call, you couldn't do your filing, you had no ambition, the simplest chore was too much.

And that was with air conditioning. Skip Langdon wondered what kind of hellhole the city had been before it was invented.

She had just come back from lunch and her ankles were

swollen. Some said it was the salt in the seafood that did it, some said just the heat. She'd noticed it sure as hell didn't happen in winter.

But no problem. In two days she'd be out of here. A line from an old song—"California Dreamin' "—popped into her head. It was about winter, but it perfectly described her state of mind. In the Crescent City the bad season was summer. Though her head was full of sea breezes instead of smog, at the moment even L.A. in a smog alert seemed preferable to New Orleans in August. And Skip had a tolerance for the heat, almost liked it.

She was aware that the fact that she'd be seeing her friend Steve Steinman probably played no small part in her wanderlust. She'd met him here at Mardi Gras and hadn't seen him since. Would he be different on his own turf? Did he live in a sterile condo or a funky old house? (Whatever it was, it couldn't be any worse than her studio on St. Philip Street.) Was he a good housekeeper? (She hated a man who wasn't.)

Was she really in love with him, or had they just gotten caught up in the moment? She felt absurdly adolescent about this vacation.

Or at any rate, she supposed she did. She hadn't dated in high school, had been too tall, too fat, too confused, and probably, to the other kids, too weird. Of course she'd been to Miggy's and Icebreakers, sixth-grade dancing school and seventh-grade subscription dances—every McGehee's girl had. But the "normal" course of events hadn't materialized.

She smiled—rather nastily—as she imagined how much that must have chagrined her social-climbing parents. It had so chagrined her at the time she hadn't noticed the neat revenge in it. But in the end, they'd won—they'd worn her down to the point she'd agreed to make her debut. If they'd known she'd end up a cop, they probably would have saved their money.

The phone jangled her out of her reverie and she saw that

she'd doodled a pathetic paraphrase, "August is the cruelest month," without realizing it.

"Langdon. Homicide."

She might be semi-conscious, but she wasn't dead yet. It still gave her a thrill to say that, to listen to herself proclaiming what she was, to feel she'd made it in her hometown. Informally, she was a detective now, and she had been for a month. Technically, she was still a patrol officer, since "detective" wasn't a rank in the New Orleans department, just a description.

At Mardi Gras, she'd been a rookie walking a beat (literally walking—VCD, the Vieux Carré District, was the only walking beat in town). A week later she'd almost resigned—and now here she was in homicide. She still only half believed it.

It was the desk officer on the phone. Some French Quarter apartment manager had had some kind of crazy suspicion about one of his tenants. Two guys from VCD had responded and found a body.

That was bad. She was the only one in the office and her vacation started in two days. Her sergeant, Sylvia Cappello, had tried not to get her in too deep before she left—most homicides that weren't solved in the first week didn't get solved—but it looked as if the plan might have backfired.

It was an old building, poorly kept, the real-estate market being so soft no one could afford to fix anything up.

One of the VCD guys was smoking out front, making Skip long momentarily for her uniform. (She'd had to buy clothes for her transfer, having had hardly a rag in her closet before it came through.) At the moment, she was wearing a basic-black skirt—she'd bought three of them—with a beige silk blouse and a pair of flats. She had had the courage not to wear heels, but a rare moment of social insight had suggested she really couldn't skip pantyhose. So at the moment her legs felt like sweaty sausages.

3

"Hi, I'm Langdon."

The uniform smiled. He was cute. "Apartment four."

She hoped to God the AC was on.

A man called down the stairwell, "Are you a friend of Linda Lee's?"

She shook her head, tried to look friendly as the old guy came into view. "I'm from homicide." She showed her badge.

He looked nearly eighty, thin, with shrunken shoulders. He frowned, but not so much, she thought, with displeasure as with the fear of giving it. He reminded her of her grandfather, her father's father back in Mississippi.

He extended his hand. "Curtis Ogletree. I'm the manager. Thought you might want to talk to me."

"Thanks. In a minute I'll knock on your door if I may— I'll just have a look first."

"I better go in with you."

"That's okay. I can handle it."

But he tried to follow her. A true Southern man, she thought, determined to do his duty no matter how unpleasant for himself, how inconvenient for others. By *God*, he was going to be helpful. Her grandfather had driven her nuts, actually removing her paper dolls from her tiny hands, cutting the clothes out himself, never understanding why she screamed in rage and frustration.

Who knew what Curtis Ogletree felt responsible for? Perhaps he didn't think he should leave the owner's property unattended; more likely, he was trying to be gallant, to protect a lady about to be in distress. Perhaps he thought he'd catch her if she fainted. The corners of her mouth twitched even as she soothed and shooed him—he was about five feet nine, 140 pounds; she was six feet tall and didn't tell her weight.

She sighed, closing the door of the woman's apartment— Linda Lee, Ogletree had called her, but Skip didn't know if it was a first and last name or two firsts. Instantly, her gorge

4

rose. Yes, the air conditioner was on, had probably been on for days, but Linda Lee hadn't died today or even yesterday. Skip clapped a tissue over her mouth and nose. Her eyes watered. The door opened behind her, the cute officer's partner arriving, a guy with a beer gut.

"Pretty bad, huh?"

"Why don't you wait outside?"

He shot her a grateful look, and she hoped he'd remember one day when she needed a favor.

She drew close to Linda Lee (if that was her name), a white female adult. Very white indeed. Short hairdo, almost prim. Not much makeup. Her neck had what might be bruises on it, but they were faint, possibly due to lividity. Purge, or white froth, had come out of her mouth and nose. There was no blood, no wounds that Skip could see, and there was nothing around her neck. But there were those marks, as if she'd been strangled. Strangled bare-handed.

She was wearing olive-drab baggy pants and a shirt open over a tank top, as if she were going out at night, expecting a cool breeze off the river. Or perhaps, Skip thought, she had chubby arms and she was self-conscious about them. A small, fashionable black bag was still slung over her shoulder, crossing her chest in mugger-foiling mode. More evidence that she was going out—or she'd already been.

Had she opened the door to her boyfriend, had they fought? Had he arrived with a snootful, to accuse her of cheating on him? Or had she been out and come home with someone who'd strangled her?

Either way, the bag was chilling, struck a perfunctory note that gave Skip goose bumps. No preamble, no foreplay. No signs of a struggle. Just murder. Skip looked at Linda Lee's hands. Surely she had fought her attacker. There would be skin under the nails.

Skip didn't see any. Maybe Linda Lee hadn't thought to scratch, had only grabbed and pulled.

She lay nearly underneath a table just inside the living

5

room. On the table was a lamp, a tray for mail, and a neat pile of books. On the wall above the table was a red *A*, written in what looked like lipstick.

Skip looked around the room—ordinary furniture, on the cheap side; posters tacked to the walls and one old-fashioned landscape, maybe painted by a relative or bought at a garage sale. Nothing special here, but the room was neat and looked cared for. Not the room of a crazy artist, an out-of-it alcoholic, or an obviously disturbed person—not even the room of a free spirit. Not the room of a person who painted on her wall with lipstick.

Why *A*? And why lipstick? To simulate blood? Was it intended to be a scarlet *A* with the same meaning as the original? Skip dismissed the idea as preposterous. She hadn't been in homicide long, but already she found it inconceivable that anyone would make a literary allusion in the midst of snuffing someone. Still, a jealous lover . . .

It was a weird town and the Quarter was plain wacko.

Technically, the victim had to be declared dead before any homicide investigation could start, and then the crime lab had to go over the place and photograph it. But Skip took a cursory look around the apartment. There was only a bedroom and kitchen, both neat, the bed made up, no dishes in the sink. Seemingly nothing out of place. Excellent. Maybe there'd be a calendar someplace with the names of recent dates, maybe letters from a rejected lover.

Skip left the two district officers to wait for the crime lab and went up to see Curtis Ogletree. Green plush overstuffed chairs and sofa shared space with small tables stained a reddish color, possibly to simulate maple. One of the tables had a magazine rack built into it, and one side of the magazine rack was a fake wagon wheel, spokes and all. The furniture seemed nearly as old as he was, or half as old anyway, which would have made it about forty, but it was in perfect condition. Mr. Ogletree had put down a tan rug.

It was a comfortable, masculine room, one in which Skip

imagined Mr. Ogletree spent most of his time. "I've got coffee on," he said.

Coffee! It must be ninety-eight in the shade.

"Great," she said. "I'd love some." She noticed his hands shook as he handed her a cup, and felt a sudden wave of sympathy.

"I'm sorry you had to go through this."

He waved impatiently, shooing the sentiment, his frown growing deeper. "Please. It's my job."

If he's the murderer, no problem. The more he frowns, the more he's lying.

But she knew she was playing mind games with herself; he would probably lie only about how easy it was to do something hard—especially something for someone else, at great inconvenience to himself.

He looked a wreck. His face was drawn, probably with the effort of concealing the loathing and horror he felt.

Maybe it would help him to talk about it.

"Most people don't see dead bodies except lying in coffins in their Sunday clothes. I know it was a shock for me the first time—and it never really got any easier."

His frown was so fierce she wondered if he was going to hit her. His words and voice were gentle: "I guess it's different for men."

She was making things worse.

She took out her notebook, crossed her legs, leaned back, and pretended to give him an appraising look, ever-so-slightly suspicious. She made her voice crisp: "How did you happen to discover the body?"

"A lady from her office came—Lucy McKinnon. I have her number; would you like it?"

"Please."

He rummaged in a pocket and handed over the number. "She said Linda Lee hadn't showed up for work Friday or today and didn't answer her phone or her doorbell. Wanted to know if she'd moved out. I said no, but I'd let her know

7

if I found out anything—that's why she gave me the phone number.

"Then I went down there and knocked on Linda Lee's door myself. Now, I know I'm not s'posed to enter a tenant's apartment without giving notice—I hope I'm not in trouble—"

"Of course not."

"—but Miss Kitty was so pitiful. I could hear her meowin' like she'd lost her best friend right *at* the door, like she knew I was there and she needed to talk to me."

"Linda Lee had a cat?"

"Beautiful white longhair. I just couldn't resist—'course, I did knock first, but that poor animal was just so *pitiful*. All I did was try the doorknob—didn't even have to unlock it. And when it opened I couldn't understand why I hadn't noticed the odor—guess I had and just thought it was garbage. There she was, lying on the floor right in my line of vision. And Miss Kitty was all over me, rubbin' against my legs like I was a hundred pound bag of catnip."

"Did you go in?"

He flushed. "Well, I didn't."

Skip knew what he wanted to hear, and she provided it. "You did exactly the right thing."

"There might have been something. . . ."

"No, there wasn't. You knew she was dead. A ten-year-old kid would have known. Anyway, if you *had* gone in, it would have interfered with the investigation. Where's the cat, incidentally?"

"Oh, I . . . well, I hope I didn't do wrong. I brought her here and fed her. Then she went under the bed and hasn't come out yet. Don't blame her, do you?"

"You had cat food?"

"I, uh . . . gave her some chicken. What's going to happen to her?"

"I guess that'll be up to Linda Lee's relatives. Meanwhile, we could call the humane society."

8

"Oh, no, I'll take care of her. I mean, if that's all right."

"I think that's fine. But I have to ask you something painful, Mr. Ogletree. Did you see the body well enough to be able to identify it?"

"It isn't Linda Lee?"

Skip's heart sank. Not only didn't she know that, she didn't even know who Linda Lee was.

"Well, sir, you're the only person who knows Linda Lee who's seen the body."

Ogletree flushed, obviously once again embarrassed at not having done a good enough job.

"It's okay. Someone else can identify her."

"I'll look again if you like." His frown was two deep slices flanking his nose.

"No need, sir."

"I'll be glad to."

Sure you would, Mr. Ogletree. If ever anyone gave the lie to studies linking stress and early death, it's got to be you. You probably also eat an oyster po' boy a day, never exercise, and drink a six-pack before breakfast. I bet you live to a hundred and twelve.

She said, "Tell me about Linda Lee. What was her full name?"

"Linda Lee Strickland from Indianola, Mississippi. She moved in about six weeks ago, right from Indianola, didn't even have a job yet. Then she went to work for that restaurant-supply place . . . I forget their name."

"Simonetti's."

"Got a good job, she said. I don't really know—maybe she just said that so I wouldn't worry about the rent."

"How well did you know her?"

"Pretty well, I guess. I used to take over little seafood scraps for Miss Kitty and we'd talk awhile. Come to think of it, I guess I could tell you about every cat she ever had and all the cute things they did, but I don't really know much else about her. I sure wish I could help you on that, but I don't think I can."

"Did you meet any of her friends?"

"I never saw anyone there. She was a quiet girl—real good tenant."

"Was she friendly with anyone else in the building?"

"I don't know anything about her personal business."

He spoke so primly Skip suspected the other tenants were men. Sure enough, they were Mr. Davies, who "traveled for" a cosmetics company, and Mr. Palmer, who worked "for the city."

Honorifics only. Curtis Ogletree, you should be in a museum.

After reassuring him once more that he'd done just fine, Skip returned to Linda Lee's. The body was gone; Paul Gottschalk from the crime lab had removed the purse and said she could go through it.

In it was a wallet containing Linda Lee Strickland's credit cards and driver's license, comb, blusher, and address book. No lipstick.

No lipstick? Did the asshole open the bag, take out her lipstick, write the A *on the wall and leave with it? Keep it for a souvenir, maybe?*

"Paul, was she wearing lipstick?"

"You mean you didn't notice?"

"I don't think she was."

"She was. Tiny trace left. Like she'd put it on a long time before and maybe eaten or drunk something that took it off." He sounded bored, nodded at the *A* on the wall. "We're comparing samples."

"Any other lipsticks found in the house?"

He shrugged. "Two or three. Wrong colors, but we're checking anyway, Officer Langdon."

"Excuse me, but do I detect a note of testiness? Am I being pushy or something?"

"Shit." He shrugged again. "It's the heat."

10

Understanding completely (but resenting the fact that he hadn't apologized), she more or less tiptoed around after that, trying to figure out who Linda Lee Strickland had been.

Everything screamed small-town girl without much money or education. A nice respectable girl from a blue-collar family grown into a woman who had to get married or go back to school if she didn't want to live on the edge of poverty the rest of her life.

Apparently, Linda Lee had been working on the former; the only books in the apartment were the ones on the front table, most of which had titles like *Smart Love*. There were two by John Bradshaw on other subjects, but all the rest seemed to be self-help books geared to relationships. Skip sighed. Linda Lee had been Cinderella looking for her prince. But what had she had to offer him?

It was almost eerie how little of herself she'd left in the apartment. There were no magazines, no letters—she had probably gotten her news from television, and phoned her relatives rather than writing.

The address book was the only thing remotely useful—and all it contained were Curtis Ogletree's number, that of Simonetti's Restaurant Supply, and ten or twelve more in Indianola, Mississippi. Neither of the building's other occupants, Mr. Davies nor Mr. Palmer, was home. Skip canvassed neighbors in nearby buildings, those few who weren't sweating it out nine to five, but no one had known Linda Lee, had ever seen anyone of her description, or had heard or seen anything relevant.

So Skip went over to Simonetti's and asked for Lucy McKinnon. McKinnon was an older woman, apparently what passed for an office manager at the small operation, and she seemed to have taken quite a shine to Linda Lee, who'd answered the phone and done clerical work. A "gal Friday" in less enlightened times.

She'd often asked Linda Lee to lunch, but Linda Lee had usually said she "had plans." McKinnon thought that a little

11

odd, since often Linda Lee walked out of the office carrying her brown bag. But not too odd—it occurred to her that Linda Lee couldn't afford to go out for lunch but didn't want to say so. Or perhaps met someone for picnics. McKinnon doubted that, though, because sometimes she brown-bagged it in the rain.

Skip went back to the office, hoping the coroner had had time to notify Linda Lee's next of kin, Mr. and Mrs. Garner Strickland of Indianola, Mississippi.

Two

WHAT DID YOU say to a small-town woman whose daughter had been murdered after less than two months in the big city?

If you were Southern, you said you wished there was something you could say, and please let you know if there was anything you could do. Even Skip knew that and she knew virtually nothing about how to be Southern. You had to say that, when all the while what you really wanted was for her to do something for you. Tell you everything.

As it happened, Skip had found no one was more motor-mouthed than those suffering the first pangs of grief. Later they would talk only about themselves—what they'd been doing when they got the call, how the news had been broken, how they'd reacted. But at this stage they'd talk about the victim.

Linda Lee was a good girl, took care of her baby brother

when she was only six and a half, didn't make straight A's but did well enough, active in the MYF ("that's Methodist Youth Fellowship"), and didn't deserve the life she'd had. Her marriage hadn't worked out and now she was dead.

Skip tried to keep her voice neutral. "She was married?"

"Five years. To Harry Beaver. Everybody liked Harry. He seemed like a wonderful husband for Linda Lee."

"But he wasn't?"

"Well, see, Harry drank. Nobody knew it, of course, because he was always so jolly and nice. I mean we knew he *drank*; we just never saw him drunk. Did you know you can be a complete alcoholic and never get, you know, commode-huggin' or anything? When she told us, that did help explain why she never did get pregnant. I guess if you're always full of booze—oh, well I shouldn't talk about that. And also why he never had no real ambition. Like to broke Linda Lee's heart, though." She stopped to get control. "Oh, that poor, poor girl."

"How long have they been divorced?"

"Oh, I don't even think it's final yet. She filed just before she left town."

"How did Harry take it?"

"Well, he was broken up about it. He just loved that little girl to death."

"Do you know how I could reach him?"

"Oh, are you gon' break the news? Thank you so much— I just don't think I could stand to do that. Here's his number." She rattled it off. "Or else you might try over to the sheriff's office. Harry's a deputy here in Sunflower County."

"Mrs. Strickland, could I just ask you something? Do you know if your daughter had any enemies?"

"Linda Lee? She was the most popular girl in town."

"I see. Then perhaps someone was jealous of her."

"I didn't mean she ran around. I meant people liked her."

"Did she know anyone whose name began with *A*?"

"I beg your pardon?"

"I can't tell you why I'm asking, but it's important."

"First or last name?"

"Either one."

"I sure can't think of anyone, except maybe Tommy Axelrod, used to live next door to us. But he and his folks left town about ten years ago. Linda Lee used to babysit for him. 'Course, she knew his folks too, but that was different."

"Has she heard from Tommy at all?"

"I don't think so."

"Does the letter A mean anything else to you?"

"Nothin' except 'angel,' and that's what my baby was." A freshet of tears drowned her voice.

Skip kept her on the phone long enough to assign Miss Kitty to Mr. Ogletree. Then she phoned the Sunflower County sheriff's department, and got a lieutenant named Mike Bilbo who said Harry Beaver was out. He said Harry was a good officer and didn't have a mean bone in his body, but he hated to see what was gon' happen when he found out somebody'd killed Linda Lee. They'd been living apart for six months before Linda Lee left town, but Harry never could accept it—said Linda Lee'd come back to him, it was just a phase she was going through.

Not only had Harry been at work every day of the last week, but he was reliable as a Japanese car, never did miss a day. Bilbo had personally seen him at church on Sunday and a barbecue Saturday evenin'.

So if he'd killed his ex-wife, he'd have needed wings.

Time to discuss the case with Cappello and Joe, a not unpleasant thought. She called Joe "lieutenant" now, out of respect for his rank, but she still thought of him as "Joe," a friend. A warm friend. He'd turned into the kind of executive who liked to shoot the breeze with his detectives, find out how each case was going, help out when he could, and she looked forward to running things by him, enjoyed the hell out of their rapport.

Cappello wasn't nearly so warm. She was all business,

almost brusque, but she was a dynamite officer. When Skip got her transfer, she'd wanted Cappello for a partner, but had ended up working under her instead. Which was okay. Very much okay. Skip had wanted to learn from her; this way she could do that and still work alone, a situation she cherished sometimes. Skip found she tended to re-invent police work with each new problem, and she didn't always like to be observed. Cappello was a straight by-the-book type who might not appreciate a lot of free-wheeling creativity.

Skip checked with Cappello, then Joe. Both were free and ready to listen. Neither said a word until she got to the part about the *A*. Joe had started to look grim at the mention of the bag slung over Linda Lee's shoulder, and the *A* did even less for his mood.

"I got a bad feeling, Skip. Writing on the wall isn't normal."

She bit her tongue, forebore to say the obvious. She understood what he meant, and murmured, "No."

"Look, girl with a good reputation, in town for six weeks, doesn't know anybody—it doesn't wash. How does a girl like that get killed in her own apartment? If nobody's mad at her, and nobody knows her, who's gonna kill her? Pervert, right? That's bad enough, but she had all her clothes on. All right then, maybe not a pervert. So what's left?"

Skip shifted uncomfortably. "Another kind of crazy."

"Yeah. That's what I'm worried about. Somebody she let into her apartment; somebody who didn't grab her on the street; guy who looks okay to some girl from Mississippi. Where does she meet a guy like that?"

"At a bar maybe. I don't know."

"Okay, a bar. But why'd he kill *her*?"

Skip sighed. "She was there."

Joe wagged his head back and forth, as if to rid it of the thoughts it was generating. "This ain't normal. It just isn't, that's all."

15

"Maybe it was someone she knew—maybe the *A* meant something between them."

"Yeah. And maybe you want to go see your boyfriend so bad your judgment's messed up."

Skip smiled. "Oh, it's not that bad." She produced a snapshot of Linda Lee, taken from an envelope in a vanity drawer. "I thought I could show this around."

"Yeah, but where?"

That was the problem. As an army marches on its stomach, New Orleans staggers on its liver. If every cop in Louisiana were set end to end on a cat's cradle of a bar tour, they still couldn't cover the territory.

"Bars," she said. "But selectively. Maybe she had a favorite near where she lived. Also, I could hit other places in her neighborhood. The corner store, stuff like that."

Joe shook his head. "And hope somebody just happened to see her talking to the murderer? I hate to say it, but I don't see it being very productive. What do you think, Sergeant?"

Cappello shrugged. "Try the neighbors again. That's all I can think of."

"Okay. I'll do it tonight." But it didn't feel like enough. Not by a long shot.

Still, it was a good night to be a cop, to have any assignment at all. She had a great excuse for cutting short her brother's engagement party.

Later, driving to Commander's Palace in a silk dress—as tarted up as she ever got—she thought about what Joe had said when she'd told him that: "You don't want to go? Why not just skip the whole thing?"

He had seemed genuinely puzzled. Would a normal person do that, she wondered? Her relations with her family were so abnormal she didn't have the least idea. Her dad hadn't spoken to her since she enrolled in the academy. Her mother, whose lifetime ambition was to achieve greater and greater social prominence, preferably through her children,

16

had virtually no use for her either. And her brother Conrad was a joke.

New Orleans was a city rife with types, losers, and weirdos, and Conrad didn't fit in—he was a misplaced, latter-day Sammy Glick, clawing his way to who-knew-what in a milieu where ambition was considered almost embarrassing. Skip knew perfectly well he had about as much interest in her as in one of the roaches that skittered over the city's kitchen counters—and as much regard for her. She returned the sentiment.

And yet he'd had to invite her; her mother'd felt obligated to phone and beg her to come; and Skip had known there was no choice. Otherwise it wouldn't look right. The bride-to-be might ask ticklish questions. The Langdons wouldn't look normal.

She wondered what the hell "normal" really was. And why she was helping Conrad with his own egregious social-climbing—for she had every idea that's what the engagement was all about.

She was doing it because she couldn't bear too much more familial disapproval, she thought. Did anyone ever grow up?

Joe must have—he hadn't seen why she couldn't just cash out of the whole sordid affair. But surely that wasn't the usual thing in the South. You did what you did because things had always been done that way and because someone else wanted you to. Not because there was any point in hell in it.

She took a deep breath.

Come on, you wouldn't be a cop if that were true.

She answered herself: *It isn't always true, just too often for comfort.*

Ah, comfort. What about that one? Where did you go to find that one? Out in the stratosphere, she supposed, where "normal" lived. She wasn't going to find it here tonight.

It was a small party—just her family and the bride's—which was going to make it interesting. Her dad really couldn't ignore her without drawing attention to himself,

17

which would brand him the odd man out in front of people he wanted to impress. The Whites were from Baton Rouge, but they were related to the Gilliats, a very important family, the one that Conrad no doubt thought he was marrying into. He had met his betrothed at their house.

Skip's mother had told her Camille had some kind of job at the Gilliats' shipping company, but Skip hardly expected her to rise to CEO. Within two years, she'd bet, she'd be a permanently retired shipping exec and full-time mommy with a wandering eye.

The rest were already seated. That was good. She waved the gentlemen back down when they made to stand, which relieved her father of the dreadful responsibility of a duty kiss. To smooth things over, she babbled.

"So sorry I'm late—I can only stay for a drink. We got a very strange case today and I have to work."

"What do you do, Skip?" asked Mrs. White.

Oh, no—Conrad hadn't briefed them. She saw her father flush, her mother's fingers tighten on her glass.

Camille said, "She's a homicide detective—can you believe it? Skippy, you just can't know how I've been dying to meet you—we've never had anything remotely so exciting in our family."

And so the talk politely turned to her "interesting" career choice.

Camille was short and cute: short, curly brown hair, blue eyes, tiny little nose, milky skin—skin to kill for, as a matter of fact. She wore a halter-top blue dress that perfectly set off a figure that belonged on a teenager. She couldn't have been sexier if she'd worn a lace teddy and couldn't have been more proper in a business suit.

She was the sort of woman guys like Conrad must construct from their own dreams of perfection. When Conrad introduced her to his senior partners, their eyes were going to light up like the neon nipples of a sign on Bourbon Street. In the first second they knew her, they were going to flash forward, seeing her fitting in at social events through the decades, tossing her head and making precisely the right coquettish remark, never embarrassing, just borderline-bawdy. Just perfect.

Conrad had probably told her about his sister the black sheep and the little problem with Dad. And, of course, she'd figured out the perfect way to handle it.

"How did you get promoted to homicide? I mean, you're so young—it's a big honor, isn't it?"

"I had a friend." It was true. If it weren't for Joe Tarantino, she'd have left the police department in the first place, and in the second place she'd still be giving drunks directions in VCD. Joe had talked her into staying on, had said she had terrific potential, that she was a good officer who was going to be excellent. A few months later there'd been some personnel changes and Joe was head of homicide now. Skip had nearly fainted when he'd had her transferred to his division. He hadn't been bullshitting. He'd meant it. He really thought she was good.

She'd never been a student, having flunked out of Newcomb and barely made it through Ole Miss. Before that, she'd so poorly understood her environment that her parents had made her feel wildly incompetent—and she was, she'd wryly admitted since. But police work was something she could do. She was big and she was physically adept; maybe in this atmosphere her size and strength gave her the confidence to use the brains that really were what made her good. She didn't know. All she knew was she felt she'd come home.

"You can't fool me, Skippy. I've heard about you."

Aghast, Skip glanced at her father. But he was smiling benignly on the whole domestic scene. Camille was handling the whole thing as adeptly as Conrad must have known she would.

"Alison Gaillard just thinks you're the greatest thing since sliced bread. She's always telling Skippy Langdon stories."

Her mother raised an eyebrow—she'd probably had no idea her daughter had renewed an old acquaintanceship with Alison, and that was going to raise Skip about a hundred points in her estimation. Her dad looked positively giddy.

She wondered if it would be impolitic to ask Camille if she'd ever considered joining the diplomatic corps and decided it would probably break the mood.

She admitted to herself that she liked the girl. What wasn't to like? Nothing that showed, that was for sure, but there was certainly something suspect about her—she was about to throw away a perfectly good life on Conrad Langdon. Something had to be wrong with her.

Skip ordered a Perrier.

"Yes," said the waiter, "Perrier." He gave it the American pronunciation, not so subtly correcting her. Skip's thoughts turned instantly to Steve Steinman. That was the sort of thing that could keep him going for an entire afternoon. Why in New Orleans, with its touted French heritage? he would ask. She would explain that it was probably because there was a Perrier Street that was more Perri-than-thou rather than Perriay, and that would get him going again. As far as he was concerned, New Orleans was Mars.

"What are *you* smiling about?" Conrad managed to make it an accusation.

Oh, certain things the Kama Sutra doesn't even mention.

She considered it, but in the end wimped out. "Just having fun."

Camille said, "Tell us about your new case."

"Oh, gosh, I can't really. Not at this stage."

"Skippy." It was a voice she hadn't heard in nearly a quarter-century—her mother's, commanding a small child. The message was clear: *For once, your stupid "career" is doing us some good. Don't screw this up as usual.*

She gave her mother what she hoped would pass for a big

friendly smile; it felt more like a baring of teeth. "Sorry, Mother; rules is rules."

Her dad said, "Oh, come on, Skippy. You know it won't go any farther."

Skip was close enough to childhood to be resentful. For nearly two decades you had to follow rules you didn't even know existed half the time, with nasty consequences if you didn't; then suddenly the enforcers turned criminal.

She breathed deeply. "It's not really dinner-table talk."

Mrs. White, who lived up to her name perfectly, with pale skin and prematurely gray hair that looked more blond than otherwise, said, "Ooh, then, by all means tell us. I never miss 'Murder She Wrote.' "

Dear God.

"Well, a baby died. He was born addicted to crack, and he was in the hospital for months and then the mother took him home and he was back in the hospital the next morning with half a dozen broken bones." It had been her case, but it was three months old.

A flush, only partly from his bourbon and water, spread over Camille's father's face. "They should pack them all up and send them back to Africa."

"It was a white family."

"A what?"

"White, Mr. White." Half of it had been.

She looked around at the downcast faces of her parents and Camille, the furious one of Conrad. "I'm sorry. Police work just isn't pretty."

Her mother's mouth pursed. No one said anything.

The waiter hovered. "Ready to order?"

Skip said, "I really have to go."

They all said good-bye, perfectly polite except for her dad, who seemed once again to have tuned out her existence. Camille insisted on walking her out.

"Listen, I'm really sorry about my dad. I hope you won't think we're all that way."

21

What on earth can Conrad have done to deserve this paragon? Do you suppose he can fuck?

She hugged Camille and wondered if they could be friends.

After a quick change at home—to khaki slacks and a white shirt—she once again rang Mr. Palmer and Mr. Davies, Linda Lee's most immediate neighbors. Mr. Davies, the one who traveled, thought he'd seen Linda Lee once, but he wasn't really sure. He'd certainly never heard any noise from her apartment. Mr. Palmer had spoken to her once or twice and thought her very nice; he was horrified she'd been murdered—that's the kind of city it was nowadays—but couldn't shed the slightest glimmer of light.

Plenty of people in nearby buildings hadn't been home that afternoon. Skip tried them now. Most were home and none knew anything.

It was only eight-thirty and she'd practically wrapped up her entire investigation. She went over to Mama Rosa's and got a meatball sandwich. What Joe had said was right—it probably wouldn't be the least bit productive to show Linda Lee's picture around, but neither would going home and turning on the tube. She couldn't believe this woman hadn't known anyone in the neighborhood. Somebody, somewhere must know her, know something about her.

First she went into every place that was open within a six-block radius—and got nothing. Okay, she'd come back tomorrow, when more places were open.

Next, bars. She tried to put herself in Linda Lee's place.

Where would I go if I were new in town, didn't know anyone, and wanted a drink?

Home.

Okay, that bespeaks wanting something more than a drink. Just to get out of the house maybe. What else? Local color? Company? Music? Guys?

If guys, then what? A quick and dirty lay? True love?

True love! Who'd go to a bar to find love?

22

But the answer was all too obvious. Someone with no place else to go. Someone with no other ideas and very little imagination. Someone stupid. Linda Lee might easily have been the first, and even the second. She might have been stupid too. But with those books about relationships, Skip didn't think she'd have gone out looking for cheap sex, and probably not love either. More likely she'd wanted a change of scenery, some conviviality, a little noise, maybe some music—anything but the same four walls and the dead quiet, a quiet she knew wasn't about to be cut by the sound of a ringing phone.

So almost any place would do. Someplace nearby, convenient, would be the obvious choice. Good. There were probably no more than eight or nine hundred bars in the Quarter.

Pat O'Brien's was perfect—colorful and completely safe, full of tourists, lots of activity, and a beautiful courtyard. No one could be lonely at Pat O'Brien's. But if Linda Lee had been there, no one had seen her.

Oh, well, it was a good place to start—kind of got the blood up. Cosimo's was a thought, the Absinthe Bar, the Napoleon House; probably not a hotel bar and no place with a cover. Would she have walked all the way to Snug Harbor and Café Brasil? Probably not. Even keeping it fairly local and fairly selective, eliminating the hotel bars and obvious tourist traps, it was going on two o'clock and she'd chewed off her lipstick by the time she hit the Abbey. Shit! Claude was working. With utter amazement, she realized she hadn't thought of him in months.

"Skip! Whereyat, babe?" He leaned over for a kiss.

"Beat. Can I have a Coke?" He got her one.

"Haven't seen you around, dawlin'." Not a word of reproof. And why should there be? He probably hadn't thought of her in months either. He was six-five, and had a gorgeous mustache and the cutest butt in the parish. Who knew how many women he had, not counting his wife.

"Fell in love."

"Nice guy?"

She nodded. "It's more than I can say for you."

He laughed loudly, showing teeth like piano keys. There were times when she simply hadn't been able to resist him. "You got my number, honey."

She showed him the snapshot. "Do you know this girl?"

"Uh-uh. I don't think so. Something happen to her?"

"Why do you think that?"

"I don't know. A lot of weirdos out there."

"Any in here?"

He rolled his eyes. "Don't get me started."

"Sure you don't know her?"

He stared at the picture again. "Not really—she's not that different-looking. You know?"

She knew. The whole idea was crazy. She didn't even know what night to ask about. "Listen, I gotta go."

"Take care of yourself." She could have sworn she saw affection in his eyes. All those months they'd been sometime lovers and it had never occurred to her they were friends. She guessed they were.

Three

SONNY GERARD ORDERED a second gin and tonic, strolled out to the patio, and came back in, sitting once again at the bar. He rubbed the knot between his shoulders with his left hand, wondering when the gin was going to start working. It was a great muscle relaxant, but that wasn't the whole point—he also wanted to obliterate his feelings, to be in a place where no one knew him and he knew no one, where he could play Clint Black on the jukebox and lean on the machine if he wanted to, letting the bass pulsate through his fingertips, turning him into somebody else. Somebody simple, somebody with a dozer hat and love of country-western music, somebody with a girlfriend named Rae Lynn and nothing to do but drive a truck or work on an assembly line.

He could pretend here. Here nobody knew about all the stuff he was supposed to be; it was like a secret window he could open and get a breath of air. He did it about once a month—told everybody he knew he had an emergency with someone else, like a teenage girl who says she's sleeping over at a girlfriend's when she's somewhere she shouldn't be.

It was a one-time Quarter tourist bar turned neighborhood hangout—now so ordinary nobody Sonny knew was ever going to wander in for any reason, even slumming. He never spoke to anyone when he came here, just had a few drinks and listened to the kind of music he was supposed to hate and didn't think about a goddamn thing most of the time.

Tonight he was thinking all too hard—about what it would have been like to be born in Lafayette or Natchitoches or even Slidell, into a blue-collar family without a care in the world except making some kind of crummy salary, just enough to get along, and maybe going to church on Sunday to make up for drinking too much and cheating on his wife.

What could it have been like to have a childhood in which he didn't have to make all A's, then didn't have to keep up a 3.8 average, get into the best fraternity, get into med school, get the prettiest girl, all that stuff you had to do if you were Sonny Gerard? He wondered if other people who were born not to be ordinary thought about it at all. About what a burden it was. What a pain in the ass.

He thought about it all the time. Did the triumphs outweigh the effort of it? Yes. They did. That was why he kept it up—that and the fact that he truly wanted to do what was right. It would have been nice if he'd never known about it—his life as Sonny Gerard. If he'd been born Joe Blow and the question hadn't come up.

"Sonny? Aren't you Sonny?"

He turned. Standing beside him was a woman he knew from somewhere but couldn't quite place. "Do I know you?"

"I'm Di. From the program. Maybe you don't remember me."

"Di. Of course." They hadn't spoken before, but he'd noticed her, found her very attractive. "Buy you a drink?"

"Oh." She looked dismayed, as if he'd insulted her.

"Hi, Di," said the bartender.

"Hi, Floyd. The usual." She gave him two dollars. To Sonny, she said, "I guess you took me by surprise. I don't drink. I live across the street." The bartender laid a stack of quarters in front of her. "Floyd gives me change for the washer and dryer."

"You're doing laundry tonight?" She was wearing jeans and a T-shirt, a low-cut T-shirt showing cleavage.

"I was, but it's so hot." She sat down and fanned her face.

"A Coke or something?"

"Ice water."

Sonny ordered another gin and tonic for himself. "Maybe we should go out on the patio."

"I can only stay a minute."

Up close, he saw the tiny lines under her eyes, the softness of her half-exposed breasts, and realized she was probably as old as his mother. What could he possibly have to say to her? From her right ear hung a star, from her left a crescent.

"Di for Diana? The goddess of the moon?"

"And the Huntress. Did you know she was supposed to be immune to falling in love?"

"Are you?"

"I'm not even named Diana."

"Diane."

She shook her head.

"Diamond."

"Diamara."

"Ah." He took a sip of gin, not knowing what to say next. "Diamara."

"My birth name was Jacqueline." She pronounced it Zhakleen.

"That's a beautiful name."

"It wasn't me. I'm born again."

"How did you come up with Diamara?"

"You were almost right the first time. I am partly named for Diana but, I have to admit, partly for diamonds, and Mara is a name for the goddess."

"Mara or Mera?"

"I just pronounce it Diamera. It's really spelled with an *a*. I had to do it that way so it would come out a master number."

Sonny knew there must be a way to answer her. He tried to think what it could be.

But she said, "Do you know anything about numerology?"

"Oh, yeah. Numerology. I had a girlfriend once who was into it. Something about names and numbers. But you aren't supposed to change your name, are you? Isn't that part of the deal? You have to use the one you were born with?"

She smiled, a priestess passing on the word. "I do it my way. That's the way a nine person is, which is what I am; meaning my reality number is nine."

"Uh, could you run the system by me again?"

"Let's do your name. Okay—Sonny: *S* is one, *o* is six, *n* is five, the second *n* is five, and *y* is seven. Twenty-four, right? So that makes six—two plus four. That's your key number. *S* is your cornerstone, so that's one, and *o* is your instinctive desire, which is the same as your key. A six has a strong sense of duty and responsibility. Is that you?''

Sonny felt a twinge of guilt. "Usually, I guess."

"You could be a banker, maybe, or a musician; or a doctor or lawyer."

Sonny's head was awhirl. There was something wonderfully elfish about this woman, with her tangle of black curls, full breasts, and tiny waist. She might be twice his age, but she looked like a teenager, seemed more like the sister he'd never had. He was on the verge of asking, in envy, how she could put aside her reason, simply dive in and play such charming games with herself, when it occurred to him the question might be rude. He didn't know exactly how, but he knew there were things about her he didn't understand. He had a feeling answers wouldn't necessarily come from direct questions.

He wanted to know more, but he felt like a kid around her, didn't have a clue how to keep her with him.

"What name do you want?"

"Me?"

"Besides Sonny?"

"I don't know. Arthur, maybe."

"Because of the king?"

He nodded. How had she known that?

"What else? You need a backup."

"How about Jean-Paul?"

"Jean-Paul?" She laughed, a pixie laugh. "Arthur was easy. Why Jean-Paul?"

"From Jean-Paul Belmondo."

"Ah, the movie star. You don't look old enough to remember him."

He was offended—he'd hoped she wouldn't mention age. "You don't have to be old to see old movies."

"Why do you want his name?"

"I don't know. I like his style . . . something about his eyes."

28

"Yeah. Like he could get away with anything." She looked straight at him and they laughed, together, in sync. She was definitely flirting.

He felt strangely powerful. He, Sonny Gerard, had done something to win this stunning woman's attention. He couldn't think what. How could he keep it?

She picked up her quarters. "I'll see which one works."

"Which—uh—what?"

"I'll look them up."

It was only after she was gone that he realized that she was going to analyze the names he'd picked according to that crazy system of hers. It made him laugh.

The encounter had done more for him than his whole bar-as-window system ever had before. He felt strong, fresh, masculine—like a man, not the terrified boy he felt like most of the time, the boy who was the truth he struggled so hard to conceal.

It wasn't working either. Someone else knew, and she was trying hard to help him, but he hated it that she knew, that he was so transparent. He felt as if Di didn't see him that way.

Damn! He didn't know her last name. How could he see her again?

Forget it, Sonny, he told himself. *No way you're going to see her again. You're just drunk. Go home.*

"Hi, Missy."

She looked like every girl in Georgia. Blond. So many of them here were dark, like everyone in New York and Pennsylvania. This one had almost certainly been head cheerleader in high school, and probably homecoming queen, had gone on to pledge some good sorority at LSU and now probably worked as a teacher or maybe a clothing-store clerk. Just something until she got married.

A piece of fluff—slender, blue-eyed, perfect WASP features. If there had been one single thing about her that was different, that set her apart from a million other young women, she could have been a TV star; probably she wouldn't make it in movies, you had to have talent for that. But even for TV she needed a beauty mark or something.

She said, "I'm going through something really hard right now. I'm trying to let go. Well, not let go, exactly, just loosen my grip, sort of.

"I'm trying not to be too smothering, not to hang on too hard."

Her voice was like a flower petal, her perfect face marred by her earnestness. "I'm trying to recognize the fact that not everyone needs as much attention as I do, and that maybe I don't really need it myself. But I'm not really there yet. I'm still fighting it. I've been with the same man for a year. . . ."

Damn!

He hoped no one had heard his sudden intake of breath. It wasn't fair—the good ones were always taken; he'd been watching her for weeks.

Oh, get a grip, Abe.

He looked around to see if any of the other men looked similarly disappointed and saw that they didn't. They looked as earnest as Missy, their sympathetic brows creased with concern.

I should have known. She's always with that guy.

Well, she wasn't tonight. "I know that my boyfriend needs time to himself, and that it isn't personal when he doesn't want to be with me every day, all day. . . . I mean, we both work, but when we're not working, we don't have to be together all the time. I know that, I really do."

She was too young anyway, and a shade too perfect—perfection was blandness. He'd be sick of her in five minutes.

"I'm doing okay with that. It's just that lately he's seemed really distant sometimes. I keep wondering if something's bothering him and telling myself that it's not my problem. He and I are two different people. If he's having a problem,

30

it's something he has to work out for himself, it's nothing I can help him with.''

Suddenly he saw through her as clearly as if she were made of Lucite: *She thinks she's the problem. She's afraid he's going to dump her.*

Adrenaline surged through him. She'd be vulnerable now; it was a perfect time to move in.

She gave a self-deprecating little laugh. ''I'm a social worker. I spend all day every day trying to solve people's problems. I think I should be able to solve his and everybody else's as well. Sick, isn't it?''

No one answered. It was forbidden.

''It's the hardest thing I've ever done, not to meddle; not to try to help when I know I could. He has to go through this thing alone, whatever it is. I think it's something like a mid-life crisis. Except he's only twenty-six.''

Before Abe could stop himself, he snickered. You weren't supposed to do that, but it didn't matter—a few others chuckled indulgently, laughing with, not at, because that was the way it was done here. She threw back her head, tossing the blond hair out of her face, and laughed with the others. She was flushed, maybe embarrassed.

''My mother died when I was twelve; there were three kids in my family younger than me, and I was all the mom they had till my dad remarried a few years ago. I've been a mother all my life. How am I supposed to stop now?''

The inevitable tear or two spilled.

''But I know I have to, because it's inappropriate to act as the parent to another adult. He doesn't need that and he doesn't want that. And neither do I.''

She paused to blow her nose.

''Except I do.'' Laughter again. ''Well, that's what I'm fighting. I guess that's all I have to say.''

The leader said it was time to stop. This was the part Abe hated. The group stood and joined hands. Someone volunteered to lead the prayer. Then there was the ritual wagging of joined hands that accompanied the chant.

At first he hadn't said the chant, but it got easier every time; he said it now as heartily as anyone else, his gorge rising hardly at all.

Four

SONNY WATCHED HER as she slept, pale hair falling away from her face. He was hectored by guilt over his adventure of the night before. He hadn't intended to see her, in fact had told her he couldn't, but his encounter with the gypsy-like Di had left him too restless to sleep alone. He'd phoned Missy and told her he was lonely.

That she would see him hadn't been in doubt. Missy was Missy—always ready to help no matter how shabbily she was treated. She was such a lovely person, a truly good person—a near-perfect person, to Sonny's way of thinking, and he wanted to treat her like a princess. She was the perfect woman to marry, and when he'd asked her, she'd accepted as if she couldn't believe her good fortune. But he knew he was getting the better part of the deal. And even so, sometimes he couldn't imagine himself married.

Sleepily she stirred and reached for his penis. It came alive in her hand and he felt guilty about even that. He didn't want to make love to her. But he caressed her as if she were the greatest treasure of some forgotten empire, till her cheeks were flushed and she writhed like a lure on the end of a line, and then he entered her as gently as if she'd break. Her body shuddered and she seized his buttocks, eyes open, fiery with passion. He could at least give her this much.

He closed his own eyes, rocking her, and the woman under him was Di, lush tendrils like corkscrews round her olive face. He felt his cheeks go hot with his shame, opened his eyes, and said Missy's name. She smiled and said she loved him. He said it back to her and hated himself.

When it was over, she said, "I don't think you know how beautiful you are."

"Men aren't supposed to be beautiful." He disliked compliments.

"You're the sort of person who deserves a wife who'll make love to him three times a day for the rest of his life."

"How about one who cooks?"

"Cooks too."

"Cooks what?"

"Oh, maybe Oysters Rockefeller for breakfast. How would that be? Exotic, unexpected things. I'm going to work twenty-four hours a day at making you happy."

"Stop. I'm getting embarrassed."

"I know."

Blue eyes looked into blue eyes. "You know?"

"You don't think you deserve it, do you? A woman who'll love you and take care of you?"

He shook his head. "No." It came out a whisper.

"Oh, Sonny, you do, you do. You're a wonderful person, do you know that?"

He sat up, turning away from her. "Oh, Missy!"

"Okay, okay, I'll shut up." She touched her lips to each of his vertebrae in turn, opened her legs, wound them around his body, and simply sat that way, arms around his chest, kissing his neck.

The breasts against his shoulder blades were small and round, as firm as only the breasts of women under twenty-

five are firm. Diamara's would be much larger, not round at
all anymore, as soft as down pillows.

He shook his head to clear it, forgetting Missy at his neck.

"Ow."

"What?"

"Bit my tongue."

"I'm sorry, Missy. God, I'm such a fuck-up!"

"You are not, Sonny Gerard! Don't even think that. You're
the pride of your goddamn stuck-up family, and you've earned
it, precious. Do you realize how hard you work? It's not
normal. It's not natural. You're going to keel over one day."

"Do me a favor, Missy. Don't call me precious, okay?"

"Why not?"

"It's a name for a little kid."

"But you *are* precious."

He headed for the shower, feeling slightly depressed, hoping against hope for a good day. Yesterday had been one
Room Four after another, sometimes two at a time.

At least for once he'd had a full night's sleep.

Though you could tell it only from the roof, Charity was
actually a giant, nineteen-floor *H*. From the street it merely
looked like some out-of-control antique, urban sprawl in mi-
crocosm, the hospital that ate New Orleans. But Charity
wasn't about to devour anything. Nurses hated working there,
and many wouldn't. It was still a good teaching hospital with
one of the best trauma units in the country, but it was per-
ennially short-staffed and underfunded.

The building itself was so outdated you could hardly believe it had elevators, much less elevators with robot voices
(which it did). Above the fourteenth floor, there was no hospital, only the now-empty call rooms where residents had
once resided, and a couple of ancient operating theaters.
Sonny had explored every inch of the place, knew which of
the call rooms had keys above the doors and could be entered
for a catnap, when you could make speeches to imaginary

audiences in the operating theaters. (Now and then meetings were held in them.)

The first time he'd seen the waiting room, where, despite emergencies and imagined ones, many waited the better part of a day, he'd thought: *Calcutta*. The place looked caught in time, a scene from a Thirties movie that should have been hung with cobwebs. People moaned on gurneys or in their chairs, held broken arms against their bodies, drooped in misery and boredom.

Sonny could feel himself absorbing their pain. He'd had a dream once, of being a flasher—he'd opened his trenchcoat and his skin came open as well, exposing his heart, liver, intestines, everything that needed protection. Being in the room was like that, like the dream come true. He was open, vulnerable, couldn't separate himself from the misery in the air, couldn't get his skin zipped up.

Half an hour later, behind the closed doors of the trauma room, where he'd watched as a team stabilized a man found beaten up in the street, where he'd seen a nasty cut stitched, where the hospital bustle mixed reassuringly with the misery, making inroads, he was fine.

It was a pretty normal reaction so far as he could tell. Even Missy had had it. The touted medical armor didn't take months to develop, it came on you almost immediately. You couldn't go around with your skin open, you had to close up.

But this rotation was still the worst for him—the worst by far, the only thing he'd ever gotten into that made him doubt himself.

His uncle had come over once to find his parents fighting, arguing before a party. "Robson Gerard," he'd intoned, "you are a physician!"

When his dad left his guests and came to tuck him in, Sonny asked, "Why did Uncle Bick say that?"

"Because doctors are supposed to do better than other people—didn't you know that?"

"No. Why are they supposed to?"

"They just are, Sonny boy. That's why you have to be such a good boy—because you're going to be one someday."

"How do you know?"

"I just do." He had drawn a finger down Sonny's nose and left him then.

In medical school they taught you by example not to show reaction—anger was okay, but nothing else, never anything else. Even in your own family you didn't show weakness, didn't say you felt for a patient, you hurt for him, a little of you died when he did.

Was it really that way, or just the way he perceived it? Maybe no one else was weak, or felt for the patients, ever— maybe it wasn't all just a front. Maybe he really was different. And if he was, he couldn't be a doctor.

And even if he wasn't, but didn't conquer it, he still couldn't be a doctor. And if he couldn't be a doctor, he couldn't be Sonny Gerard. Sonny Gerard was born and bred to be a doctor. Both his grandfathers had been doctors, and so had all their sons and so would all their sons be (except for Sonny's brother Robbie, who had never fit in). With that one exception, it was what Gerards did, all they did, and Robbie had paid by becoming a family outcast. Not that he seemed to give a damn, but he had *chosen* not to follow the family path, hadn't flunked out, as it appeared Sonny was about to do.

He'd started getting squeamish in the neonatal intensive-care unit, doing heel sticks on those unbelievably tiny babies—all night stabbing babies, night after night. He hadn't been ready for that, but he'd steeled himself, prayed about it. He got through it. Got through it easily—it was just one of the things you had to do if you were a doctor. He even heard other people talk about it. This was normal, that baby-stabbing would get to you. The other thing wasn't.

It had started with the woman who came in with nausea

and vomiting about six months ago—not the first person he'd seen die, not by a long shot. But he'd felt the mass in her stomach and gotten the resident to order the CAT scan. She loved him—all the old ladies loved him—black or white, he treated them all the same, spoke quietly, calmly, didn't try to kid around and call them beautiful. She asked to see him every day he was there—he couldn't run away from it—and in a week she was dead.

Here in this rotation, in the emergency room, they lost about three a week. Usually, he was fine. It was as the folklore had it—adrenaline kicked in and the patient became only a medical problem. Nothing else. But frequently they had the medical students do the chest compressions. At first he could dissociate when he was doing that, could do it so well he could even see himself as the charge resident, orchestrating the thing. Now he was beginning to lose it a little. It was starting to get to him.

The distressing thing about the whole situation was that it shouldn't be that big a deal—a cosmetic surgeon who lost patients wouldn't be in practice for long. In other words, if he could just get through medical school, he was never going to have a problem with this. But pretty soon one of two things was going to happen. Someone would notice him turning pale, shaking—and it would all go up in smoke. Or worse, he would get worse.

"Room Four now!"

Sonny's stomach did a quick flip, but stabilized. He felt okay, excited, the way you were supposed to feel. Anything could happen—they could save this one. What was he thinking of? They usually did. It was a Tuesday morning, so it probably wasn't a gunshot wound—maybe an accident.

Gloves and goggles were going on.

The team was standing around the table, IV's already hanging, each ready to take what he needed from the crash cart, to do his or her part, simple as ABC:

A. Airway—make sure he's able to breathe.

37

B. Breathing and blood—if he's not breathing, put a tube in and breathe for him; if he is, look for blood; get blood tests, dipstick his urine for blood.

C. Circulation—hook heart to monitor; shock chest if in fibrillation.

D. Disability—is he awake or comatose? Can he move his arms and legs?

They had it down not to a science, more like a recipe.

The paramedics wheeled the victim in. Sonny stood in the hall, watched with med students and others. A Room Four was a show.

It was an accident—he'd guessed right. A hit-and-run victim, a pedestrian, the paramedics said. She must have weighed three hundred pounds.

The team performed like the Moscow Ballet—stabilized her, patched her up, put her back together, working like a bunch of robots invented for the purpose. It made you proud to be a doctor.

The charge resident took off his goggles, stepped into the hall.

"Okay, Sonny, let's take her up to seven." For a CAT scan.

She was breathing okay, but still unconscious, just lying there sleeping like a baby.

Seven was the most cheerful floor in the hospital—tiled in midnight blue, all recently redone. It was cold here—had to be for the equipment—and very quiet. No one was around except for the C-T tech.

"Uh-oh," she said. "Got one for me?"

"A big one."

"Damn! I've got to go to the little girls' room."

"Go ahead," said the resident. "Plenty of time." He began to inject the dye for the CAT scan.

The patient's chest heaved. She wheezed.

"Jesus! She's allergic."

Red blotches were popping out on her arms. Her mouth

38

worked as she fought for breath, the terrible sounds of "strider" caught in her throat.

"Sonny! Get the epinephrine!"

"Where do they keep it?"

"Just find it, goddammit! And get us some help."

Sonny started rummaging. There had to be a kit somewhere.

"Where the hell is that tech?"

The resident had started CPR. It would keep her breathing, but they could stop the thing if Sonny could find the epinephrine.

"Get us some help, dammit!"

Sonny picked up the phone. "Code Thirty-three," he said. "Seventh floor."

He looked some more for the kit. Where the *hell* was that tech?

"How're we doing?" The tech was back, smiling.

"She's gone into anaphylactic shock. Where's the epinephrine?"

Her smile faded along with her languor. She moved quickly, had the epinephrine kit in hand in five seconds, maybe less. "Put it in her IV," said the resident.

"It's fallen out."

"What?"

"This lady weighs about half a ton, and you're doing chest compressions—what do you expect?"

There wasn't time to start sticking her arm experimentally. Three minutes must have passed already.

"Goddamn! Jesus shit!" The resident was falling apart.

Sonny said, "Under her tongue."

The resident gave him a look of pure hate, as if he'd killed the patient. But he opened her mouth and lifted her tongue, where he knew he'd find a vein. It was too late; her body shuddered and gave up.

He refused to accept it, injected the stuff anyway. Sonny knew he would have done the same thing. "Sonny. Chest compressions.'' He and the resident did them together. And that was how they found them when they answered the code, still pumping rhythmically, the resident pale but resigned, Sonny's face fierce in its desperation.

Later on the roof, gulping air he could practically drink, it was so humid, that fairly burned as it entered his lungs, Sonny thought of gentle hands smoothing out the furrow between his eyes, massaging the muscles of his face, making it all go away. Not Missy's. Missy's ministrations would come with a thousand kisses, a thousand words of praise and admonitions that it wasn't his fault, a thousand suggestions on how to handle it in life, in his profession, in his heart of hearts. Missy would not rest until she had split every atom of his psyche, pieced each one back together, and re-arranged them to make a rosy new picture.

All he wanted was the fingers.

Five

SKIP HADN'T CLOSED the Goodwill sofa she slept on, instead had made it up as if it were a real bed in an actual bedroom instead of nearly the only thing in her studio apartment. She needed the surface for packing, and for Jimmy Dee Scoggin, her neighbor and landlord, who reclined as she worked.

The air was scented with pot smoke, Skip abstaining but getting an atmospheric high. ''Officer Darlin', it doesn't have to be like this, you know. Some squalid apartment out of *The*

Day of the Locust, that bear of a human crawling all over your petite little person. . . . "

"Dee-Dee, what is it with you and Steve?" Frustrated, she threw her hair-dryer so hard it thumped against the suitcase. "You've never asked me to travel with you before."

He bestirred himself to grab her wrist, bring it to his lips, and nibble. "I'm in love with your itsy-bitsy bone structure."

She jerked away. "Oh, cut it out."

"Do I detect a note of genuine irritation? Darling, is it our first fight?"

"Dammit, yes. I could have taken *two* vacations. I'd love to have gone diving with you, no matter if I didn't have your full and complete attention. I'd especially love it at your expense. You invited me just to tease me."

"True. True, I did."

She faced him. "And to keep me from seeing Steve."

"Don't be ridiculous." But he rolled off the bed and went to the kitchen, anything so he didn't have to look her in the eye. She couldn't understand why Jimmy Dee hated Steve so much. For months he'd been telling her she had to get out, trying to get her to buy clothes she could wear on dates, even introducing her once to one of his straight friends, and the minute she took his advice he got huffy about it.

"Dixie?"

"No thanks."

She heard the top pop open. "I just think you could have found somebody more . . .

"More what? Go ahead and say it."

"Okay. More your own size."

"Oh, can it, Dee-Dee—if you and I made love, I'd crush you."

"Yeah, but I'd love it so *much*."

"More what else, landlord?"

"More local."

"Oh, pish-tush—you'd really hate that."

Not only was the conversation inane, they'd had it about fifty times lately. She needed it and she knew Dee-Dee did too. She'd realized, once she caught on to how jealous he was of Steve, that Jimmy Dee really loved her. She was half his age, twice his size, and not his type—he preferred men— but something in her had touched him. They had both been depressed when she moved in—Skip for so many reasons she kept losing track of them, Jimmy Dee because he'd lost friends and knew he'd lose more, because he'd taken a vow of celibacy, because he'd seen his whole world come apart with the AIDS epidemic. He had taken Skip on as a project.

Now that she had Steve, they spoke this way to each other— it was easier on both of them than spewing mush, gave them a vocabulary they hadn't previously had for expressing affection.

"I just want you to be happy," he said.

Skip feigned vomiting and Jimmy Dee changed the subject. "So how come Joe's letting you go in the middle of a case?"

"I got down on my knees and begged."

"Is that all you did down there?"

"No. I unzipped his fly and . . ." She stopped, licking her lips. ". . . and then . . ."

"Yes?"

"I slipped my hand in . . ."

"Go on."

". . . and let go of the stack of bills I was holding."

"You disappoint me, Tiny One."

"I know. I should have gone to law school—I'd be a much better liar today."

"Now if *I'd* told that one . . ."

"Spare me, Counselor." She shrugged, returning to Jimmy Dee's nearly forgotten question. "He let me make the choice. Three days and three nights—"

"I notice you're looking a little wan."

"—and I haven't gotten diddly. He doesn't think I'm going

to get anything, and neither do I." She sighed and held up a pair of walking shorts. "Okay for L.A.?"

"If you wear them with some kind of metallic-spattered T-shirt."

"I'm pretty upset about it, to tell you the truth."

"But it's nothing a bear of a man can't fix."

"I'm not kidding, Dee-Dee. It's a professional failure. Not a trace. Not lead one. Every idea exhausted and nowhere else to go. It was such a nasty murder, too."

"Don't think about it, Snookums. Think about hard cocks and firm asses."

"Obviously you don't understand the spiritual nature of my relationship."

Jimmy Dee took a deep drag on his joint, held the smoke and said: "How was she killed?"

"Strangled bare-handed. By somebody who probably wore gloves."

"Was she raped?"

"I thought you said not to think about it."

"I changed my mind. You need to talk." He touched her wrist.

Without knowing she was going to, she sat on the bed, her packing forgotten. "I do. You're right, I do." The words poured out. "Dee-Dee, it's the weirdest thing. There was no evidence of sexual assault, no sign of a struggle, no trace of drugs or alcohol. Not a thing in her stomach but coffee. No pregnancy. Nothing! And she doesn't know a soul in town except her landlord and the people at the office."

"Gotta watch those landlords."

"Hers couldn't strangle a gerbil. And let me tell you something else. There wasn't any physical evidence either. Like the guy wasn't even there long enough to leave hairs or fibers."

"And no prints, of course."

"Not only no prints, but no surfaces had been obviously wiped. Like he'd worn gloves. And it's August, Dee-Dee."

43

"In other words, we're talking premeditation."

"Yeah." She sighed. "I wonder if she had a date with him. You have coffee on a first date, don't you?"

"You're asking me?"

"They had coffee, he brought her home, and then he strangled her."

"If I were heterosexual, I guess I'd say, 'I've had those kinds of dates.' "

"Right. Everybody jokes about it. Nobody does it. You don't strangle someone you don't know."

"Unless you're crazy."

"Nobody she knows got her a blind date, so where'd she meet the guy?"

"Maybe she advertised—or answered an ad."

Skip shrugged. "No rough drafts of ads lying around; no copies of *Gambit*; no receipts, bills, telephone messages, or any other kinds of notes that might indicate that. She could have run into a stranger on the street who said, 'You're gorgeous; let's have coffee.' "

For once in his life, Dee-Dee looked grave. "That's probably what happened."

"Well, how the hell am I supposed to track the guy down?"

"Maybe she belonged to a church group. Or a singles club."

Skip stood in frustration and started throwing panties and nylons into her bag. "For Christ's sake, Dee-Dee. I've been working on this thing for three days—don't you think I thought of that?"

"My. Aren't we touchy."

"Sorry. I feel like a failure, that's all."

He rolled over on his stomach. "Guess you need a vacation."

"I feel weird about that—I don't even know if I can enjoy it."

The phone rang. Jimmy Dee answered and handed it over.

It was Jim Hodges, another homicide detective. "Bad news. Real bad news."

"Oh, shit. Another scarlet *A*."

"I just thought you'd want to know."

"Are you there now? I'm coming."

"Forget it, Skip. I got it handled."

"I'm not going to L.A."

"Hey, don't be a martyr. I wouldn't have called if I thought you were going to act crazy."

"Jim, you've got to give it to me, you owe me—I took one for you when your wife was in the hospital."

"Aren't you looking at things a little bit backwards?" Nevertheless he gave her the address.

"You didn't want to go anyway," said Jimmy Dee when she had hung up. He ruffled her hair and left with the slightly smug expression he got after smoking half a joint by himself.

Steve hadn't been home when she called, a good thing in a way—there wasn't time to talk—but she ached to hear his voice even for a moment, to be reassured he'd be there when she could come.

As she drove, she found him more and more on her mind. It was odd, she thought, that when she was on her way to him, all but on the plane, all she could think about was Linda Lee, and now that she had work to do, he wouldn't leave her alone.

Two patrol cars were parked in front of the tiny house off Elysian Fields, a house so badly in need of paint you could tell it in the dark.

Every light in the living room was on, and Skip saw that Gottschalk from the crime lab was already at work. Hodges, a sad-looking black man, was shaking his head, looking even more miserable than usual. Skip had noticed that no matter how long some officers worked homicide, they never got hardened. "The day I get used to it," Joe had told her, "is the day I quit the department."

The corpse was crumpled near the far end of the room, not barely inside the door as before. There were two other important differences, the first almost mind-boggling, it seemed to Skip—the victim was a man.

Even without sexual assault, she'd been so sure the killer was the sort of lunatic who preyed on women. And now she knew why she'd been reluctant to take her vacation—she'd known, deep down, that he'd do it again. But she'd imagined a kind of slaughter of the innocents—young women victims like Linda Lee without enough street-smarts not to talk to strangers.

She was looking now at a man in his late fifties, maybe early sixties. Like Linda Lee, he'd been dead awhile. He had strangulation marks on his neck and a jagged cut on his arm. A knife lay on the living room floor, a brown stain on the blade. The second difference was the *A* on the wall—it wasn't scarlet at all, but matched the stain on the knife.

Even that wasn't the weirdest part of the scene. Beside the body, as if the victim had dropped it when he was attacked, was a child's teddy bear.

That alarmed her. "Is there a kid here?" she blurted. Hodges said, "I had the same thought. Nobody home but Tom."

"Tom?"

He inclined his head toward the floor. "That's Tom Mabus, a waiter at the Orleans House. Had the same job for fifteen years, never missed a day."

"You know him?"

"No, but I got you a witness. I had a bet with Cappello—she said you were going to want this one. So, okay, it's yours. Since I owe you one. You must have some understanding boyfriend."

"Thanks, Jim."

He gave her an avuncular look: *You'll outgrow this eager-beaver stuff.*

"Where's my witness?"

"In one of the patrol cars, not feeling too good. He's Tom's boss." He looked at his notes. "A Mr. Derek Brown. Tom didn't show up for work; he investigated—found the body." He laughed. "Don't think he's ever seen one before."

"Okay. Let me look around and then I'll get to him. Are you out of here?"

He looked almost regretful. "If you really want this turkey."

The furniture was old and dusty, smelled mildewy. Everything was shabby, poorly kept. The sheets on the unmade bed were gray. It looked like the house of a man who didn't know how to take care of it, perhaps a man whose wife had recently died. Alternatively, maybe it was the home of a depressed person, someone with barely enough energy to go to work, come home, turn on the TV. Or maybe an alcoholic. No one very happy.

Derek Brown, sweating and mopping his face every few seconds, was ten or twenty years Tom's junior, with thinning blond hair and a narrow strip of mustache. His breath was coming in gulps and he was pale.

"You need air," said Skip. "Want to come out and talk to me?"

He shook his head. "I need to sit down."

"I'll get you a chair." She went inside and brought out two straight-backed dining room chairs. "You can't stay in there. It's like a sauna."

It wasn't unlike a sauna in the evening air. Brown's light blue suit was damp and limp. "I should have got somebody to come with me," he said. "I knew when Tom didn't answer the phone it was bad. Real bad. I'm not saying I didn't half-expect to find him dead, but not like this." He shook his head, willing away the grisly spectacle.

"Had he been ill?"

"It's not that. It's that he never misses work."

"What can you tell me about him?"

"Tom? There's not much to tell, I guess." Again, he shook his head. "He was a sports fan."

"That's what he talked about? Sports?"

"Yeah. Loved to keep up."

"What about his personal life?"

"He lived alone, we all knew that. Last year when he got the flu, we were all worried about him, I remember that." He brightened. "But he had a daughter. She came and took care of him."

"Do you know her name?"

"Yeah. Just can't call it to mind, that's all. Give me a minute."

"Okay. Do you know who his friends were? Did he belong to any social groups? Church?"

He shook his head. "Edna! That's his daughter. Edna. I know it because it's the only name he ever mentioned. He talked about her a little, but nobody else."

"Grandchildren?"

Brown looked puzzled. "I don't know. Seems like he would have said if he had any. Shown pictures and all."

"He didn't?"

"Did you notice the teddy bear in there?"

"Yeah. What do you think that's about?"

"That's what I was going to ask you."

"Do you know if he knew a woman named Linda Lee Strickland? Young woman, pretty. Blond. Did you ever see him with anyone like that?"

"Are you kidding? Tom Mabus?"

Later, she found the neighbors were pretty much of the same mind—Tom Mabus was the last person in the world anyone would want to know, much less murder. He offended no one and apparently interested no one. He was a nice man, a quiet man, never had friends over, didn't go out much, watched television a lot. No one had seen anyone with him the day before—or ever—except for his daughter.

* * *

48

There was an Edna Purcell in his address book who lived on the West Bank, in Marrero.

It was a modest neighborhood, a modest house, but still better than the one she'd grown up in if she'd been raised in Tom Mabus's.

She was overweight, plain, tired-looking. She had on no makeup and wore a pink quilted robe, though the suffocating mugginess still hung in the air.

Inside, a massive man with heavy eyebrows sat in front of a TV, a Dixie beer in his hand. True to stereotype, he wore a T-shirt stretched over his belly, thick chest hair escaping at the top. His forehead protruded.

The house was like a refrigerator; Skip marveled to think of the Purcells' electric bills.

"Darryl, Daddy's dead." Her face was a mask; she hadn't taken it in yet.

Her husband looked at her with such sudden and unexpected tenderness it tore at Skip's heart. "Oh, honey."

The look on her husband's face was enough; she got it, and fell into his outstretched arms, belated sobs escaping her. Skip stood awkwardly in the background.

Finally, Darryl Purcell said, "Edna, I think this lady wants to talk to you," and the Southerner in Edna, the perfect-hostess-in-any-circumstances, dried her eyes and turned to her guest.

"I'm sorry. Won't you sit down?" She introduced her husband. "Can I get you anything?"

Skip shook her head, sitting on the edge of the beige velour sofa. She had told Edna only that her father had been murdered, and now she gave the details.

Darryl's face turned dark. "What kind of animal would do a thing like that? Tom Mabus never hurt one soul in his entire life, never did a thing except go to work and come home."

"I wonder if it could have been someone he knew."

Darryl said, "He didn't know anybody."

"Did he belong to any social clubs, or maybe a church? A bowling league? Anything?"

Edna shook her head. "We tried and tried to get him interested in something. He's been a loner ever since Mama died ten years ago. Seemed like he never got over it. Never cleaned the house, always kept the shades down, even in the daytime. . . ."

"That house never would have got cleaned at all if Edna didn't do it for him every now and then."

"We asked him to live with us, but he wouldn't. He lost weight and looked sadder and sadder, I swear, as the years went by. I guess he was one of those people who aren't happy unless they have someone to take care of."

"I beg your pardon?"

"Well, Mama was a handful."

Darryl snorted. "Alcoholic."

Edna nodded. "Yes, she was. He had to work real hard, raising me, taking care of the house, doing everything Mama was supposed to be doing. And then when I was gone, seemed like she got even worse. But after she died, he never had no interest in anything—not even much in me, to tell you the truth. I guess he really loved her."

"Don't see how anyone could."

"Darryl!"

"I'm sorry, Sugarplum. But you know how she was."

"Are you his only child?"

Edna nodded.

"Do you have children?"

Darryl withdrew, stony. Edna said, "Our daughter's autistic. She doesn't live with us."

"I'm sorry. I asked because your father had a teddy bear."

"A teddy bear?" Darryl sounded furious. Edna was silent.

"A teddy bear was found near the body, as if he'd been

50

holding it when he was attacked. I'm wondering—do you know of any children he was close to?"

"No, I don't. He was always so sad about Rochelle."

"Your daughter?"

Edna nodded. "I wanted him to go into therapy."

"Sheeit!" said Darryl.

Edna cast him a furious look. "He was miserable, Darryl. You never saw an unhappier man."

"Should have gone to church."

Edna looked at Skip beseechingly. "He wouldn't even do that. Wouldn't do a thing to help himself."

"Did he ever mention a Linda Lee Strickland?"

Edna and Darryl simply stared.

Six

THE MORNING DAWNED hot as the night before, and Skip awoke in clammy sheets. After Edna's meat freezer of a home, she had slept with only the breeze from the ceiling fan, naked and lonely. She hit the snooze alarm and lay in bed awhile, thinking of Steve and missing him, enjoying one of the principal pleasures of the long-distance romance.

Thirty minutes later, in a crisp white blouse and slate-blue skirt, carrying her suit jacket, she arrived at work, lewd and lonesome thoughts forgotten.

She was puzzling about the case, looking forward to talking it over with Cappello and Joe, getting some ideas—she was out of her own.

But her stomach lurched as she arrived on the third floor. The halls were full of reporters and television cameras—why, she didn't know, but it couldn't be good. She pushed through, into homicide. Cappello was in Joe's office.

"Langdon! In here!" Joe sounded furious.

"What is it? Did somebody leak the scarlet *A*'s?"

"Worse. I swear to God it's worse."

With a pair of tweezers, he handed Skip a letter, typed on plain white paper. "Look at this."

It said:

Dear Broadcaster:

You probably remember me. The first time, I wrote to the print media, but there was no television then. I also used an axe. That, of course, would be messy in this day and age and I have two perfectly good hands to strangle with. So forget the axe, but I'm still who I am. My signature is an *A*, written in blood. I kill whom I need to kill, both women and men.

As I mentioned before, they never caught me and they never will. I am not a human being, but an extraterrestrial. (Or perhaps that is the best way you can understand it.) I am what you Orleanians used to call the Axeman—make no mistake, I'm back.

It's me.

I'm baaaaaack.

Hi, Mom.

Honeee, I'm hooome.

I have killed twice this time, in the Quarter and near Gentilly. Ask the police. I left my signature.

Maybe you know my song. It has two names: "The Mysterious Axeman's Jazz" is my preference, but it's also called "Don't Scare Me, Papa." *I am no one's papa!* I am the Axeman! I am the walrus! (Just kidding.)

Here's the deal: It's the same as before. Jazz is the life-blood of this great city of ours—it was then and it is now. It's the only constant, the only universal. My spaceship lands

Tuesday, and I'll be out for blood. (Did you know we extra-terrestrials are vampires?) But I have an endless supply of infinite mercy and I will show it to anyone in whose home a jazz band is playing between the hours of 7 P.M. and daylight. Take heed—you will be spared!

But no matter if you aren't, my infinite mercy extends to my victims. I am quick and I am painless. Ask Linda Lee and Tom.

THE AXEMAN

Skip said, "I don't believe what I just read."

"Believe it, Langdon. Every station in town got one."

"How modern." She caught her breath. "Could I ask a question?"

"What's it all about? No problem, ask away. Everybody else in town has. Do you have any idea how many bozos were here when I got to work, waving that damn thing? Fortunately, we were able to have a constructive exchange of information, because some of them were on to the original."

"Original what, Lieutenant? You've lost me."

"Read this and blow your mind."

The document he handed her was a photocopy of a page in a book. The relevant part, a letter, had been highlighted:

Hell, March 13, 1919

Editor of the *Times-Picayune*
New Orleans, La.

Esteemed Mortal:

They have never caught me and they never will. They have never seen me, for I am invisible, even as the ether that surrounds your earth. I am not a human being, but a spirit and a fell demon from the hottest hell. I am what you Orleanians and your foolish police call the Axeman.

When I see fit, I shall come again and claim other victims. I alone know whom they shall be. I shall leave no clue except my bloody axe, besmeared with the blood and brains of he whom I have sent below to keep me company.

If you wish you may tell the police to be careful not to rile me. Of course, I am a reasonable spirit. I take no offense at the way they have conducted their investigations in the past. In fact, they have been so utterly stupid as to amuse not only me, but his Satanic Majesty, Francis Josef, etc. But tell them to beware. Let them not try to discover what I am, for it were better that they were never born than to incur the wrath of the Axeman. I don't think there is any need of such a warning, for I feel sure the police will always dodge me, as they have in the past. They are wise and know how to keep away from all harm.

Undoubtedly you Orleanians think of me as a most horrible murderer, which I am, but I could be much worse if I wanted to. If I wished, I could pay a visit to your city every night. At will I could slay thousands of your best citizens, for I am in close relationship with the Angel of Death.

Now, to be exact, at 12:15 (earthly time) on next Tuesday night, I am going to pass over New Orleans. In my infinite mercy, I am going to make a little proposition to you people. Here it is:

I am very fond of jazz music, and I swear by all the devils in the nether regions that every person shall be spared in whose home a jazz band is in full swing at the time I have just mentioned. If everyone has a jazz band going, well, then, so much the better for you people. One thing is certain, and that is that some of those people who do not jazz it on Tuesday night (if there be any) will get the axe.

Well, as I am cold and crave the warmth of my native Tartarus, and as it is about time that I leave your earthly home, I will cease my discourse. Hoping that thou wilt publish this, that it may go well with thee, I have been, am and will be the worst spirit that ever existed in either fact or realm of fancy.

THE AXEMAN

"This is ringing a bell." Skip put her hand to her head and thought. "Eugenie Viguerie's sixth-grade history project."

"That's got to be right. I don't think I heard about it till eighth grade, but you went to a better school than I did."

"Jesus H. Christ!" she said as she understood what the first letter was all about.

"So, Langdon." Joe looked weary. "You wouldn't remember any details, would you?"

"He was a serial killer. I never put that together before. A serial killer before there were any."

"Either that or the bogeyman. Look, somebody at one of the stations already researched it and I promised him a press conference if he clued me in." He looked sheepish. "I have to do one anyway—look at that pack of wolves out there. Here are the relevant facts. In 1918 somebody started breaking into people's houses and axing them—some lived, some died, but nobody could identify him. The cops looked back into the records and found there'd been some similar cases in 1911, but I guess they didn't catch on. These did."

"Citizen panic attack?"

"More or less, but the weird thing was, most of the victims seemed to be Italian grocers. They never caught the guy—the murders stopped about eighteen months after they started. But later the widow of one of the victims killed somebody who might have been him—somebody who'd been blackmailing Italians, went to jail in 1911, got paroled in 1918."

"So how about the letter—was anyone killed on party night?"

"No." Joe sighed. "But some composer did write a piece about the whole deal—like it says in the new letter. And a good time was had by all, of course. A real good time. Langdon, you ever been to a hurricane party?"

"Sure. Hasn't everyone?"

"You, Cappello?"

She shrugged. "Of course."

"You two see what I'm getting at? This is the kind of town where people think it's a real good idea to blow it all out just because a storm's on the way. Can you imagine what next Tuesday's gonna be like?"

"Murder."

"Yeah. Unless we get him by then."

"How about our letter?"

He shrugged, knowing what she meant but obviously wanting to hedge his answer. "I hate to say it, but I guess it's got to be him. Nobody else knows about the scarlet *A*'s. A little piece about Linda Lee ran in the paper, but nobody knows about Tom Mabus. He had to have mailed it day before yesterday, before Tom's body was even discovered."

Skip's scalp prickled. "This guy's really crazy."

But unexpectedly, Joe grinned. "I like the spaceman angle. Do me a favor, okay? Put out an APB on a little blue guy."

She wasn't in the mood. The reality of the situation was still sinking in—she hadn't yet had time to assimilate it and wall off a piece of herself. "What are we really going to do?"

"Well, Skip, I think I might have to give you some help." She noticed he'd dropped "Langdon" and gone back to his normal form of address. Curious, she thought. As she got more stressed out, he was getting more relaxed.

I guess that's what good lieutenants do—take the pressure off the generals.

"The national media are going to be all over this thing, you realize that? Like stink on—"

"Shrimp," said Cappello quickly.

"Maggots on garbage," Joe said. "And I gotta tell you something else—I'm worried about this asshole. We got a major-league problem on our hands and I got a feeling it's going to get worse before it gets better. So here's what I'm going to do. I'm assigning a five-person team to this deal—not counting the consultant.''

''Who's the consultant?''

''Later,'' he said. ''Ten-thirty in the conference room.''

As she was leaving, he said, ''Oh, Langdon, one more thing. Can you work with Frank O'Rourke?''

''No problem.'' She heard the chill in her own voice.

She was third in the conference room. O'Rourke was there already—handsome, nasty Frank O'Rourke, who delighted, it seemed, in sabotaging Skip. He was a veteran homicide detective and a natural for the Axeman team—much more so than Skip.

Jim Hodges sat with him—a solid guy who might have regretted giving his case away. But that probably wasn't why Joe had picked him. He was a hard worker and a team player—everybody liked to work with him.

The others filed in in a minute—Cappello and Sergeant Adam Abasolo, apparently detailed to homicide for the biggie. He was known as a whiz, soon to take the lieutenant's test and certain to be promoted to head of his division, which was sex crimes. Abasolo—tall, slender, and wiry, with dark hair and blue eyes—looked a little like a thug and a little like a movie star. He was single and known to fancy the ladies—thin blond ones, usually from good families.

Joe arrived looking pale and harried. Briefly, he outlined the case, describing the two murders and the letter. ''As you know,'' he said, ''we've never had a case like this in New Orleans.''

''Yes we have,'' said Cappello. ''The original Axeman.''

''What, you don't think it's the same guy?'' asked Hodges. ''Funny-looking little dude with great big Bambi eyes?''

O'Rourke said, ''That's Abasolo. He's supposed to be on our side.''

Joe wasn't in the mood for banter. He spoke as if no one else had. ''I've brought in some outside help on this—a consultant working at Tulane right now. Someone we were very lucky to get—an expert in forensic psychology. In fact, a nationally known expert on serial killers.''

''You talkin' a shrink, Joe?'' asked Hodges.

Joe nodded, looking a little guilty, as if he'd betrayed the police code of ethics. ''I think she's going to be a tremendous help to us, and I want you all to listen carefully to what she has to say, and to utilize her services to the maximum.''

''Man, you must *really* be desperate.'' By virtue of his age, Hodges could get away with remarks others couldn't.

Nervously, Joe glanced at his watch. ''She ought to be here now.'' He left the room.

O'Rourke said, ''This ought to be right up your alley, Langdon. Everybody Uptown goes to shrinks, don't they?''

''I wouldn't know, Frank; I don't live Uptown.''

Joe returned with Dr. Cindy Lou Wootten, possibly the only non-blonde in the Western hemisphere who could make Abasolo's eyes go dark with lust at a second's viewing. Skip thought she'd never seen such a naked statement on a man's face. In spite of herself, she found it sexy.

Dr. Wootten (''Call me Cindy Lou, I'm just a psychologist'') was easily the best-looking woman Skip had personally seen (not counting the likes of Meryl Streep and Kim Basinger), and Skip had gone to Ole Miss, where everyone looked like a Streep or a Basinger. Wootten was spectacular, and it wasn't only her beauty—Skip was willing to bet she wasn't ''just'' anything, despite her self-deprecation.

She was about five feet ten, thin, willowy, with straight Lauren Bacall hair, high cheekbones, and clothes that managed to be both crisp and fashionable; also to look like a million dollars. Her jewelry was tasteful and expensive; even in the heat, her makeup was perfection. She was black.

She carried herself like the first woman president, exuded a confidence that made Skip squirm with envy. She talked like an actress portraying a tough public defender given to street slang to get through to her clients. Or so it seemed to Skip, so incongruous was her earthy speech with her sophisticated appearance.

"Anybody here thinking, 'This broad's no expert on crime, I know as much about crime as she does,' has got another think coming. I grew up in Detroit, ladies and gentlemen, I was an expert before I was two and a half; and you could say I had some hands-on expertise by the time I was fourteen.

"But just in case you think that's all, I've got a few meaningless graduate degrees in psychology, I did my clinical internship in a federal prison, I'm well-published in the forensic end of the field, and I've consulted for the FBI. You wonder what I'm doing here, I got a grant; we academics'll go anywhere for a free ride, or anyway, I used to think that before I experienced the Crescent City in August. Whoo-ee, never again. Now let's talk about the Axeman." She took a breath.

"This guy doesn't look like a sex killer. He kills men, he kills women, he doesn't care; and he leaves their clothes on. So right away we got a little problem. Most of what we know about serial killers comes from an FBI study of thirty-six convicted sexual murderers. Although they were all sexual killers, and we think our man isn't—or our woman, if that's the case—all we can do is use what we've got.

"Okay now. I don't mind telling you up front, the FBI looks at things a little differently from the way a psychologist might. They're not so much interested in why a person murders as how he does it. So the data we've got is descriptive. Only problem is, when I give you the lists of characteristics the study isolated, some of you are going to see yourselves in there. A lot of the responding murderers were daydreamers and compulsive masturbators as children, for instance. Anybody like that here?"

An uncomfortable titter riffled through the room.

"But then they were bed-wetters and fire-setters, too. They

destroyed property, some of them, and engaged in self-mutilation. You don't see all that every day.''

"Hold it a minute," said Hodges. "When we get a suspect, how're we supposed to know in advance if he liked to masturbate when he was a kid?''

"Easy," said O'Rourke. "Forget the ones who spent their childhood in a coma.''

This time the laughter was more of a catharsis—for some of the officers. Skip and Cappello weren't among them.

"Well, you've got a point there," said Cindy Lou. "What you can look for are things like psychiatric problems, substance abuse, criminality, maybe a sporadic work record.''

"Give me a break," said O'Rourke. "Whose brother-in-law doesn't have a sporadic work record?''

Cindy Lou shrugged. "Your best bet's classic police work—checking criminal records.''

"Thanks a *lot*."

She ignored him. "Okay, there's something we need to look at right off the bat. Your crime scenes. The FBI classifies offenders as organized and disorganized.

"The organized offender plans. If he's a rapist, maybe he uses a condom so the police can't analyze his sperm. He's going to wear gloves, maybe, or wipe off his fingerprints. Maybe he takes the body away from the crime scene. The important thing is this: He plans the crime in such a way as to avoid getting caught. He's usually smart.

"The disorganized offender maybe isn't so bright. He leaves a sloppy crime scene—fingerprints, footprints, every kind of thing. Sometimes he can't resist keeping the bodies. One guy made drums and seat covers out of two women he kept around for eight years. After killing them, of course.''

The requisite groan rose.

"This kind of killer might use a weapon found at the scene and left there. Now, your guy brought his weapon—his hands—and probably wore gloves. But he did use available materials for his *A*—a lipstick in one case, and blood in another, obtained with a knife he found at the scene. So what does that suggest to you?''

Cappello said, ''Can you have a combination?''

''Good. You sure can and in fact it's pretty common. We'd know more about the Axeman if we knew how he was getting his victims, but just from the simple, clean crime scenes he left, I'd say he seems more like the organized type. Would you agree? Especially the officers who were there—Langdon? Hodges?''

Both nodded. Hodges said, ''I don't know how much planning went into it, but it definitely didn't look like any maniac had been there. More like an executioner. Did his job, did it well, and split.''

''Okay. Leaning toward organized then. Unfortunately, a disorganized killer might be easier to spot—might look a little crazier if you want to use that term. Your organized killer is usually intelligent, socially and sexually competent, has a car in good condition, and does some kind of skilled work.''

O'Rourke said, ''Shee-it. How do you know that?''

Cindy Lou smiled. ''That's the profile. But remember, the Axeman's probably a combination. When you get to know him a little better, you might find out he's high in the birth order, his father has a stable work history, he uses alcohol when he kills, he lives with a partner, he kills when he's under precipitating stress, and he follows the crime in the news media.'' She smiled. ''Or you might not. The main thing is, I probably wouldn't look for somebody on the fringes, a social outcast type. This person probably functions pretty well in the world.

''Even if the profile didn't say he was bright, I think the letter would indicate that. He's got enough education to know about the original Axeman and enough brains to haul the story out again.''

Skip said, ''What about the E.T. thing?''

''Two possibilities that I can see. First of all, he might

believe it. But I don't think so. These weirdos don't usually become spacemen—more likely they see them or hear them. And this one doesn't seem the type for that—that would be more the disorganized profile. The other thought is that it's just a clever update on the original. Which fits with the organized profile. But you know what I don't like? All that extremely childish stuff—'I'm baaack' and that kind of mess. We're talking a case of very arrested development here."

"I thought it was funny," said O'Rourke.

"We're talking two cases."

Joe said quickly, "What about the *A*?"

"The *A* suggests a need to be recognized and the letter confirms that. But this dude's wily. Maybe he's lying about it standing for 'Axeman.' It's funny he picked that name when he doesn't use an axe."

"But that was the name of the historical killer," said Cappello.

"Then why not use the historical weapon? There's a false note there someplace. There's a piece of every criminal— even little kids who raid cookie jars—that wants to confess. Maybe this guy started to write his name and some sane self-protective part of him pulled him back—and then he dreamed up the Axeman thing as a cover."

"Adam Abasolo," said Hodges.

Cindy Lou looked Abasolo in the eye. "You do look kind of dangerous."

Joe said, "Where do you think we should look for this creep?"

"These organized types tend to move around. I think I'd check with the police departments in the immediate area— maybe there've been similar crimes."

Joe nodded. "We'd better do recent releases too." He sighed. "And new arrests. Somebody with a similar record may have just gone to jail in another parish."

Since the letter had just arrived, Skip doubted it. But she

knew it had to be checked. There'd be literally hundreds of names.

They divided up sheriff's offices, and Joe assigned Hodges to the State Department of Corrections. It was boring, tedious work. But it was the best bet they had.

"I'll have the veggie muff."

"I beg your pardon?"

"It's like a muffelatta without the poisons."

Sonny settled on a more conventional sandwich, and when they were seated on a bench outside, he with a Coke, she with bubbly water, he found himself wondering what the hell he was doing here. Every restaurant in the city was airconditioned and they were eating outside.

Di said, "What a gorgeous day! I'm so glad you came by. I probably wouldn't have come out at all, all day long, if you hadn't turned up. We miss so much staying inside, don't you think?"

"I guess we do. I would have missed you, anyway." He was embarrassed the instant it was out. He had come by her house to figure out who she was, to leave a note, to try to make contact sometime in the future, but without much hope. She had been on her balcony watering her star jasmine, and on impulse he'd asked her to lunch.

But then had begun the long negotiation that had ended in this odd nibbling on a bench outside a health-food deli on Esplanade. "I only eat live foods," she had said.

"Oysters?" That was all he could think of.

She had laughed. "Sprouts and things."

"Is that a live veggie muff?" he said now. "I don't see any sprouts."

She laughed again, a laugh like a flute. He thought of the nymph who had been named Syrinx after a musical instrument (or perhaps she had been enchanted and changed into one). "I say 'live' when I really mean 'raw.' Raw foods are live to me."

"Ah. Raw eggs. Steak tartare."

She made a face. "You're teasing, right?"

"Uh-huh. If you think a muffelatta's poison, I guess you must be a vegetarian. Don't you even eat dairy products?"

She shook her head.

"What's the theory behind that?" He congratulated himself. He'd found a subject she liked; he was talking to her and she was answering, not treating him like a dope or a child.

"Eating can change the world, did you know that? When you only eat live foods, like I do, the photosynthesis happens in your body and you begin to feel this *energy*. You feel all these cosmic connections." She hugged herself. "Oh, Sonny, such a change is coming in the next ten years! We're just at the beginning of it."

He was speechless, but she seemed to take his silence for rapt attention.

"You have to understand that the plants are here for a purpose. The old way, eating animals, is going now, fading out—have you noticed?"

"I do seem to know a lot more vegetarians nowadays."

She nodded. "The plants are here to teach us something, to enlighten us."

"Hey, listen, I went to Carrot U myself. First I had Professor Plum for Consciousness 101, but he was just an old fruit. Then I took Good Vibes from Dr. Zucchini, but he squashed all my ideas. So then I went out for the cornball team and life was just . . ." He paused, searching. ". . . a bowl of cherries."

She put a hand on his knee. "Sonny, you're delightful, you know that?"

He knew it was true. She brought out something in him, he didn't know what. He could almost feel the flow of energy she talked about. Who was he to say she was wrong? Even he knew doctors knew nothing about nutrition. She talked like a Venusian, but maybe this elfin, slightly nutty woman knew more than he did. He could never have thought of all those puns with Missy. Being around Di energized him, kicked something into gear.

"I'll bet you're a writer," she said. "You're so clever! A poet, maybe."

He preened. He wasn't clever. He was smart, sure, like all the Gerards were smart, smart like a scientist, but his brother was the clever one, the only Gerard who was different. Before now, he'd no more thought he could make up a line of poetry than wrestle an alligator.

He said, "No. Just a student." He'd meant to leave it at that, not mention the suddenly mundane thing he actually did, but he realized that "student" alone sounded absurdly young. "A medical student," he added.

"In that case, be Jean-Paul."

"Excuse me?"

"I checked on those names for you. Jean-Paul is an eight—philosophical and mature; intense, determined. That could work for a doctor."

"You checked on those names for me?" He was so immensely flattered he had hardly heard what she said.

"In either case, Arthur or Jean-Paul, your cornerstone would be one. Very creative and original. A visionary, really."

Now he was embarrassed. Surely he didn't deserve this much attention. And he was no visionary. More like a plodder. He wanted to get the spotlight off him before it revealed unpleasant truths. He said, "What do you do, Di?"

"Me? You mean my job?"

He nodded.

"I'm going to meetings right now. I go to three most days—I'm playing hooky today, but I'll go tonight. I think I can go to two—two really good ones."

"I see."

"I guess I'd have to say my job right now is healing myself."

Absently Abe wrapped the last crusts of his dreary sandwich in aluminum foil, not thinking about the task, looking miserably out his office window.

Shit, I hate this place, he thought.

He wouldn't have to be here at all if it weren't for goddamn Cynthia. Cynthia controlled the universe.

Mine, anyway. And there's not a goddamn thing I can do about it.

He had eaten staring glumly at the facade of the building across the street, possibly the only ugly building in the entire town, its architecture being possibly the only thing in town he could stand.

Now he walked to the window and looked down on the street, wanting to take a walk but knowing the heat was killing.

A lovely woman walked by—a lithe, very young one in a blue cotton dress. A blonde. He felt an unreasonable hunger rise up in his loins, a scary, uncontrollable tidal wave of a thing. He sat down again, dizzy, overwhelmed by the wave.

He knew her number—Missy's, not that girl's. He had gotten it from the list. But she wouldn't be home. What was the point?

Automatically, he dialed it, the act performed by the robot that had taken over his body, that was being run by that tidal wave, that wouldn't be stopped. Her machine answered—and then there was a click and she said, ''Hello?''

''I didn't think you'd be home.''

''It's my lunch hour,'' she said. ''I forgot something.''

''Missy, this is Abe. Abe from the program.''

''Abe.'' He could hear her taking a breath, searching her memory banks. ''I think I know you.''

''I was at Al-Anon Monday. I just wanted to tell you I was really inspired by what you said.''

''Thank you.'' She was hesitant, sounded properly flattered.

"I thought . . . Well, I'm going through something too. I'd like to talk to you."

"I remember you now. You're the one with the bald spot."

Oh, Jesus.

Catching herself in mid-faux pas, she kept talking. "Oh, I didn't mean . . . It's really cute, I mean. My uncle has a bald spot. It's sexy. Really. It's nice."

"You really think so?"

"I really do."

"Well, listen, would you indulge an ancient, ancient old man and—"

"You're not old."

"You wouldn't be ashamed to be seen with me?"

Silence.

"I mean, would you like to have lunch Monday?"

Seven

"EXCUSE ME?"

Since no one else was in the office, Skip was taking advantage of the solitude to check her teeth for bits of spinach, and re-apply lipstick. She planned to spend the afternoon re-interviewing Strickland's and Mabus's neighbors, catching any she might have missed.

She was staring at her own reflection, not too much caring for it, probing teeth with tongue, when she heard the timid inquiry.

"Yow!" She almost dropped the mirror. Looking up, she

saw that the intruder was a tired-looking woman, a little overweight, with hair frizzed on the ends by an inferior perm now about six months old. She wore walking shorts and running shoes. "You startled me."

"I guess I should have said something before I got so close—I'm Mary Shoemaker."

Skip stood and offered her hand. "Skip Langdon."

"They told me homicide was this way."

"Yes. Everybody's out but me, and I was just leaving. Who were you looking for?"

"Somebody on the Axeman case?" She looked as undecided as she sounded.

"I could probably help you. Would you like to sit down?"

Gingerly, Shoemaker sat, and leaned toward Skip. "I have this crazy idea about the murders. I don't know. . . ." She flushed in embarrassment. "I don't know if it's relevant, but I just thought I ought to tell somebody."

Skip nodded encouragingly, smiling on the outside, groaning inwardly.

"Linda Lee Strickland? You know, the girl who was murdered?"

Skip nodded.

"When I saw her picture in the paper, I thought I knew her. I just couldn't place her, that's all. But I did know Tom Mabus. I heard all about the murder on the way to Schwegmann's—on the radio?" She had the Southern woman's tic of ending statements with question marks. Once again, Skip felt obliged to nod.

"Poor Tom—I didn't know him very well, but he was somebody who was working very hard and I respected him for that. Well, anyway, when I heard his death was connected to that girl's, I remembered where I knew her. They were both in the program."

Skip searched her mind for relevant "programs," but didn't come up with anything.

"Programs, I should say," said Mary Shoemaker. "I think

the AA people just say 'program,' but everybody else is usually in more than one.''

''More than one what?''

''Oh. The twelve-step programs? You know them? Like AA and OA and everything?''

''I know AA. . . .''

''OA is Overeaters Anonymous. And then there's Al-Anon and Coda. . . . There's lots of them.''

Skip's pulse pounded in her head. ''Ms. Shoemaker, would you mind looking at some pictures for me?''

She pulled out a picture of Tom Mabus, one she'd gotten from his daughter, and three other pictures as well. She laid them out for Mary Shoemaker.

''Do you know any of these men?''

She pointed to Mabus's picture. ''That's Tom. But he was younger then. It's an old picture, isn't it?''

''Ms. Shoemaker, you certainly did the right thing by coming in today. I think this information could be very important, and I'd like to introduce you to somebody else if you have a moment.''

She got Cappello, took Shoemaker to Joe's office, and let her tell her story. Cappello was as excited as she was, literally licking her lips. ''Ms. Shoemaker, which one of these programs are you a member of?''

''Oh, I go to lots of meetings—Coda and Al-Anon, mostly, and OA; but I've been to Emotions Anonymous and once I went to Sex Anonymous.'' She blushed. ''I mean, I don't really have that problem—you know, sex addiction?—but a friend took me.''

''Okay, let's start at the beginning. Coda is . . . ?''

''Codependents Anonymous. And Al-Anon is technically for spouses of alcoholics, but anybody can go. People who aren't alcoholics even go to the regular AA meetings now.''

Skip watched Joe struggle with that. Finally, he said, ''Why?''

''You get inspired by other people's stories.''

"But why not just go to Al-Anon or Coda or something?"

"Well, they probably do that too, but maybe there isn't a meeting at the right time or place or something."

"You mean you don't just join a group and go to that one?"

"Oh, no. It's not formal at all. You just go to any meeting you want."

Skip was getting a bad feeling and she could sense the others were too. Cappello asked the question on both their minds. "Can you remember where you met Linda Lee and Tom?"

"Well, I saw Tom a lot. You probably wonder how I knew his last name."

"I beg your pardon?"

"Oh, maybe you didn't know we don't use last names. In the program? But Tom and I went to lunch after a meeting and he paid with a credit card." She sat back, looking embarrassed. "I peeked."

"Lunch. So it was a daytime meeting. Do you remember which one?"

"That was Al-Anon, I think. At the Perrier Club—that's a place where a lot of the meetings are held. Anyway, I know I saw him at lots of meetings. And I'm not sure where I saw Linda Lee. I never talked to her—I just know her face."

"So Tom went to Al-Anon."

"He did, but I'm starting to think I'm not really explaining myself very well. He probably went to lots of meetings."

"How many?"

"Well, I usually go to two or three a day."

Joe couldn't control a snort. "Two or three a day! What else do you do?"

The heretofore meek Mary Shoemaker straightened her back and said with dignity, "I don't think that's any of your business."

"Oh. Sorry. I was just surprised, that's all. Do you know of any other friends Tom had?"

70

She thought for a moment. "No, I really don't. When I said I saw him a lot, I didn't mean I talked to him a lot. But one day I was really impressed with his share and I told him so. And that's how we ended up having lunch. I kind of think he was a loner? A real nice man, though."

"And you're sure the program was where you saw Linda Lee?"

Once again she gave it her full attention. Finally, she said, "I don't go anywhere else except the grocery store and to take my kids to school."

Before she left she gave them a list of her favorite meetings and past favorites—eleven in all.

And then Skip got on the phone.

In an hour, after many misunderstandings, well-meanings, and speakings at cross-purposes, she had information that made her heart sink. She watched Cappello's face fall as she reported.

"These things are called anonymous because they are. You don't sign up for membership, you don't pay dues, and as Shoemaker said, you use only your first name. Needless to say, they don't exactly call the roll. They do pass around a phone list, so you can get in touch with Susie Q. across the room if you need someone to talk to. But of course that's voluntary, like everything else. Nobody has to get on it."

"Murder Anonymous," said Cappello, looking as if her mother'd just died.

"Yeah. You just walk in and you say 'I'm John and I'm codependent,' or maybe you don't. Some people never share at all." Seeing her puzzled look, Skip said, "Sharing means talking. But you don't have to do it. So say you want to find some lonely people to kill. You saw Mary Shoemaker. From what I gather, these things are full of people like her—nothing and nobody in their lives, and nothing to do except go to meetings. They're like churches used to be; or market day in small towns. I don't know—they're a whole social phenomenon.

71

"So say you want a good place to find somebody to kill—somebody who couldn't be connected with you because you don't even know their last name, and nobody knows your name at all. Do you walk in and say, 'I'm the Axeman and I'm homicidal'? What you do is walk in on a roomful of sitting ducks. And then you walk in on another roomful of them. I hate to say it, Sylvia, but you know how many of these things there are in New Orleans? Hundreds. There's more than a hundred Al-Anon meetings and four hundred and five AA meetings alone. So that's about five hundred. So far I've unearthed eleven programs besides those two main ones, but there may be more. Lots of the programs don't even have permanent phone numbers, so I couldn't find out yet how many there are."

Cappello sighed. "You've got to be kidding."

"I've got more bad news. I sort of remember a long time ago my friend Alison Gaillard advised me once to go to AA because that's where you met all the best guys. I thought she was kidding."

"Shit!"

"Well, I called her back."

Alison had said, "Skippy, honey, that was years ago. You don't have to go to AA to meet guys. Everybody's doing Coda this year."

"Including you?"

"Why should I? I'm married."

Cappello said "Shit!" again. "You mean we're talking about a bunch of neurotics cruising each other?"

"Hey," said Skip, "our first thought was a bar, remember?"

"Yeah, but if it's that kind of deal, how do you explain Tom Mabus?"

"Maybe he saw something—like Linda Lee with the Axeman. Anyway, yes to cruising, but that's not exactly the whole story. I gave Cindy Lou a call too. Want to know what she said?"

"Yeah, from the horse's mouth—in half an hour. Get the whole team together."

Cindy Lou brought books with her—books with names like *Codependent No More!* and *Beyond Codependency*. She also brought some by John Bradshaw, including the ones Skip had seen in Linda Lee's apartment.

When Joe had brought everyone up to date on Mary Shoemaker, he let her take over.

"Ladies and gentlemen, we are talking large. We are talking the biggest thing since VCRs—maybe since the great god television itself. If you aren't addictive, then you're almost certainly codependent, and if you aren't codependent, you're nobody."

"Be there or be square," said Hodges.

"Well, not exactly. It's not like you've got any choice about it. See, the people who write these books say ninety-six percent of the population's codependent. They don't say who the other four percent are, but you can bet you haven't met them and aren't likely to. They're basically saying we're a very unhealthy society and a lot of the things we hold up as real great qualities are sick, sick, sick. So people go to these meetings to unlearn everything they learned as kids."

Cappello said, "I thought therapists were the chic thing."

"This stuff's free." Cindy Lou looked around the room. "Anybody in here codependent?"

O'Rourke snorted. "I don't even *know* any alcoholics."

"You don't have to know any alcoholics. That's a big misunderstanding about this whole deal. You can be codependent as hell even if you live alone and don't form relationships or friendships. It's a dumb word, 'codependent.' Doesn't work, really. But the reason I asked that was just to see something. These groups are anonymous, and I don't want to blow anyone's anonymity, but I'm willing to bet there's somebody in here who's been to at least one meeting of one of these things, maybe who goes regularly."

"I'm Adam," said Abasolo, "and I'm an alcoholic."

"I was in Alateen," said Cappello quietly. "I still go to ACOA—that's Adult Children of Alcoholics."

Cindy Lou nodded. "Just about everybody's got some kind of contact with them. I bet somebody else in here's got a relative who's hooked on Al-Anon."

O'Rourke said, "You got it. My ex-wife. And she's as bitchy as ever."

"Well, now, that's an interesting point you bring up. One of the objects of the exercise, reduced to simplest terms, is to quit being too nice to people. Look here." She opened one of the books she'd brought, turned a few pages. "What do you see?"

"Looks like lists."

"That's right. Lists of characteristics that make you co-dependent. You read this stuff, you see why they say just about everybody's got the bug—anything you can name, especially anything that's real common behavior in America, is probably here. Listen to this—page eighty-nine: 'Code-pendents tend to blame themselves for everything.' Two pages later: 'Codependents frequently blame other people for their problems.' Here's two right together: They tend to be 'extremely responsible,' or 'extremely irresponsible.' "

Hodges whistled. "Kind of slips through your fingers, doesn't it?"

But O'Rourke was interested. "What does that have to do with being too nice?"

And Skip blurted, "Is it *about* anything or is it just a bunch of words?"

"It is about something. These people tend to get a little obsessive—and they'd be the first to admit that obsessiveness is a sure sign of codependency—but basically they're onto something. They have all these lists of different ways you can react to being codependent, but as far as I can figure out, the bottom line's this: If you're codependent, you're minding everybody's business but your own."

"Sheee-it," said Abasolo.

"Yeah?" said Cindy Lou. "You ever feel like you're the only one in your district doing any work? Maybe you can't figure out why all these old guys twice your age don't get half as much work done as you do. You worry about that at all? Spend any time thinking of ways to make them shape up? The codependency folks talk about being obsessed with controlling other people's behavior."

He reddened.

"Maybe you're codependent, baby. Besides being an alcoholic."

Skip hid her smile with a hand. She'd liked Cindy Lou that morning, but her attitude was deepening to something approaching worship.

Cindy Lou went on with her lecture. "That's why I say it's the bottom line. Everybody's got that one. In this society, we're all busy taking up the slack for everybody else, sometimes just with our own secret knowledge that we're superior, like Adam over there; sometimes we mind their business to the point where we're trying to guess what they want next and give it to them before they even know."

With a jolt, Skip remembered Curtis Ogletree, Linda Lee's landlord.

"I've heard this crap before and it makes me sick," said Abasolo. "Recovery spillover, I call it. AA meetings are getting so they're full of assholes mouthing all that garbage, nattering on about their fathers and mothers, telling their boring dreams, carrying on about their damn 'recovery'—I hate that word, 'recovery.' I'm a drunk, I'm not a recovering drunk, and I'm goddamn sick and tired of having my meetings co-opted. See, they come from all these other programs for any goddamn thing you're 'addicted' to. Sex Anonymous; Emotions Anonymous. Jesus! I almost died of my addiction and it pisses me off to hear the word trivialized."

"A not uncommon AA view," said Cindy Lou, completely unfazed. "The steps were formed for dealing with substance addiction and are now being applied to the theory I was just describing, plus a lot of iffy-sounding non-substance 'addictions,' like work, shopping, and food. Can you be addicted to food? AA people have their doubts it's the same thing. However, like it or not, some two hundred other groups have adopted the AA model. Nationwide, there are from two million to twenty million people in the recovery movement, depending on how you count.''

"Well, look, Dr. Wootten," said O'Rourke. "I'm sure this is all very interesting, but aren't you here to advise us about the Axeman? Are you saying his psychological profile's 'codependent'? If ninety-six percent of the population's codependent, do we really need an 'expert' to come in here and tell us he's just like everybody else?''

"Oh, that wasn't about the Axeman. That was about communication. I just taught you people a new language you're going to be needing. Now I'm going to teach you one more thing. You go into a twelve-step program, you better be ready to turn over your problems to a higher power. And that's what I'm going to do now.''

Joe laughed. "I don't think they mean lieutenants, Cindy Lou.''

"Well, I do. And when you're done with my problems, you can do my laundry.''

He turned to the others. "Okay, we've finally got a link between the two victims, and frankly, we haven't got another damn thing. Officer Langdon's been on the phone all afternoon and here's the deal. There are at least thirteen twelve-step programs in this town and hundreds of meetings—well over five hundred, maybe more like a thousand. Only one member from each meeting—the intergroup representative—is known to the larger organization. And because of the tradition of anonymity, the program people won't tell us who any of *them* are. Even if we could get a court order for the information, we'd then have several hundred people to interview who would know only the people in their own groups by first names and wouldn't even tell us those."

"Because of the tradition of anonymity," said O'Rourke, sounding disgusted.

"So we're going to go to the meetings and look at the phone lists for any Toms and Linda Lees."

"You gotta be kidding!"

"Right, Frank, I'm making a great big joke. Now tell me what you want to do instead."

O'Rourke said nothing.

"Anybody else got any better ideas?"

"Okay, I appreciate the fact that it's going to be time-consuming and may lead nowhere, but it's the only place we've got to go and we're going there." He went back to his original lecture. "So far as Langdon can tell, neither Mabus nor Strickland was a drinker. And Mary Shoemaker doesn't go to AA, Narcotics Anonymous, Cocaine Anonymous, or Gamblers Anonymous. She does go to Tough Love, which is a parents' group, but neither Tom nor Linda Lee had children or teenagers. So for now, we're going to skip those programs and concentrate on the others.

"We've got a list of the ones Shoemaker likes and a promise from her not to blow anyone's cover, so we're going to start out with Mary's Greatest Hits. And Langdon found out Mabus was off only on Thursday and Friday nights. So we're going to concentrate specially on the Thursday and Friday meetings. But we know he went to daytime ones as well, and Strickland could have gone any night of the week, so we'll try to cover everything we can.

"This is Thursday and it's four o'clock. Some meetings are right after work and some are later—I want everybody in here to go to two tonight, and then we'll see where we are. Here are the lists and the assignments."

O'Rourke said, "Are we undercover, or what?"

"To the extent you can be—because of the anonymity tradition some of these people may balk if you say who you are.

But we all know how small this town is. You may run into somebody you know, but remember, even policemen have a right to go to these things. You're there because you're Frank and you're codependent, so far as anybody knows, but don't 'share'; keep a low profile. Remember, no one knows about the twelve-step connection except the Axeman, so there's no reason for anyone else to suspect anything, therefore no reason for gossip to get around."

They began picking up their things. Cindy Lou walked over to O'Rourke and stood very close. She said, "Frank, can I ask you something? Is it women you hate, or black people?"

O'Rourke reddened, for once apparently at a loss.

Eight

SKIP HAD ASKED for Overeaters Anonymous, partly because she was intrigued and partly because she thought if she already had it, O'Rourke wouldn't make jokes about how she ought to. He hadn't either, but that was probably because he had a new target in Cindy Lou. His excuse for hating Skip had been that she was from Uptown, and maybe he had really thought it was true, but now it seemed more as if he simply had a chip on his shoulder where women were concerned.

And Cindy Lou could handle him. *Delighted to have you aboard, Cindy Lou.*

She looked forward to the OA meeting—maybe it would be like Weight Watchers, which she'd already done with semi-success. She liked to be around overweight people, especially women—most women she knew in New Orleans were so damn slender. She didn't know if it was in the genes or the result of constant secret dieting. Their tiny bones and fluttery mannerisms made her feel like an ostrich in a flock of finches.

Skip was six feet tall and had never been thin, had thought of herself as fat for years. Green eyes and a head-turning mop of curly brown hair were all she had, according to Langdon family mythology (and Conrad had some unflattering things to say about the hair). But she'd gotten in shape before she joined the police department and now she was "Juno-esque" if you listened to Jimmy Dee. In her own opinion she could still stand to lose a few pounds—twenty, maybe.

The meeting was in a church and she was almost late. They hadn't started yet, but it looked as if most of the chairs were filled. Strangely, there weren't all that many fat people here, a notable exception being the guy in the small chair in the back. . . . Good God! A four-hundred-pounder. On the other hand, quite a few people looked as if they were recovering away to nothing.

Quickly she sat on the floor, more or less behind one of the chairs, devoutly wishing the person in it were fat, because the last person in the world she wanted to see was sitting across the room. Her mother. She was talking to the woman next to her, her face in profile, and Skip didn't think she'd been spotted yet, but she would be; the group wasn't nearly large enough to hide in.

Her mother! It wasn't her day.

A woman who seemed to be the leader said her name was Leslie, she was a compulsive overeater, and it was time to begin. Then followed a complicated ritual—the reading of the steps, the traditions, a sort of welcome or statement of purpose—in all, quite a few more documents than Skip had any interest in. And there was the Serenity Prayer: "God, grant me the serenity to accept the things I can't change, the courage to change the things I can, and the wisdom to know the difference.''

Skip found herself fidgeting, slightly embarrassed, hostile. She had wondered if it would be like a cult and found that it was exactly as she imagined one would be—the silly rituals, the rapt faces of the true believers, the utter lack of humor, the deep sense of purpose. Her skin crawled.

''I'm really grateful for the opportunity to lead the meeting this week,'' said Leslie, ''because of something that happened to me this week. But I want to go back farther than that. I was a thin little girl, and everybody always told me how pretty I was, and then I got chubby when I was about nine or ten, and then they didn't talk like that anymore. They said I had beautiful skin or beautiful eyes and I knew that was all they could think of to say because I wasn't beautiful anymore.''

Skip found it hard to imagine that Leslie ever hadn't been beautiful. She was forty perhaps, and beautiful now, dark, with high cheekbones, not afraid to let the first streaks of gray show. From the looks of her body, she worked out every day. She was absolutely the sort who made Skip feel like an ostrich, and she would have killed to look like her. How dare this woman speak so trivially, concern herself with such a pathetic excuse for an issue, when she didn't have an excess ounce on her?

Leslie paused in her narrative. ''We were Jewish. I didn't know anyone else who was. All the girls I knew were tiny little blondes. And then I started growing. Everybody said when I got my growth I'd lose my baby fat, but I didn't. Whenever I was with them, I kept getting this weird image— of this great, lumbering female Godzilla walking through a field of Barbie dolls.'' She made such a funny Godzilla face that Skip forgot herself and laughed loudly. Quickly she caught herself—surely her mother would know her laugh.

''I thought that what being Jewish was about was being ugly. Being fat. I brought my friend Nancy home from school one time, and she said, 'Oh, Leslie, I never smelled anything like your house. I hate my mother's cooking—we never have anything but bologna sandwiches for lunch and overcooked roast beef for dinner.' I don't know why her mom wasn't home cooking gumbo all day.'' She paused to accommodate the titter that passed through the room.

''My mother didn't cook. We had a maid who did, but my mother taught her how to make all the Jewish dishes so no Jew had to cook on holidays. And she also made all the great New Orleans things and a pretty mean spaghetti. But when Nancy said that, I realized that it was bad to eat good food, that I could look like Nancy if only I would deprive myself, as she was naturally deprived, on account of growing up in a Gentile household.

''I wanted to stop eating but I couldn't. I'd starve myself for a while and then I'd binge. And then I learned how to throw up after bingeing. Anyway, to make a long story short, I ended up almost dying. I spent a long time in a hospital, and I was really grateful to be there and to have discovered this program and my higher power.

''Meanwhile, my friend Nancy had long since married someone from Pennsylvania and moved away. And then she got divorced and came back. I was really happy to see her and felt like we really had a friendship this time. I mean I felt good about myself and didn't have to feel inferior because I was Godzilla anymore, and it was great. I'd been abstinent for a long time and I thought I really had a lot of recovery.

''But anyway, what happened this week was, my husband moved out. He told me six months ago he was in love with Nancy and said he didn't want to break up our home and asked me to go into therapy with him and everything like that. . . .''

Her voice was steady, her delivery matter-of-fact—not overly dramatic, not wooden. ''But none of it worked, and he moved out and moved in with Nancy. And last night I almost asked him, I almost called him up and said, 'Is it because of my thighs?' '' She laughed, and so did everyone else, apparently glad for the momentary tension release.

"And then when I didn't call him, even though I've been abstinent for . . . well, eighteen months this time, I almost went into relapse. It's so hard not to get into that trap of eating to make yourself feel better because your self-image is bad because you're so fat. Stuffing your face along with your feelings. I had one hand on the refrigerator door when the phone rang and it was Sudie asking me to lead the meeting tonight, and I thought, I can't go into relapse *now*. So that's how my higher power works for me. Realistically, I know I'm not fat, but I know I will be if I'm not careful. And so because I'm feeling that way, I guess I'd like to hear from other people about self-image. Right now is a really hard time for me and I'm just glad I have this group, that's all. Thank you.''

Skip felt tears in her eyes, almost felt she should applaud, wondered what would happen next. Would people tell Leslie what a great gal she was and how she shouldn't feel so bad about herself?

They didn't.

Several raised their hands and Leslie recognized the Toyota-size guy. He said his name was Robert.

"Hi, Robert," chorused the group.

"You know how there's supposed to be a thin guy inside every fat guy? Well, I never had one. My dad was fat, my mom's fat, my uncles are fat, my grandfather was fat, and my bother was fat. We're Vic.'' His audience laughed politely, knowing he referred to a local cartoon character who was a food giant.

"Can you imagine what our refrigerator looked like when I was growing up? You couldn't even conceive of the size of pots my mother made red beans in. And she never cooked one pot, it was always two.

"It was like growing up in the desert and never seeing a tree. You think the whole world's made of sand and scorpions. I don't think I ever saw a thin person until I was in first grade. Then the kids started to call me names. You know what? I didn't even mind because I had a *great* self-image. I thought fat was how you were supposed to be. I didn't feel ugly at all because everybody at home always told me I was handsome.

"My father died a few years ago, and that was sad, but I did fine for myself. I married a gorgeous, lovely woman and had two beautiful children. I never paid any attention at all to what those doctors said. Sure people died early in our family, that was just our genes. But two months ago my brother died. My brother did fine too. You know what? He also had a lovely wife and two beautiful children. You know what else? He was two years younger than I am. So I'm trying to get a new self-image. I'm trying to imagine what I'd look like thin. I've lost ten pounds, I'm working on it. I know I'm not supposed to work so hard, that my higher power will take care of it, but I'm new to this program, and I don't really know my higher power yet, and I've never surrendered a day in my life. It's a real hard thing, but I'm just glad to be here. I know there's a thin guy in there somewhere and I really want him to get to know his kids, and be able to see them go off to college and get married." His voice broke. Blinking back tears, he said, "That's all. Thank you."

Once again, people responded only by raising their hands. To Skip's horror, Leslie recognized Skip's mother.

"I'm Elizabeth and I'm a compulsive overeater."

"Hi, Elizabeth."

"I'm wearing black," she said, "even though it's the middle of the summer. If I weren't wearing black, I'd be wearing vertical stripes.

"Right now I'm only about five pounds overweight. Usually I'm ten. Lately, I've been trying really hard to accept myself as a person who weighs ten pounds over her ideal weight, but I'm afraid if I did that, I'd gain another ten pounds.

"I recently figured out what I've been eating about all these years and that makes me feel empty, like I need to fill up. I know I eat because I'm nervous. Deep down I'm afraid people won't like me; they won't accept me. I haven't got the right dress, I didn't use the right fork, I don't belong to the right clubs. I'm different. I feel really different from everybody else. I feel like somebody's going to find out about me—that I'm really from Mars and I'm just faking it. Actually, I'm from Monroe. In this town that might as well be Mars."

Skip noticed a hard set to her mother's mouth. She had worked hard, Elizabeth had, at becoming a fixture in New Orleans society, had devoted her life to it (had nearly ruined Skip's life trying to make her into a social asset). Being from Monroe was a bigger hardship for her than it would have been for the average citizen. Ordinarily, Skip's lip would have curled with distaste—she hadn't a moment's time for her mother's social-climbing—but larger, more disturbing emotions roiled within her.

A piece of her felt for Elizabeth, saw her in a new light. Her voice was different from her social voice or her mother voice. Could it be that this was what she really sounded like, stripped down to plain Elizabeth Langdon, no roles? Skip honestly didn't think she'd have recognized this voice over the phone. It sounded sincere, not a word she associated with her mother.

Elizabeth used everything and everyone to get what she wanted, yet covered her ruthlessness with a patina of dizziness. She was a genius at organizing a charity drive, but hopeless, for instance, at cooking. It was as if so much of her energy went·into her life's work she had none left for life. The notion of her mother as a feeling person, someone with insecurities, touched Skip's heart.

But Elizabeth's portrayal of herself as alienated, out of it, different from everyone else, was unbelievable, out of the question. It made Skip furious. She felt angry spots pop red on her cheeks. Her mother had spoken in that unfamiliar voice, the one that sounded . . . sincere.

But that isn't how she is, it's the way I am. Skip was the one kidnapped by aliens and dumped in foreign territory—all Elizabeth had done was move from Monroe. It wasn't fair, and that wasn't half the story. Skip had been bullied, browbeaten, and beleaguered all her life by a harpy of a mother trying to get her to conform, to be like everyone else, when Skip had no more idea how to do it than she knew how to summon the flying saucer that had set her down on an inhospitable landscape.

How dare Elizabeth, if she knew how it felt! Worse, how dare she claim feelings in common with Skip? That was almost the toughest part to take.

Oh, Skip, don't be such a baby.

She scrunched down smaller, hoping her mother couldn't see her, and tried to get her mind off herself. Fortunately, conditions were right. The next speaker told riotous stories of stealing cakes, eating them in locked bathrooms, replacing them so no one would know—but getting the flavors wrong.

When it was over, Skip knew the jig was up: everyone stood and joined hands in a circle. She was trapped—couldn't leave without making a spectacle of herself and couldn't hide in the circle. But Elizabeth gave no sign she saw her.

To Skip's horror, everyone closed eyes, bowed heads, and said the Lord's Prayer.

Then things got worse. A squeeze went around the circle. Skip felt both her hands being jerked up and down. "Keep coming back," said the group in unison and in rhythm with the jerks. "It works if you work it." Two last emphatic jerks.

She felt embarrassed and used. Was "used" the right word? "Manipulated," perhaps. At any rate, forced to participate in something that wasn't her idea, to conform. She hadn't been given a choice and it made her mad.

Her mother left, eyes straight ahead, but most people stayed to socialize. Skip found the phone lists—kept, she was glad to see, in a spiral notebook, which meant those of many past meetings were available. Quickly, she looked over the last four or five for "any Toms or Linda Lees," as Joe had put it, and found two Toms. Better still, she discreetly removed last week's.

She left starving and picked up a shrimp po' boy on the way home. She couldn't help wolfing it, in fact felt compelled to, and decided OA wasn't for her. Or maybe she just felt compelled, period. Compelled to stay in motion, to avoid stopping and thinking about what she'd been through. She compared the phone numbers of the two OA Toms with Tom Mabus's number—no match. She started dialing numbers from the pilfered list, trying to coax out last names, saying she was looking for a friend named Linda Lee. In a few minutes she'd reached seven answering machines and four human beings, two of whom had revealed last names and none of whom knew a Linda Lee (though one had once met a Linda at a meeting).

When she took a break to get a Diet Coke, the phone rang and she cringed.

No wonder I'm being so compulsive about the damn phone list.

But it wasn't her mother.

"Skippy, it's Alison."

"Alison Gaillard, guess what? I went to OA today."

"You want to meet a *fat* guy? Anyway, I thought you were already booked."

"Alison, have you ever noticed I could stand to lose a few pounds?"

"A lot of people in OA are thin—especially the women."

"How do you know?"

"Oh, all right. So I went a few times."

"Is everyone in town into this stuff?"

"Didn't I tell you? But a lot of people dropped out. You may have heard, those people don't drink."

"I thought that was just AA."

"It's just not a party crowd. Which brings me to the reason I called. I'm having an Axeman party. Come and protect the rest of us. You could even wear your uniform."

"Oh, for Christ's sake."

"Did I say something wrong?"

"I'm sorry. I knew it was going to happen. I was just thinking what a nightmare that whole thing's going to be—if we don't catch him by then. Sort of a mini–Mardi Gras."

"Listen, Skippy, the party's on even if you do. Please come!"

"I have a horrible feeling I'm going to be working."

"I hope not—you won't believe the band we're having."

And then the dreaded call did come.

"Skippy, I thought I ought to let you know I saw you at the meeting." Skip stifled a sigh as she realized her mother's voice was back to normal—too sugary, trying too hard to please; phony as Naugahyde. "I know why you were there and I just wanted to let you know I won't blow your cover."

The TV words sounded strange with no *r*'s, pillowed into a softness that belied their origin.

"Mother. Thanks for calling. I guess you noticed I was hiding."

"That's why I didn't speak to you."

"Well, thank you for that. But I need to ask you something important—what do you mean you know why I was there?"

"Well, you just said you were hiding."

"Did you mean you thought I was on a case?"

"Of course I thought you were on a case. You wouldn't be caught dead at a meeting like that."

Did she dare press it anymore? She thought not. There was no way an Uptown matron could know which case she was on. But she had to hand it to her mother—she had great instincts. Any other mom would see her overweight daughter at OA and rejoice. How had Elizabeth figured it out? She decided, for the moment, not to ask.

"I didn't think you would either."

"Well, there's a lot you don't know about me."

"I liked the way you talked in there."

"Well, it wasn't for you, it was for me. I didn't see you till later. And I was mortified."

"Mortified! Why?"

"What I said was personal."

Oh, brother. "Well, I'm sorry I overheard it. But I really liked it. You sounded so real."

"Real! What do you mean by that?"

"I just liked it, that's all."

"Well, I don't mean to pry, but I was wondering about your case. If the police are coming to OA meetings, it must mean something."

Oh, it does; it does. And what do you do when you have a potential great source with a mouth like a tuba and not an ethical bone in her body?

Run for cover.

"Can you keep a secret?"

"Skippy, please. Did I ever tell you what Santa was bringing?"

"Well, look, I really can't discuss departmental business, but you know how women go to those meetings and kind of put their purses down and get all involved and don't pay attention?"

"You're looking for a pickpocket."

"Well, I can't really say, but anyway, whatever it is, we've had several complaints. And I mean *several*. I just think I need to warn you to be careful when you go to the meetings. In fact . . ."

"What, Skippy?"

"Maybe you should consider not going for a while."

"Because of a *pickpocket*?"

Damn, she'd gone too far. "Just a thought, that's all."

"It's not a pickpocket! Skip Langdon, you tell me what this is all about."

It was the voice of a parent speaking to a five-year-old—a bullying parent, and she heard it as such. Normally, she realized, she would simply have responded without recognizing it, but the professional dilemma was giving her distance. She was still so busy trying to resolve her problem that she could listen to what was happening, be objective about it. *I must have heard that voice a thousand times*, she thought, and realized with a pang how different it was from the one she'd heard in the meeting.

"I'm really sorry, Mother, but you know I can't discuss department business."

"You lied to me!"

"Mother, I really need your help. Were you serious about not blowing my cover?"

"Well, if there's danger, I think people ought to know about it."

She spoke slowly, hoping her voice sounded calm. "Listen, it can't hurt to watch your purse, can it? It would really help me if we could leave it at that right now."

"How dumb do you think I am, Margaret Langdon? Do you think I've forgotten you're in homicide?"

Oh, shit!

But, exasperated, she found herself laughing. "I forgot you knew. Okay, I'll tell you the truth. I was there for the same reason you were."

"I know you weren't. Even if you are fat as a pig, you wouldn't go to OA any more than you'd go to church on Sunday. The way you neglect your spiritual life is just outrageous."

"That's not true, Mother. I'm praying for a higher power to come to my rescue right now."

But when she'd finally gotten off the phone, it didn't seem funny at all. She noticed she was sweating, even though the AC was on high. Her hands trembled. She hadn't realized Elizabeth still had so much power over her.

She stripped to her underwear and sat on the floor, closing her eyes and taking deep breaths. She had a dozen books on meditation, wanted its promised solace like some people want to quit smoking, but she could never seem to sit still long enough to make it work. At the moment attempts to empty her mind resulted only in the ping-ponging of disjointed thoughts.

Was her mother in danger? Had she sacrificed the personal for the professional?

Surely, surely, surely not. There's a million twelve-step groups. What are the chances the killer's in that one?

But something Elizabeth had said echoed in her mind: *There's a lot you don't know about me.*

Maybe she went to three meetings a day, like Mary Shoemaker. Skip dismissed the thought: *Anyone who'd make that remark about my "spiritual life" couldn't possibly have one.*

That was the ping; the pong said, *You don't really know.*

And the ping said, *Don't be silly. You're just feeling guilty because she manipulated you into it.*

Over it all reverberated the part that really counted, the part that would be there for a long time, the phrase that even Steve Steinman wouldn't be able to kiss away:

Fat as a pig!
Fat as a pig!
Fat as a pig!

Nine

"I'M DI, AND I'm codependent."

"Hi, Di."

Di was a gorgeous woman, a woman of a certain age, but what age that was Skip couldn't have said—thirties to fifties was the best she could do. It hardly mattered. She had probably been ordinary at birth, awkward at twelve, and magnificent at fifteen; she would die magnificent so long as she didn't let her hair go gray. In ten or twenty years, even that wouldn't hurt.

She was small, a quality about which Skip was ambivalent at best. Yet she was so perfectly proportioned, so oddly beautiful in that dark, strange way of Southern women, that even tall people couldn't miss her. She wore black jeans and a T-shirt with a hand-painted parrot on it, a lavender parrot. Her expensive, many-strapped sandals showed plenty of toe cleavage; her toenail polish matched her parrot. A lesser dresser, Skip thought, would also have worn lavender eye shadow, but Di had chosen a dull gold. She was as well turned out as she was beautiful. The odd thing about her was the oversized doll in her lap.

This was obviously a hugely popular meeting—there were probably fifty people in the small, stuffy room, sitting either on the floor or on half-size chairs meant for children. It was a Sunday-school room in a Baptist church, a cheerful yellow room, the walls decked with children's drawings, a room apparently chosen for ambience rather than comfort.

Skip had chosen the floor over one of the tiny chairs, but still she felt huge and awkward, wildly uncomfortable, restless as a kid in Sunday school. Maybe that was part of the deal. It didn't matter a damn because this was where she wanted to be. Fully a third of the people in the room, not one of whom was a child or even a teenager, cuddled teddy bears or dolls.

Mary Shoemaker had described the group a little—it was Codependents Anonymous (Coda, to initiates) with an inner-child focus—but she hadn't mentioned anything about toys. And why should she have? Tom Mabus's teddy bear was one of those details that hadn't been given to the press.

Di led the group through virtually the same twelve-step ritual Skip had so detested at OA, but this time she found herself relaxing a little, almost getting used to it. Di said the subject was vulnerability.

"I talked to my daughter today," she said, "and she said to me, 'Mom, you're still a kid, you're always going to be a kid.' And I was hurt. Isn't that weird? Nothing is more important to me than this group. Some of you know how hard I've worked to let my kid out, to really experience things like a child again, but when she said that, I thought, 'You're supposed to be a mother, not a kid. If your kid thinks you're a kid, there must be something wrong with you.' And I realized how vulnerable my inner child still is, how much more work I have to do, reassuring her and letting her know she's loved."

There was more, some of which Skip followed and some of which she didn't. Mostly, she found herself distracted, wondering why the hell a grown woman would be so hurt by something her daughter said.

Fat as a pig! came at her like a slap in the face, and with it the memory of her feelings when she'd heard her mother share, some of them adult, lots of them childish.

So that's it. Your inner child is the part of you that didn't grow up, that kicks in when your parents run the same old familiar numbers on it.

But *was* that it? Di was talking about something that had happened with her daughter, not her mother. And what did the dolls and teddy bears mean?

"I'm Leon and I'm codependent."

"Hi, Leon."

Despite the heat, Leon wore a coat and tie, the tie loose at the neck.

He could have just taken it off.

But she suspected Leon hardly ever took off his tie, maybe slept in it, if the worry lines around his mouth were any indication. She remembered Cindy Lou's remarks about obsessiveness. Leon looked as if he had it in spades. He had thinning blond hair and a wiry body, could have been attractive if he'd known how to smile.

"We don't have vulnerability in my family. We work in banks or maybe shipping companies and we rise to the top." He said the last four words in a mock bass and he did smile. And he was attractive.

The teddy bear in his lap was the size of a two-year-old. He stroked it as if it were a real animal.

"We don't get hurt, we get mad. We're an entire family of rage-aholics. If somebody says to us, 'Hey, Leon, baby, it kind of gets to me the way you always forget my birthday and never come home till midnight and always have to go to the office on Saturday, and I think I'll divorce you now,' do we get upset? Do we say, 'Hey, I'm losing my wife, I must have really screwed up, this really hurts'? Not in my family we don't. We stuff all our feelings of hurt and guilt and spew out bile. After we yell at her awhile, we say, 'You know, she never was good enough for the likes of us. Her family comes from New Iberia and her fanny's too big and always was.'

93

And then we say, 'If she thinks she's getting a penny of our money, she's out of her pathetic Cajun mind.' ''

Skip realized she knew who he was. He was Leon Wheatley, whose divorce was infamous Uptown; for days while it was happening, Alison Gaillard had fed her chilling stories of Wheatley arrogance and penuriousness. But here was Leon, from one of the fanciest families in New Orleans, making what amounted to a public confession with a teddy bear on his lap.

''We always make it the other guy's fault. We'll do anything to keep from admitting we might be hurt. We don't have an inner child. In fact, we never get to *be* children even when we're under ten. So I'm having to kind of . . .'' He paused, sweating from the effort, Skip thought, of what he was saying ''. . . give *birth* to one. He feels bad sometimes and I let him do that. I just let him know that's okay, it's okay to feel bad. Nothing like that's ever been okay in my family.''

His voice was almost a whisper by the time he was done. He was still caressing the bear with strong, sensual strokes that he seemed to be using to distract himself. There was something weird about it, something raw and embarrassing—as if he were doing it to the bear because it was what he wanted for himself. Skip wanted to hug him, to comfort him, and understood that his need was so strong, had been so openly expressed, that it was practically impossible not to feel that way.

Leon Wheatley!

She couldn't believe any adult on the planet could do what he'd just done in front of strangers, and certainly not Leon Wheatley.

Again, she wanted to applaud, to go up and clap him on the back. Half of what he'd said made no sense at all to her, but the way he said it had seemed so real, had reminded her so much of Elizabeth speaking, that she couldn't help being moved.

A man named Abe shared next, another tall wiry one,

wearing glasses. "I was the kind of kid who always got everything I wanted. I mean I came from that kind of family.'

I bet. You've got that smug voice guys get whose mothers told them every day how great they were.

And I'm jealous.

"I'm trying to deal now with what happens when you can't have what you want. I realize my kid just never developed those muscles—the ones that handle vulnerability. There's a lot of things I want right now that I can't have. I don't even want to live in this city, but I have to now. I don't want to be the age I am; I want things I can't get anymore."

Things! You mean women, right?

"I have to talk to my kid; I say, 'Listen, I'm trying to be a good parent—to you, and to my own birth-children—but it isn't easy because I'm kind of a kid myself.' "

Skip decided this wasn't getting her any clearer on the concept and let her mind wander. She thought Abe seemed to be talking to someone in particular, and looked where he was looking. A lovely young blonde, no doubt the sort he couldn't get anymore, might be the object of his affection, but she looked as if she was with the young man sitting next to her. (Of course *he* might be the target, but Skip didn't think so.)

They were a gorgeous pair—very WASP, very Southern, a Kappa, probably, and a Sigma Chi, barely out of LSU. She wondered what they were doing here. They seemed too young and beautiful to have problems.

There were a lot of good-looking people here. She wondered if they were there to cruise, even whether this particular meeting had a reputation for having good pickings. It was certainly an odd idea, given the things that were coming out of people's mouths. Could a woman who'd just heard Abe possibly be interested in him?

Sure, if she were codependent. She'd probably want to help.

A guy in the corner was eyeing her. No question, he was

95

interested. He was staring at her, trying to get her attention. He was a beefy guy wearing cowboy boots when it must be ninety-five outside. His shoulders strained his shirt fabric. He was quite a bit older than Skip, late forties maybe, but he was dressed young—jeans, boots . . . no, it wasn't the clothes. It was the expression. His head had the round look heads get when a certain portion of hair has gone, but no one would think of this man as balding—simply round-headed. He had a mustache like a pirate's. He had a pirate's expression. Skip realized he reminded her of Clark Gable as Rhett Butler. But it was purely attitude, not appearance. He was a walking testosterone bomb, and Skip could feel the radiation from clear across the room.

The young blonde raised her hand. She was Missy and she was codependent.

"I know my higher power is working for me tonight because of what Leon said about his family. I just want to thank you for that, Leon. I found it so moving because I know a family like that, and a person who suffers from all that Superman stuff. But my instinct is not to say that's his problem and he's got to deal with it, it's to take it on as my problem. But that's not even the worst of it. Instead of trying to help in a constructive way, a way that might say, 'Listen, you're great the way you are,' my instinct is to help him become Superman."

The young man sitting next to her was either having a heat stroke or nearly fainting from embarrassment.

"I'm so vulnerable to his feelings, his wants and desires. Sometimes I feel like I don't know where his skin stops and mine starts."

Skip had a sudden flash: *She's my brother's fiancée. Camille. They're peas in a pod.*

"It's really, really hard for me to be saying this stuff right now, because I know how much he'd consider it an invasion of privacy. But I know I have to do it, for me. It's like the kid in me just got forgotten. I was born grown up, always taking care of everybody. And you know what? It's so hard to get her to talk to me. I have pictures. . . ."

She fished snapshots from her purse, held them up—pictures of an adorable towhead.

"I've started keeping these with me so I can look at her when I talk to her. But in my mind's eye she wears a little power suit and little baby high heels—I can't even see my own kid. I ask her what she wants and you know what she says? 'Whatever you want.' She's just like me—another people-pleasing little dork." Her face twisted, as if she hated herself, and Skip wondered how that was possible; she was every man's fantasy woman, every mom's fantasy daughter, every woman's best friend, the one who brought chicken soup when you had the flu.

"See how judgmental I am about myself?" She had turned red, as embarrassed as her companion. "But I'm working on it. I'm really trying." She paused, getting ready to sum up. "I guess that's all. Except that I'm really grateful to be here tonight."

Even as the next speaker began, the pirate, Skip kept watching her, fascinated that anyone could strip herself so naked in public, could let herself be so vulnerable so publicly. She thought Di's subject particularly interesting in view of what was happening here. Missy wiped tears that streamed briefly, smiled at her companion, the very picture of bravery, and gave her attention to the pirate. She reminded Skip not only of Camille, but of Melanie in *Gone with the Wind*. Noble to a fault. The flower of Southern womanhood. She'd had no idea before tonight what these women were all about.

The pirate was named Alex. His voice, like his manner, had a touch of a swagger in it. She was uncomfortably attracted to him, instinctively didn't warm to him, but couldn't help responding sexually.

He was saying that he didn't think men were taught much about vulnerability, indeed that the notion had never entered his head until recently.

"I suddenly found myself at the mercy of the fates. I always thought I could control my life. It was easy. I could just use my talents and skills—the stuff men *are* taught—and there wouldn't be any problems. I held all the cards. But I had a couple of reversals—me, *Alex*." He waited for his audience to snicker. "That kind of stuff doesn't happen to me." He lowered his voice. "And then my mother died. I've spent the last year learning what it is to be powerless, to live a life that's become unmanageable. But it's really hard for me to admit that."

Skip recognized a paraphrase of the first of the twelve steps, admitting powerlessness, but it seemed not so much that as a rote repetition. Saying he found it hard to admit, she thought, was supposed to be a kind of admission of vulnerability, an asking for help, a courageous confession that a macho man was having trouble. Why did it sound like a clever performance?

"But I'm like Missy," he continued. "I'm working on it."

Sure you are.

She wondered why she was so suspicious of him, and figured it was because he was so attractive. It paid to suspect attractive men if you were Skip Langdon.

I wonder if I should go to Sex Anonymous?

No, I'm not addicted to sex. I'm just a girl who can't say no.

She hated herself for wondering if Alex was still watching her as she went to introduce herself to Di; she certainly wasn't going to turn around to check. She chatted briefly and, once again finding the notebook setup, managed to tear out last week's phone list, which she was stuffing into her purse when she heard a voice at her elbow.

"Joining us for coffee?"

It wasn't Alex, but Abe. "I beg your pardon?"

Di said, "After the meeting, we usually get together for coffee at PJ's. Join us, won't you?"

Abe and Alex both came, and Missy without her companion. Seeing Missy alone, Abe quickly abandoned Skip and sat next to the one she was sure was his first choice. Another attractive woman, a redhead in pink jeans, plopped down purposefully next to Alex. Good. That meant she could sit by Di and pump her.

She was glad Leon hadn't joined them. If she knew who he was, he probably knew her too—that was the way with New Orleans, which might as well have been a village. She had always taken that for granted, but for once it didn't ring true. It was true for her and for Leon, and certainly true for Alison Gaillard, but it hadn't been true for Linda Lee Strickland or Tom Mabus, must not be true for most of the people at these meetings.

She thought it might have been more accurate for most of them to say they were lonely instead of codependent. But even if you were part of the village, you could be lonely. *I'm lonely.*

She would have given her father's fortune to see Steve Steinman that night. Something about the way this thing worked was making her melancholy.

Or horny. Maybe that's all it is. All these stupid hormones in the air.

Di asked, "Have you been in New Orleans long?"

"I was born here, but I moved away. I came back about a year and a half ago. And you?"

"Born here. Went to LSU, moved back. Are you going to a lot of meetings?"

This wasn't the way Skip meant it to go. She meant to do the interrogating. But she guessed it was normal for Di to take the initiative, considering she was the new one. She had a semi-cover story ready and waiting.

But surprisingly, she didn't need it. All Di's questions related to Skip's experience with twelve-step programs; she supposed the eschewing of personal questions was a form of protocol, of respecting people's anonymity, and found it refreshing.

"Is the group usually the size it was tonight?" she asked.

"Usually. Sometimes it's bigger."

"I was just wondering—I know somebody from another meeting who goes sometimes. Tom—do you know him?"

Di looked pensive. "Tom. No, it doesn't ring a bell. He might be one of those people who never share."

She pronounced hardly any *r*'s at all; her voice was like butterfly wings. Skip had an overwhelming urge to trust her. She fought it hard.

Abe said, "Can I walk you ladies to your cars? Somebody got murdered in the Quarter a couple of weeks ago."

"Oh, the Axeman. That's a weird one."

But no one took the bait.

"I've got a seat on the back of my hog," said Alex.

"Macho man," said Di.

And as Skip walked to her car with Abe, Di, and Missy, Alex sailed by on a Harley-Davidson, the redhead on the back, holding on to his middle. Skip was glad it wasn't she. Touching Alex wouldn't be a good idea at all.

Di pulled out right in front of her. Skip, who'd started to fret about how to find out people's last names, quickly jotted down her license number.

At home, she took a cursory look at the phone list. There was no Linda Lee on it, but there were two Toms. Excited, remembering the teddy bear, she looked up Tom Mabus's number—sure enough, it matched that of one of the Toms.

Ten

THE NEXT MORNING she told Joe about the teddy-bear meeting and could have sworn she saw a fleeting pleased look in his eye. Especially when she told him Tom had been there. Then she got busy with the list.

Di first. Her car was registered to a Jacqueline Breaux, but the phone book showed a D. Breaux at Di's address. Skip called with a phony accent and a story about an amazing windfall prize for Jacqueline. Chatty as any other Southerner, Di confided that she'd recently opted for Diamara.

One down. A satisfied feeling.

Going down the list, she found some people had last names on their message-machine tapes. For some, she simply said, "Is this the Smith residence?" and they'd answer with the right name. Some she had to call back with more complicated ruses. There were twenty-three people on the list—almost certainly not all the people who'd been to the meeting and probably not all the people who usually came, but the murders had been in the last week. The list might mean something.

Soon she had sixteen full names. She ran them through the computer, and two had sheets. They were two she'd already met—Jacqueline (a.k.a. Diamara) Breaux and Alexander Bignell. Di and Alex. Di had a conviction for child abuse and Alex had once been arrested for assault, but the case had never come to trial.

101

Hardly able to walk fast enough, she went to the records room to pull the report on Di. The case was eighteen years old—a generation ago. But Jimmy Comer, the deputy D.A. who'd handled it, was still around. Still around and still mad about it, once he refreshed his recollection. "Nice woman," he said. "Oh, yeah, real nice woman. Married to a rich guy too. Walt Hindman." He paused.

"Hindman Construction," said Skip.

"Yeah. Can you beat that? Family like that, I just don't get it. What happened, kid got out of line and she beat him. He started yelling, she couldn't stand the noise—so she choked him till he shut up."

"Choked him?"

"A neighbor saw the marks on his neck."

The Axeman team met at one o'clock.

O'Rourke had been to meetings for "One-armed blind people, survivors of junkie parents, and impotent dwarves with personality problems," and thought the whole thing was a crock.

"I think you ought to try that last one again," said Cindy Lou, cracking everyone up and once again causing Skip to turn purple with envy. O'Rourke was so much easier to take with Cindy Lou around to put him in his place, but why couldn't she do it herself? She didn't think of herself as timid, but she couldn't bring herself to come down hard, even on creeps who deserved it.

"Okay," said Joe. "Let's cut to the chase. Langdon's onto something. Anybody else got something that looks good?"

"I found Jesus at Al-Anon," said Hodges. "Does that count?"

"Not unless you think you're him. Hit it, Skip."

"Remember Mabus's teddy bear? I went to this group where a bunch of adults were sitting around holding teddy bears and dolls."

"Ah," said Cindy Lou. "Nurturing their inner child."

"Bull!" said O'Rourke.

"In your case, it'd be more like an outer child."

O'Rourke was really taking it on the nose. When the chuckles had subsided, Skip said, "Mabus was at the meeting last week, but we don't know about Linda Lee. Two people who appear to attend regularly have very interesting records. I've Xeroxed the phone list from last week, and written in as many last names as I could get." She passed out copies.

"Oh, my God!" Cappello sucked in her breath. "My next-door neighbor's on here. Janet Acree. She's got three out-of-control kids and a drunk for a husband. Works as a lab tech."

"Good," said Joe. "That one's yours. Anybody else know anybody?"

No one spoke.

"Okay, Cindy Lou. Any reason you can think of why a serial killer would be in a group like this inner-child thing?"

"Only because he could be anonymous there. But that doesn't narrow it down, does it?"

O'Rourke snorted. "I just love psychologists."

"O'Rourke," said Joe, "give us five minutes on the theory of the inner child."

"You gotta be kidding."

"Okay, Cindy Lou, you do it."

Inwardly, Skip cheered. She'd never known that Joe, usually such a placater, could cut through shit so cleanly.

Well, he's desperate. He's got a serial killer on his hands.

"Your inner child's the part of you that'll never grow up, and you don't want it to. It's your most playful, spontaneous, creative part—when it's healthy," said Cindy Lou. "But the theory is that if you didn't get your needs met as a kid it may not be healthy. And so it's the part of you that's scared when there's really no reason to be scared, or maybe tries to get attention when it's inappropriate. In other words, as an adult you may act out like a kid that needs attention and security. The inner child may be more or less running your life. So now you've got to give it what it didn't get.''

Skip said, ''They talk about talking to 'my kid.' ''

''Yeah, they do that. They ask it what it wants and what they can do for it, even go out and buy it stuff—that's partly what the teddy bears are about.''

''More,'' said Skip, ''on the teddy bears.''

''Well, when a little kid feels scared or anxious, it hugs its teddy bear. So if you've got a part of you that's scared, you don't deny it's there, which is what most adults do. Right, O'Rourke?'' She smiled at him, but didn't wait for an answer. ''You acknowledge it and let the kid in you hug the teddy bear.''

Skip thought of Leon Wheatley stroking his bear.

''Also, you're actually comforting your inner child when you do that because the bear represents the child; it's like an outer form of it.''

O'Rourke said, ''You really believe that crap?''

''I'm giving you theory, man. That's what I get paid for, okay?'' She leaned across the table. ''And by the way—in case you've forgotten, I get paid a lot more than you do.''

O'Rourke mumbled something: ''Cunt,'' Skip thought.

She said, ''What's wrong, you leave your teddy bear at home? Why don't you just suck your thumb?''

Joe said, ''That's enough, Langdon.''

''Sorry.'' In a way she was, but it had felt good to stand up to the creep, even though she knew it was unprofessional. Sure, he was unprofessional, but he was probably going nowhere. Every time the subject came up, she tried to remember that. It wasn't easy.

''Okay,'' said Joe. ''Here's what we're going to do. Langdon will try to make contact with everyone she can from the inner-child group. The rest of you will keep going to groups, and getting the phone lists. When we see duplications of names on the phone lists—between the inner-child group and others—we'll pay particular attention to those meetings. In addition, we're all going to split up the names on the phone lists and start on extensive background checks. What they've been doing all their lives, and particularly the days of the two murders.

"And that's just for openers. We're getting big play in the national news, and frankly, the mayor's breathing down my neck. This is still tourist central, you know. All we need's a reputation for having a serial killer stalking the streets and we can kiss our pathetic little salaries good-bye because the tourists are going to stay away from here like it was San Francisco after the earthquake. And the cupboard's going to be bare. Sure, this is only two murders and we've got a whole city out there, but this is big, guys. It's the biggest thing we got going by far. This asshole's not done and he's going to have us looking like assholes if we don't nail him.

"So here's what I want you to do. I want you to do everything I said and then I want you to pretend you're not a cop. Just be Vic or Nat'ly watching the six o'clock news and saying, 'If da cops was smart, here's what dey'd do.' You know how people do that? Ever notice they know so much more than we do? Well, for once, just let your mind wander. Think of something unorthodox. Not illegal, okay? Just different. Off the wall."

Abasolo said, "You saying be creative, Lieutenant?"

"I'm saying be creative, Sergeant. Any questions?"

"Yeah," said O'Rourke. "Why'd we have to know that inner-child stuff?"

"Because if we don't catch this bird before next Thursday, you're all in that meeting. That's one. Two is this: Langdon may not be the only one socializing with these knuckleheads. Anybody looks good, we may need to get to know them close-up. And you've got to speak their language. Want to do some role-playing? Speak to your kid, Frank. Come on." He was kidding, not baiting, and for some reason Frank got into it, wanting to repair the bond with Joe, Skip thought.

"What do I call the brat?"

"You're getting warm," said Cindy Lou.

"Now. How're we're doing with arrests and releases?"

Hodges shrugged. "Still checking."

"Anybody else have anything?"

Shrugs went round the room. Nobody had any leads.

"Okay, we may have the meeting narrowed down, so I'm taking a couple of you out of the twelve-step programs. Langdon and Abasolo, stay with it. Hodges and O'Rourke—do arrests and releases full time."

"Shit," said O'Rourke. "That's only about a three-year job."

Joe actually smiled; he could take O'Rourke better than most people. "No problem, Frank. Take it one day at a time."

Skip phoned her mother. "I need some advice."

It was the phrase Elizabeth most loved to hear, and she responded as enthusiastically as her daughter expected—with an invitation to tea.

I suppose that means she's codependent, the way she jumps at this stuff. I'm starting to get this.

When she arrived, the truth of it shocked her. Her mother had spent the few minutes it took Skip to get to State Street rushing out to get Skip's favorite Pepperidge Farm cookies. She was still patting sofa pillows, fluffing them for her guest, when Skip arrived.

I never measured up. She.hates me. Why is she trying so hard?

Because she doesn't notice her effect on other people. It doesn't occur to her that she behaves as if she hates me. She takes my reaction as a sign that she doesn't measure up. She's trying to prove herself to me the same way she tries with everybody else.

The idea nearly struck her dumb. After all these years, a possible explanation!

"Skippy? Is something wrong with your hearing? All those

106

pistols at the firing range—I knew something like this would happen."

"Sorry. I was looking at that bird out there. Could I, uh, have some milk in my tea? I'll get it."

She needed a minute or two to process her revelation.

Her mother assumed a deeply hurt expression. "Milk? You never *used* to take milk in your tea?"

Oh, God. Was I right or what?

She summoned a grin. "It's okay, Mother. A temporary affectation. I'll be over it soon."

As she headed toward the kitchen, she thought, *That's right. Make yourself wrong.*

She had a sudden flash of herself at three or four, playing out the same scene, except that the baby Skip was contemporary—dressed in tiny black Reeboks and a Bart Simpson T-shirt. *Yow. It's my inner child. What should I say to it?*

She heard her mother's shoes clicking behind her. Elizabeth's face was grim. "Skip, I just remembered I forgot to get milk. There's some in there, but it might be sour."

Skip made her voice deliberately hearty. "Well, gosh, who needs milk, anyway? I've been drinking black tea for nearly a quarter of a century and I can still drink black tea."

"Hardly that long. I don't think you drank tea at all until you were out of high school."

Skip turned around and headed again for the living room, feeling tired and somehow invaded. Her mother always purported to know more about Skip than she did about herself, and would argue about it if given the chance. Skip desperately wanted to avoid an edifying discussion about the age at which she had first drunk tea.

Elizabeth said, "You always had hot chocolate for breakfast."

"I always wanted it. I was never allowed it on grounds it was too fattening."

Oh, no. I'm doing it.

107

"Oh, you had it all right. Look at you now." And her mother smiled as if to show she meant no harm.

"Well, Mother, the reason I called was because I need some twelve-step advice."

"For your case."

"Yes. Do you mind?"

Elizabeth shook her head. Her mouth was set in a way that let Skip know she'd done something wrong, but she had no idea what. Probably just the old story—being a cop in the first place.

"By the way, this is completely confidential. Is that okay too? I mean, you probably shouldn't even tell Daddy."

Her mother perked up at that.

It's because she thinks I need her. That's what gets to her.

And she had a moment of deeply pitying her mother, thinking what a horribly vulnerable position hers was, how easily manipulated she must be. And yet knowing that she herself couldn't do the manipulating, wasn't yet able to stand up to her even in an adult way, in fact was still terrified of Elizabeth's own manipulations.

"I don't really know how to approach these people. I need to talk to some of them without letting them know I'm a police officer. What I'm wondering is, can I just call them?"

"Of course. That's what the phone lists are for. But you're not going to do anything to embarrass me, are you?"

"I beg your pardon?"

"You know what I mean."

"I'm afraid I don't." It had always been like this. She was supposed to know things she didn't.

"I'm friends with those people, Skippy. Well, at any rate, we're acquainted. If you question them and they find out you're my daughter, it'll reflect on me."

"Oh, I see what the problem is. I'm concentrating on another meeting. Another program entirely. Not yours at all."

"How do I know the people in it aren't in mine as well?"

108

"None of them were there the other day. That's all I can tell you."

"I don't know if it's good enough."

Skip felt as if she'd fallen into a spider's web and couldn't disentangle herself.

She rose to go. "Listen, I'm really sorry if I've upset you. I promise I'll stay away from your territory."

Her mother looked suddenly stricken. "But didn't you want me to help you?"

"You have helped me, Mother. I wanted to know if it was okay for me to call people out of the blue, if they'd think that was odd."

"Well, it might be a little odd if you haven't actually talked with them."

"But if I have I can call them? Do I need to have a problem? Or can I just ask if they want to get together?"

"I think you can do that. I'm pretty sure you can. No one's ever called me, but"—she cast down her eyes, would have blushed if she did that sort of thing—"I wear a wedding ring."

"I see."

"Really, I think you can. I think quite a bit of romance happens in these groups." She pronounced it *ro*mance.

"But do women call each other—for coffee, maybe?"

"Probably. I don't see why not." She was looking enthusiastic, eager to please. Skip realized her mother was probably socially isolated from these people—that to have any kind of relationship she had to volunteer her services, to "help," and that that wasn't what these groups were about. But she'd pretend she knew the answer to get Skip's approval.

Skip sighed. The answer didn't matter much anyway—she was going to have to talk to her assigned suspects one way or another. At her request, when they divided up the background checks, she'd been given Missy, her boyfriend, Alex, Di, and Abe. She'd made personal contact with all except Missy and the boyfriend, and she had a feeling about those

109

two, especially about Missy—that they were like her mother, they'd talk too much just to be accommodating.

But by far the best suspects were Alex and Di, because of their priors. To get in the mood she drove by their respective houses.

To her surprise, the pirate on the Harley-Davidson lived out in Lakeview, in Ozzie-and-Harriet land, the last place she could imagine him. His street was the very exemplar of Fifties domesticity, overhung with shade trees, divided by a neutral ground, so tame kids here probably walked instead of ran. The houses were modest, the yards nasty-neat.

Despite all that rampant sexual energy, Alex must be very, very married. Anyone who'd live here had to be.

In the light of day she could see that Di's building wasn't a funky one like hers. It was new, but, like all Quarter buildings, perfectly in keeping with the prevailing architecture. Inside, it was probably a palace of mod. cons., mirrored closet doors, and jets in the bathtub.

As long as she was so near home, she went there to make a phone call. I wonder, she thought as she opened the door to nothing in particular, if I should get a pet.

No. Jimmy Dee would be jealous.

She called Eileen Moreland at the *Times-Picayune*. "Would you consider doing a favor for a long-lost Kappa sister?"

"Not if it's Skippy Langdon, who never gave a goddamn about Kappa or even the school or the whole United States of America, for all I know."

"You recognized my voice after all these years."

"You've been on my mind, to tell you the truth. Actually, I was going to call you."

"What for?"

"Well, you know they keep me in the women's ghetto here. So I'm always trying to think up interesting features— I think you'd be one."

"Me!"

"You're in homicide, I hear. How about something like 'The Lady Always Gets Her Man'?"

"News travels fast. But here's some more. There are several women in homicide."

"Better still. I'll do them all."

Great. Just what she needed when she was semi-undercover on the biggest murder case in the city.

"I don't know; I'm kind of publicity-shy." *Especially right now.*

"Oh, come on, Skippy. I get so bored around here."

"Let me think about it. Fair enough?"

"Oh, pooh."

"By the way, are outsiders ever allowed to use your library?"

"I could get you in. Especially if you'd think real hard about that interview."

"Well, you know I will."

It was weird; whenever she talked to true Southern belles, Skip found herself picking up their speech habits.

An hour later, she knew nothing more about Di or Abe and precious little else about Missy. But Missy's name had been mentioned once, as the date of Sonny Gerard, in a picture caption. The young man in the picture was the one with her at the meeting, and Skip knew exactly who he was now. Everybody, especially everybody whose father was a doctor, knew his dad, "Bull" Gerard, possibly the best plastic surgeon in the city. Certainly everyone who'd gone to McGehee's did—he'd bobbed half the noses in the school.

And then there was Alex. Alex was a celebrity of sorts. Even Skip had heard of him, she realized, though she hadn't recognized his name till she had it in context—and anyway, she'd had no idea he was in New Orleans. He was Alexander Bignell, the hot pop psychologist and author of seven self-help books based on his workshops.

So far as Skip could tell from the clips and from previous things she'd read about him, he'd been sort of a prince—never quite king—of pop psychology. But his eighth book, *Fake It Till You Make It*—just out a year ago—had denounced all of his previous work, that of most of his colleagues, and in fact a good part of modern psychology. In it, he'd more or less admitted to being a charlatan and suggested that so was everyone else in the field and all their ancestors as well—including Freud and Jung.

The *Picayune* reviewer seemed to think he'd gone crazy. A wire story that had run with the review indicated that so did the psychology establishment. A third story explained the assault charge—he'd apparently slugged the reviewer at a literary reception, but the journalist had declined to press charges.

Skip dashed out to the nearest bookstore to get his book and got John Bradshaw's latest as well. Then she went back to phone a few suspects.

"Di, it's Skip. From last night? I really enjoyed talking to you, and I'm kind of new in all this; I was just wondering—"

"I could sense you were new, but you know what, they're really right when they say, 'Keep coming back.' I know it sounds stupid, but it really does work. Listen, I know what you're feeling, though. At first you kind of need somebody to talk to; I mean, the whole thing is so overwhelming."

"I was wondering if we could get together. Tonight maybe."

"Tonight! My goodness. Well, let me see—I do have a meeting. . . ."

"After your meeting?"

Skip heard pages ruffle, presumably pages of Di's calendar.

"Okay. I could do that."

In a way it had been almost too easy, but she realized she'd come across as a soul in trouble. By tonight she was going to have to have a problem.

She tried Missy next, but her phone was busy. She took a

deep breath and dialed Alex. He said, "Skip? Skip? Oh, yeah, the one with the curls."

"Big broad. Does that help?"

"What can I do for you, big lady?"

"Well, I've just realized I'm a fan of yours."

"Uh, well, I don't quite . . ."

"You're Alexander Bignell, aren't you? I know you from your book photo."

"You've got to be kidding. You've actually read one of those pieces of shit?"

"All of them. Even *Fake It Till You Make It*. You're a complicated guy."

"Well, listen, I'm flattered, but I gotta go now."

"When can I get my book signed?"

"I don't do that shit anymore. I'm just plain Alex and I'm codependent, okay?"

"You know, I really think your argument's . . ." She was acutely conscious of the expectant silence as she searched for the right word—strong, but not gushy; oh hell, gushy. . . . "I think it's kind of, well—brilliant, really."

"You know, Skip, you might be a cut above the average Bayou babe."

"And then again I might be a shameless flatterer interested only in your body."

"I like shamelessness in a woman."

"Are you free for breakfast tomorrow? I really do want to get my book signed."

"Breakfast, hell! What about my body?"

She closed the deal but hung up sweating, and not because of the weather. Flattery didn't come anywhere near natural to her.

She tried Missy again, got her. "Missy, I loved what you said last night. I was wondering—I'm not exactly new in town, but I've moved back after some time away. I haven't made any friends yet, and you and your friend looked so nice. I just wondered . . . I mean, are the two of you ever free for coffee?''

She made her voice small and pitiful. Missy the perennial rescuer came running immediately—she was meeting Sonny for coffee at three the next day, and Skip could join them.

Abe was the easiest of all. ''Listen, I hope you don't take this the wrong way, but I really think you're attractive, and I wondered . . .'' He asked her to dinner the next night.

That done, she called Cappello and told her where she stood. ''Langdon,'' she said, ''a *date*? Breakfast, no big deal, but dinner? What are you hoping to find out?''

''I don't know. Have you got any better ideas?''

''Sure. Routine background checks.''

''I'm doing those too.''

Cappello sighed. ''Don't wear yourself out, Skip.''

Skip had known she'd react like that. She wondered herself if this was creative police work or just plain goofy. But who cared? As long as she didn't wear herself out, it really didn't matter. It beat sitting home feeling helpless.

Eleven

TALKING TO DI, Skip had said, ''I can't think of any- where to meet except the Napoleon House.''

And Di had said, ''I hate the Napoleon House.''

''Where shall we meet, then?''

''There isn't anyplace else.''

There were hundreds of other places, but no one in the

Quarter could ever think of one that was half as convenient, and secretly even Di probably liked it. Even with as much wear and tear as its customers put on it, it retained its graciousness. It was a serene corner, never mind the peeling plaster (or maybe that was the best part). Except for the fact that alcohol was most assuredly served there—by the barrel, it seemed—it was probably as good a place as any for two ladies on a spiritual path to meet.

Di, twenty minutes late, arrived apologetic—someone had wanted to talk to her. A male someone was Skip's guess. She couldn't tell Di's age, but knew she'd have admirers at ninety.

"Let me buy you a drink."

"I never drink, but . . ." Her eyes fluttered as she saw Skip's Pimm's cup, icy sweat dripping down the glass, its slice of cucumber crisp and erect. "You know what, I think I'll have a glass of wine. I have one about every six months."

Skip smiled. "And hamburgers too, I'll bet, if you're like most people. Not *much* red meat, but every now and then the tiniest treat."

"Oh, no. I eat only live foods."

No way I'm taking that bait, thought Skip. "I know what you mean," she said, hoping she sounded as if she did. "Listen, it was nice of you to see me tonight. I'm not feeling too good about things."

She let a beat go by, to give her companion a chance to beg her to pour her story out.

Instead Di gave her a big smile and a pat on the forearm. "Oh, don't be down—everything's getting so much *better*! Listen, we're really, really onto something in these groups of ours and I just know they're going to work for you. Don't you feel it? Did you feel it last night?"

It seemed such a wildly inappropriate response to what Skip had said that she hardly knew how to answer. Finally she settled on "You must have just come from a really good meeting."

115

"Oh, I did. I did! I'm so sorry you're feeling bad—I know I must sound heartless, but it isn't that."

Delighted to hear it.

"It's that I've been there. I started going to these meetings because I felt like you do. I guess I was depressed. Oh, I hate that word, it's so clinical. Anyway, I felt like you're feeling now. And look at me now. Have you ever seen a happier person? I'm just trying to tell you—by example, my own living example—that you'll be better, that the whole Earth is getting better, not worse; we're going to be saved, the world really isn't going to end, no matter how it seems. Really. It's a new age."

"I don't know, Di. The Age of Aquarius was supposed to be dawning a few years back—isn't it a little soon for another one?"

Di laughed her curiously flute-like laugh. "I think it *is* the Age of Aquarius, coming to flower. The Earth is going to be saved and the youthening is coming."

"The youthening? Is that something I should know about?"

"Oh, it's just a word I use. It's not a movement or anything. I just mean we're all getting younger. Don't you feel it?"

"I'm not sure." She took a long swallow of her drink, kind of a short vacation. "Well, to tell you the truth, I guess I really don't."

"You will, though. Because everything is connected and you won't be able to miss it. These groups we go to, for instance; they're all connected to other groups. And the whole thing is connected to a worldwide movement that's setting new paradigms."

So foreign were the words that Skip couldn't even be sure Di was speaking English, but she found herself feeling oddly buoyant, wanting to believe it, whatever it was.

"Things are getting better," Di continued. "Things are definitely getting better. I am a goddess and I decree it."

116

She smiled so seductively that Skip really thought she could buy the whole thing. The crazy, cock-eyed optimism was catching. Skip sipped again. "A goddess," she said.

"Of course. All women are goddesses. The faster we can accept that fact, the sooner the youthening can take place, because, of course, to recognize our divinity is to acknowledge our own immortality."

Skip decided for the moment to treat her as if she were sane. "Let me get something straight," she said. "Are you saying you actually believe we're immortal?"

Di laughed, and the sound was like wind chimes. Expensive ones. "You must think I'm crazy. Of course I don't mean literally immortal—not in linear time (except for being reborn, of course). I mean in real time. Linear time has nothing to do with the cycles of time, which are real time, as you'll know if you're tuned in to the valence of the youthening, and live food, and nurturing the inner child. Which I know you are because of where I met you."

"Well, I'm trying to get tuned in. But last night was only my first meeting. I really think it's going to be important to me to feel close to the people there."

"Oh, I do *too*. And don't you find you do when they share?"

"I felt very simpatico with you. I found myself wondering about you and wanting to know more."

Di didn't answer, merely basked in expected praise like the goddess she was, used to but still enjoying the adoration of the multitudes.

Come to think of it, Skip thought, *that's not so far from a perfect definition of the Southern belle.*

"You mentioned a daughter. I noticed because—" Skip stopped in mid-sentence. She had been about to remark that the daughter must be about her age, but suddenly realized that a woman expecting a magical "youthening" might not care to be reminded she had grown children.

"Did I?" said Di. "Sometimes I feel like I'm channeling
117

in there. I never really know what I'm going to say and I can't remember it afterward.''

"You definitely mentioned a daughter. I just wondered what she's like; how old she is.''

"Oh, I never discuss age.'' She brought her glass to her lips, pulled it away at the last minute. "Because it's so false. It means nothing in real time.''

"Of course.'' She let a beat pass, wondering where to go next. "Do you have any other children?'' she said at last. The child who'd been attacked had been a boy.

"The hardest lesson we'll ever learn is that we're all children, don't you think? But the most valuable. That's what the inner-child group's all about and why I love it so much.''

Skip had the sensation of trying to catch feathers borne on a light breeze. She searched for a subject that would bring the goddess to Earth. Perhaps now was the time for the "problem'' she'd brought.

"Sometimes,'' she said, "my life seems so empty.''

"Oh, no! You're a goddess; remember that.''

"Could I ask you a personal question?''

Di nodded slightly, but only very slightly.

"You're a person who seems to have everything—looks, brains. You do seem like a goddess. But what does a goddess do all day? Do you work?''

Di laughed her pretty laugh. "My work right now is healing myself.''

"Oh, I'm sorry. Have you been ill?''

"I prefer to use the term 'dis-ease.' As in 'not at ease with oneself'; perhaps 'not at ease with one's inner child.' Today I went and had my hair tested. Have you done that yet?''

"No. I never even heard of it.''

"They can analyze your hair for toxins. Everybody should do it—particularly in this kind of world. I had too much selenium.'' She gave Skip a cheery smile; apparently, it wasn't serious. "Listen, the other thing—have you read Bradshaw's book on the inner child?''

118

"Not yet, but it's next on my list." After *Fake It Till You Make It*.

"I'll lend it to you. It'll really help a lot."

It was a clever feint, but Skip refused to be distracted. "Listen, I feel bad about your illness. Doctors are so expensive."

"Oh, I don't go to M.D.'s. Not anymore, I mean." Skip caught a flicker of something—anger? "I try to go to three meetings a day."

Was that a non sequitur? Had she changed the subject, or was she speaking to it? Skip said, "Instead of doctors?"

"Sort of." And Di laughed again, which seemed her normal procedure when she'd thoroughly confused her questioner.

It's as if she knows.

"Tell me about yourself."

There it was. It had to come sometime. Skip shrugged, trying to hide her nervousness. "There's not much to tell. I guess if there were, I wouldn't be going to Coda."

"Oh, not necessarily. Remember Leon from the other night? He's from an extremely prominent family. Very high-powered sort of guy."

"No kidding! He seemed very nice."

"A little old for my taste."

"I thought age didn't matter."

"State of preservation does." Her mouth turned up in a way that could only be described as lecherous. Skip went with the mood.

"I know what you mean. Speaking of which, I'm not usually attracted to older guys, but . . ."

"Don't tell me. Alex."

"I guess he's got quite a fan club."

"He doesn't do it for me at all. But everyone under thirty goes nuts for him."

"What's his story, anyhow?"

She shrugged. "I don't know. He claims to be 'an unsuccessful writer.' Sounds right to me."

"And he goes through the ladies like so many pairs of socks, I guess."

"Oh, Skip, they all do." She picked up her glass again and stared at it, as if summoning the nerve to take a sip. "Are you married?"

"No. Are you?"

"No, and never again. I *wish* I hadn't done that. I should have followed my bliss. You're so lucky, Skip! You can do anything you want. Or do you work?"

"I just have a civil-service job." Quickly, she looked at the table, as if too ashamed of her job to meet Di's eyes. "Nothing to make my family proud."

But Di seemed to have lost interest. She was looking at her untouched glass. "You know," she said, "I don't think I'm a drinker anymore."

"Would you like something else?"

"No, thanks. I think I'd better go home. Do you want to come with me and get the book?"

Skip was so taken aback, she almost forgot which book. She made a quick call to let Cappello know where she was going.

Di's apartment was exactly as she'd imagined it except that she hadn't expected the fireplace. It gave a homey touch but would be about as useful in this city as a snowplow.

But if the place itself was conventional, the eccentricity of the furnishings compensated nicely. The coffee table was covered with a velvet cloth in which crescents and stars had been worked in silver thread, and on the cloth reposed a large crystal ball. Tarot cards were laid out, apparently from Di's last reading. Three large crystal bowls—actually bells for meditation—stood on a sideboard. A bust of Apollo topped a bookcase. Sandalwood scented the air. Candles covered nearly every surface.

Yet care had been taken not to let the mystical trappings become heavy, weight the room's essential femininity. The walls were painted apricot; damask drapes striped in apricot and white flanked the French doors, a simple cornice between them. A Victorian settee was covered in tangerine, piled high with pillows. The other furniture was also old but light, walnut or cherry. The candles, all forty-odd of them, had been chosen for their perfect complementary colors—either white or shades of yellow and orange, or dark green for contrast. A single art object hung on the walls, a metal sculpture painted white and touched with gilt, a cut-out of a graceful woman in flowing gauze. She was winged, but no angel; more like a fairy. Her airy quality reminded Skip of her owner.

"This is quite something."

"What?" Di was lighting some of her candles. "Oh, my decor. I'm a priestess of voodoo, you know."

"Oh." Were there white voodoo priestesses? Skip supposed so. "I got the impression meetings were pretty much your whole life."

"Far from it, my friend. Far from it. I'm a hypnotherapist some of the time. And kind of an amateur nutritionist."

"Ah, yes. Live foods."

"I might surprise you with some of the things I do "

Oh, Lord. You certainly might.

"Now where's that book?"

Together, they surveyed her bookcase. It contained a better selection of New Age writings than any three bookstores in New Orleans, and quite a few books on breast cancer; more, Skip thought, than anyone would have who had merely a passing interest in it. But there were no books on either voodoo or hypnosis.

Twelve

THERE WERE A lot of popular meetings in the Quarter, it seemed. Alex had one at eight that morning and had agreed to meet Skip at Café du Monde. It meant sitting outside, but at seven o'clock New Orleans in August was bearable, even right on the river, where the air hung like a curtain, sultry and entangling.

He was late, no doubt to make an entrance, Skip thought when he pulled up on his hog. Even though the temperature would soon climb to ninety, perhaps to a hundred, he'd tied a bandanna around his neck. He'd tucked a blue work shirt into tight jeans, and if he'd asked her to make love under the table, she'd have had a hard time turning him down.

She had his book on the table, thinking that would flatter him, but he turned it over even before he sat down—and then, seeing his photo on the back cover, turned it front side up again.

"Did you really read that thing?" he said.

She nodded. "You're awfully modest for a best-selling author."

"Not best-selling." He dismissed the notion with a wave. "I know the publicity says that. Maybe I made some bestseller list somewhere, and that's how they justify it, but if you saw my royalty statements, you wouldn't die of envy."

After they had ordered their café au lait and beignets, Skip presented the book for signing.

But Alex said, "Not just yet. Let's talk first. You make me nervous."

"Little ol' me?"

Alex didn't smile. He squinched his eyebrows into a nasty scowl. "Yeah. Little ol' you. I keep wondering who you are."

"I didn't know I was that threatening."

"You're a psychologist. I hate psychologists."

"Oh, my God!" She wanted to give the impression she was taking him seriously, but this was too much. Before she could stop it, a belly laugh rumbled up and out. "A psychologist! Why on earth do you think that?"

Mr. Macho now wore a bewildered, slightly hurt look, the look of a man who's been made light of, and Skip regretted her amusement. She touched his wrist, knowing even as she did it that he would probably take any physical contact as a sexual signal, but thinking it necessary to establish rapport. "Because you've read the books," he said.

"You're the last guy in the world I'd have suspected of having a self-esteem problem. Does it occur to you that many members of the general public have read the books?"

He sighed. "You have no idea how much I wish that were true. What are you?"

Somehow her flattery ruse was backfiring. "Why," she asked, "do I feel like I did something wrong by asking for your autograph?"

"We really have to talk." This time he grabbed her wrist, didn't merely touch it lightly as she had touched his, and it was sexual, was the first of many little moves he'd make if their acquaintanceship continued. Curiously, she found herself relieved—if he was attracted to her, it made him a supplicant in a mild sort of way, gave her a little edge. "You could really blow things for me."

She leaned back, hoping it made her less threatening. "I don't understand."

123

"I'm undercover here. Nobody in New Orleans knows I write these things."

"But it was in the paper. I remember."

"You remember?"

"What's so weird about that? You're an author I admire and I saw a piece about you. That's why I read it."

"Listen, lady, if you remember, you're the only one in this godforsaken place who does."

"I take it you're not happy here."

"Jesus! Are you sure you're not a psychologist?"

"I just hate to see people unhappy, that's all. Go ahead; call me codependent."

"Okay, okay. But don't change the subject. Can I trust you?"

"With your bank account, probably not. Not to attack you in a candlelit room, maybe not. Not to lie to you—not entirely. But to buy you breakfast, sure. I said I would and my word's good."

He smiled. "You're not stupid. I like that."

"Hush my mouf, honey, all us Southerners are stupid."

"I meant can I trust you to keep a secret."

"Ah. You don't want anyone to know you're Alexander Bignell."

"Right."

"I don't get it. What's the big deal?"

"You just said your word's good, right?"

"Yes."

"Okay. This can't go any further."

"Of course not." She shrugged as if the matter was of no more importance than the plot of a movie.

"I'm writing a book about the twelve-step programs."

Skip sat up straight. "Of course! That's the only thing that makes sense. And you're free to come and go as you please because all anyone knows is your first name."

"So how about it, kid?" He grabbed her wrist again, squeezed this time, a bit more intimately. "Can I trust you?"

124

"Certainly. I gave you my word."

"I'll buy breakfast, then."

"Don't be silly. I gave my word on that one. But I still need to get a couple of things straight. I was wondering—isn't there some kind of rule that what's said in the groups doesn't go outside them?"

He shrugged. "I don't give a damn about that."

"Wow. Hard guy."

"Look, if I think these things are crap and they're just ripping people's feelings off because they really don't do a damn bit of good and just get your hopes up, then why would I give a good goddamn what their rules are?"

"How do you know I'm not a dedicated twelve-stepper who'll betray you?"

"You just said I could trust you." He smiled again, obviously relaxing, and the smile had more than a hint of sensuality in it. "Besides, I've got a feeling."

Right. A feeling a little judicious attention is all you need to get me on your side. And I think I know what sort of attention.

She said, "Well, you're right. The other night was my first meeting."

"You had the look of a virgin."

"Had is right. I was about twelve at the time."

He gave her an appreciative look. "Women in New Orleans don't talk like that. You want wit and spirit, go to New York."

"You're looking in the wrong places, sweetheart. The wit and spirit of the Southern woman are famous throughout the land. But you're not going to find either one in Al-Anon. Those people take themselves seriously."

"Sometimes they can be funny."

"I thought you thought nobody in the whole town is funny."

"Jesus, this is a shitty town!" He spoke with such sudden violence that Skip jumped. He noticed and tweaked her arm

125

again. He was touching her entirely too much. "I didn't mean to scare you."

"What's so bad about my hometown?"

"Everything's bad about it. It's a smelly backwater without an intellectual for five states around."

"Yeah, but it's got charm."

"Shit! It's got falling-down buildings, cholesterol instead of food, and brimstone instead of weather."

There were times when she felt like that herself. But this morning she'd gotten up early to have the city's trademark breakfast by the river, and a slight breeze ruffled her hair, drying the sweat. She felt good; at peace with this place. Even, for the moment, at home.

"So why are you here, Mr. New Yorker? They've got twelve-step programs everywhere."

"I've had financial reversals. Or haven't you heard?"

"How would I have heard in this backwater?"

"My last book didn't sell for shit. That one." He pointed at her lap. "Nobody wanted to hear that stuff."

He paused a moment while Skip tried to think of something to say. "Idiots!" he said. "They just want a lot of false hope and stupid sermonettes. Nobody can face the truth about all this crap. They want everything to be rosy and they don't want to listen to anybody who says it isn't." His sudden anger shocked her, seemed out of proportion.

She felt much as she had when she was talking with Di—as if she were in the presence of some insanity too mild to notice at first glance, but unmistakable up close. And the Axeman would be that way, she thought; he would probably pass as a solid citizen; a little eccentric, perhaps, but wasn't everybody?

Why was it that way?

Because in a sense Alex was right, she thought. If your breakfast companion was a little nuts, you didn't want to think about it too hard—you didn't want to think about where "a little nuts" might take him. You wanted to think a nationally known author couldn't possibly be a murderer; these things just didn't happen.

He said, "I grew up here, you know."

It was all she could do not to ask him what schools he'd gone to.

He yawned. "Things are cheap here now. And they've got as much of what I need as anywhere."

"Material for research, you mean."

"Yes. Pretty clever setup when you get down to it. Except I have to live in this hellhole. What do you do here?"

"You mean what kind of work?"

"I don't know. Half the people I've met in these programs don't seem to do a goddamn thing except go to one meeting after another. What's your poison?"

"I work. Petty bureaucrat." She wrinkled her nose. "Civil-service job." She held her breath. If he asked the next obvious question, she'd have to say she was a cop—it would be too dangerous to lie.

"What do you do for fun?"

She thought about it, decided to tell the truth. "Precious little. I guess mostly I'm trying to adjust to the place I don't know if I fit in either. Mostly I don't, I guess."

"And so you thought you'd toddle on down to Coda and make some new friends. You wouldn't be the first." He swallowed the last beignet nearly whole.

"I'll bet you've made a few little friends there yourself."

He gave her his pirate's smile. "It's all research. Anyway, I'm new in town—or newly returned—and I live alone—why not?"

"You live alone?"

"Do I seem like the married type to you?"

No, but your house does. Instead, she said, "Where do you live?"

"Uptown." His chin dropped a little and Skip took note of it. It probably happened whenever he was lying. She hoped she'd remember that. "Why do you ask?"

"In the meeting you said your mother died. I wondered if you inherited property."

"That's not your business." He didn't sound angry, just stating a fact. But stating it very clearly; setting boundaries, as the twelve-steppers said. (As he'd no doubt said himself in earlier books.)

"Come on, I didn't ask you what schools you went to."

"Why did I get the impression you were changing the subject? About who's married and who's not—you, for instance."

"Not married."

"Otherwise involved?"

"Um-hmm."

"How heavily?"

She spread her hands, not knowing how to answer.

"Good. Want to go out tonight?"

"Otherwise involved."

"No problem. Monday."

She made her smile discreet, eager not to seem too eager. "Okay, Monday."

"I want to be alone with you." He touched the back of his hand to her cheek.

In a way she found the gesture repulsive, the sentiment a little scary. Alex struck her as someone in the grip of a giant ego without a lot of brains for backup, as well as a man caught in a peculiar maelstrom of anger, a condition she sensed he didn't even begin to comprehend. She didn't like the man and she was wary of him, even a little frightened; yet her stomach flopped when he touched her face.

Thirteen

SHE MEANDERED OVER to the Voodoo Museum on Conti Street. A young black woman with beads and corn rows was minding the store, reading a book on herbal medicine. Plenty of herbs were being offered for sale in the museum's gift shop, along with touristy gris-gris, incense, and a few books.

"I wonder if you know a woman named Di? Diamara Breaux?"

"Am I supposed to?" The young woman had a full mouth, wore no lipstick, and could have been a movie star.

"I don't know. I thought maybe this might be a kind of center for people who're into voodoo."

The voodoo woman shrugged.

"I need to find her."

"I don't know her." Her mouth hardened and she went back to her book.

Skip hadn't mentioned her job because she didn't want to tip Di's voodoo friends that a cop was asking about her. But she believed this woman; she seemed authentically not to give a damn.

She pulled out her badge. "I'm Skip Langdon. New Orleans police."

"Oh." The woman laid the book down, her face serene.

"Good book?"

"I'm sorry. I thought you were a weirdo. We get 'em in here."

"Could I ask your name?"

"Kendra. Kendra Guillory."

"Pretty name. Listen, you're not in trouble and neither is the woman I asked about. I'm just trying to verify whether she's really who she says she is. I gather by your book that you work here because you're interested."

Guillory waited.

Skip wondered why she felt so embarrassed. She had a feeling there was something secret about practicing voodoo, that people didn't like being asked about it. "I don't know how to say this, exactly," she said, "but is there a sort of voodoo community in New Orleans? Do people who practice get together? Do they know each other?"

"We prefer to call it Voudun."

"Sorry."

She shrugged again. "This woman says she's a priestess, right? She offers to do spells and gris-gris for a price—is that the idea?"

"I can't really talk about that."

"I hate these frauds, I swear I do. We don't do it for money. It's a religion. People don't get that. You know what she probably did? She probably read a couple of books"—she swept an arm around—"and now she says she can raise the dead or something. Maybe she channels Marie Laveau. You wouldn't believe some of these people."

"You're sure you don't know her?"

"Don't know the name. What's she look like?"

"White. Very small, black hair with a lot of curls, perfect figure—extremely pretty woman. Maybe forty, maybe fifty; I don't know."

"Look, membership is secret. If she were an initiate, I couldn't tell you. But I hate these damn frauds. So, okay, I don't know her."

"Well, that's a big help. How do I know you're not protecting her?"

"You don't. But I'm trying to help you."

"Do white people do this stuff? Just tell me that."

"Whooo! You'd better believe it. Here's something—have you seen her altar?"

"Her altar?"

"Yeah. If she's for real, she'll have an altar with spirit water on it, maybe an ancestor picture, some statues and shells or something. It'd be kind of spooky-looking, I guess; to you. There's one in the museum—you can go look if you want."

"Where would she have it?"

Guillory shrugged. "Could be anywhere in her house."

Skip cursed herself for not taking an investigative trip to the bathroom. "How about stars and crescents?"

"On her altar?"

"On some kind of velvet cloth with a crystal ball on it."

Guillory rolled her eyes. "Forget it. Look, I'll even make some calls for you."

Skip perused the literature, catching up on the seven African Powers while Guillory made her calls.

"Nothing," she said finally. "If she were really practicing, she'd have to shop at a botanica. There's only one, and there's one magic shop where you can get incense and stuff. I just checked them out. Nobody's ever seen this babe." Guillory's earrings were made of brown feathers with white dots. They swung with the rhythm of her indignation.

"Uh-oh. Maybe you should put a gris-gris on her."

"That's not what we do. This museum is here for educational purposes and I'm going to educate you right now. Listen to this and listen good—we don't go around hexing people. You ever heard of Elleggua the Trickster? I saw you looking at those books, maybe you have by now. You start hexing, what do you think Elleggua's going to do? He's probably going to remind you that what goes around comes around: If that woman's a fraud, let him deal with her; I don't want him dealing with me."

131

She was frowning, and failing so utterly in her efforts to look fierce that for the first time Skip realized she probably wasn't even twenty yet.

Feeling silly and not a little intrigued, she asked Guillory to recommend a couple of books, and bought them.

Then she went home and called Cindy Lou.

"Hey, girl. You caught this creep yet?"

"You mind being called on Saturday?"

"Hell, no. It's good to hear from you. I could feel left out if I let myself."

"That's how I spend my life. There's a lot of good guys in that department, but somehow I always end up working with O'Rourke."

"Hodges is kind of crotchety too. But Adam Abasolo—now, there's a fox."

Thinking of Steve Steinman, she said, "I kind of like teddy bears."

"Honey, I know what you mean. And they're so good for the inner child. But you didn't call me up for girl talk, I bet."

"I need professional help."

"My meter's running."

"How can I find out if somebody who says she's a therapist really is?"

"Look in the phone book, maybe?"

"Oh, shit." She hadn't looked, somehow assuming that wasn't Di's style. "Hold on a minute." As she checked, she filled Cindy Lou in on Di and her two peculiar last-minute statements of the night before. "Anyway," she finished, "the voodoo folks don't know her. And now I've checked the phone book. She's not under 'psychotherapists.' Are there organizations she ought to belong to? She says she does hypnotism—does she have to have some kind of certificate for that?"

"So far as I know, in Louisiana anybody can hang out their shingle and say they're a hypnotherapist. But most of them know each other—you could see if they know her. And

132

yes, there are organizations she might join. If she's a therapist who happens to know hypnotism, she'd have to be licensed to be in private practice.''

Skip asked who did the licensing and made a note to follow up first thing Monday morning.

Cindy Lou said, ''Listen, you get into anything interesting, call me up. You know what? I like working with you. There's not that many people appreciate my sense of humor. You always laugh in meetings.''

Skip couldn't stifle a smile, though no one could see it. Cindy Lou liked working with her. Cindy Lou had specifically asked to work with her. Her hero had spoken kindly.

''Hey, girl, I've got an idea. I guess I can't do it, but you can. Or maybe it's routine—I don't know. I was thinking about not just asking people's neighbors about them or whatever you do, but visiting their families. Seeing where they come from.''

''I beg your pardon?''

''You could use some kind of ruse. Just kind of check out the scene.''

''I don't see what you're getting at.''

''Well, if you run into something really ugly, you could concentrate on that person. A serial killer doesn't just come out of nowhere—he comes out of hatred and meanness. You know that FBI study? They put together a chart of family background characteristics based on their interviews. The stuff they found the killers had in common varied from thirty-three percent to seventy-four percent. Guess what was seventy-four? History of psychological abuse. Next was seventy-two percent—'negative relationship with male caretaker figures.' You could look for that kind of stuff. You might get a feeling about someone.''

''Police work—'' She stopped. She'd almost said, ''Police work isn't about feelings,'' but she knew better than to speak that way to a psychologist; she'd probably be told it ought to be. There was something else as well—intuition did play a

133

part in police work; a big part. If you had a feeling somebody with a gun was behind you, you'd better duck first and then turn around. She said, "I'll think about it, Cindy Lou."

She sat by the cradled phone awhile and tried to get the idea out of her mind. It was preposterous. It could very well be a waste of time. . . .

That one didn't fly. What else was she going to do with her time?

. . . And it wasn't sound police work. That was the important one. You didn't go around questioning a suspect's intimates unless they were mad at him; if they were on speaking terms, word would get back. But in this case, what if word did get back? Did that mean he'd stop killing? Would that be so bad?

Somehow it didn't strike her that forebearing to talk to people's relatives at this point was going to make or break the case. And she liked the idea. She really liked the idea. She didn't have the least sense of what made some of these people tick. Especially Di.

And Joe had said to be creative.

She attacked the phone book.

There were enough Breauxs in it to populate the state of Rhode Island, and she didn't even know if Breaux was Di's married or maiden name, or one she'd taken for good luck. But one thing was sure—there couldn't be more than one Diamara Breaux in town. If anybody was related to her, they'd know who she was talking about.

She put on a pair of shorts and got a glass of instant iced tea. And in a scant hour and fifteen minutes had located Diamara's mother. She'd said only that she was a friend who was looking for Di. Next she'd have to think of an excuse to ask impertinent questions—if she decided to get creative.

She sat on the floor and tried to meditate. She did this a couple of times a week, often more, and hadn't yet succeeded. Today she lasted eight minutes, most of it spent trying to keep from thinking about what made Di tick.

If it was supposed to relax her, it didn't. But if she was getting in touch with her feelings, she made progress, though of a sort she didn't need. In the tiny mind-clearing interval—maybe thirty scattered seconds—she became aware of how tired she was, how much effort it took to pretend she was someone she wasn't.

Only the thought of the two victims made her get dressed and keep her coffee date with Missy and Sonny. Missy had said they worked at Charity Hospital, asked to meet her in the lobby.

She wore shorts and a T-shirt. "Hi, Skip. This is gon' have to be real informal. Sonny's on duty in the emergency room. Nothing much is going on this afternoon, but he can't really go too far. Maybe just the coffee room inside?"

Skip hesitated. Most homicide detectives spent a lot of time in Charity's accident room. If she saw someone she knew, her cover was blown. On the other hand, if she refused, she'd draw attention to herself. "Sure," she said finally, and hoped for the best.

As they headed down the corridor, she said, "Is Sonny a doctor?"

"Second-year medical student."

Skip came back quickly before Missy could ask what she did. "Are you two married?"

Missy gave her a shy smile and held up her left hand. "Not quite yet."

Skip took her hand and examined the diamond. "What a lovely ring."

"I'm a real, real lucky girl. Sometimes I can't even believe a great guy like Sonny could love me." A look flitted on and off her face, a look so sad Skip nearly winced. "This way."

Sonny was sitting on a bench in the hallway of the Accident Room, actually a complex of small treatment rooms that Skip knew only too well, as did most cops in the city. He was reading a newspaper, waiting for them.

"Honey, you remember Skip? From Thursday night?"

135

"I don't think we actually got introduced." He held out his hand. She was sure he hadn't the slightest recollection of her.

"I saw you two and I thought how nice you looked."

"That just shows how deceiving appearances can be." With his words came the disarming smile that had probably been automatic for him since he was two and a half. Or did they teach it to fraternity pledges the way medical schools taught doctors who God was? She wondered if he'd learned that lesson yet, and for the first time thought about whether or not it came easy.

Sonny led them to a closet of a coffee room with a Chez Panisse poster on the wall. What a weird thing, Skip thought, with all the great restaurants in New Orleans.

Missy had brought cups of good coffee from somewhere and served them up, saying she was sorry about the Styrofoam. She'd also picked up a bag of bakery cookies. This was a girl who had raised "nice" to a fine and delicate art. A Southern girl. Skip caught herself thinking "girl" instead of "woman" and considered the implications; she decided the judgment was right.

She thought it must be a measure of spiritual growth that at the moment she no longer felt either intimidated by these two or contemptuous of them because they were perfect. They understood the rules, had been born knowing how to be Southerners, how to fit in, how to be properly female in Missy's case, male in Sonny's, how to be homecoming queen or captain of the football team. They were golden, they were sun-kissed; they were from Mars.

Or that was her feeling some of the time about the Missys and Sonnys of the world. That was when she felt contemptuous. She knew, of course, that *she* was actually the Martian; when that bothered her, she felt intimidated. At the moment, she merely admired them. Plato would have, she felt sure—would have known them for the ideal they were.

There was only one thing wrong with this perfect picture—

she'd met them in a twelve-step program, the first step being an admission that your life was out of control. Obviously they weren't there to meet people; even if they hadn't had each other, these two didn't need mixers. Of course they were codependent—Missy noticeably so, and Sonny on the grounds that nearly everyone was, according to the experts. But the fact that they'd noticed it made them different from the usual run of perfect couples.

She decided to come out with it. "You two look so well-adjusted—I was really amazed to see you in the meeting."

Missy shook her head, smiling a little wistfully. "I wonder what 'well-adjusted' is."

Sonny said, "Well-adjusted, hell. How about sane? Who do you know who's even sane?"

"You look sane as anything to me."

Missy rested an elbow on his shoulder. "Oh, he is. You wouldn't believe how sane he is, and I don't know what on earth I'd do without him."

He gave her an uncomprehending look—one of those unbelieving looks half a couple gives when the other half has just said something along the lines of the earth being flat. "Well, what the hell do you drag me to those meetings for?"

"Honey, you might have a little bitty problem or two, but that doesn't mean you're not *sane*—one of us *has* to be."

Sonny gave Skip a self-deprecating smile, showing teeth Paul Newman might have envied. "Well, I guess you know the country song: 'I've always been crazy, but it's kept me from goin' insane.' " He spoke in a drawl that had probably caused death by melting in more than one sorority house.

But Skip failed to melt, in fact hardly noticed. Her mind was on something Missy had said, something she couldn't put her finger on. . . .

"Sonny, Skip's going to think you actually listen to that ol' stuff."

She had it—the italics, the easy endearments, the slightly-too-niceness that sometimes seemed like bossiness. It wasn't

137

New Orleans, it was the trademark of every girl at Ole Miss. She said, "Missy! I just caught your accent. You're from Mississippi, aren't you?"

"Now, how'd you do that? I thought I talked like everybody else."

"I went to Ole Miss for a little while. Where are you from?"

"Hattiesburg. Near Hattiesburg, I mean. In the sticks, really. I went to Ole Miss too."

"Not LSU? I figured both of you did and you met at a pep rally."

"Gosh, no. We met right here. We've only been together a year."

She turned her warm, loving gaze on Sonny, only to find him staring into space, eyes glazed. Skip brought him out of it. "Sonny, do you come from a medical family?"

"My dad's a doctor and my grandfather before him and my uncle, and I think my great-grandfather was one too. Anyway, as you can guess, there wasn't much choice about it." Skip thought he spoke ruefully.

"You're not enjoying med school?"

"Oh, med school's fine. Grades are what the problem is."

"Oh, Sonny! You're doing great and you know it."

He pointed a playful thumb at her. "My coach says I'm doing great."

When they asked what she did, she gave them the civil-service routine that she hoped made her sound like a postal clerk and said she hadn't made many friends at work.

Missy covered Skip's hand with hers. "You're gon' just love Coda! There's so many nice people in there."

"There certainly seem to be. Di seems very nice—the one in charge of the meeting last night."

"Oh, she's a peach."

"Do you know her very well?"

"I don't think Sonny does, 'cause he doesn't always go to coffee and I usually do. But I think she's a doll—she's my

138

sponsor. Goin' to coffee's the whole key, Skip. That's how you really get to know people.''

''I knew a man who used to go—named Tom. Did either of you know him?''

Missy shook her head, but Sonny seemed to have drifted off again. He was preoccupied perhaps, or a little depressed.

Or maybe he just resents having me horn in.

Fourteen

''MARGARET! MARGRIIIIIT!''

Only one person called her Margaret and only one person stood outside her door and yelled as loud as he pleased.

She answered the door in a towel, having just stepped from the shower.

''Oh me-oh my-oh,'' said her guest. ''It's Venus of de bayou.''

''As a matter of fact, Dee-Dee, it's the second time I've been called a goddess in twenty-four hours.''

''Do tell.'' He offered his early-evening joint, which she waved away, and strode in, closing the door.

''Your version was better. The other person said all women were goddesses.''

''Well, some are more so. May I nuzzle your neck?''

''By all means.''

After a brief caress, he said, ''What news of your oafish swain?''

''I'm cheating on him tonight.''

139

"With me, you mean? I don't recall asking."

"I wish, Dee-Dee; don't I wish. I've got a date with a character named Abe."

"Abe what?"

"I don't know. I met him in a twelve-step program. First names only."

"My dainty darling, no! You can't be going out with some anonymous meeting-cruiser! There's a killer on the loose, or haven't you heard?"

"Worse news, he's not only a suspect, he's a creep."

"Oh, Jesus, I just had a flash. A truly horrible thought came over me. You're absolutely sure you don't know this man's name?"

"Actually, I think I do. He left it on the machine when he called to confirm." She thought back. "It's Morrison."

"Oh, no! Worst fears confirmed. Abe Morrison. Awful Abe to everybody on Gravier Street."

"You know him?"

"This is for your job? Is that what this is about?"

"It's not for my health, Dee-Dee. Dress me, will you?"

He flung open her closet. "Black," he pronounced. "For deepest mourning."

"Dee-Dee, it's the middle of summer."

"This!" He pulled out a calf-length sundress, khaki green with a dropped waist.

"Why this?"

"It's olive drab. The color of his personality."

She went in the bathroom to slip it on. "Okay, Dee-Dee, I've got five minutes. Tell me who the hell he is."

"In my opinion," he shouted through the closed door, "he's quite capable of serial murder. Even mass murder. Easily capable."

Oh, shit. Abasolo would be covering her, but they both could have used a little advance warning.

"What the hell do you mean?" She burst out the door, ready to pick him up and shake the information out of him.

But he burst out laughing. "Officer Darling, you're so cute when you're terrified."

"I mean it, Jimmy Dee."

"My, my, she means it. Okay then. Maybe I overstated the case a tiny little bit. Maybe the world's primo pompous bore isn't *necessarily* a killer. But I'll tell you one damn thing—forced to remain in his company for long, *you* might become one."

She'd agreed to meet Abe at the bar in the Monteleone. Back in the shadows, she could make out Abasolo, sipping a Coke. And there was Abe—in a sport coat over an open-necked shirt.

She'd never have thought to wear a dress, would have automatically thrown on some sort of summer pants outfit if Jimmy Dee hadn't been clowning, but the dress was the right thing, she saw. Abe not only smiled when he saw her, he nodded—nodded several times, almost imperceptibly, but he very definitely did it. She felt like a blue-ribbon heifer at a 4-H show and reflected that it was a new experience—no man had done this to her before.

Probably because I haven't dated that much.

He said, "You look perfect. I like a skirt that swirls."

It was weird, but better swirling skirts than leather dog collars. And it was soon explained. He was into Cajun dancing.

They went to Michaul's, a warehouse of a restaurant with a live Cajun band and a dance floor as big as a bistro plunked down in the middle. The band was hot and skirts were aswirl. A mural of bayou scenes surrounded communal tables spread with blue-and-white checked cloths. Ceiling fans turned, though the AC was blasting. Bales of cotton hung from the ceiling, along with an authentic pirogue. A portrait of a rare swamp animal—an "Ali-posa-fisha-coona"—seemed perfectly plausible at a place that offered drinks like a "nutty Cajun (Amaretto daiquiri)."

"Trust me," said Abe. "The food's great. Women always get that look when they first walk in here—like maybe it's a place for the LSU–Ole Miss crowd."

"Do they?"

"Yeah, but they end up loving it."

"A funny thing. I'm getting the feeling I'm part of a mile-long parade."

"Hey, we're adults."

"What's that supposed to mean?"

"Why pretend we're kids on our first date?"

"I'll tell you later."

"Why not now?"

"I have to wait for the right moment."

She found herself eager for a drink before dinner, something she usually declined, preferring wine later. There was something about the situation—and not just the fact that she was a fraud—that was making her nervous. It was a weird sense that she had to perform, had to please Abe, had to make him like her whether she liked him or not. Those women who loved the place—had they lied to please him? What was it about him? Something intangible; demanding; something oddly controlling yet needy.

"Want to dance?"

"Not yet. Later maybe."

"Now, baby." He got up and pulled her to her feet.

"But I don't know how."

"Skip, you gotta get with it. Everybody's into Cajun dancing."

"Last on my block as usual."

"You gotta go to the Fais Do Do at Tipitina's. Or come here—they have lessons at six o'clock."

She would have said she'd do that, but he had dragged her to the dance floor, stuffed ear plugs in his ears ("I never dance without 'em"), and was getting into professorial mode. "Okay, here's all it is. You think it's going to be two steps

142

but it's four. You've got to take those two extra steps. Bend your knees and kind of go up and down. That's it. Got it?"

"I guess so." Dancing wasn't her strong point.

But the music was irresistible, and he was right, it was getting to be a fad. She went at it with all her heart.

"Hey," said Abe, "you can't do that."

"I can't do what?"

"You've got to go up and down when your partner does. You can't set the rhythm yourself."

Damn! Just like high school—she never could do it right. Her knees were starting to kill her. "Maybe that's enough for now."

But in Abe's opinion it wasn't. She was a near-cripple by the time they got back to the table, and, worse, felt off-balance, a failure. She caught Abasolo's eye—and could have sworn he was grinning evilly.

When they had ordered—jambalaya for him, catfish for her—Abe leaned forward. "Tell me about yourself."

No. Something in her balked at the exercise. Why did she always have to do every little thing he wanted?

"You first," she said.

"No, you."

It was a direct order. She said, "I wasn't really born here. That's just the story my parents tell. Actually, I was left behind when my spaceship took off and I've been trying to learn the language ever since."

"I see what you mean. You don't look like you fit in."

"Thanks a lot."

"Hey, from me that's a compliment. I hate this place."

But it stung. She had been trying lately to fit in better and she'd thought she was succeeding. What was it that made her stand out? She didn't ask, knowing the answer was bound to make her feel insulted.

She changed the subject. "Why do you live here if you hate it?"

"To be near my kids. I was in Atlanta before—now, there's a city! But my wife divorced me and moved here; she got the kids, of course, so I'd hardly ever have seen them if I'd stayed there. This is bad enough."

He speared a piece of lettuce, using his fork like a weapon.

"You miss your kids?"

"I miss 'em like crazy." He stared at her, letting his eyes go moist. She got the feeling he'd done it before.

"But you must see them sometimes."

"Oh, sure. It's just not like having a family."

Skip had a feeling that she was supposed to take his hand and croon, "Ooooooh, is that what you really want?"

Instead she said, "You're upset about the divorce?"

"Horribly." He tried the spearing trick again, but missed—his fork squeaked nastily on the plate.

He wants me to ask him what went wrong and whatever it was will be her fault.

"Would it be rude to ask what happened?"

"Not rude at all. Cynthia didn't want to be married anymore. Period."

"She didn't give any reason?"

"She gave lots of them, but they all amounted to the same thing—I wasn't perfect."

"And you thought you were."

Seeing him start, Skip held up a hand. "Just kidding. Really."

"Anyway, she really pulled the rug out from under me. I had a nice wife, nice home, two great kids, good job, friends—now I've got none of it. I threw away my whole career to come to a city where nothing's happening economically."

"Do you think she was right about any of the stuff she said—about your not being perfect?"

"I don't know if I really want to talk about that."

"Well, to tell you the truth, I don't blame you. I was

144

thinking you were being awfully forthcoming for someone talking to a stranger."

"You mean I don't have to?"

"Don't have to what?"

"Talk about this stuff. I thought women expected it. It's supposed to make us seem vulnerable or something."

Skip failed in all attempts to avoid laughing. "Sorry," she said when she had gained control, "but you don't seem at all vulnerable to me."

He made a fist and set it sideways on the table. "You know, I don't know what to do with you. I thought women liked to talk about themselves, so I tried to talk about you. I know they love to hear personal stuff, so I tried that. What the hell else am I supposed to do?"

"You don't have to be vulnerable to be attractive."

"What do you mean by that?"

"I just want to get to know you. You don't have to present some kind of false identity to get me to like you. We could just have a little quiet conversation, maybe."

"I've already gone through all my subjects."

"No you haven't. You could tell me about your children."

"What's to tell? Two lovely daughters. Real smart. Pretty."

"Names?"

"Why should I tell you their names?"

She wondered if a lot of his dates walked out in the middle of dinner and hailed the nearest taxi.

But probably none of the others have been cops. I could just pull out my gun and shoot him.

It was tempting, but instead she took a deep breath. "Oh, hell, let's talk about us."

He looked so shocked it was almost worth it. She said, "Are you dating anyone else?"

"I'm not even dating you."

"I got a good recommendation on you. I hear you date a lot of women from that inner-child group."

145

"Tell me something—will you just tell me something? Why do women think this kind of stuff is any of their business?"

"I really like you, Abe. I'm just trying to find out what you're all about. Isn't that reasonable?"

He looked wary. "What do you want to know?"

She smiled, trying to look as pleasant and non-threatening as a six-foot cop can look. "Oh, where you live, for instance. What part of town and whether you like it there."

"I can't take this. I just can't take it." He flung down his napkin and strode out, possibly to fling himself in front of an oncoming car. It didn't occur to Skip to follow. She ordered coffee and peanut-butter pie, hoping he wouldn't be joining her.

If it had been a genuine date, she probably would have been close to tears, but in the circumstances she could hardly keep from laughing alone and loudly, making a perfect spectacle of herself.

She made a mental note to phone Steve Steinman first thing in the morning. Thank God her real life—as opposed to her professional one—didn't require any Awful Abes or even Exciting Alexes. As Cindy Lou had said, teddy bears were so good for the inner child. . . .

Abe slipped back into his chair, face washed, hair combed. "I guess I kind of blew the evening, huh?"

"*Au contraire.* 'Memorable' is exactly the way I'd describe it."

"Listen, my wife always tried to get me to to 'open up'— that's what she called it, 'open up,' like a dentist. I don't know what it is—when women start asking me questions, I just freak."

"I can ask non-threatening questions. I promise."

"No you can't. No woman can—I mean it's not about them, it's about me."

"Abe. How about those Saints?"

"What does that mean?"

146

"What do you mean what does that mean? All I said was, how about those Saints?"

He looked at the table, apparently truly embarrassed. "I don't follow baseball."

"Or any sports, I gather."

"How'd you know that?"

"Just a guess. Here's one: Seen any good movies lately?"

"No, wait. Why'd you say that about sports? You don't think I'm not very masculine, do you?"

Are you kidding? I barely think you're human.

"Of course I do—it's just that the Saints are a football team. So that was a clue." She felt as if she were talking to a child. What on earth was wrong with this man?

But of course she knew. His inner child was a big fat mess.

On the way back to their cars, Abe reminded her that she was going to tell him why they should pretend they both dated other people.

"I was going to say," she said, "it's because it's more Southern that way—it make things smoother. But now that seems a little out of place."

"It wasn't a smooth evening, huh?"

"The food was great. And there's a cypress knee in the bathroom. I wouldn't have missed that for anything."

"Shit! I wish that bitch hadn't left me! I'm not cut out for this crap."

Fifteen

WHATEVER TINY BREEZES had stirred the city on the weekend subsided early Monday morning. Skip, who used the ceiling fan at night, hating the sterile atmosphere air conditioning produced, awoke with her hair damp, whimpering from a dream she couldn't remember. The dream had frightened her, or maybe it was the oppressive torpor of the city that had her on edge. She lay there not wanting to get up, her apprehension holding her down like a pair of strong arms. It hovered in the room, a strange and shadowy intruder, reminding her of times when something had been horribly wrong at bedtime and she'd awakened not remembering at first, but frightened and depressed, not knowing why.

What was it? She took mental inventory.

It was the Axeman. Tomorrow was the day he'd set for his personal jazzfest. Tomorrow.

And they were no closer to catching him than they'd been a week ago. Panic seized her.

The time had come for ''creative police work''—or, more accurately, for giving Cindy Lou's idea a shot. She hoped she wouldn't be sorry.

She grabbed for the phone and dialed her brother.

"Conrad, I need a favor."

"If it isn't the black sheep."

"I liked Camille."

"Everyone likes Camille."

She could hear the muffled voices of an early-morning talk show. While boning up on news and trends, Conrad was probably sipping a vegetable cocktail whipped up in his juicer. In the kitchen, another expensive machine was probably turning out a perfect cup of coffee. And for all Skip knew, Camille was working beside it, manufacturing the world's first cholesterol-free breakfast. There was no question she'd be the breakfast cook—if anyone would have a traditional relationship, Conrad would.

"Listen, I want to make a trade."

"Later. I've got a meeting."

"Two questions."

"Six tickets."

"Three."

"One question."

"Okay, four."

Their standing deal was this: When she was desperate, she pumped him about his Uptown acquaintances, in return for which she fixed his parking tickets. Since they'd hit on it, they'd gotten along better than they had in years, no doubt because each of them thought they were getting the better of the other.

She figured Conrad enjoyed the power inherent in having a flunky to fix his tickets; as for her, she didn't care how she got the information, but she did find a certain pleasure in knowing she was deceiving her brat of a brother. Because the truth of the matter was, she simply paid the damn tickets herself, thus reducing him to the status of common snitch.

"Do you know Sonny Gerard?"

"A little bit. Nice guy."

"What do you know about him?"

"Good reputation, everyone likes him, especially women."

"That's it?"

"That's the enchilada. Was it worth four tickets?"

"No."

"Tough shit." He laughed triumphantly.

"Come on. You've got to give me more than that."

"Okay. His dad's Bull Gerard the plastic surgeon."

"Give me credit for *something*, Conrad."

"Oh, yeah. You're a detective, right? Sonny's okay; his brother's the weird one."

"His brother?"

"Rob Gerard. He's an artist. He and Sonny don't speak."

"How's he weird?"

"I told you—he's an artist."

Rob was in the phone book, but it was hours too early to call an artist.

She dressed, went into the office, and ran the whole plan by Cappello. As she'd expected, the sergeant agreed—it was unconventional, but time was running out.

She called Abe's old law firm in Atlanta and the one he'd said he recently joined on Gravier Street, forebearing to use the term Awful Abe, but only barely. Both places verified his existence. Next she checked for any criminal record in Georgia but failed to find one. Finally she tracked down a Cynthia Morrison in the admissions office at UNO, the ex. Now, here was a potential source. But how did you ask a woman if her ex-husband had murderous tendencies?

On a roll, she called Hattiesburg, Mississippi, and learned not only that a Missy McClellan existed, but her dad was a former mayor running for the legislature. Good family, churchgoers, no police record; lived with an aunt in New Orleans. Skip checked one more thing—a map. She wanted to see if Hattiesburg was just down the road from Indianola, where Linda Lee had grown up. It wasn't.

Di was another matter. None of the hypnotists in the book had ever heard of her and neither had the National Guild of Hypnotists, the American Association of Professional Hypnotherapists, or the National Society of Clinical Hypnotherapists. She was licensed neither by the State Board of Certified Social Work Examiners nor by the State Board of

Examiners of Psychologists. None of which meant she wasn't a hypnotherapist, but if she was, Skip had the feeling she was the sort who just decided she was and hung out a shingle.

She reported to Joe and Cappello, "They're all screwballs—three of them out front and two who're too good to be true."

Joe said, "They sound pretty ordinary to me."

"Yeah. Ordinary screwballs. At least they're all who they say they are, except for Di. The voodoo people don't know her and neither do the headshrinkers."

"You better try to concentrate on her awhile."

"Okay." She felt a light sweat break out on her forehead: *I think I'll just ask her mom about her. Or maybe her ex-husband.* On days like this she was glad she didn't have a partner; it wouldn't suit her freewheeling style. But some things had to be run by her superiors. "By the way, tonight I have a little pretend date with Alex."

"You what?" The look on Joe's face said his own dog had bitten him.

Cappello calmed him. "It's okay. She's already been out with Abe. To what avail I'm not sure, but I'll try anything at this point."

"Abe doesn't have a criminal record. Alex hit a guy once."

"He doesn't quite check out either. Claims he lives Uptown and he doesn't. But not to worry—I can handle him. And Abasolo's backing me up."

Joe sighed. "Be sure you take a radio with you."

When they were done, she drank coffee, killing time. And at ten o'clock she took off for Rob Gerard's studio, not caring if she made him mad. Just feeling desperate.

She had a bad feeling the Axeman had been out of commission too long for comfort. The first murders had been close together. Another was due.

* * *

An ankle was tied to something—a rope, maybe, a wisp of fog, perhaps—that anchored the body to Earth. It floated aubergine and red in a dark mass that could have been space, or possibly the sea. The mass roiled and twisted, alive with tumult and agony, Skip thought, but that wasn't possible. It wasn't alive, it wasn't even real.

She was oddly unnerved by the huge painting—Rob's, surely—leaning against a brick wall. It made her throat close slightly, and not in a good way. She felt a little bit afraid, though there was no one else in the courtyard except a man so wispy she could have broken him in two. He was clearly unarmed, indeed almost undressed, wearing only a pair of faded shorts. His skin glistened, probably from a recent application of sunscreen. He was very white to be out in August with no shirt or hat. His hair glinted copper, neon in the morning sun. He sat on the ground, his back to Skip, either staring at the painting or meditating.

"Excuse me. . . ."

When he turned around, she saw that his eyes were light blue and his face, unlike his body, was biscuit-brown. His lashes and brows were bleached white. He reminded her of a leprechaun, so small was he, and so crafty-looking.

"Whoooo are youoooo?" He drew out each syllable, in a parody, she thought, of some Lewis Carroll character, some grotesque from *Alice in Wonderland*. He stood, feet apart, solid. He was a good six inches shorter than she was but he had presence.

"I'm Margaret Langdon," said Skip. "I work at De-Paul." The local mental hospital.

"How very convenient. It's time for my medication." He held out his hand.

"You're not kidding. That is, if you painted that." She nodded at the painting, knowing she was taking a big chance. If she insulted him, she was lost; if he took up the challenge, she'd established a weird rapport.

152

He didn't bat an eye. "I'm a very sick man. You have to help me." He didn't remove the open hand.

"Drop by," said Skip. "Feeding time's at three."

He was bored with the joke and was looking at her intently, starting to make her uncomfortable. "You wouldn't let me paint you, would you? Just your face. I mean it."

"Are you Rob Gerard, by any chance?"

"They've heard of me at DePaul?"

"Only in the personnel office. Your brother wants to work for us as a volunteer."

"And he gave me as a reference? Excuse me, but I'm hallucinating. Give me a Valium."

"Actually, he didn't."

"Would you like to go inside? Your upper lip's sweating and I keep wanting to lick it."

"Please."

In a moment she saw why he painted outside. He had no real studio at all, just a garage with a skylight. It would have been fine except that it was filled to the gills—with furniture (indoor and lawn), books, magazines, painting supplies, and paintings, paintings, paintings. "Maid's day off," he said. "Have a seat."

She removed a foot-high pile of magazines from a director's chair and parked herself. "Sonny didn't give you as a reference. We're like the CIA; we pry."

Rob was fiddling with a coffee-maker. "Can't have crazies taking care of crazies."

"You got it."

"Well, what if they've got a crazy in the family? Does that disqualify them?"

"You mean you?"

"The Gerards think so. Next to me, ol' Sonny ought to look like a paragon of stability."

"He does next to anybody."

"You want some coffee?"

"No thanks."

Rob poured himself some and turned to face Skip. She saw that the blue eyes were serious, looked sapphire now, deep with trouble, and there was pain etched in his face. "He's had a hard life."

"Sonny has?"

"He's the pleaser in the family. I'm the rebel."

"No kidding."

"I never get to talk to anyone about my little brother. Anybody who'll listen, anyway. Everybody thinks he's the greatest thing going."

"And you don't?"

He looked around, could find no available surface, finally sat on the floor. "Are you kidding? Who doesn't? He's perfect. He does everything right. You'll love him to death."

"I don't get it. What's wrong?"

"Are you a shrink or are you from personnel?"

She sensed he wanted a shrink, not a personnel officer. "Both, actually. Personnel sends out a psychologist to do the evaluations."

"Pretty elaborate. I didn't know DePaul was that good."

Skip tried to look insulted. "We do the best we can."

"Well, tell me something, Doctor. . . ."

"I'm not a doctor."

"Tell me something anyway. Can I paint you?"

"That's not what you were going to ask."

"All that pleasing can't be good for a person. It's got to be eating him up inside."

"You sound like you really care about him."

He mimicked her: "You sound like you took shrink lessons. Well, listen. Take ol' Sonny on. Baby brother'd be great. Nobody in the world's got more patience. Nobody's got more stability. If you're worried about somebody falling apart when the crazies do, it'll never be Sonny. You could trust Sonny with a baby. And another thing. Nobody's got more compassion. Kid weeps when he sees a wounded animal. Or used to. He's a med student now—probably toughened up. I think that's really why he became a doctor instead of mere bowing to family pressure. He hates to see suffering.''

"We've got a lot of that at DePaul.''

"Sonny probably thinks he can fix it. And you know what? He probably can, to some extent. He's never failed at anything yet.''

"Why do I detect a note of irony? Don't you two get along?''

"We don't speak, but it's nothing personal. None of the Gerards speak to me. Word came down from on high.''

"I hear the Gerards have been doctors for generations. I take it you didn't bow to family pressure.''

"Hey, we needed a secretary.''

"What?''

"You know, a scribe. Somebody had to chronicle the family history.''

Puzzled, Skip looked around her. Most of the paintings were like the one outside. Dark; disturbing; more or less abstract.

"We grew up in the same place, you know. And this is what it was like.'' His moving hand took in the panorama of ugliness he'd created. "But he's perfect. You're a shrink—explain it, okay?''

Skip talked for ten minutes on codependency, amazed she could do it and enjoying every second. Deep in her heart, though, she knew a real shrink would have kept her mouth shut.

Rob took the news without shouts of "Eureka! The secret of life at last!'' Instead he said, "You want to have lunch or anything?''

To her surprise, she did. She definitely didn't want him to paint her—she was hideous in purple—but she found herself hating to leave him.

"Sorry,'' she said. "Already booked.''
Very sorry.

He was like her—a native who was really an alien. No wonder Conrad thought he was weird.

Abe had chosen the restaurant carefully. He had agonized over it and had finally come up with Arnaud's. Probably Missy had only an hour, and probably she didn't drink, but perhaps she could be persuaded to linger, to have a Bloody Mary, maybe even a glass of wine. He had chosen Arnaud's partly because she was young and it was old; it would seem stable, maybe even intimidating. He would seem to be treating her with great care. And it was the sort of place that lent itself to a leisurely time, a gracious time; more of her time than she wanted to give if he was lucky.

He knew she would bore him, that she wouldn't have anything to say to him, but he liked to look at her and he knew how to talk to her. He'd feel okay with her—not the stupid, awkward way he felt with Skip, so huge and so . . . what?

Self-confident.

He didn't care much for self-confident people. Why the hell had he asked Skip out anyway?

Because I ask them all out.

Every fifth or sixth one went. He'd had no idea Missy would.

She came in wearing a peach miniskirt that showed off a mile of leg and a matching short top that kind of swung loose at the waist. Sometimes when she leaned a certain way you could almost see skin. He sucked in his breath.

She was looking all around, confused. He waved, realizing she didn't really know him.

"Abe?" She still wasn't sure it was he. "Am I late? I'm so sorry. I had a client and"—she shrugged—"it just went over. The time, I mean."

She was as nervous as he was.

"Thank you for coming. Would you like a drink—a sherry, maybe? Just a tiny little something."

"No thanks. But you go ahead."

156

Damn. If she'd drink, she'd lose track of time, forget she had to be back.

When they'd ordered he thanked her again for coming. "I was feeling really down and you made me feel so much better with your share the other night."

She blushed. "I guess that's what the program's for."

It really was a good way to meet women, but he wished to hell they were less sanctimonious women. "Sometimes I don't really feel like I can say what I need to in front of the whole group."

"Really? I find the group incredibly supportive."

"I don't know. Maybe I'm shy."

She looked shocked. "Shy?"

"Maybe I just don't have as much recovery as I thought I did."

He watched her face change from puzzled to sympathetic, shift before his eyes into codependent gear. *A useful word,* he thought. *I love it to death. You go to the group, the group defines what it takes to make them take off their clothes; and you go out and do it.*

He said, "I've just been feeling really vulnerable lately."

She said nothing, being far too busy melting.

"Do you have kids?"

"No, but I really want them."

He smiled, a sad smile as if through tears. "They're life's greatest pleasure. Really. You just can't know till you have them."

"How many do you have?"

"Two. Two girls." He clenched a fist. "God, I miss them!"

"Miss them! What's happened to them?"

This time he went for brave nonchalance, spreading his palms, shrugging. "Oh, the usual thing. Divorce. She got custody. It's the American way."

Her eyes burned, her cheeks flamed. "I think that's so wrong! A father is just as much a parent as a mother."

"I just feel so helpless."

"Are you working the steps?"

"I try," he said. "It's so hard."

"You've got to let your higher power take over."

He loved it. She didn't have a shitload of "recovery," that was obvious. Ten minutes flat and he'd manipulated her into giving advice. In a way this was almost more fun than getting them in bed—watching them fall all over themselves trying to do what they were going to the damn group to avoid doing.

"Oh, Missy, you're right. You're really right. It's just so damn hard to let go."

"I know. Believe me, I know."

She looked so terribly sad, so young, so much like one of his daughters that he forgot to feel triumphant as he took her hand and squeezed; as she let him touch her for the first time.

Who in the hell was this Di—a gypsy fortuneteller or Scarlett O'Hara? Sonny had actually found the courage to ask when he saw the place—the weird living room and the bedroom like something out of Tara.

Di had laughed.

Her silky, velvety, satiny, silvery, golden laugh had come to haunt him; it came to him in dreams and sometimes he thought he heard it in the street, on the wind, perhaps. It was the oddest, loveliest laugh he'd ever heard; an elf laugh, a fairy laugh, the mirth sound of a butterfly.

She had laughed and said she'd been a gypsy in another life, but not a Southern belle, never for a moment; she didn't have a submissive bone in her body.

The bed was hung with mosquito netting, he supposed, though he'd never seen any; at any rate something like gauze was wound around the four-poster bed, almost casually, yet he knew it had probably been done with the greatest of guile. The whole room was white—white and airy, like something in a dream. A full-length mirror, instead of being bolted to the wall, had been placed at a slant, a strategic slant so that vou could see what was happening in the bed, you could watch yourself undress your lady love. It was the bedroom of a queen, perhaps a goddess. He wanted to worship her.

In his church you knelt to worship and he knelt before her now. Unzipped her shorts. Pulled them off. Worshipped until she nearly lost her balance, till he had to pull her even closer into his face, digging his fingers into her soft buttocks. So soft; so amazingly soft after Missy's young hard ones. He loved digging his fingers in, loved her silky feel, loved the look of her thighs, not smooth—no cellulite, of course, but dozens of tiny little wrinkles. He wanted to lick each one.

He picked her up finally, and laid her gently on the bed. She crossed her hands over her stomach till he pulled his T-shirt over his head and, while he was doing it, pulled off her own, took off her bra as he got out of his jeans.

Gently, the ceiling fan ruffled the mosquito netting. Everything was so peaceful, so incredibly beautiful.

As he leaned over to kiss her, he saw that her abdomen was scarred. She had lovely breasts, perfectly sculptured, but he knew what he had to find under them. He took one in his mouth, sucked, licked the nipple that he knew was tattooed. It was pink; she had chosen pink like the nipples of a teenager, though the originals had undoubtedly been brown (he knew she had grown children, she talked about them in the group). Gingerly he caressed the other breast, reaching underneath, and felt the diamond-shaped scar.

He felt a sudden wave of nausea, swallowed. What was wrong with him? He was a doctor. Or he was almost one. Plenty of women had mastectomies, had reconstructions, and this one was quite sophisticated, beautifully done. In a few years he'd be learning to do it himself, he'd do hundreds of them in his career. He turned away from her.

"What is it? It's my scars, isn't it? You find me repulsive."

"No—" He looked back and saw that she'd covered her stomach, had left her breasts outside the sheet. How could he tell her it wasn't the scars, it was the cancer? It was that

159

she'd come close to death. Maybe not very close, but close enough to make him think about it. He felt tears well in his eyes. "It was thinking of you sick—I can't stand to think of you sick." He buried his face in her neck.

She said, "I feel so mutilated."

"You're not mutilated. You're beautiful. Your breasts are beautiful."

"That's what *he* said." Her voice was hard and ugly, unlike her voice, nothing like the voice of Diamara, the nymph (or possibly the goddess Diamara). It wasn't only her voice. He couldn't take in the fact that she'd spoken of another man while she was in bed with him.

"What?"

"Nothing. They are, aren't they?" She cupped them in her hands. "They're beautiful."

She kissed him, her breath like all the spices of the East. She rolled over on him and felt for his penis. It was limp. She took it in her hand, rolled it between her fingers as expertly as if she'd been taught in a *harim*. It was delicious, a rain of sweet fruits and exotic perfumes, everything strange and heavenly, even the frustration, the hideous frustration of it.

She took him in her mouth and it only got better, and a thousand times worse.

When she finally gave up, she was on the verge of tears. "I'll bet you've never been impotent before in your life."

"Di—I'm under stress. I'm really stressed out." His voice sounded like it was coming from a tunnel. He knew he didn't sound sincere. He didn't sound anything. His voice had no expression at all.

"You think I'm ugly."

"I think you're beautiful."

He threw the sheet off, intending to go down on her again, to make her happy after all, to show her how much he cared. Along with the scar, there was an ugly lump on her abdomen. He sucked in his breath, touched it, felt its hardness, its wrongness.

"What's this?"

"That's what he did to me. He botched it. He destroyed my body." She turned her head away, sunk in a sadness that seemed nearly as deep as his own, biting her lip.

She meant her doctor, and she was right. He had most assuredly botched it, botched it horribly. In a way that almost made Sonny remember what he could be, what he could do, if he could just get past this damn ER rotation. He knew himself well enough to know that he would never in his life screw up a woman's body like this. This gorgeous woman really thought she was ugly because of the butchery some amateur had performed on her. In a weird way this was giving him courage, making him want to finish what he'd started, to do his job properly.

"He didn't destroy your body," he said. "There's enough of it left to kiss." In a few minutes she was moaning as if the unfortunate incident had never occurred, once more a goddess properly worshipped.

Sixteen

"NOW, THAT ONE sounds interesting. I've always thought so." Cindy Lou meant Alex.

"Interesting how? Like he could be a murderer?" Skip had talked her into going to see Di's mother and was grilling her on the way.

"Lively but childish. Like he might be fun on a date. Except that I never go out with anyone in my field."

"Is there some special reason for that?"

She thought about it. "Naah, I don't think so. I think they just don't like me."

Skip tried to take it in, found she didn't know what to ask. Who wouldn't like Cindy Lou?

"I guess I'm too sharp-tongued," Cindy Lou supplied.

"I can see that. I'd say this was the kind of guy who went for bimbos if he didn't seem to go for anything that walks."

"Yeah, that's his rep."

"You mean you've heard of him?"

"Oh, chile, everybody's heard of him. The man's a best-seller."

"He says not."

"He's close enough so the nearest competition's wild with jealousy—or was. Sounds like his career's pretty much over, though. Burn-out case."

"But you don't see him as a suspect."

"I didn't say that. I just kind of like his style. The hog and all. You can still be a murderer and have a lot of testosterone."

"They usually do, right?"

"It makes them aggressive."

But her tone was light. It seemed to Skip she was taking neither Alex nor the others very seriously as suspects. "So," said Skip, "this is the official consultant's view, as I understand it: Di, harmless crackpot; Missy, unmitigated wimp; Sonny, obsessive medical nerd; Abe, thoroughgoing asshole; and Alex, cute."

"No, no, no. You got it all wrong. That's just gossip. Personally, I think they all sound dangerous. Di doesn't sound like she's got a real good grip on reality; Missy and Sonny are wound way too tight for comfort; and Abe and Alex are hostile as hell."

"I thought you wanted to date Alex."

"Yeah, but I have truly terrible taste."

Di's mother lived in Kenner, just outside the city, in Jefferson Parish. It was a fairly nice bedroom community, if a little on the colorless side, the sort where families with children lived. It wasn't especially where you'd expect to find an older woman living alone. And Mrs. Breaux wasn't what Skip expected, seeming far too ordinary to have spawned so exotic a daughter.

She had none of Di's gypsy looks, just smallish brown eyes and brownish hair, lightly touched with gray. It was cut short and curled tightly around a face that wore a thousand and one wrinkles and a heavy coat of orangy powder. Her legs were paper-white beneath a pair of loose pink pants that stopped slightly below the knee. She looked like any old lady from a small Southern town.

As arranged, Cindy Lou did the talking. She gave her real name and real credentials, claiming Di had applied to Tulane in some sort of therapist's capacity and they were checking her out—the Rob Gerard ploy slightly modified. She introduced Skip as her colleague.

The thing not only worked, Mrs. Breaux apparently couldn't have been more delighted if the Queen of England had come calling. For a while she bustled about, settling them into a formal living room with glasses of iced tea. Then she sat down herself, snuggling well-padded posterior into wing chair and making no bones about the fact that her day was made.

"You have a very nice house, Mrs. Breaux," said Cindy Lou.

"Isn't it lovely? It was Jackie's, of course—Diamara's, I mean. I got it in the divorce settlement. She likes the action down in the Quarter and I like the quiet out here." A shadow came over her face. "Or I thought I would. I never lived anywhere quite so fancy. Sometimes it gets a little too quiet."

163

She paused to repair her smile. "I'm so glad Jackie's going to use some of those courses she's always taking; she's such an intelligent girl. I've always said how much potential she had. But then you won't believe me—I'm her mama."

"That's why we came. Who could possibly know her better?"

"Well, you're right about that. What can I tell you?"

"Oh, I just thought we'd talk informally. The whole idea is just to get to know what kind of person she is. Why don't you tell us about your family? Starting with you, for instance."

Cindy Lou made it seem so easy—just a friendly conversation over tea.

"Oh, gosh, there's nothing interesting about me."

"Well, you know, I'd never pick you for Di's mother. She has such exotic looks, and the Cajun name—"

"Oh, Lord, yes. I was Louise Wood from Cullman, Alabama. Met Jimmy Breaux and thought I never saw anything so tall, dark, and handsome in all my days. And charming! The man could talk you out of everything you owned, and did, most of the time. He was in sales. There was a downside, though. Isn't that what they say today?"

Skip and Cindy Lou nodded, spellbound, knowing she was going to talk until she was talked out and that they were soon going to know enough about Diamara Breaux to write her biography.

"What was the downside?"

"Well, I moved here with him and everything went real well for a year or so. Then, I don't know, Jimmy just seemed to lose interest in everything; couldn't seem to get out of bed, even. Then all of a sudden he got better and next thing you know he disappeared."

"Oh, no."

"Well, that wasn't the worst of it. He started writing bad checks. Dear God, what a nightmare!"

Skip said, "Tsk tsk," but nothing else, not wanting to stem the flow.

"It kept happening, that was the really sad part. That time I was pregnant and I was still in love with him. Later on, I don't know if I was in love or not, but I had two kids—Jackie was the oldest. It was only years and years later somebody put a name to it. The long and short of it was, I married a manic-depressive." She stopped, nodded, and let it sink in. "A manic-depressive. Can you imagine?

"He'd get manic and he'd go off and, frankly, he'd turn into a con man. Then he'd get depressed and he'd come home and just lie there."

Cindy Lou said, "Sounds kind of hard on the kids."

"The amazing thing is, they took it better than any kids you could ever imagine. Now, Mary Leigh, she had some problems, but Jackie never did. You'd have thought she came from the best home in the world. Funny how kids can adjust, isn't it?"

"What was she like as a child?"

"Oh, always dreaming, always making up stories. And into everything—curiosity almost killed her—you know, like the cat? She'd do anything just to see what it felt like. More scrapes and bumps than any kid in the neighborhood—any girl, anyhow. But the main thing about her was she was always so optimistic. Mary Leigh'd make bad grades and do bad things—break things, sometimes on purpose, it seemed like. Jackie just always saw the good side—always thought things were going to turn out all right. Never had a sad day in her life, that child. Even when the girls were at the Ellzeys'."

She stopped to sip from her glass, a lecturer in mid-performance. "Jimmy'd go and he'd come back and then he'd go again, and when he came back he'd be real sick, and I could tell he really needed me. So somehow I never got around to thinking about getting divorced and maybe finding someone new. But that meant I had to keep things together

165

the best I could. I really wasn't trained for anything, but I could get a job now and then, when I needed to. But I couldn't afford to pay very much for child care. So when the girls were real young, Jackie in second grade and Mary Leigh in kindergarten, I think, I arranged for them to go and stay with some neighbors after school. That was the Ellzeys. Mary Leigh started wetting the bed a few months after they started staying there. I didn't know much about child psychology, but I knew something was wrong. Wouldn't you have thought that?''

''Um,'' said Cindy Lou. ''What was going on?''

''Well, I never found out. Mrs. Ellzey said she didn't know and the girls never would say, only just shrugged. But when I asked if they wanted to stop staying there, they both said yes, and then I quit work for a while so I could be with them and Mary Leigh stopped wetting the bed. Whatever it was, Jackie never seemed bothered.''

''It sounds like you had a really tough time.''

''Oh, it wasn't all bad—not even mostly. We had some good times too. Especially when Jimmy was home and he wasn't depressed.''

''Whatever happened to Jimmy?''

''Nothing good.''

''I wonder if you could tell me, though. For my records.''

''Well, he died. Had a heart attack when Jackie was about fifteen.''

''I'm sorry,'' said Cindy Lou.

For the first time, Mrs. Breaux's eyes misted over. ''It was probably for the best, in the end. He was a very, very unhappy man. A lot of the time, anyhow.''

Skip thought of Tom Mabus, seemingly so unhappy, so deeply depressed for so many years and then rallying, making one last stab at life just before he died.

''And Mary Leigh? Where's Mary Leigh now?''

''Mary Leigh died. Now, that really is a sad story.'' Her eyes were dark pools of regret.

166

"Oh, dear." Cindy Lou looked so sympathetic probably even O'Rourke would have spilled his guts. "When did it happen?"

"When she was nine. Or ten, was it? Nine. She was hit by a train. You have to remember this was over forty years ago and we had trains then. It was in Alabama, when we were visiting the girls' grandparents. She was on her way to the swimming pool to meet a friend. Only one person saw it, old Mrs. Cleland on her way home from the grocery store. She said Mary Leigh just stood too close to the tracks—one minute she was there and the next she was gone." She put her hand over her face, apparently to hide tears. "Mary Leigh always was in too much of a hurry. She was an impatient child right from birth. If she didn't get her bottle right *then*, she'd tune up and cry."

Skip was frankly reeling, but Cindy Lou remained impassive. She smiled, bringing Mrs. Breaux back to the present. "Di's certainly done well," she said.

Mrs. Breaux sent back the smile. "She was the first in her family to go to college. Always smart, Jackie-girl. But she didn't finish—smart, but she had a short attention span. She ended up going to nursing school instead."

"And she did finish that?"

"Oh, yes. Not that I really wanted her to. Frankly, I raised her to marry well. I never did, so I wanted my daughter to have the opportunity."

"I see. And did she?"

"She sure did." She looked as proud as if it had happened yesterday. "Married Walt Hindman. You know, of Hindman Construction?"

Skip did know, having been told by the D.A. who'd handled Di's child-abuse case. When Cindy Lou raised an eyebrow at her, she nodded ever so slightly. The Hindmans were very big in New Orleans. Their firm had been used at one time or another by practically everybody who was socially important.

"The Hindmans are a fine family," said Cindy Lou, winging it.

Mrs. Breaux nodded. "Wealthy. But in the end he turned out to be one of Jackie's bad ideas."

"He drank?"

"No, it wasn't that. He was abusive." She looked away when she said it, not meeting either woman's eyes. The momentary role of proud mom had evidently crumbled under a desperate need to talk turkey—which seemed to fade as swiftly as it had emerged. "Jackie sure got two lovely children out of it, though." She got up and walked to a table at the rear of the room, extracting two framed pictures from a large collection. One she gave to Cindy Lou, one to Skip. Skip got a brown-haired, wholesome-looking girl, somewhere in her late twenties or early thirties. "That's LiLi," said Mrs. Breaux. "Isn't she a beauty?"

"A doll." Cindy Lou traded with her.

"And that's Bennett." The young man in the picture was a little younger—twenty-five, perhaps—and nearly blond. He looked so much like Sonny Gerard that Skip gasped before she caught herself.

"What a hunk," she said.

When Di's mother had returned the photos to their altar, Cindy Lou said, "Tell me, Mrs. Breaux, where did Di study hypotherapy?"

"Well, to tell you the truth, I don't know. I suppose that was one of those courses she took and just never mentioned—she takes so many, you know."

Skip spoke up. "There's a question I'm afraid we have to ask—just a formality, of course, but it's one of those things. I wonder . . . has Di ever been arrested?"

Mrs. Breaux flushed slowly scarlet, from neck to hairline. Tears sprang to her eyes. "How dare you bring that up!"

Skip said nothing, silently entreating her companion to continue the role of the nice cop. Cindy Lou was a natural.

"Oh, Mrs. Breaux, we're so sorry to upset you," she said. "May I get you a glass of water?"

Mrs. Breaux shook her head, probably now as much in the grip of embarrassment as anything else.

Skip said, "I'm sorry, it's just something we have to know."

"I know it can't be all that bad, Mrs. Breaux," said Cindy Lou. "It doesn't mean we'd keep her from getting the job. We just have to know, that's all."

"The charges were dropped."

"You see? I knew it couldn't be that bad."

"I'm sorry, I really can't talk about that." And even Cindy Lou couldn't persuade her.

When they were in the car, Cindy Lou said, "I wonder what it was like growing up in that family? I'll bet those kids had a hell of a ride."

"Manic-depressive dad, you mean?"

"And the day-care debacle. But there might be more. I mean, Mary Leigh did kill herself."

"Mary Leigh killed herself? How do you get that?"

"She was standing too close to the tracks and then she wasn't there? How does a train run over you if you haven't actually stepped onto the tracks?"

"Jesus. I missed that."

"Every family's got one—an accident that was really a suicide, a suicide that was obviously a murder. . . ."

"Oh, come on."

"We had one in ours—a generation back. Great-Grandma is supposed to have walked right into the furnace in her house, but guess what? Great-Granddaddy was home all the time."

"You think he pushed her?"

"She had no history of sleepwalking, drugs, or alcohol. Just one day she walked into the furnace."

Skip shrugged. "Could have happened."

"Well, how come she didn't walk right out again? Or how come he didn't hear her screams and come pull her out? 'Cause he closed the door and leaned against it, that's why."

169

"What kind of furnace was that?"

"Oh, who knows? Maybe it was really a fireplace of some sort—it's oral tradition, that's all."

"And you think it really happened."

"All I know is, when the old folks get drunk, they get to whispering. *They* think it happened. All except my grandpa and my great-uncle—their kids, get the point? You can never believe it of the people you're close to. Suicide's worse—to admit it happened means you contributed to it. And Di's sister committed suicide. So by definition, Di grew up in a family situation that was pretty intolerable."

"She's sounding more like a victim than a criminal."

"Criminals are victims, haven't you heard?" Though Skip didn't speak, she held up her hand—a gorgeously manicured one. "I know it sounds like liberal hogwash, but it happens to be true. They come from nasty families. And not all of them are from the ghetto either."

"So you think Di's family could have produced a murderer?"

"After what we just heard? Not a doubt in my mind." They drove in silence for a few minutes. And then Cindy Lou said, "But just about any American family might. Particularly any Southern family."

"What makes you think we're worse than the rest of the country?"

"Living here. You're such a bunch of blamers. I swear to God I've never seen anything like it. Somebody's always taking the heat for something, and if they're not, they're cringing and saying, 'It wasn't me, it wasn't me,' hiding under a table and scared to death."

For the second time since she'd met him, Skip thought of old Mr. Ogletree, the manager of Linda Lee's apartment house. He'd seemed terrified he was going to be accused of something.

Come to think of it, she'd spent her childhood in a similar state.

Seventeen

"DRESS ME, DEE-DEE."

It was a ritual they'd played out repeatedly—Jimmy Dee smoking a joint while Skip got ready to go out, picking out her outfit as he had when she went out with Abe. The conceit was that although she was a woman and supposed to be born to it, she didn't know the first thing about clothes; the truth was, it was more than a conceit.

He delved into her closet. "Hmm. No leather."

"Too hot for it, anyway."

"Oh, hell. Jeans and a T-shirt. What else can you wear on a motorcycle in August?"

"You disappoint me."

"Not half as much as your wardrobe disappoints me."

Casually, she flipped him off and went into the bathroom to pull on her jeans.

This was part of the ritual also—her dressing in the bathroom, both of them hollering through the door. "I've decided to have an Axeman party."

"Oh, Jimmy Dee, give me a break."

"What are you complaining about? Having parties assures *no* violence, or haven't you grasped that?"

"Oh, great. No violence. Sure. Like there's never any violence at Mardi Gras."

"Come on. This is your opportunity to flush this animal out."

She came back in.

"No," he said. "Definitely not. Not baby pink." He meant her T-shirt.

"You're always saying my clothes aren't feminine enough."

"I am not. I'm always saying they aren't chic enough. And baby pink is definitely not chic."

"Rats. Steve gave me this."

"Dump him. He'll only crush your little baby bones."

She sighed. "I think he's dumped me. He didn't call all weekend."

"Oh, do let me console you with large bottles of spirits and boxes of chocolates."

She pawed through her T-shirt drawer. "How about a little red convertible?"

"Anything."

"How about this?" She was holding up a purple T-shirt from last year's JazzFest.

"Perfect. How many Axeman parties are you going to?"

"None, I expect. I'm working."

"Well, how many are you invited to?"

"One—Allison Gaillard's. Oh, wait—did you invite me to yours?" She went back into the bathroom.

"Not yet, but you'll only find out about it and get your dainty feelings hurt. So I guess you can come."

"Two then."

"*Pathetic*. Surely you jest."

"How many are you invited to?"

"Seven. Excluding my own."

"Well, here's the thing. You're popular and I'm not." She spoke the casual words, but she was starting to feel panicky, and it wasn't about her social status.

"We've *got* to get you launched socially."

She returned wearing the purple shirt. "Dee-Dee, are you really going to seven parties?"

"Certainly not. I said I was invited, not going."

"Oh, God. It's going to be a living nightmare."

Her landlord left her in a cloud of marijuana smoke. She'd refused to toke on his joint (since she was working), but she breathed deeply, hoping for a tiny high or at least an imaginary one. And then she went out to meet her date, once again at the Monteleone. Again, she detected Abasolo in the background. And again she drew praise for her outfit. "Oh, good," said Alex, "you're dressed correctly."

"I knew you'd bring the Rolls. Where are we going?"

"It's a surprise." She hoped Abasolo could keep up.

When they had drunk their obligatory drink (Perrier for both of them), and mounted the hog, she spaced out the danger for a moment. The all-too-human truth was she quite enjoyed having her arms around Alex's waist, her crotch against his butt. She thought how odd it was that a man and woman who hardly knew each other should be so entwined publicly, with society's sanction.

A block or two later she reprimanded herself for her crudeness, imagining that most people would focus on the wind in their faces. So she turned her attention to that and found it almost as sensual. They were nearly on the causeway before she realized that was where they were going.

"What's going on? Are we going across the lake?"

"Uh-huh."

"Why? What's over there?"

"Surprise."

Her scalp prickled, though she knew Abasolo was covering her. The weight of the gun in her backpack was comforting, but she felt helpless heading out of the city. She couldn't have said why, she just had a feeling.

The nearly twenty-four miles of the causeway seemed like a thousand, but they turned off quickly on the Covington side, into a darkly wooded area. She could smell pine in the velvet air, air that was still brushing her face like wings. If she'd been with Steve Steinman, it would have been heaven; as it was, she was aware of a clammy coat of sweat on her body.

Jesus, I must have been crazy. What in hell made me think I could handle him?

Another voice said: *Oh, shut up. This is his idea of a romantic evening. He doesn't know you find him repulsive.*

Repulsive? How about terrifying?

She couldn't shake the fear. Half of her said there wasn't a thing wrong with a man taking a woman to a romantic place on a date; the other half argued that she wasn't a woman on a date, she was a cop in the middle of nowhere with a suspect.

She'd told Joe she could handle him and she'd have to do it. It would be too stupid to die this way.

They stopped in front of a house—a house in the middle of what seemed a huge forest but was actually a residential area studded with similar yuppie palaces. This one was a two-story frame house, in keeping with other examples of Covington architecture, beautifully kept, and, if the outside was any indication, furnished with relentless good taste. That was how people in New Orleans dressed and how they decorated their houses—soporifically, to Skip's mind, but no one could call it tacky.

Alex parked his hog.

"Whose house is this?"

"It belongs to some friends of mine. They lent it to me."

"They're not home?" *Inane question,* she thought. *Of course they're not home. The place is dark as a cave.*

He shook his head. "They're in Europe. It's all ours."

"All ours for exactly what purpose?"

"For dinner. White wine or red?"

"I don't know—why don't we just go to a restaurant?"

"I just told you what's going to happen. I've spent all day shopping. I'm cooking dinner. Are you going to join me?"

174

Oh, well, at least he's in touch with his inner child.

The sudden petulant turn, unpredictable as it was, annoyed rather than alarmed her. She'd seen this in men before, and none of them had been murderers.

She took a deep breath, thinking of Abasolo. He'd go nuts if they went in there—Alex could kill her and he'd never know. *Trust me,* she murmured silently, and said to Alex, "I'm going to join you. With pleasure." She even took his arm as they walked to the back door.

He unlocked the door, and as they slipped in, almost sneaking, she felt the air conditioner. Another of his preparations, apparently.

The light went on. She could see that she was standing in an up-to-the-minute kitchen done in the ubiquitous black and white of up-to-the-minute kitchens. "Lovely."

There were no curtains, the place being too isolated to have to worry about privacy. Great. As long as she kept lights blazing in every room she entered, Abasolo's sanity had a fighting chance.

"Want a look at the rest?"

It was as she'd imagined—perfect but predictable. Wing chairs. A few antiques but a lot more reproductions. Family portraits. Laura Ashley prints in the bedrooms. Muted colors. No original art. Nothing out of place. No sign that children lived here, or even adults who did anything more than sleep. A gorgeous place to bring a date—a lot like a hotel room, just bigger and nicer. Skip wondered again about the house at Lakeview.

Back in the kitchen, Alex poured her a glass of California Chardonnay, which she accepted for the sake of appearances and sipped after they'd clinked glasses. She sat on an Italian-style barstool while he pulled out fish, salad makings, and vegetables, hoping he wouldn't notice she'd quit sipping.

"This is such a lot of trouble to go to."

"Aren't you worth it?"

She tried out a flirtatious smile, but couldn't manage more

175

than a grimace. He stepped toward her, took her hands in his. "What's wrong? You look so nervous."

"I think we're moving too fast."

"We're not moving an inch. All we're doing is having a glass of wine."

"I know, but we're in the middle of nowhere." She desperately wanted to back away from him, an impossibility in a sitting position.

She braced herself for another outburst. Instead he stepped away, shrugging, once again attending to his salad greens. "Hey, don't think a thing about it. I've done it every night this week. Sometimes I score, sometimes I don't."

Involuntarily, she laughed. How could this man be a murderer? "Candor," she said, "will get you nowhere."

"I guess that's my problem. We could take a walk after dinner."

"Listen, what's wrong with your apartment in the city? Why come all the way out here?"

"Echh, you should see the place. Besides, the Campbells have black satin sheets."

"Who are they, anyway? How do you know them?"

"The Campbells? The same way I know you—from the inner-child group. They're very large in the whole thing—in fact, they've given several parties for us here. Frankly, they must be pretty hard up for friends."

"New in town?"

"Yeah. What's that about? Who'd move to this decaying, beat-up old place?"

"You, for one."

"Yes, but that was because of the decay, not in spite of it. Anyway, they're your basic boring, middle-class jerks with nothing better to do than go to these stupid groups all the time and no better friends than me to take care of their insipid hideaway that looks like a motel."

Though the sentiments weren't wildly different from hers,

his harshness seemed to vibrate in the artificially cooled air, the Campbells' air, lent in the spirit of friendship.

Well, it's the Southern way, Skip thought. *Not only are we blamers, we're backbiters, a culture of backbiters.*

But there was something different about Alex's style. It seemed nastier, for one thing, but what else? After a moment it came to her; it was usually Southern women who were treacherous. And not all of them, either, only the wildly unhappy ones who'd gotten trapped in the steel-magnolia syndrome and resented it in bilious undercurrents that made their families miserable and erupted at funerals and weddings—any inappropriate time guaranteed to embarrass everyone present.

What was Alex's excuse?

"Let's don't talk about boring people," he said.

"I like the Chardonnay," said Skip. "A little too oaky, but . . ."

"Oh, stop! I hate boring subjects."

"What are boring subjects?"

"Food, wine, and football."

"What's interesting?"

"Sex."

"Sorry I asked."

"You know what? They hate me in Germany. I got a royalty statement today. My book hasn't sold a single copy. Not one." He turned around to deliver the announcement, smiling as if he'd just announced he'd made a million dollars.

"I'm sorry."

"People don't get it."

"Dolts."

"Where did you go to college?"

"Ole Miss."

"And before that?"

"McGehee's."

"My first girlfriend went to McGehee's. Caroline Bousquet."

"There must have been dozens since; hundreds. How on earth do you keep them straight?"

"What have you heard about me?"

"What do you mean?"

"People say I'd mount a dog. It's not true."

Skip searched vainly for another topic, desperately wanting to leave this one. Nothing came into her mind but food, wine, and football.

"I mean, do I want to go to bed with every pretty woman I see? Yes. Do you blame me? It's not the same thing. Caroline Bousquet was the most perverse woman I've ever met. And she was seventeen at the time."

"Have you ever been married?"

"I can't ever imagine being really relaxed with another human being. Can you?"

"Was that a no?"

He only shrugged.

"You must have been in love."

"I was, but the woman was a relative. It was sad—the saddest thing that ever happened to me." He had a way of announcing catastrophes with a dazzling show of teeth, just the happiest guy in the world. "Did you know Caroline?"

"No." *Thank heaven. Because I'm about to know everything about her.*

"She made me a slave. We did things I've never done with anyone else."

"What things?" She hadn't meant to ask. She was falling under a spell of morbid fascination.

"She said she wouldn't sleep with me unless I did everything she told me to. She'd set time limits in which I had to bring her to orgasm."

Ah, so that's it. I'm supposed to think he can perform miracles on the black satins.

"Other stuff too. Things I thought were disgusting—not even sexual. She made them sexual. Have you been married?"

"No."

"Why not?"

"Way too young."

He put the fish on and began sautéing. Skip was glad of the respite. She searched for silverware and set the table for two.

"Do you like rough sex?"

He moved toward her, in each hand a plate with a serving of fish. From several feet away, she could feel the restlessness, the raw energy of the man. Very deliberately she put down her wine glass. He was like a dragon blowing hot breath.

"Alex, this is moving much too fast."

"Sit down and eat. Later I'll show you the moon in the woods. It's why I brought you here. Have you lived with anyone?"

"No."

"This man you mentioned at breakfast. Is he jealous?"

"Not very."

I'm not even sure he's still in the picture.

"Have you ever been with anyone really jealous, someone violent?"

She shook her head, not liking the way this was going.

"You'd think you could see it coming, wouldn't you? But you can't. It's just like betrayal."

She seized on what seemed, by comparison, a relatively safe topic. "Have you been betrayed a lot?"

He showed teeth, as usual when something was wrong. "Just about every day I get betrayed. Do you think I'm doing something wrong?"

What the hell is going on here? Is he playing stupid sex games or is he violent? Or is it me?

"Betrayed by whom?" she said. "By women?"

"By everyone. My publisher wouldn't do *Fake It Till You Make It.* I had to sell it to a stranger. You want to look at the moon?"

No!

But how to say it?

"Let's go," he said.

"No coffee?"

"Later."

She grabbed her backpack and slung it over her shoulder.

"Women and their purses," he said. "What earthly use do you think you're going to have for that?"

"I might want to hit you with it."

"So you do like to play rough." He tweaked her ear. "Let me get a flashlight."

It had been just dark when they'd arrived and by now the moon had had plenty of time to rise. There was much more light, quite a lot now, but trees blocked out the sky. Alex said they'd have to walk to a clearing to get a really good view of the moon. He led the way down a well-worn path, hardly needing the flashlight. There was the faint scent of ozone in the air and Skip worried momentarily whether it would rain before they could get home on the bike.

Alex said, "Here we are." She stepped into the clearing—a small one with a rustic bench in the middle—and automatically looked up.

"It's full!" Full and gorgeous. She hoped the Axeman wasn't susceptible to its pull.

"Jesus, what the hell is that?" Alex stepped backward, nearly landing on her foot, and trained his flashlight on the ground.

"It looks like a chicken."

It was, and there was another one lying beside it, both dead. Near these two were others, arranged more or less in a pile, or perhaps just left as they fell.

Skip wanted to bend down to examine them, but didn't dare put herself at such a disadvantage. The heads of some were grotesquely askew. Alex kicked one; the head flopped, leaving no doubt the neck was broken.

He said, "The Axeman strikes again."

180

Skip's forearms erupted in goose bumps. "The Axeman?"

"He strangles his victims, doesn't he?"

"Yes, but the last I heard he wasn't killing chickens."

"Well, somebody strangled those." He knelt and picked up one chicken after another, feeling their necks. Skip knelt also, keeping her distance, also feeling the carcasses. No question. Strangled.

"They must be freshly killed," said Alex. "They don't stink yet, and in this heat . . ."

"You act like you're conducting an investigation."

"That's it. I am Hercule Poirot, gearing up my little gray cells."

"Hey, you don't think this is creepy at all?"

"You got down and touched them. The average woman wouldn't do that."

She shrugged, trying like hell for casualness. "They're only chickens."

"They've been murdered."

"Oh, come on, Alex."

"What other explanation could there be? And, by the way, who did it? The Campbells aren't home—I'm the only one who's supposed to be here."

She looked him square in the eye: "Did you do it?"

A glimpse of what could have been surprise passed over his features, and then he started laughing; loudly and inappropriately. She felt for the gun in her backpack, ready just in case. When he'd gained control, he said, "You're something, you know that? There's a mad strangler loose in this town, you're all alone with me, and you just asked if I strangled a dozen chickens."

"Just curious."

"You aren't acting even a little afraid."

"I'll ask again. Did you do it?"

"Come here." He reached for her, his eyes suddenly soft with desire.

"Not now, Alex. Are you crazy? Let's get out of here."

181

"Okay." He waved her ahead of him.

"Uh-uh. Women and children last."

Alex stood still. "This guy could still be here."

"*Let's go.*"

He moved toward her again. "Getting scared? Are you finally getting a little nervous? Do you want my arms around you?"

"Alex, this is no time for kidding around."

"Take my hand."

"I'll just follow you."

He shrugged, but turned on the flashlight and started down the path. After a few moments, he reached back for her. "Come on; take my hand."

"I'm okay. Really."

"But I'm scared."

"Oh, give me a break. You're a guy with a Harley."

He laughed again. "I've never met a woman like you."

As soon as they were off the path, in the area that would have been a yard if one had been planted, he stopped and reached for her, hands high, catching her shoulders.

Too close to the neck for comfort.

"I want you."

She shook him off. "This isn't the time for that."

"Feel my cock."

"No!" But she sneaked a look and what she saw made her palms sweat. It was graphically obvious that this was a man on whom the sight of strangled chickens had had a strong erotic effect. She was planning what to say, what calming, non-threatening tack to take, when suddenly his breath was in her face, his arms going around her. She struggled and his arms tightened. She kicked his shin.

"Whoa!" he hollered, but hung on. She broke from his grasp.

"Don't even think about it, Alex. I'm almost as big as you are and in much better shape."

"Run. Let me chase you."

Her scalp prickled. She strove for control. "Could I ask you a question? What's so exciting about a bunch of dead chickens?"

"It isn't the chickens. It's you."

"Well, listen, I have a headache."

"I guess I read the situation wrong."

"I said no. How do you get clearer than that?"

He shrugged. "I thought you meant yes."

Struggling to keep her cool, she said, "Now we each know what the other meant. I think we should go, don't you?"

"We have to clean up."

As they worked, they listened to an oldies radio station (chosen by Alex) and even danced a little. It all seemed so normal and friendly that she started to relax. There was something offbeat about Alex's sexuality, that was for sure, but at least he didn't seem to be a rapist. He probably wasn't lying—he probably really had misread the situation, though if you asked her, he hadn't done any reading at all, simply acted on impulse. That didn't make him all that different from lots of other men.

As she hung up her dishcloth, she felt his arms once again go around her waist, his lips brush her check. "For Christ's sake, Alex, enough's enough!"

His arms tightened. "You're so sexy when you're trying not to be."

She smashed an elbow into his ribs, broke his grip, and stepped out of range. He lunged, but again she stepped away.

"You crazy bastard!"

"You like it rough, don't you? I can tell when a woman does."

She didn't like the confined way she felt here. Her scalp was prickling again, and she was uncomfortably aware that he stood between her and her backpack. She started circling, hoping to get it, momentarily playing his game. He circled with her, obviously enjoying it.

She grabbed the pack and ran for the door. He caught her

there, but she shook him off and made for the hog. He was close behind her, caught her quickly. He tackled her at the waist, bringing her down on top of him, rolling her over, holding her down, kissing her.

"Get off of me, you asshole, or I swear to God I'll knee you in the balls."

Thinking about it later, she wondered why she gave him the warning, why she didn't just knee him, and thought that even then she hadn't been really terrified, hadn't yet been convinced he wasn't just playing a game—a perverse, dangerous, almost unbelievably stupid game, but not rape.

"Don't call me an asshole. I really hate it when people call me an asshole." He rolled off her, and the second she was free she was on her feet and walking.

"Thanks for a fascinating evening, Alex."

"Where do you think you're going?"

"I'm hitchhiking home. It's safer."

"Come on. I can't leave you here."

"Goddammit," she called over her shoulder, "I could have you arrested for what you just did."

"I thought it was what you wanted."

She bit down the next thing it came to her to call him— "sicko"—and settled for "Sorry, I don't have sex on the first date." The words echoed in the dark.

"Well, why didn't you tell me?" Once again his voice was petulant.

She didn't answer.

"How about the second date?"

She started running toward the main road, knowing he couldn't follow before he'd turned out the lights and locked up. But something crashed out of the brush, nearly sending her up the nearest tree.

Eighteen

"SKIP!"

"Adam." She stopped, panting, heart in throat. "Let's get out of here before he sees us together."

When she had recovered her breath, she thanked Abasolo for sticking close to her, and for giving her a chance to handle it when Alex jumped her.

"That wasn't exactly on purpose." He was smiling; his fine teeth gleamed in the dark. "I was just about on him when you yelled—scared me as much as you did him. I mean when you said, 'knee you in the balls,' I paid *attention*."

Knowing it was a compliment, that he was saying he knew she hadn't needed him, Skip gave him a friendly cuff. "Oh, shut up."

"You saw the chickens?" she said.

"Yeah. Ugly."

"What do you think of him—Alex?"

"The guy's not normal."

"But is he the Axeman?"

"Well, he didn't try to kill you."

"Come on, I'm almost as big as he is. Maybe he was working up to it."

"Maybe."

The Covington police were incredulous. They said there were a lot of perverts around, but "ain't nobody in St. Tammany Parish mean enough to murder a flock of innocent

185

chickens.'' They said, sure, the New Orleans crime-lab people could come collect the chickens, they'd be happy about that. But were things so quiet the New Orleans department had nothing better to do than investigate fowl deeds in another parish?

Neighbors confirmed that the Campbells were in Europe and that they'd been told an Alex Bignell would be in and out. Some had heard his hog, but no one had seen him or anyone else on the property. No one had heard the hog—or any vehicle—earlier that day. A careful inspection of the chicken graveyard failed to turn up a scarlet *A*.

Skip was feeling let down when Abasolo finally dropped her off at home.

She played her messages. Her old friend Cookie Lamoreaux had phoned, asking her to an Axeman party the next night; and so had Di, which surprised her. She hadn't thought of twelve-steppers as raging party animals.

She checked her inner-child phone lists, old ones she'd gotten from Di. They showed that the Campbells were indeed regulars at the meetings.

What did it all mean? Heedless of the hour—it was now after one—she phoned Cindy Lou and asked.

''Chickens?'' squealed the woman she admired most in the world. ''You're calling me about chickens?''

''Serial murderers kill animals, don't they?''

''Yes, or they're cruel to them. That's part of the profile, both as children and adults.''

''Well, at the risk of repeating myself, what do you think it means?''

Fully awake now, Cindy Lou sounded serious. ''I hate to say it, babe, but realistically speaking, I think it's got to be the Axeman, and I think it confirms he's in the group—or she is, if you want to be picky about it. One of the victims came out of the group, the owners of the house are big in the group, they've had parties for the group at the house, and the whole group probably knows they're not at home. Now what does that add up to?''

"Exactly what we were thinking. But why kill chickens?''

"Listen, Skip, I know you don't want to hear this, but that could be pre-crime behavior. We know about one guy that knocked off neighborhood dogs before committing murder.''

"But why now? After he's already killed two people?''

"Hell if I know.''

"Well, sorry I woke you up.''

"But I've sure as hell got an opinion on who it is.''

She had given Cindy Lou an account of the whole evening, including some parts left out of her report to Cappello. "Alex, by any chance?''

"Yeah, but there's one thing that doesn't make sense if he's it. Why aren't you dead?''

But she knew the answer; must have known it intuitively all the time she was with him. Because the Axeman was smart. He wouldn't kill her at a house to which he was known to have the key. Maybe he liked to play with his victims first.

At 8:15 A.M., as soon as Alex had roared away on his hog, Skip marched up to his door with a clipboard, rang the doorbell, and awaited her first glimpse of the long-suffering Mrs. Bignell. Instead, a dried-out old coot answered the door, so shockingly indicative of what Alex's rough handsomeness would shrink down to that she drew in her breath.

Wearing khakis and a salmon-colored shirt with an alligator on it, he was a dapper old thing even at this time of day. She spoke to him in the ingratiating interrogatives of the true Southern girl (if not woman).

"Mr. Bignell? I'm from the planning department? I wonder if we could talk a little?''

"Sure, sure. Good mornin', good mornin'." His manner was hearty. "Come in, won't you? Would you like some coffee?''

She said she would and was led into a bachelor kitchen, more redolent with the smell of yesterday's coffee grounds than with the new brew. He seated her across from him at a yellow Formica table and, while he got her coffee, kept up a running commentary on the weather.

"You ever seen anything this hot? I mean, it's been hot before, but not like this. I'm tellin' you we got to get those rocks back on the moon."

Finally, he sat down and asked what he could do her for. She gave him a spiel about possible plans for developing the neighborhood and how "the department" wanted the neighbors' opinions first.

"Development!" He made the word a sneer. "You mean high-rises. Forget that crap."

"I can see you're not the one Carol Meier talked to. Whoever that was seemed to take a different attitude."

"Elec!"

"Beg pardon?"

"My worthless son."

"I didn't quite catch the name."

"Elec. Short for Alexander."

She had heard it lots of times as a child, had never known it came from Alexander. Hearing it now, she felt the twinge of inadequacy she always did when confronted with things Southern that she didn't get. Was this simply a mispronunciation of Alex or another nickname?

"Could be." She flipped through pages, finally saying, "August ninth. A Thursday." Since Linda Lee had missed work on Friday, the presumption was that she'd died Thursday night.

"Nope. I was home. I always watch 'Cheers,' don't miss it for any reason."

"Could Carol have talked to you, then?"

"Is she good-looking?"

"Mr. Bignell!"

"Now, you call me Lamar, you hear? I asked because if

188

she was good-looking—looked anything like you, for instance—I'd have remembered.''

"Must have been someone else."

"Nope. My son's never been here after seven o'clock—not once the whole three months he's been here."

"Oh, well, that explains it, then. We sent someone around another night—the Tuesday after, I think the fourteenth, and nobody was home at all." Tom Mabus had been killed the day before his body was found.

"Well, Elec wasn't, you can bet on that. I bet I was, though. Prob'ly answerin' a call of nature. Sometimes . . .''

She changed the subject quickly. "I wonder if I could ask how many residents live here?"

"Just two—me and ol' Elec."

She smiled encouragement, knowing her smile was watts and watts away from belle quality, but hoping that at his age he was too blind to notice.

"Just the two of us now," he said. "Wife died six months ago. Boy come to help me. Ha! Lotta help *he* is."

"Oh?"

"How'd I *get* a boy like that? Just answer me that one. Other people's boys are doctors, lawyers, mechanics, plumbers. You know what mine is? He's a psychologist."

"I always thought that was a pretty respectable profession."

"Well, that ain't the whole story. Ain't the whole story by a long shot. That's what he was trained to do, and if he did it, wouldn't be the best thing, but wouldn't be the worst either. Kind of sissy profession—silly too, 'specially when you think of Elec in it. Things that boy doesn't know about how people's minds work'd fill a whole library. But that's the worst you can say. It's a job, anyway. I wouldn't call it a profession. Only trouble is, he doesn't do it. Now he's got up on his hind legs, rared back, and said the whole thing's a crock. And him with a Ph.D.!''

"Umm. Umm." (This was one of the few Southernisms

189

Skip knew. It was something she'd heard black people say when white people went raving on about something or other.)

"Boy's fresh out of money. S'posed to support me in my old age and here I am supportin' him." He got up and rummaged in a cabinet until he'd found a box of supermarket doughnuts, which he opened unceremoniously on the table. "Take two, they're small," he said. "And butter 'em while they're hot."

"Thanks." She eyed them warily.

"What do you think of a boy like that? Tell me, I'd like to know."

For once, I feel kind of sorry for him. Aloud, she said, "Maybe he's just changing careers."

He snorted. "Changing careers! You know what he says he's doing? Says he's working on a book! Now, who does Elec think he is, trying to write a book?"

Was it possible he really didn't know his son was a highly successful author? "Well, I don't know," she said cautiously. "Maybe he took a writing course or something."

For some reason that tickled Lamar's funny bone. He slapped his knee and had himself a good old laugh. "You're all right, you know that? He ought to, that's for sure. See, Elec's written a book or two before; but piss-poor? You can't even imagine. All kind of whiny stuff that just shows what's wrong with America today. My son the grown-up crybaby. No wonder those books never did a damn thing. *Really* stumped his toe on that last one. I don't think it sold but three copies in the whole country, and his mother bought one of them—not me, nosiree, I wouldn't waste *my* money. And now here he is tryin' to write another one—or says he is. I got no idea what that boy does all day."

"As long as he's home at night."

"Home at night! Well, that's a good one. I'd like to know the last time he was home at night. Can't really expect it, though. Him and me never did get along. You know, even when he was a little boy he wouldn't do right. Other boys liked to play cowboys and war and everything, what did Elec do? Always lyin' around with his nose in a book. I knew he wasn't ever gon' be a man's man. Always Mr. Intellexshul. Always thought he knew better'n his old man. Don't know what his mama saw in him.''

"They were close, were they?"

"Well, we got divorced early on and he spent most of his time with her. Guess that was all the comp'ny she had—had to make the most of it. He'd come stay with me and wouldn't lift a finger, that boy. Way she spoiled him'd make you want to puke.''

"You must have remarried, then. You mentioned your wife's dying last year.''

"Did. I remarried the same old woman. If you can feature such a thing.'' Once more he laughed and slapped his leg. "We wasn't really apart that long, tell you the truth. Minute Elec left home, that woman wanted me back. She just never could stand to be alone, that was her problem.''

"Oh, Lamar, you can't fool me—I'll bet you were glad to have somebody to take care of you.''

"You shore are right about that! Lordy, lordy, those years we were separated, I never even learned to open a can of soup for myself! Why, I had dust mice looked like cocker spaniels!'' He was laughing up a storm now, hugely enjoying himself—to the point that Skip wondered if he hadn't doctored his coffee.

She looked at her clipboard as if prompting herself. "What kind of work do you do, Lamar?"

"Little as possible.''

"Don't blame you. Don't blame you a bit.'' She waited, but he didn't continue. "Are you retired?"

"I guess so,'' he said. "Wife had some decent insurance. Miss her, though. She had a mouth on her, but I miss her. Never thought I would.''

"You married her twice—you must have liked her.''

"Best woman I ever saw. But you know about women.''

Skip got ready. She knew what was coming.

"Can't live with 'em," he said. "Can't live without 'em."

He got up, found a brown bottle, and held it up to her. "Want a little something in that coffee?"

When she shook her head, he poured an amber stream into his.

She consulted her clipboard again, inventing as she went along. "It says here this is a two-income family."

He nodded. "Jonelle worked. Night nurse at Touro."

"And you, sir?"

"Well, I did this and that. That time we were divorced, I set up as a painting contractor. Pretty good, too. But you know what? There's not a good way to paint, not a good way in the world. You've either got to spray it, roll it, or brush it on. None of 'em work worth a damn, compared to everything else—you know, like cars and computers and things. So I got me some ideas. I did some inventin', got some patents."

"Ah."

"Problem was gettin' the parts manufactured. Make a long story short, I just never figured out how to do it." He took a sip of his coffee. "Oh, well. Why should I work? My wife did. Keep 'em barefoot, pregnant, and bringin' home a paycheck, you got a happy woman. You just got to make one thing clear—she better turn that check over to little ol' you."

Skip had heard Allison Gaillard flirt-tease and she could more or less simulate the cadences. "Now, Lamar," she said, letting one corner of her mouth turn up, but not the other, going heavy on the eye contact. "Is that what she did?" Her syllables were low and soft, as gently coaxing as if she were begging him to touch her breasts.

He laughed. That tone always made them laugh when Allison did it. *It worked,* she thought with surprise. " 'Course she didn't. But what you gon' do? Can't live with 'em. Can't live without 'em."

"Lamar, you're a character, you know that? I bet living with you was the hardest thing she ever did."

192

He twisted himself into a pretzel, just dying laughing at what he apparently thought was affectionate joshing. While he was splitting his sides, she thought about Steve Steinman and how much fun it would be to tell him she'd finally gotten the hang of being Southern, that all you had to do was dip your dart in curare, then wrap it up in silk and velvet before you threw it. Your victims never knew what hit them—even when they were taking it out on their own victims. Before you knew it, there was poison all over the parish, but also yards and yards, miles and miles, of gorgeous, tattered fabric.

When Lamar saw her to the door, he kept her there for five minutes, extracting promises to visit again, swearing he was going to write to her boss and tell what a good interviewer she was, how she'd gotten all his secrets without even trying. Sweat was running down his face by the time he let her go. "Whew," he said. "Weather's out of control. We gotta get those rocks back on the moon."

What all that accomplished she wasn't sure, except that, so far, Alex's dad hadn't alibied him for the night of either murder. If he were ever arrested, of course, it might be a whole different story—suddenly Lamar might claim he and his son had spent the evening playing gin rummy.

With the Axeman's JazzFest only hours away, her palms sweating as if she were about to have her appendix out, and no idea what else to do, she decided to talk to Abe's ex-wife and to Missy's aunt.

Cynthia Morrison had other ideas. A pinched brunette with too much red lipstick, she said she was sorry, she and her ex-husband were "on terms that prohibit giving personal references."

"To tell you the truth," said Skip, "he didn't give you as a reference. His law firm has applied for a contract with the city, and frankly it would be very embarrassing if they got the job and something surfaced later. Your ex-husband would

193

be the man assigned to the position, and we just don't know enough about him. He seems to be new in town, and to tell you the truth, nobody really knows him but you."

"Are you kidding? Know somebody you're married to? I'm the last person in town who knows the guy."

Skip wasn't about to quit now. "It sounds as if you know him a little too well."

Morrison drew in her breath, made her face a mask. "He's the father of my children. I'm not going to stand in the way of his getting a job."

"I'm getting the feeling you're withholding something."

"Not at all. Provided it's a middle-level job at an unimportant agency, I'm sure he'll do it perfectly well."

"Does he have any history of violence, Mrs. Morrison?"

She sucked in her breath again, and this time there was a note of alarm in her voice. "Why do you ask?"

"Just routine."

"I'm sorry. I really can't help you."

Was there something there or was she just being ornery? Morrison swallowed and spoke again. "None that I know of."

But do you suspect something? Skip couldn't read her. It was obvious she wanted to get at Abe somehow or other— was she wrestling with her conscience, trying not to lie? Holding something back to protect her children? Or was she afraid of him?

Ms. Sally Enright, aunt of Missy McClellan, lived on the top floor of a wonderful old Queen Anne house that was now a duplex. It was a funny arrangement, Skip thought, a girl in the city living with an aunt. But if she could see anyone doing it, it was Missy.

I just wonder what Auntie thinks when her young niece spends the night with her boyfriend.

But the minute she walked in, she could see that Ms. Enright was no ordinary Southern aunt. She was blond, overweight, dressed in a pair of black shorts and a pink tube top that would have fit Missy, and rather beautiful. She had the kind of skin that looked as if it would break if you touched it, but was unmarked by wrinkles (though she must have been on the lying side of forty-five). Her hair was caught up in a ponytail on the right side of her head—a ponytail that swung halfway down her back. Her feet were bare, unless you counted the toenail polish. Her face was heart-shaped and she was one of those heavy women who don't gain weight above the neck.

"Come in." She led Skip into the most interesting room she'd seen in New Orleans. The walls were covered with traditional art—masks, sculptures, paintings, and artifacts from just about everywhere, as far as Skip could see. There was one deep, comfortable sofa, but other than that, the furniture was equally exotic, much of it Asian. The rugs were many and colorful—Chinese, Persian, Iraqi—and an antique Chinese kimono was encased in a corner of the room, displayed as an artwork.

"What is it?" said Enright, and Skip realized she'd gasped.

"No wing chairs."

Enright laughed.

"It's a breathtaking room."

"I travel a lot." She sat down and motioned Skip to do the same.

Deciding on a different strategy for this interview, Skip had already identified herself as a police officer. But Missy's aunt seemed far sharper than she'd expected. She wasn't sure her plan would work.

Playing for time, she said, "You travel for your work?"

"Sort of. I run a business out of my home—designing clothes that I have made up in various cheap-labor countries. And then, of course, I have to go to more exotic countries still to get inspiration." She paused only for a second, having made the clear statement that she was in the middle of her workday. "How can I help you, Officer?"

"I'm investigating a string of burglaries in your neighborhood."

"Damn!"

"I know. The last thing you want to hear about."

Enright got up and walked to the door. "I've really got to do something about this door."

It was one of those with a window in it, a window that could be broken, the deadbolt turned by a hand reaching inside. "You're not kidding—with all this art."

"What should I do?"

Skip was about to suggest calling the department's community-relations officer when she remembered she was posing as someone from burglary. She shrugged. "You could have the whole door replaced."

"That's it! It's ugly, anyway. I could buy a beautiful door."

Hoping she was sufficiently distracted, Skip seized the moment, giving the dates of the two murders. "I was wondering if you saw or heard anything on either of the nights the burglaries occurred—the ninth and the fourteenth."

"Excuse me a moment." She padded off and came back with a leather Filofax. "Let's see—last Tuesday and Thursday." Her voice turned wry. "I've really got to give you guys credit for promptness."

Skip felt a blush starting. "We've been kind of overloaded."

"Oh, I know—so many of the damn things." She waved a hand, letting Skip see that her nails had been painted with the natural colors reversed—white with pink half-moons. "What time were the burglaries?"

"Well after dark, we think. Let's say after nine." After the latest twelve-step meetings were over.

Enright sighed. "I was home both nights. Some social life, huh? Didn't hear a thing. Who got hit, by the way? The Livingstons?"

"To tell you the truth, I can't talk about it."

"I just thought it was across the street, since you're asking me."

"Could I ask if anyone else lives here?"

"Just my darling niece, Missy McClellan." Her friendly features softened even more. "Missy McClellan from Hattiesburg, Mississippi?" She said the sentence with a question mark, like a Hattiesburg girl. "Poor Missy."

"Poor Missy?"

She waved her *trompe l'oeil* hand again. "Little girl in the big city. Very earnest. I love her to death in spite of it."

"Can you remember if she was home on those nights?"

"Gosh." She was quiet for a moment. "She's almost never home—she's got a boyfriend, and that's not the half of it."

"Oh?"

"She's 'in recovery.' Or don't you know the phrase? God, grant me the serenity to put up with it."

"You mean from drugs or something?"

"No, no. That's just a phrase they use in those damn meetings she goes to. She goes to at least one a day, can you fathom that? I mean, is there a group for meeting addiction? There's one for everything else." She snapped her fingers. "Wait a minute."

She left again, came back carrying schedules of several different meetings.

"She's had these tacked up on her bulletin board forever."

Some had been circled in red, presumably Missy's favorites. "Tuesday and Thursday both. Well, she probably wasn't home."

Skip wondered if Sally Enright had noticed what she had—that Missy apparently attended a group for incest survivors.

Cappello caught her as she arrived back at the office: "Task-force meeting in fifteen minutes. Assignments for the big night."

Everyone looked about as desperate as she felt. No one

had come up with a single fact that pointed to one suspect over another. Except for Skip and Abasolo.

Joe was in very nearly the worst shape of all. He seemed to be holding panic just below the surface. Something bad was bothering him. It was the pile of dead chickens. He turned to Skip. "How would you feel," he blurted, "about being used as bait?"

"You mean make myself an easy target for Alex?" She'd already thought of it.

"Look, I'll lay odds he's it. We can put guys on him, but we just don't know who might get in his path that can't take care of themselves. You can."

"I was going to suggest it myself." *If I managed to get up the nerve. I didn't think you'd go for it.*

She had thought Joe would find her too inexperienced, might not quite trust her with something this big. "The only thing is, he probably hates me after last night."

"All the more reason to kill you. Okay, Langdon has an invitation to *the* party—the teddy bears' picnic itself. It's at Diamara Breaux's house, starting at seven P.M. I want you all to be there. Langdon is specifically assigned to Alex. Abasolo, you take Di. These are still our best two suspects. Cappello and Hodges, play it by ear. O'Rourke, park outside and cover Langdon if she leaves with Alex. If he leaves alone, he's your baby. Let him out of your sight and you're dead. Langdon, what's your plan?"

She shrugged. "I guess I'll call him and ask for a date. If he says no, I'll try to cozy up to him at Di's. If he doesn't go for it . . ."

"See that he does. Okay, everybody, I'll be in the office, monitoring everyone's whereabouts. You all have your assignments. I want you calling in every forty-five minutes."

They discussed a few more details, deciding on staggered call-in times, setting them for each officer. But they adjourned unsatisfied, still worried. It was a good plan as far as it went, but they all knew concentrating on Alex might be a mistake—there were about twenty other suspects that were nearly as good.

Alex wasn't home. Thanking her stars he didn't share a machine with his dad, Skip left a message saying she was sorry they hadn't had a chance to "really get together" the night before and asking to see him that night.

The she consulted her twelve-step schedules. On the third try she found Alex hunkered down and looking bored at an Al-Anon meeting at a church on the river side of Magazine.

He brightened and signaled when she walked in.

Through the remaining half-hour of the meeting she sweated, wondering how the hell she, Skip Langdon, was going to be seductive enough to get him to forgive, forget, and agree to see her that night.

In the end she relied on everything she'd ever seen in the movies. She stood very close to him, touching his arm, touching her thigh to his, as she apologized for her precipitous behavior the night before. She said she'd been thinking about him all day and she really wanted to see him that night; she felt she'd made a big mistake. She licked her lips, having read somewhere that men think that's a seduction signal. She'd never felt like a bigger ass in her life.

But it worked, after a fashion. At least the apology did— she wasn't sure about the sexual grandstanding. Because Alex, suddenly, was treating her like his best pal, practically hitting her on the arm like a great old comrade. He happily made a date with her, but didn't seem the least bit interested in being alone with her. He wanted to go to Di's party and hit a few others as well. She wondered about that, but he did ask her to meet him at the first stop. That might be a good sign—the Axeman would want to keep his quarry in sight, yet not be seen arriving with her.

As she drove home, hoping to find something that vaguely resembled a party outfit, she reflected that her rejection of the night before certainly hadn't seemed to hurt his feelings. She wondered if he had any.

Nineteen

DI HADN'T HIRED a whole jazz band, but a single clarinetist was tooting away in an atmosphere oddly subdued, to Skip's way of thinking.

When she had helped herself to fruit juice, she realized why—it was the first New Orleans party she'd ever been to at which no liquor was served. She felt as if she were in church.

So this is how twelve-steppers boogie down.

She went to the refreshment table. No oysters here—live food though they might be—but there were lots of nice green-pepper slices and bits of cauliflower, plenty of chips without salt, and a couple of vegetable dips. Nothing, Skip noticed, containing any dairy products. There was something resembling cheese, but a bite convinced her it was some sort of soy concoction.

All the crackers and pita were whole wheat. But there was hope—it was apparently a potluck and people were still bringing things.

A man with hair combed over his bald spot seemed intent on methodically devouring everything on the table. As fast as something was put down, he ate it, peppering the air with staccato, bossy questions. "Does this have wheat in it? Does anybody still eat wheat? Is that hummus ready yet? Who's that blonde in the miniskirt?"

She wondered if he was in OA.

"Skip? I want you to meet somebody." It was Missy, taking care of the lonely newcomer. "This is Chris."

"Hi, Chris."

Chris didn't answer, but Missy said, "Chris is an architect at that firm down on that corner—you know the one. He built half the buildings on the West Bank. And not only that, he teaches yoga and he's an expert horseback rider. *And* a gourmet cook. And his sister just moved to town, she's a lovely girl too, and Chris is a single father with two kids, seven and ten."

There was certainly enough conversational material there. "Hi," said Skip again.

Again Chris said nothing.

Sonny was hovering near his lady love, looking rather askance, she thought, at his apple juice.

"Ich! It's an animal." The man with the bald spot spat into his napkin. Apparently somebody'd brought some clam dip.

She saw Jim Hodges in the kitchen. Moving closer, she heard someone say, "How do you know Di?"

And he answered, "I don't. To tell you the truth, I'm a friend of the clarinetist."

Who knew? It might even be true.

Adam Abasolo came in with a huge spray of flowers. Di opened the card, pronounced them from "Ernest," proclaimed that she didn't know Ernest, and then fell hook, line, and sinker for whatever brand of flattery Abasolo was handing out.

Skip saw her take his arm and lead him to the ersatz bar. Out of the corner of her eye, she thought she caught something—an involuntary movement perhaps. But pivoting quickly, she saw only Sonny, staring at the bar as if he wished he could turn water into wine.

The hum of conversation wasn't picking up. *Do these people talk, or are they all like Chris?* she wondered. *And if they do, what do they talk about?* She took a tour around the room.

"Janet Shirley's the best. Non-force manipulation. You never feel a thing."

"But Jenny Walker does X rays. Don't you think you need X rays?"

Evidently a conversation about chiropractors.

". . . so I left the workshop three days early. I couldn't concentrate on Asian medicine with the worst cold in Louisiana history."

Workshops. Of course. The speaker wore crystal earrings.

"What she does then is she takes a piece of your clothing and she can tell you how many husbands you've had and which of them were alcoholic."

Psychics.

"I really can't digest anything but broccoli anymore and sometimes a little bit of rice. My system's just too sensitive, too finely tuned."

Anorexia?

"No, really. Enlightenment through sex. And it's a lightning path, too. You can do it in one lifetime."

Seduction.

And the speaker was her date. He was talking to a slim young blonde with blue eyes that hadn't seen much beyond a Catholic girls' school. She wore her hair in a pageboy tucked behind her ears so you couldn't see how wet it was back there. Skip's nerve endings stood on end. If he took her home, went into her house, they couldn't follow. He could strangle her and they'd know when he went in and when he left, but she'd still be dead.

She kissed Alex on the cheek, hoping to put the girl off. "Skippy, baby." He put an arm around her, pal-like, and kept talking to the girl, ignoring Skip. In turn, she wrapped her arm around him, rubbed his love handles. She leaned against him, nuzzled an ear, then danced out of reach, hop-

202

ing she'd be more attractive that way. Unfortunately, she ran—literally—into Abe.

"Hi." He had a mouthful of guacamole, but that didn't stop him from talking. "Great party, huh?"

"A little quiet, maybe."

"I was just thinking that. Say, there's only this one guy. Do you think the Axeman'll count that as a band?"

She was surprised to realize it was the first mention of the party's purpose.

"Abe, do you think there really is an Axeman?"

"You mean did the media make him up? Hey, two people died." His voice was angry, his face starting to get red.

"You don't have to get mad. I was just making conversation."

"Well, I didn't think that was funny."

"Sorry."

Abruptly, he left her. Di arrived with Jillian, very short, very fat, wearing a vintage dress, strapless and black, with humongous boobs spilling out of it. Because she was so short, everyone was literally forced to look down her dress. Things jiggled.

"You're a newcomer?" Her voice was tiny—such a baby sound you could hardly believe it belonged to an adult. She stroked Skip's arm as if she were an animal.

"Yes. I moved to town fairly recently. You?"

Jillian smiled and rocked on her feet, not answering at first. She didn't seem to want to talk. Finally she said, "I don't really live here. I'm a student."

"And what are you studying?"

"Law." She smiled and sort of purred. "I want to be a criminal lawyer. A prosecutor." Said in that tiny voice it was laughable.

"Interesting field."

She smiled and purred some more, still stroking Skip's arm.

"Excuse me, would you? I have to find someone."

"I really liked what you told me."

Skip hadn't told her a thing. *I wonder if I should have mentioned chiropractors. Or vegetables maybe. I know—new paradigms.*

The crowd was getting thicker now, and the musician was taking a break. Tapes had been substituted and people were starting to dance. *Oh, boy. Bunch of honkies on fruit juice. Get down, you party animals!*

It was starting to look like a party, but it still didn't sound right. For fun, she started a few more conversations, and she saw that it wasn't just the lack of booze or the right subject that was responsible. She dragged out her vegetables and her paradigms, but a lot of these people were like Jillian and Chris. You talked to them; they didn't really talk back. Just smiled and nodded, sometimes rocked; often purred. Seemed eager to please, even overly nice. But really didn't try to connect. She wondered if they were on something, but couldn't think what it might be, unless it was the high you get from fasting.

On the whole, she thought, *I'd rather be in Chalmette.*

She looked around for Alex, didn't see him. Her heart in her mouth, she threaded her way through the crowd, probably looking as tense as she felt, because Abasolo caught her eye and pointed to the bathroom.

Alex came out, hair combed, face washed.

"Looking good," she said, and meant it.

"Let's get out of here."

Oh, boy. Now the fun begins.

"Meet me at . . ."

"Actually, I walked over."

"Okay. We'll go together." He had acquiesced awfully easily. Did that mean she wasn't the target, that he didn't mind being seen with her?

"Tell you what, though. I'll meet you outside in a minute."

She went out, signaled O'Rourke in a car across the street,

and waited, noticing that the streets were mobbed with Axe-man revelers. Many wore T-shirts bearing the skull and crossed axes that some enterprising entrepreneur had made the official emblem of the evening.

For fun (Alex's idea) they took a tour around the Quarter. Banners with skulls and crossed axes hung like bunting from the balconies. Jazz blared. Camera crews crawled merrily through the streets, taping, interviewing, shining lights, stirring up excitement. Vendors hawked not only T-shirts but rubber axes, souvenir plastic clarinets, saxophones, complete ceramic jazz bands, and theatrical blood, which was also in evidence on plenty of jolly celebrants. The T-shirts said festive things like I SURVIVED THE AX ATTACK and THEY ALL AXED FOR YOU. It beat hell out of Mardi Gras.

It was the music that was responsible, and a little bit the impromptu, outlaw, defiant nature of the thing. A kind of people's JazzFest overlaid with black humor.

But Skip's mood darkened as Alex headed Uptown. She had an uneasy feeling about the route they were taking. Her horror mounted as he turned onto a familiar street. Jesus! She was right. They were going to Cookie Lamoreaux's. How on earth did those two know each other?

"Alex, I've really got to pee. See you inside, okay?" She jumped off the hog and left him to secure it, O'Rourke to take over if he got on it and split. She would know lots of people here, stood a major chance of getting her cover blown.

Sure enough, Cookie himself, three sheets to the wind, was standing on the porch trying to get a breath of air. The evening was so close she wished him luck. The sounds of a full and very good jazz band emanated from the old house.

"Detective Langdon! I've been waiting for you."

She put a finger to her lips, raced up the stairs, kissed him on the mouth, and whispered, "I'm not a cop tonight, okay? Pass the word. It's important, Cookie. Pretty please."

"Kojak! You undercover or something? This sounds serious."

"It is."

"You mean the Axeman's *here*? At Chez Lamoreaux its l'il ol' self? Fabulous, Officer. Just fabulous. You mean we're at *the* Axeman party?" He thought a minute. "But he can't be. We got the band and everything."

"Cookie, I'm not kidding. Here comes my date and he just can't know. Listen, I'll owe you. I'll do something big for you. I'll fix all your tickets." The way she fixed Conrad's.

"Listen, Marcelle's here."

"You've got to tell her, Cookie. You've got to warn her. You've got to warn everybody."

"We've got a surprise for you." He looked crestfallen.

"Here he comes, dammit."

Cookie hollered, "Hey, Big Al!" To Skip he said, "Big Al's your date? You're dating that guy?"

Alex was upon them. "Cookie! Whereyat?"

The two guys gave each other high five, followed by further complicated hand maneuvers.

Marcelle Gautier appeared at the door, singsonging in the high, thin voice usually reserved for children. "Skippy! I've got a surprise for yooooouuuu!"

Skip slipped quickly in the door, hoping Cookie would distract Alex for a few minutes more.

"Marcelle, listen . . ."

But she wasn't about to listen. She stepped aside to reveal her surprise—an eager-looking Steve Steinman. Skip nearly fell apart, she was so glad to see him—and so horrified.

She could only stutter: "Steve . . . what . . ."

"Muhammed came to the mountain," he said.

"Gosh, I'm glad to see you."

He opened his arms for a bear hug, but he wasn't getting any hello kiss—not yet. She found his ear instead of his mouth. "Listen, I'm working. The guy I'm with is a suspect." She knew she shouldn't have said it, but there didn't seem any other way. "How are you at keeping a secret?"

206

"You mean I didn't come all the way from California just to see you?"

"Right. And if I hang on him and act interested, it's for a good cause, okay?"

"No."

"And I'm definitely not a police officer."

"When can I see you?"

"Tomorrow."

"No good."

"You won't be here?"

"I will. But it's not soon enough."

Alex came in then and suddenly she felt angry. This was no time to be conducting a love affair. She introduced the men, watched them bristle at each other—it was hate at first sight, and Skip didn't think it was because of jealousy. It had more to do with Alex's being a jerk and Steve's not hiding the fact that he'd deduced it.

"I need a drink," Alex said, looking thirstily toward the bar. Though he'd barely touched her all evening, he chose that moment to grab her butt by way of good-bye. And off he strode, not offering drinks to anyone else.

"Nice date," said Steve.

"Let's catch up. I have to keep an eye on him."

"Oh, great. A real romantic encounter."

"Excuse me. I'm working a homicide case."

"Well, excuse me. Sorry to get in your way."

She sighed, starting after her quarry, Steve at her side. It was a weird town, the sort where people gave parties at the behest of serial killers. Steve wasn't even a native—professed, in fact, to be utterly confused about the place—and even he wasn't taking the Axeman seriously.

Oh, well, he'd probably had a couple of drinks and so had everyone else. It was hard to imagine a murderer walking into your party.

Steve said, "That guy's not the Axeman."

And it was hard to imagine that a person with whom you

had just shaken hands could be a murderer. "Why do you say that?" she asked.

"He doesn't have the look in his eye."

"Are you suddenly psychic?"

"If you were with a murderer, you'd know it. You'd get a clue. There'd be something."

"How about all the ones who're always described by their neighbors as nice, gentle guys?"

"Those neighbors are people who haven't been paying attention."

She wondered who he would pick as the Axeman from her list of suspects—no one, probably. On a whim, she said, "I went out with Alex last night too. He tried to get rough with me."

"Case of arrested development."

"Well, what do you think a murderer is?"

"Someone smoldering inside."

"Alex is one of the angriest guys I've ever met."

"No he's not. He doesn't give a shit about anything."

That was how he looked, all right. But who wouldn't be angry if he'd been put down by his father all his life? And after her morning's experience, she had no doubt Alex had. But lots of people had—what made one a murderer and another a politician? It bothered her that she'd probably never know.

Even if Alex tried to kill her later that night, if he were arrested and stood trial, she wouldn't know what it was in his personality, in his past, in the childhood insults he'd had to endure, that had flipped him over the line. What made Rob Gerard an artist and Sonny a doctor? Why was Missy a conformist while her aunt was free and creative? Did even Sally Enright, did Rob Gerard have their struggles with reality? (Judging from Rob's paintings, one of them did.) Because the music was so loud, she had plenty of time to ruminate on the nature of crime. Alex was dancing with everyone, permitting her to watch him and chat with Steve at the same time, which should have been ideal. Except that they had to shout to hear each other. Except that the situation was so awkward neither could relax.

They were edgy with each other, Skip preoccupied and slightly annoyed at the distraction, Steve deeply disappointed. It was a good surprise, it was a lovely surprise, she told herself. And yet why had he thought she wouldn't be working?

She found herself fighting a need to make things better for him, to soothe and comfort, when her attention needed to be on the suspect she was sitting on. She had to make sure she kept Alex's interest, that he didn't bug out with some likelier prospect. She excused herself to dance with him, first fast, then slow, both sexy. Now there was no question she was his target for the night, though whether for murder or sex was certainly in question.

Her mind was a mess, racing in all different directions—partly on the danger of Alex finding out her identity; partly on Steve, who was probably sulking; partly on her guilt, not only at abandoning Steve but at making a spectacle of herself with another man. She took deep breaths and tried to focus.

"Let's blow this joint."

Exactly what she wanted to hear.

"I want to be alone with you," he said.

Better still. No more parties. H-hour.

They went to the borrowed apartment Cappello had arranged. It had a Futon on the floor and little else for furnishings, but Alex didn't give the decor a glance. They were barely inside, the door just clicking shut, when he started tearing at her blouse.

Her heart pumped hard against her chest; this must have been exactly what happened with Linda Lee—the quick attack just inside the door.

"Alex, what are you doing?"

"Tearing your clothes off."

"I think I need to catch my breath."

He was kissing her shoulder, biting it a little, starting to pull her hair. "No you don't."

"Alex, I don't know about this."

"Quit talking." His mouth found hers.

She couldn't quit talking for long—that could mean real disaster. She pulled away from the kiss.

"Alex, I don't think I can do this."

"Do what?"

"Have sex with you."

He stepped away from her. "What the hell are you talking about?"

He was suddenly transformed from pushy suitor to crazy man. Black fury seeped out of him; his voice was a raspy shout.

"I guess I'm getting cold feet."

"You bitch!" An unhealthy redness flooded his face.

"I'm sorry."

"After manhandling me all night!"

"All of a sudden you seem a little too much for me."

"Shit, I could have had the young blonde."

"Why didn't you?"

"Fuck!" He took a spin around the room, stomping. "You fat, ugly *bitch*!"

"You like to insult women, don't you, Alex? And pull their hair and bite. What else do you like to do?"

"Oh, no. You're not going to get me to fall for that again. You're like some high-school girl on a date."

She took a step closer to him, poised, ready. But he didn't move. Finally, he said, "You want to know what you need? A spanking."

She tried getting mad, yelling as loud as she could, anything to provoke him. She knew she was walking a thin line, maybe stepping over to the edge of entrapment, but she went ahead. "Don't you talk to me like that, you airhead. All you want to do is rough somebody up!"

"Shut up." He grabbed her neck with one hand.

"Take your hand off me."

To her consternation, he did. But she wasn't done yet. "You're the Axeman, aren't you? Oh, Jesus! Oh, no!" She moved, scared and crablike, toward the kitchen. "Don't come near me—leave me alone!" Her voice was shrill, harsh and terrified.

But he didn't move, instead looked at her with pity. "You're crazy, you know that? You're really crazy. I don't know why I didn't see it before."

He pushed past her and clattered down the stairs.

Cappello and Hodges burst out of the bedroom. The signal had been a simple one: "Help." If she'd needed it, she would have asked for it.

They radioed O'Rourke: Stay on him.

They phoned Joe. When he was done swearing, he said, "Pack it in, Langdon. Tell the other two to back up O'Rourke."

"But, Joe . . ."

"Yeah, I know how you feel. But trust me—you're stressed out and you're a lot more tired than you think you are. See you in the morning."

Feeling sad and let down, she watched her colleagues, still in full adrenaline rush, take off down the stairs. She felt she had failed. Felt like a kid on Christmas Eve, sent to bed while the grown-ups stayed up to do mysterious things. Felt like a kid, period. Her own adrenaline was still pumping. She longed for the thrill of the chase. And yet, she told herself, things would wind down soon. It was nearly one, and even in the City That Care Forgot, tomorrow was a workday.

Half an hour later, at home, the phone rang. Her heart leaped. But it was only Jimmy Dee begging her to come to his party. He had seen her light go on, and she was touched. Why not go over?

It was as crowded as Cookie's, but a lot more colorful. Jimmy Dee, a partner in a very proper law firm, remained, in some circles, discreetly in the closet. Skip was perfectly

211

aware that his nightly shows of camping it up were purely for her benefit, that the city was full of women who hadn't yet given up hope.

He kept his gay and his straight friends separate; his Uptown friends and his Quarter friends; his artist friends and his lawyer friends; his weird friends and his button-down friends. Tonight he'd invited the gays, Quarter-crawlers, artists, and weirdos. There were enough costumes for a Mardi Gras party. Jack the Ripper was there; so were Charles Manson and Ted Bundy. They wore appropriate clothing (blood-smeared, for one thing) and name tags.

Jimmy Dee had decorated with black bunting, black balloons, the requisite skulls and axes, and a life-sized mannequin strangled with a scarf, a scarlet *A* on its white shirtfront.

"Real tasteful," said Skip.

He gave her a big, wet kiss. "What are you doing home, Officer Darling?"

She sighed. "We didn't get him, Jimmy Dee."

"The night's young."

"I've been sent to bed." She felt embarrassed to say it.

"Well, come to the buffet. I brought out the warm blood at midnight . . . let's see. Ah, yes, still some left." He handed her a cup of it.

"What is this? Bloody Mary soup?"

He looked crestfallen. "Got it in one, Officer."

"It's delicious." The night was still warm. What she wanted was a gin and tonic, but the soup was probably better for her. Most of the alcohol would have cooked off, no doubt Jimmy Dee's subtle way of sobering up his guests to go home.

She looked around to see if anyone she was dying to see was there and wished for Steve Steinman. She'd thought of phoning him when she was called off the job and decided it was way too late. Even if anyone at Cookie's was up to answering the phone, she couldn't handle the big reunion scene. She was too let down, barely up to a cup of soup at her neighbor's party. The adrenaline had started wearing off. In a few minutes, she'd be sleeping as soundly as the dummy in the corner. Where *had* Jimmy Dee gotten such a thing?

"Hey, Skip. You know Carlton Lattimore?"

She turned around to see Cindy Lou Wootten with the father of her best friend from high school, arms around each other, obviously entwined in more than one way. A perfect end to a perfect evening.

She nodded stiffly. "Hello, Mr. Lattimore."

"You don't have to blush, honey. Lynn and I are separated."

To her horror, Skip knew he was speaking literally—she *was* blushing, her face hot with the shame of a child who's caught the adults at play. "I didn't know you two knew each other," she said.

Cindy Lou said, "Nobody did, till tonight. It's our maiden public appearance."

"And how do you know Jimmy Dee?"

"Oh, we don't. We came with some friends of mine."

Of course. Certainly not friends of Carlton's. Jimmy Dee was probably as horrified to see him as Skip was. Carlton was a stuffy old coot—and old he really was, even for the dad of a friend. He was also loaded, married to a younger woman, and not the sort to get divorced—for financial was well as social reasons. And he would no more be seen in public with a black woman than spit in his soup. What the hell was wrong with both these people?

She answered mechanically as Cindy Lou asked her a thousand questions about how the night had gone, whether the Axeman had shown himself, if an arrest had been made. It was too much. Not only had she failed professionally, but Cindy Lou had failed her. She was the closest thing Skip had to an idol, and she turned out to be not only human, but not very bright in a certain area. Granted it was the area in which almost no one is very bright, but it didn't help Skip's mood any.

She slunk off to bed as soon as she could extricate herself.

And was gratified to find a good-night message from Steve Steinman on her machine: He loved her. Even if she did go out with murderers.

Twenty

THE NEXT MORNING Joe was jubilant. To him, the bottom line had been getting through the night without a body on page one of the *Picayune*.

She wished she could match his mood. A body still might turn up.

And they still didn't have a good suspect. Alex, their best bet, had gone straight home after he left Skip. Di had never left her apartment. Cappello had followed Sonny and Missy to one other party, then home. Abe had stayed late at Di's, and O'Rourke, returning from following Alex home, had followed Abe to a few bars, then home.

"We got through this," Joe told the task force, "and we should all be proud. But we have to hit this investigation even harder now. We have to think of new ways to go, ways to kick this thing out of neutral, get it into high gear."

But what was left? They were already backgrounding everybody they could trace who'd lately been to the inner-child group. So far, connections with the victims just weren't emerging.

"The group meets tomorrow night and I want you all there."

Skip said, "I just had a thought."

O'Rourke said, "Oh, shit."

"Can it, O'Rourke," said Joe.

"I was thinking," Skip continued, too excited even to be annoyed, "that Cindy Lou might go to the group too. She could meet all these types and give a better evaluation of them."

Joe turned to Cindy Lou: "What do you think?"

She shrugged. "Worth a try, I guess." Her enthusiasm would not have inspired regiments.

Later, she got Skip aside. "So what's the deal on Carlton Lattimore?"

"He'll never leave his wife, Cindy Lou."

"He has left her."

"He'll go back."

Cindy Lou sighed.

"You can do better."

"What the hell's wrong with me?" Cindy Lou said, and turned away to hide her tears.

Skip had a sadness of her own: *No one is ever who you hope they'll be*.

He'd had enough. That was it. He was never going back. Abe crumpled his phone messages, tossed them in the wastebasket. Perfect shot.

Shit. Last night had been an unmitigated fiasco. Skip had left with Alex. The new blonde had been a bimbo, probably never dated anyone over thirty. And Missy had been with Mr. Beautiful-but-Dumb. He was starting to think they were two of a kind. He'd gone prowling after leaving Di's, had actually gone into the Quarter, that was how desperate he was. But all the women there were cheap and country. Probably had AIDS and herpes both.

Why did it have to be this way? Why did he have to be in this goddamn hellhole? He knew for a fact that two people in the firm had had parties last night, and he hadn't been invited to either. That was the way New Orleans was. Closed.

Tighter than a strongbox unless you'd been born here or at least gone to Tulane.

Or weren't Jewish. That was probably a big part of it. They hated him here because he was Jewish. Not that he was really Jewish, gave a damn about it or anything, but nobody'd asked him, had they? They just assumed he was and that was that.

Mary Ann had been like that. His first girlfriend. He could still remember her from seventh grade. A beautiful little blonde with blue eyes, the most popular girl in the class. She called him every night for two weeks, and then they went to the movies, his mother driving. And after that, she didn't call anymore. His mother said it was because her mother had recognized her when she picked Mary Ann up, and knew she was Jewish, knew Abe was. So that was the end of it.

After that he'd given up girls for a while, and when he finally emerged as a dater, he chose only Jewish girls—dark-haired, which he didn't like, brown-eyed when he preferred blue. But he didn't mind the colors so much as the fact that their hair was not only dark but usually curly. He was uncomfortably reminded of black people's hair. He liked straight, silky hair, to this day couldn't understand why women got perms.

He'd noticed something right away about the Jewish girls in high school. Those who'd already had their noses done wouldn't go out with him, invariably chose guys on the football team or class officers. That was the way they were—snotty bitches. The others were bad enough, but these were ball-breakers. There was no other word for it. They always had to choose the movie, always had to pick the place to go afterward. One of them had done him at the drive-in, though. But the bitch wouldn't fuck, that was as far as she went. He'd gotten her a really great birthday present too—a single pearl on a chain.

When he looked back on it, it was ironic. Half the grown-up ones wouldn't go down on you, or expected you to do it to them every time. He didn't mind on a first date or something, just to get things rolling, but it was too much work. He certainly wasn't going to keep doing it over and over again, as if it was his idea of a million laughs. It was a disgusting practice, gooey and smothery. Jesus, you could end up with hairs caught in your teeth. While a penis was perfectly smooth and sanitary. Hell, he'd suck his own if he could reach it. (But no one else's, of course—talk about revolting.)

Who needed Jewish princesses? He'd graduated to the blondes and redheads when he got to Princeton. They liked his Southern accent.

After college he thought it was time to get serious. First there was Inge, the nurse he would have married if the cunt hadn't been so fucking interested in ending up with a doctor.

Then there was Amy, the secretary with the perky ass. Amy had dumped him for a senior partner in the firm. That wouldn't have been so bad except that the guy was sixty-five and married. What was wrong with chicks, anyhow?

It never got any better. Finally, he'd married Cynthia, mostly because she wasn't Jewish and therefore didn't judge him on the basis of income and status in the firm. She looked good. She wanted children. She could cook. She liked to fuck. What could go wrong?

She was a bitch, was what could go wrong. He should do half the cooking, he should help with the children, he should mow the lawn; shit, she even wanted him to help her paint the bathroom, go shopping for furniture—there was no end to the crap she could dream up. And all to control him. She wasn't happy unless she was controlling some man. That was what she really loved in life.

He'd gotten so he couldn't stand to fuck her. Just didn't want to at all. She'd take off her clothes and he'd remember what she looked like giving birth. (He'd had to watch, it was fashionable.) She'd put on perfume and he'd get little whiffs of baby shit.

That was marriage and the hell with it. He wasn't doing it

217

again. He was finding some hot little number who loved kids and getting her to move in with him. How hard could that be? He was a prominent lawyer.

But he wasn't and he never would be. Not in New Orleans. And it was all that bitch Cynthia's fault. In Atlanta he was hot shit.

And in Atlanta the women were prettier. Softer. More like flowers. There had to be some women like that here, but where? Not in these damn twelve-step programs. Certainly not in that stupid teddy-bear group. He was fed up with all that ritual crap anyway. It was too Christian. Who needed it? He'd thought the girls who went there might be disease-free, that was all. They didn't smoke, didn't drink, hardly ate anything, they could probably stay out of the wrong beds. And there was also a bottom line: He didn't know where else to go.

Nobody was introducing him to anybody or inviting him anywhere. What the hell was he supposed to do?

Something. Not that crap anymore. Maybe he could volunteer, get on some committees. But the women would be too old, probably married. Maybe he could take a class. There had to be something. He was through with teddy bears.

His phone rang and who should it be but the Bitch of the Bayou, otherwise known as Cynthia.

"Abe, how are you? I've been worried about you."

Sure she had. "Great, Cynthia. What can I do for you?"

"Listen, Jocelyn's really having trouble with her math homework and I can't help her with it. You're good at that sort of thing. I thought maybe you could work with her."

"I have been."

"I meant this week."

"They're with you this week, Cynthia. Surely you don't expect me to come over there."

"I could bring them over tomorrow night. . . ."

"No."

"What do you mean no? You're the one who followed me

218

here from Atlanta, 'just to be near the girls.' Frankly, I'm starting to doubt your motives."

"What other motive could I possibly have had? It's not like I like being here, you know."

"Torturing me."

"Cynthia, if you have a point, would you get to it, please?"

"I have a date tomorrow night."

"Hip, hip, hooray."

"Listen, Mr. Prominent Attorney, do you have any idea how hard it is for women in this town? While you're going out every night with a different blond tramp, I'm sitting home watching TV without even the girls half the time because they're at your fucking house. For once I have a date, okay? And it happens to coincide with Jocelyn having terrible trouble with her math. So if your precious daughters mean so goddamn much to you, you can just goddamn take them for one night."

"Cynthia, do you happen to recall telling me I should see a shrink? Do you happen to recall about a million suggestions you have made in the last few years about how I can improve myself? It may interest you to know that I'm deeply involved with a group that meets every Thursday night and is devoted to spirituality and self-improvement."

She spat out a grim snicker. "Oh, sure you are. Honest Abe strikes again."

"I really don't care what you do and don't believe. I can't be at your beck and call every time you don't care to take care of your own children, and I suggest you get a babysitter."

"I've tried. Don't you think I've tried?" Her voice got shriller on each word.

"It's really not my problem."

And then the first sob came over the phone and he knew that once again it was easier to do what she wanted than put up with her crap. It was starting already: "It's the first time!

The first goddamn time since I've been here! Do you want me to be a dried-up old crone?"

"Okay, okay. Take it easy."

Shit. Now he'd have to get a baby-sitter. Because there was no question he was going to the meeting. She'd ask the girls if he'd gone out, and if he hadn't, she'd say he'd been lying and throw it back in his face. This way, he'd have taken the girls at a huge sacrifice to himself. There should be some leverage in that.

The monitor showed the flat line of asystole, cardiac stand-still. The guy had a nasty gunshot wound, probably wouldn't make it.

The defibrillator sounded its little alarm; it was charged.

"Everybody clear; I'm going to shock him." Sonny moved away from the table.

Two hundred joules. Nothing.

Three hundred. Still flat.

Three-sixty. Sonny's pulse was going crazy. The uneven peaks and valleys of normal sinus rhythm appeared on the screen.

"Okay," said the resident. "Call the lab and tell them he's going to surgery. Get that blood upstairs."

The guy had a good chance. Sonny had to shake his head to get the hang of it, had to come out of a kind of trance. He'd been so sure this one was going to go. So sure. He must have fallen into that weird half-trance to protect himself against it.

Great. A fat lot of good it would have done if the guy had died. He'd still have to come out of it and he'd still feel just as bad as he ever did. But never mind, who the hell cared? He felt great now. It really did feel good when you saved them. This was what being a doc was all about. This was why people did it. (People other than the Gerards.)

He'd been such lousy company lately that he hunted up

Missy, thinking to tell her . . . what? Well, just how good he felt. To "share" that, he thought with a smirk.

"Can you take a break?"

She looked at her watch. "Five, ten minutes."

"Let's go."

"Where?"

"The roof."

But once in the elevator he had a better idea. He knew a room, several of them, in fact, with keys hidden over the doors—the old call rooms.

"Where are we going?"

"In here." He hustled her into one.

"Why?" She had on a tiny lime-green miniskirt, a crisp white blouse—a madonna in a mini. She was so beautiful. Why didn't he notice it more often?

He felt so tender, so choked up with love for her, he could barely whisper. "I want to make love to you." It came out a croak.

"Sonny!" Her voice was a schoolteacher's, shrill and punishing.

He put his arms around her, kissed her. Her arms didn't go around him. "Sonny, are you crazy?"

"Yes. Yes. I'm absolutely crazy." He took her arms and put them around his shoulders, prompting her. He ground his groin into hers.

"What the hell is wrong with you?"

Missy never talked like that. Not Missy McClellan, the woman he loved, who was so afraid of displeasing anyone, he'd never heard her raise her voice. Never even heard her say "hell."

Oddly, it made her more human, endeared her to him all the more.

"Everything's right with me. We just saved a guy and nature's juices are flowing in my veins." He was kissing her shoulder, nibbling her ear.

221

"Sonny Gerard, will you for once act like the grown-up I wish you were?"

Feeling slapped, he stared at her. "What did you say?"

"I have to get back to work."

"Shit. Well, just shit."

He sat on the bed, dejected, not believing what was happening.

"For once I feel good, for once I want to share something with you, and this is what I get!"

Instantly, she was sitting beside him, massaging his temple. He'd hardly seen what was happening, she'd moved so fast. "Oh, Sonny, I'm so sorry. It's just that it's in the middle of the workday. I've got clients to see."

His beeper went off. Another emergency. Maybe another chance to save someone's life. Maybe death instead; the patient's and his own, that little death he always experienced, a draining of his own, along with the slipping-away of the patient on the table. A sick lurch in his belly, a panic that lasted, that wouldn't go away. He'd have to go in a minute.

"You bitch!"

"What?"

She probably hadn't even known he knew the word.

"Bitch! Do you know how you made me feel?"

Her mouth twisted, her whole face started to writhe in pain. She was going to cry. It made him furious. He had no idea why, had no notion Missy could rouse such a feeling in him.

"Sonny, don't!"

Startled, he looked behind him, sure she was warning him of something, some danger to both of them, she sounded so frightened. . . .

But even as he turned his head, he realized that his hand was moving down, that it had been up, at shoulder level, coming at her, ready to hit.

That wasn't all. He looked at it, not believing. The fingers were curled in a fist.

Twenty-one

"I'M SORRY, ALEX."

"Shit." His first publisher had turned down his last book, and now his second one was throwing him out. He had given his agent a fifty-page proposal for the twelve-step debunker, and the assholes weren't going to buy it. He couldn't believe it.

His agent said, "You know, I really don't think there's a market for this one."

"That's what you said about the last one."

"Well?"

"Jared, you're such a know-it-all."

"Let's put it this way. I think I know the market. People buy self-help books for a reason. They want help. They feel bad and they want to feel better. They don't want to be told nothing works."

"But nothing does."

"Maybe not for you."

"Me?" What the hell was Jared talking about? "What have I got to do with it?"

"Alex, you gotta consider therapy." Just like that.

Like Hollywood's idea of an agent, not a thing like the real person Alex had worked with for ten years, who'd made him a pile of money and then slogged through rice paddies to sell his last book, which hadn't made money, and who was wimping out just as Alex was on the verge of a comeback.

"Jared, are you doing coke again?"

'Do you realize I owe my recovery to these programs you've got so much contempt for?''

"I bet you never took a teddy bear to a meeting."

"Alex, I like you, I really do. We've been together a long time. But I've got to tell you the truth. Something's wrong with you. You've hit some kind of block of hatred in yourself and you can't get around it."

What the hell is the man talking about?

"You know what I think, Alex? I think you hate yourself. You need to get in touch with who you really hate."

He had actually said, "get in touch with." Next, he would tell Alex he was "stuffing his feelings."

"You sound like Bradshaw and those other assholes." Alex couldn't keep the sadness out of his voice.

That was what the book was about, of course—why it had to be published. Because the world was getting fuller and fuller of assholes who swallowed everything whole, who bought the same old party line, who believed anything any self-help author told them, no matter how big a charlatan he was. Alex should know. He'd been the biggest charlatan in the business.

If you disagreed with somebody, you must hate yourself. If you tried to be honest for once, you needed therapy.

Et tu, Jared? Jesus! Maybe it was time to get another agent.

"Elec, you done those dishes yet?"

"Dad, say 'Al.' "

"Al."

"Say Alice."

"Alice."

"Your former wife is your what?"

"Ex. I see what you're gittin' at."

"So why can't you just say Alex?"

"No such name. It's Elec. I oughta know. I named you. Why haven't you done those dishes?"

"When I came here, nobody'd done the dishes in two weeks. Place smelled like a garbage dump."

"If that's the way I want to run my house, how's that any of your business?"

"You treat me like I'm still ten years old."

"Well, you act like it."

"Look, let's be adults, okay? I came here to help you out."

"Shee-it. You came here to leech. That's all you been doin', just leechin', leechin', leechin'! You can't do a thing needs doin', just out screwin' day and night, day and night. What's the matter with you, boy?"

He picked up the telephone book, held it at waist level, calculating, and drop-kicked it at Alex's chest.

Shocked, Alex didn't move, just let the thing hit him. Stood there stunned. What was wrong with the old man? He'd always been crazy, but not violent. This was the second time in a week he'd lost it. Two days ago he'd actually thrown a punch at him, and over something just as trivial. Alex had grabbed his wrist and then watched Lamar get this very puzzled look on his face, as if he couldn't remember what he was mad about.

"Hey, Dad," he said now, "what's going on?"

His dad's face was purple. "What do you mean, what's going on?" He was yelling.

Alex spoke softly, for once slightly humbled before his father. "It's not really that bad, is it? I'll do the dishes if that's what you really want."

"You'll get out of my house is what you'll do! You'll get yourself a decent job; you'll quit fooling around with this book crap. Lies, is all that is. Lies, lies, lies! You couldn't write your way out of a whore's mouth! You ain't never written a word in your whole miserable, worthless life."

He picked up one of the aluminum and yellow plastic chairs, seemed about to bring it down on the table.

"Dad, don't! You'll hurt yourself!"

Alex stepped forward and took the chair from Lamar. Once again the old man looked confused, as if he couldn't quite

225

remember how things had taken this turn. "You were a pretty baby," he said. "You know that?"

"Dad, could I ask you something?"

"Just get out of here."

Alex went into his bedroom and brought back a copy of *Fake It Till You Make It*. "Do you recognize this?"

"What do you mean, do I recognize that?"

"Do you know what it is?"

"You crazy, boy? Do I know what it *is*? What planet are you from?"

"I know you know it's a book. I mean, do you recognize the title and author?"

"You gone nuts or somethin'? What are you doin' to me?"

Alex was sick and tired of being patient. "Who wrote the book, Dad?"

"You got old-timers' or somethin', Elec? Don't you even recognize your own damn garbage?"

He threw the book into the living room, not giving a damn if he broke the spine, or a window, or a lifetime of vows. Why in hell did he have to live with the world's only seventy-five-year-old six-year-old?

As his rage rose, so did his libido. Damn that Skip Langdon! If it hadn't been for her, it wouldn't be like this. He wanted a woman and he wanted her now. Hell, he'd settle for a teenage girl if it weren't against the law. He didn't care. As long as she was female and ready.

He strode out, banging his boots on the wood floor, slamming every door he could find whether it was on his way or not, and jumped on his hog.

The white walls of Casamento's were as soothing as Skip had known they'd be. It was a sentimental favorite of hers and Steve's—he was crazy for the fried oysters and she liked the scrubbed tiles, the trailing philodendrons.

"I don't know why I didn't come."

"Listen, kiddo, this is the biggest case of your career. You don't have to apologize."

She stopped dead. He was right, but she hadn't known that when she canceled her plans. She's just felt she had to see the thing through no matter what.

"You're a good cop," he said, with real admiration in his voice.

She realized he couldn't possibly know whether she was a good cop or not, but still . . . a lot of people would have gone ahead and taken their vacations. What instinct had told her not to? She couldn't have known the case would get national attention, would terrify the town and spawn a mini-jazzfest. All she had known was that the same asshole had killed a nice young woman and a nice old man who had a teddy bear. Maybe it was the teddy bear that got her, so forlorn on the floor beside its dead owner.

But she wasn't given to sentimentality. It wasn't that. Steve was right, she thought with surprise. A good cop—a really good cop—wouldn't have left, would have seen the case through no matter what, would have gotten the Mabus case even though it wasn't really hers; wouldn't have quit in the middle.

Am I really a good cop?

Probably.

She was taken aback.

Really?

She'd never been a good anything in her life—not student, not daughter, not a damn thing. She was used to not being good.

But there was plenty of evidence she was good at this. Joe had handpicked her for homicide; he had chosen her for the task force; he was already urging her to take the sergeant's exam next time it was given.

Why did she have a tendency to listen to the likes of O'Rourke instead of to her own good sense? She didn't know, but it was there, it was true. And she felt a sudden wave of affection for Steve for being on her side.

She wanted to say, "Steve, I love you. I want you, I want to fuck you under the table."

She couldn't even say the first part.

"What's the matter? Did I say something wrong?"

She shook her head. "Got a pearl." She took the tiny gray thing out of her mouth. "Think it's good luck?"

He shrugged.

"Thanks for saying I'm a good cop." That was as far as she could go, and she hated it. Her insides were full of affection for him, love for him, that ached to get out, and she didn't know how to release it. If they could make love, if they'd done that instead of opting for a more conventional lunch, wouldn't he know? Wouldn't he be able to tell? She knew the answer was no; sex wasn't love, more often than not didn't mean a thing to most people. She had to tell him or she'd blow apart. She had to tell him sometime, but not today. Not while she was trying to solve the damn case. Later.

"So how's the case coming?"

"Bad. I'm getting desperate."

"He didn't kill anyone last night. Maybe he's done."

Skip's stomach flopped. "I don't think so. I've got a bad feeling."

"Since when does a cop date suspects?" The question popped like an angry blister, splattering her with bits of doubt and hostility.

"Steve!"

He said nothing, just glared at her.

"You know it wasn't a real date." She stared down at her plate.

"Somehow I have a hard time believing the famous Dr. Alexander Bignell is really a murder suspect. Somehow it's easier to believe he's a smart, famous, rich, sophisticated guy you'd rather stay home and date than come to California to see me."

"Oh, God."

"Listen, Skip, I had a few drinks last night and I was really looking forward to seeing you. I guess I'd have swallowed anything. But in the cold light of day, when I finally put it together who the guy is, it got a little obvious. I'm going home on the red-eye tonight."

"Don't!" She grabbed his hand.

"Don't?" He was clearly puzzled. He just stared at her, neither reclaiming his hand nor curling his fingers around hers.

"Steve, don't you understand how far I've gone already, telling you what I did? Maybe I'm a good cop and maybe I'm not. A good cop doesn't talk about her cases."

"Jesus shit." His fingers curled.

"You understand?"

"You have beautiful eyes, you know that?"

"They're pleading now." She squeezed his hand.

"Shit. You're telling me Bignell really is a suspect? One of the most famous psychologists in the country is actually suspected of killing two people and writing a crazy letter?"

"Shhhh." All she could think of was being overheard.

"Is that what you're telling me?"

She nodded very slightly, knowing she'd already answered, still feeling guilty about it.

"Let's walk."

"I have to get back to work."

When they were in the car, he said, "Alexander Bignell!" Like an explosion.

"Alex. Elec to his daddy."

"What in hell does that mean?"

"I don't know. Just a Southern pronunciation."

"Is he it? I mean is this one of those cases where the police know who the killer is, they just haven't got proof yet?"

"I wish. Can you keep a secret?"

"Sure."

"We've narrowed it down to about thirty suspects."

"Oh, come on. You can't stop now."

"I shouldn't have told you any of this and you know it."

"Tell me more."

"Kiss me."

They ended up necking in front of Casamento's.

"At least no one can see in," said Skip when she stopped to breathe. "We're steaming up the windows."

"Would you care?"

"Not if Second District station weren't right across the street," she said. "Which it is. Give me my purse, will you? I've probably got lipstick everywhere."

As she pulled out her makeup bag, a folded paper dropped on the seat.

"What's this?" Steve opened it up, not asking permission. "Oh, shit. Suddenly I get it."

Skip grabbed it from him—it was a schedule of CODA meetings, the teddy-bear group starred and underlined.

"That's what you meant by thirty suspects—they all go to this damn thing, don't they?"

"As a matter of fact, I've been going myself."

He kept on as if she hadn't spoken. "Oh, baby, have you got yourself a case. 'Murder Anonymous.' 'Twelve Steps to Murder.' 'Hi. I'm Alex and I'm a compulsive killer.' Promise me one thing. Sell me the movie rights."

"Shut up, dammit." She was trying to wipe smeared lipstick off her chin.

"I'm serious. It'd be a hell of a movie."

"Aren't you forgetting something? I haven't solved it yet."

He wasn't listening. "So that's what the *A* is for."

"What, Alex? I hate to tell you, but half the suspects have *A* names and so does one of the cops on the task force."

"It might be for 'Anonymous.' "

"Why not Axeman?"

"Why not?"

"Oh, who the hell knows? We don't know what the *A* means and we've been working on it twenty-four hours a day. What makes you think you can come in and figure it out in twenty minutes?"

"Touchy, aren't you?"

Skip's lipstick slid off-target, half-melted in the heat. "*Damn*, it's hot."

Di had bought a cat candle for attracting power, wisdom, and spiritual helpers. She had set up her altar the way it said you were supposed to do it in the voodoo book she had bought last May and finally gotten around to. And then she had taken a purple bath for power, adding mustard seed and washing with two whole eggs. She hadn't been able to find the recommended dragon's blood incense and instead had substituted lavender, which seemed purplish enough.

Now she was naked—all the books said you should practice magic in the nude, and she adored being naked. She had smudged her living room with sage. (She could have used tobacco, the book said, but how gross.) She had done the door, then the corners, clockwise, and then herself. She had lit rose incense, her favorite. (The book had recommended only a "nice" one.)

She had sprinkled the corners with "spirit water," in which she had had to use her Giorgio perfume. (She could have used a "spirit" like rum or Pernod, but since she didn't drink she didn't have any. And the book had been very specific—if you used perfume, it had to be good perfume.) Actually, she hated the Giorgio in its original strength—it had been given to her by a hopeful who hadn't realized his hopes. But it was certainly "good," and didn't smell too bad diluted down to spirit water.

She didn't have a chalice, so she held a wine glass of spirit water, about to invoke the powers of the four directions. She was loving the mingled scents of sage and rose and Giorgio florals, reveling in her nakedness, her beauty, knowing how

231

lovely she looked, arms outstretched with the chalice so that her breasts lifted, so involved, so powerful she could almost forget her hideous scar and the lump that marred her smoothness.

She was starting to feel a strange ache in her pelvis, the beginnings of desire, but she wasn't sure why. Was her own naked body turning her on? Or was it the energy of the magic she was creating? She began to chant, calling the East, making it up as she went along.

O Santana dawn ozone, scirocco zephyr khamsin, blow! Blow like a dragon's breath at first light, powerful and stirring. . . .

She was loving it, feeling herself truly talented at this, a great priestess genuinely inspired, when someone hollered, "Di, for Christ's sake! What the hell are you yelling in there? You all right?"

You couldn't be nude in air conditioning. She had had to open one of the French doors, the ones in the bedroom. Apparently someone was standing underneath the balcony there.

Furious, she threw on the caftan she had doffed for her ritual, strode into the bedroom, leaving the spirits of the East blowing lonesome through her circle.

"Who's down there?"

"It's me. Alex. I thought you might like some company."

There had been a time when she hadn't been able to resist, when he had come nearly every afternoon and they had sweated together in her fairy-tale bed. But that was before she'd found out how many other women he was sleeping with. Well, actually not how many—there was no way to know how many—just that she was one of a vast, panting crowd. She'd never said what was wrong, had just stopped being available.

No. Now that she thought of it, it hadn't been quite like that. Before she'd started seeing Sonny, she was seeing a gorgeous young black from Al-Anon, in fact still saw him now and then. She'd forgotten about Alex, but she'd never said a word to him. He'd just stopped coming around. Damn him! She hated being the rejected one.

"I'm busy," she said, her voice icy.

"It's three o'clock. Time for one of our three o'clock specials."

She hiked the caftan up, showing as much leg as possible, and stepped out onto the balcony.

"I'm sorry, Alex. I'm otherwise engaged."

"Wait. Di . . ."

But she had stepped back in and closed the French door. Even if she had to turn on the air conditioner, which meant she had to keep the caftan on, she wasn't opening the damn thing again. Alex could go find another afternoon delight.

Damn! Now he was leaning on her doorbell. What did it take to make him understand he wasn't welcome?

She put on a tape of Tibetan temple bells, turned it up loud, let the buzzer become part of the music. If that didn't get her into a trance fast, nothing would.

Then she smudged again, sprinkled again, called the quarters, and sat in a half-lotus. Leon Wheatley had been scheduled to speak at the inner-child group that night, but he had a summer cold. She'd spent the morning on the phone, trying to find another speaker, but hadn't succeeded. She probably could have gotten Abe, or maybe Alex, but somehow she didn't trust either of them—they were given to grandstanding. And Sonny and Missy were too green. So she'd have to do it herself.

She had made the circle, taken the power bath, because she wanted to meditate, to feel her inner rhythms, listen to her inner voice, really know what she was supposed to talk about, what the universe wanted. She knew she was powerful today. She had proof. She had started to feel sexual and a man had appeared to answer her needs. But she had conserved that energy, put it instead to sacred use.

The subject came as soon as she went into a trance, perhaps brought by Alex, who had in turn been brought by the powers of air, the spirits of the East that had come when she called. There were no coincidences; Di knew that.

The subject was disappointment, betrayal; loss of innocence.

Twenty-two

EVERYONE ON THE task force was at the inner-child meeting. Cindy Lou was there as well, already drawing glances from Alex and Abe. To Skip's horror, Steve Steinman was sitting next to Missy McClellan.

It was just like Steve to come. She'd long since decided it was really she who interested him, that he wasn't just a cop groupie, but he wouldn't have been a filmmaker if he hadn't been a voyeur at heart. Except that Steve wasn't the kind of voyeur who watched other people having sex. It wasn't even violence that especially interested him. It was adventure, the thrill of an unfolding tale. He had probably been serious about buying Skip's story if she solved the case.

She tried not to be annoyed. It was a free country and the twelve-step programs were open to anyone. He had as much right to be there as she did. But he knew what she was doing there, knew the Axeman was probably in the room, probably guessed that others in the room were also officers. There was something about it that she didn't like, that made her feel as if she were onstage. And there was something else—fear that he'd somehow give the police away.

What if he did? She shrugged mental shoulders. Maybe it was time they made themselves known, got people nervous and talking. Anyway, thanks to her "creative" police work, the one person who mattered might already know Skip was dangerous.

They had already said the Serenity Prayer and now Di was going through the opening rituals—the twelve steps, the twelve promises, the twelve traditions, a dozen of this, a dozen of that. She was having different people read selected bits, people she'd pre-chosen rather than simply passing the materials around, letting people read at random. Di was very precise, very controlling, Skip realized.

When the boring part, as Skip thought of the opening, had ended, Di said she would be the speaker that night because Leon couldn't make it. Convenient, Skip thought, since the speaker, she'd noticed, got to speak longer than others who shared. Di seemed a fan of the spotlight. Tonight she'd brought a baby doll, a toy about the size of a real baby, in a little white dress and cap. She was holding it in the burp position, stroking its back, symbolically comforting her inner child.

"I learned about betrayal early," she said, "when I lost my parents. My father simply left home whenever he felt like it; we never knew when he was going to go again or whether he was ever going to come back. And finally he didn't come back. When I was a teenager. He'd been gone three years before my mother mentioned it."

She went on for a while about the pain of being left by her father and then she started in on her mother: "She felt she had to work. I don't know if this was true. I don't know if my father sent money or not. All I know is I felt rejected. I thought it was a choice she made to get away from me, to get out of the house so she wouldn't have to be around me. But maybe she really needed to. She could have; I don't know.

"What I do know is that she could have been more careful

about the places she left me. It wasn't called 'day-care' in those days, but there were places where kids went after school if their parents worked.'' She started to tear up. ''I don't know if they were all bad, but I was beaten at three out of the four I was sent to. Once with a belt, once with a shoe; once I was turned over a man's lap and spanked. I was nine at the time. He did it in front of all the other kids. Beating wasn't all either. They treated you like dirt. If you were a kid, you were nothing. They'd say, 'Wash the dishes,' and you had to—for twenty-five people—or they'd beat you again. You had to do anything they told you.''

She sobbed, getting more and more into herself as a kid out of Dickens, while Skip mentally compared her story with her mother's. They were different, but not wildly different, about what you might expect from a mom who needed to believe she'd done the best for her kid and a kid who felt abused. It was curious, though, that Di hadn't mentioned the sister. Surely her suicide must have been one of the traumatic events of Di's life. Why was she leaving it out?

''So that was my first experience with betrayal; there was my dad's first, then my mother's. I had to accept the loss of my parents, realize that neither of them really loved me. Maybe they thought they did, but they didn't. They were always telling me to be a big girl, to act like a big girl, not to cry because big girls didn't cry. They never let me be myself and never asked who I really was. They just wanted me to be what they wanted, a big girl who didn't cry even when she got deserted by her parents and beaten by strangers. That's why I'm so grateful for this group and so glad to be able to cry now.''

Skip wrote down ''grateful'' and put a one beside it. She'd decided to count how many people expressed their gratitude before the meeting was over; she also wrote ''stuffing feelings,'' ''inner rhythms,'' and ''higher power.'' There was an art to sharing, she was beginning to see, and it had to do with using the correct terms.

"I've read that true adults can't be betrayed. That they pay attention to their feelings rather than stuffing them." Here Skip gave the proper term a one. "That they can catch on to what's happening early, that they protect themselves, take care of themselves, don't let people take advantage of them."

Was she ever going to shut her face? Even one or two of the regulars began restlessly to cross and uncross their legs.

"But maybe in some ways we never grow up. I was betrayed recently—lost my innocence a second time. And it was as if my kid was in control—the adult me didn't know what to do, couldn't stop it."

Skip perked up. Undoubtedly this would be a story of a love affair gone wrong, possibly with someone in the room. And then if they were lucky, maybe that person would "share" his side. She didn't know how much closer this got them to catching a murderer, but it was a diversion.

"I had breast cancer," said Di, "and I came through it just fine. The irony of it was that my real ordeal started after my recovery. For the next six months I kept finding fibroid lumps in my other breast, and it scared me to death every time."

Some of the men in the room paled.

"Finally it came time for my reconstruction, and the doctors all agreed that with my history the best thing was this operation in which they amputate the other breast and start from scratch."

Skip heard several gasps.

"They build you two whole new breasts out of tissue from your abdomen. My plastic surgeon said it was really great because you got a tummy tuck along with your reconstruction. But he didn't tell me I was going to have a hideous scar. That was the first thing.

"The second thing was, I noticed I couldn't get out of bed without drawing my knees all the way up to my chin. The first time I went to the doctor, he looked at my breasts and said, 'Those are the prettiest ones I've ever done.' I said I

237

didn't seem to have any muscle tone in my stomach anymore, and he said, 'Well, of course not, dear. You don't have any muscles.' And then he picked up one of my breasts, almost fondling it, and said to his nurse, 'Didn't I do a beautiful job?'

"I said, 'What do you mean, I don't have any muscles?' and he said, 'Well, I cut your muscles when I did the surgery. Now you've got a flat tummy and you'll never have to do sit-ups again.' Then he laughed. And he said, 'You *can't* do sit-ups again. But you've got one of the prettiest pairs of tits in the parish.' " She stopped and sobbed into a tissue. Then she said, just to make sure everyone got it, "He treated my body like a piece of sculpture he was working on!"

"Then great big ugly lumps popped out on my stomach. Fist-sized lumps. Several of them. And it hurt. It felt like something was loose in there. He said, 'Oh, you think you're in so much pain; all you ever do is think about yourself. Well, you've got a really weak abdominal wall. This time I'm going to put nylon netting in there to reinforce it. That'll hold you!' So I had to have another operation, and it didn't hold. Now I have nylon netting in my stomach and another ugly lump. Every time I go to see my doctor he tells me I've just got the weakest abdominal wall he's ever seen, but I sure have pretty tits. So it's my fault half the operation didn't work, but all to his credit the other half did.

"When he says that, I feel shamed just like I did when I was a little kid and I got beaten just because some pervert wanted to make a little girl lie down on his lap. I know it's not my fault my body's ugly now, I tell myself it's not my fault, I know this man has betrayed me, has violated all his oaths—don't they have to say, 'First, do no harm,' or something like that? I know he's the one at fault and yet I still find he intimidates me, I don't know how to tell him to stop leering at the part of the body he likes—that he 'created'— and I don't know how to stand up for myself with him. It's as if I'm so discouraged, so unhappy about the whole thing,

I'm nine years old again.'' She paused and screamed, ''And I can't grow up!'' The sentence came out with a new sob.

Everyone was quiet for a minute, taking it in. Skip felt shaken, ashamed of herself for imagining romantic trifling, and almost on the verge of tears herself. But she felt angry at Di as well. She wanted to shake her and say, ''Quit complaining and do something! Sue! Call the Board of Medical Examiners. At the very least curse him out.''

And that, she told herself, is codependency in action. Of *course* you know how to run Di's life. No problem.

Di said, ''Thank you. I just needed to put that out.''

Sonny raised his hand, announced he was Sonny and he was codependent and was told hi.

''I guess you can be betrayed by someone who doesn't mean to betray you,'' he said, and stopped, gathering his thoughts. It was a while before he started again, and it occurred to Skip that this was difficult for him, that perhaps he hadn't done it before.

''The worst thing that ever happened to me happened when I was four years old. I guess that's loss of innocence. It felt more like loss of a limb or a vital organ. But it was like I grew up, I learned what the world was like when I was only four.''

His face was starting to contort with the effort it cost him not to cry. Skip felt her whole body starting to soften, her heart opening to him. There were things she hated about these groups, but many things she liked. What she liked best was when a successful, self-assured man made himself vulnerable, actually talked, in a roomful of people, about feelings.

They never talk to us, she thought. *To women.*

''There was only one person I really loved, who I thought really loved me. Well, let's put it this way—there was only one person who was nice to me, and that was my grandfather.'' His voice was going out of control. ''He died at home, but first . . .'' He started to sob, letting himself do it. Skip wondered why not just Sonny, but any of them, did it. Cried in front of strangers. Told these horribly painful stories. "First he was sick. He was sick for a long time. I was just a baby so it seemed like forever to me. Maybe it was six months, maybe two or three. I don't know.

"It seemed like a game at first, having my grandpa home all day." He stopped and smiled through his tears. "I didn't call him Grandpa. It's funny I can talk about this part of it, but I'm embarrassed to tell you what I really called him. Anyway, he was home all day and that made me happy, but then I noticed he couldn't walk; he wasn't just pretending, he really couldn't. And he got so he didn't look like himself. Sometimes he'd want me to sit by him for a long time, just holding his hand. But I'd get bored—you know how kids are—and I couldn't do it very long.

"And then he got so he'd just lie there and moan. I'd get down on the floor and moan with him. Sometimes I'd get under his bed." He smiled again, quite the Southern gentleman, rising to the occasion. "I was about the most miserable little kid you ever saw. And then one day he told me he was going to get well. He was a doctor. My father's a doctor, we're all doctors. So he said he was going to get well and I was happy again." He contorted his face, squeezing his eyes shut. A tear or two escaped despite his best efforts. The words seemed squeezed out too: "And that was the day he died."

Sonny opened his eyes. "Thank you."

Skip felt as if someone had been messing in her chest with a Roto-Rooter. She looked at Missy, sitting across the room from Sonny, not next to him as usual. Her body was shaking; she was holding a tissue to her mouth. Steve, next to her, was almost pale, looked as if he wanted to flee and probably did. *Take that,* she thought. *Nobody asked you to come.*

A couple of people talked whom Skip didn't know—she noticed Abasolo and O'Rourke perking up—and then Abe did.

"I hardly knew my father," he said, looking down at his

240

bare lap—no teddy bear for Abe. "He thought the way to show his . . . affection was to work sixteen hours a day so we could have a pool and a color TV set before anyone else in town did."

Points for sincerity, thought Skip. *You almost brought yourself to say the l word.*

"We were reform Jews," he continued. "Reform Jews worship the TV set."

A little on the rehearsed side.

"It was a bad feeling when I really got that; when I understood that for my parents nothing was important except the things they could get. And I was just one of their things. Another possession to be shown off as part of their success. So I thought I had to do what they wanted to make them look good. Make all A's, get into Harvard, that kind of stuff."

Bet you didn't get into Harvard, but you're hoping everyone'll think you did.

"I didn't know what I was doing, but in a way I turned out just like them. I married a woman I don't think I ever really . . . uh . . . had any affection for. I guess I thought of her the way my parents thought of me—as just another possession."

This sounds real. Do my ears deceive me?

"And I guess I got what I deserved. Betrayal breeds betrayal." He paused for a long time. "She's a bitch."

A quickly stifled gasp went round the room.

"I guess I'm upset tonight because she called and tried to keep me from coming. She had the kids and she made me take them. You know why? Because she had a date. She went back on our agreement because she had a date. So I had to take the kids and get a baby-sitter just so she could go out on her damn date. And that was after she made me move to this burg in the first place. She uses the kids as a bludgeon." He paused again, building tension. "Well, I picked her. I suppose it's no more than I deserve."

You're not kidding.

241

"Thanks. I guess I'm a little angry tonight."

Backward, Abe. Skip had noticed that one of the conventions of these meetings was that often, before people started to share, they'd say how they were feeling. She liked it. It was honest and it prepared you—if they were sad or angry or something else hard to deal with, you were ready. Abe might not have understood how he felt at first, had probably meant to grab group sympathy on the coattails of the others, to use it for whatever advantage he could (possibly getting laid or maybe setting up a murder victim), but he had talked it through, however unwittingly, and at least figured out how he did feel. She gave him credit for that. A lot of people didn't know.

I wonder if that's one of the reasons people do this.

Nah. Not Abe. He'd never do anything without an ulterior motive.

Missy was speaking now, distractedly. Her eyes kept darting to Sonny and her voice kept failing her, kept coming out whispery and unwilling, but she seemed bent on getting something out.

"I'm having the kind of night I've had all my life. I came here determined to talk about something I need to talk about and I find myself so wrapped up in someone else's problems I can hardly remember what it is. And it's real important to me. I really need to say this, out front, in this group, but really what I want to do is keep my mouth shut so maybe we'll get out of here early and I can start comforting the person I'm worried about.

"And it's me I should be worried about. Me I should have my attention on. But I think if I put my attention on somebody else, then maybe we'll get closer and closer and I'll find myself that way. I'll be reflected in the golden light of his love and that's how I'll know I exist and I'm worthwhile. Now I know that isn't true. I know that I won't find myself, that really what'll happen is I'll lose myself. Just like it's always been. Intellectually I know that, but I still feel that way, do you understand?

"Listen to me asking for your approval. What's wrong with me? I'm sorry. I want to talk. I want to say that when I heard the subject was betrayal, I knew my higher power was working because that's what I need to talk about and what I would have talked about tonight even if the subject had been Good Things About Childhood."

Skip looked at Sonny. His eyes were on her, seeming to say, "Go, Missy!" She hoped Missy was watching, knew she had such a staunch supporter.

"Well, there were a lot of good things about my childhood. We had money and my dad was prominent in the town we lived in and I was always popular in school, always the kid chosen to be the lead in the school play and later the homecoming queen. And why shouldn't I have been? I worked so hard to please everybody.

"Because I knew that what I was doing with my dad was bad; really, really, really bad. And I knew he wouldn't do it if I weren't the kind of girl who was bad."

She looked at her hands in her lap, tossed her head like a coltish teenager, started again. "I don't know when it started. I can't ever remember a Sunday when he didn't say, 'You look so pretty in your little dress. Climb up here and give me some sugar, Missy.' And he'd pat his lap and I'd climb up."

Skip could see perspiration on her upper lip, more starting at her hairline.

"And he'd put his hand up my dress." She said it so quietly they'd all have missed it, except that everyone in the room knew by now what was coming. Skip looked around the room. O'Rourke's eyes seemed to have sunk about three inches into his head, his body to have withdrawn itself into the tiny curve of the narrow chair. He looked half his usual size, and still shrinking. For once Skip suspected the man of having a human feeling deep in his toe or somewhere. Hodges held his head in his hands, clearly willing the thing to go away, just go away.

Abasolo was cool. He'd been going to AA for years—there was probably nothing he hadn't heard.

"My mother'd be in the kitchen. He'd say it was our secret. The books say they all say that, but they don't have to, I don't know why they bother. No one would tell. No one would tell anyone, even her mother. It makes you feel so shamed. So humiliated. So small. You think the only way you can possibly function in the world is to make sure no one knows, no one ever finds out."

She stopped, apparently remembering she was telling her own story and she was supposed to say "I"; the books said so. "At least that's how I felt. Telling it is the hardest thing I've ever done. My therapist knows. My boyfriend knows. My incest group knows. And I'm not dead and I'm still functioning in the world." It took her a while to get control of her face. "And now you know."

A weird thing happened. Skip had been to certain meetings in which, if someone said he'd done something appropriate to the program—an overeater who'd "been abstinent for twenty-three days," say—everyone applauded. She hadn't been to this meeting enough to know if there was such a custom here, but nonetheless the whole group broke spontaneously into applause, including O'Rourke and Abasolo. Everyone seemed to need the release.

It was a hard act to follow, but these people weren't into one-upping. None of them seemed to have a problem so trivial it couldn't be aired. Everyone, it seemed, had been betrayed by their parents, either by abuse or neglect, and had gone on to repeat the cycle, finding new betrayers in adulthood.

Alex's problem was just huge. "I didn't get what I wanted today. My mother left my father when I was very young, and

I guess I'm really afraid of women leaving me. It's a funny thing—my father and I never got along that well, but I guess I was used to him. Being without him was like being without one of my toes or something. He might be an asshole, but he's my asshole if you know what I mean."

Nervous laughter fluttered through the room.

"I thought that once you made a commitment to someone, you stuck with them. But she didn't and I guess I can't really forgive her for that. I guess I thought I could make him like me if I could spend more time with him. So maybe I blame women for taking away my father. I don't know.

"Today I really felt bad—I had a bad break in business and I really needed someone to talk to. So I went to see an old friend and she wouldn't see me. Sure, she might have had something else to do"—he twitched his shoulders, shrugging off the preposterous idea—"but I couldn't help feeling the way I felt. The shrinks say there are no inappropriate feelings, so it can't be wrong, the way I felt. Can it? I felt really bad, really rejected, really—well, betrayed, really. I really needed her and she wasn't there."

Really? thought Skip. She wondered if these groups could function without that word. It could make anyone sound sincere.

Without it Alex would have been in big trouble. Because he didn't sound hurt, he sounded angry.

Twenty-three

THERE WERE A few new faces at PJ's for coffee that night—Cindy Lou's black gorgeous one and Steve's familiar one, for two. And the carefully made-up ones of two other women, shining with eagerness to chat up the new guy.

Or maybe that was just Skip's proprietary assessment. Nini, plump, snow-skinned, with blacker hair than nature ever made, was clutching her breasts, one in each red-taloned hand. But not seductively; out of obvious distress. "Oh, Di, you poor thing, what a horrible story. What a terrible thing to have happen to you."

"You were so brave," said Peggy, hands ruffling brown curls, so nervous Skip wondered if she'd recently quit smoking. "I don't know what it is about this place."

"This place?" asked Cindy Lou.

"The quality of medical care. I had real bad PMS and they told me I'd have to have a hysterectomy. So I called my old doctor in Minneapolis and she told me to take vitamin B6. I told that to my doctor here and you know what he said? He said, 'Oh, sure, go ahead and take the vitamins if you really want to; but in New Orleans women usually want hysterectomies.'"

Steve gave her the smile she seemed to be craving. "Did they work?"

She returned the smile with added wattage: "Like a miracle. I'm the only woman in town with non-raging hormones.''

It looked as if Nini'd lost out if Steve was what she'd come for, but apparently he wasn't. "Di, I really have to ask you something. I'm thinking of having a breast reduction and your story terrified me. Just the way you described that man . . .'' She dug in her fingernails and squeezed, apparently unaware of the spectacle she was creating. "I got the willies the worst kind of way. The thing is, I've got a weird feeling about this guy I went to. I mean, everybody says he's the best, but I just don't know. What if . . . I mean, I swear to God, I'd rather go around with *these*''—she literally held them up, and an impressive pair they were, too—''the rest of my life.'' Finally she blurted, "Could you possibly consider telling me who it was?''

''Oh, gosh. I don't think so,'' said Di. "I don't think I should.''

''Oh.'' Nini looked as if she were fighting tears.

''Why not?'' said Missy.

''I don't know. I don't want to get sued.''

Alex said, "Why would you get sued?''

''What if it got in the paper or something?''

''You're the one who should sue, not him.''

''I don't know. I just don't feel I should.'' Di had turned pink; she looked so uncomfortable, Skip wondered if she'd made the whole thing up.

Cindy Lou said, "Di, why are you protecting this man? He maimed you, he mutilated you, he insulted you, he injured you, and he's obviously caused you great mental anguish. He can't sue you and you know it. You've got nothing to fear from him, but he ought to worry about you, girl. I bet he does, too. And here are you are saving his ass. Now, I know you're codependent 'cause you said so, but that's not a good enough reason. I want to know why you're protecting this criminal.''

''You're right!'' Di had slammed a hand on the table,

247

causing everyone's coffee to shimmy and spill. Shocked at herself, she apologized and removed the fractious hand with her other, as if it were a miscreant pet. "You're absolutely right," she said again. "Why the hell am I shielding him? He can keep on doing that and doing that . . ."

"Unless somebody speaks up," said Cindy Lou.

"Okay. Okay, here goes. I'm saying it in front of witnesses, okay? Everybody listening? It was Robson Gerard. Also known as 'Bull.' "

Nini squealed. She was apparently given to dramatic displays. "That's him! That's my doctor!" She couldn't know the "criminal" was Sonny's father.

Possibly no one else but Missy and Sonny knew either, since last names weren't used in the group. Did Di know? Skip glanced at Sonny and Missy, who were taking it as she might have expected—they were rigid, staring straight ahead, not looking at Di, not looking at anyone.

Di was holding Nini's hands now. "Oh, Nini, I'm so glad I told. Don't go to him. Don't let that monster touch you."

"Oh, Di, oh, Di. What if I had? Oh, my God, what if I had?"

Steve caught Skip's attention and rolled his eyes—the whole thing was just too Southern for words.

Cindy Lou had an innocent look. Innocent verging on smug.

Skip felt hands massaging her shoulders, and then soft breath in her ear. "Let's get out of here," whispered Alex.

"What's wrong—you don't like mutilation stories?"

"I've got to talk to you."

The way he'd stomped out of the apartment the night before, she'd never have expected him to speak another word to her. *Surely,* she thought, *the average man would have quit by now, would have put me down as a mental case or a nasty tease.*

Okay. Maybe he's got something on his mind besides an-

other try. She reached for her purse, for the reassuring heft of her .38.

"Meet me at Bruno's." A bar in the same block.

"Five minutes."

There was no one to cover her but Steve or Cindy Lou. Choosing brute strength, she dropped Steve a note: "Pretend you're going to the men's room. Follow me to Bruno's. Stay out of sight."

Alex was waiting with a gin and tonic for her, which she took and pretended to sip.

She said, "I thought you thought I was crazy."

"I was wondering something," he said. "Why haven't you mentioned you're a cop?"

"Oh. Someone at Cookie's told you."

"That's not all they told me. I found out how your dad's Don Langdon, the society doc, and how you went to McGehee's, and how you're the black sheep of your family. I heard all that stuff and I got into thinking you were really down on yourself."

She was taken aback. "I beg your pardon?"

"Look, you're so used to thinking of me as the next thing to a rapist, you forget I'm a psychologist. You don't share in the group. You never talk about your work. You just say you have a dumb civil-service job. You've obviously got a self-esteem problem because you aren't a success.

"I thought that's why you kept blowing hot and cold. You wanted to have sex with me, but you didn't think you could handle it. Then last night on the way home I figured out what was really going on. The way you weren't a bit freaked out by those chickens. The way you always keep your backpack with you. How you asked me to go out last night, just like you hadn't practically kneed me in the balls the night before."

"I only threatened to."

"I finally got it. You saw the chickens and you thought I did it. I even mentioned the Axeman, neatly bringing him

249

together with the chickens. So you decided I was the guy. And instead of telling your sergeant or whatever you're supposed to do, you thought you'd do a little unofficial sleuthing. Think how great it would look if humble Skip Langdon, the one with the self-esteem problem, brought in the Axeman all by herself. So you tried. But you freaked yourself out and ended up sniveling.''

''Not a nice way to put it, Alex.''

''But true.''

''Well, at least you don't think I'm crazy anymore.''

''No, but I still think you've got a self-esteem problem. You're ashamed to admit what you do for a living.''

''I guess you're right, in a way. I'm not ready for people to know.''

''You've got to face it, Skip. If it's not what you want to do, then you've got to quit doing it.''

''I'm almost ready to talk about it in the group.''

''Talk about it to me.''

She put her untouched drink on the bar. ''I really can't. I've got a date. But I do promise to quit stuffing my feelings. And with the help of my higher power, I'm going to try to open up more to my recovery. I guess that's all I really have to say, except that I'm just really grateful to be here tonight and I want to thank you for sharing.''

''Always leave 'em laughing.'' He gave her a friendly wave as she left.

He came out seconds later, followed by Steve, having apparently taken just time enough to throw some money on the bar, and looked both ways. For her? Was he trying to catch up with her?

Or follow her?

He went back to the coffeehouse, started to straddle the hog, then shrugged and went back in, maybe remembering Nini and Peggy.

Skip gave Steve the high sign and watched him follow. Then she got in her car and waited. Sonny came in without

Missy, maybe having taken her home and come back. For about forty-five minutes nothing else happened, and then Alex left with Peggy astride his bike. He took her to her car and went home, having apparently struck out yet again. The lights were out, which Skip assumed meant Lamar was asleep, which probably meant Alex would stay home.

Home, then? Did that mean she could go home? She didn't dare.

She went back to PJ's to see if any coffee-drinkers were left. There were none.

Home now?

Yes.

Home to a message from Steve: "I want to see you."

It all fell away—her tiredness, her despair of ever catching this creep, her worry, even, momentarily, her puzzlement about Alex. Desire mushroomed in her; not sexual desire, but simple desire to see Steve, to be with him, to be with someone she loved.

She phoned him at Cookie's, invited him over, and stepped into the shower. She met him at the downstairs entrance in a white terrycloth robe, hair dripping, feet in thongs.

"Miss Elegance."

"Mmmm." She couldn't be bothered answering. She just wanted to bury her face in his neck.

"But you smell good."

She'd thought they'd talk first, but later wondered why she had thought that. She would have opened her robe and thrown her legs around his waist, ridden him right there in the tiny, dingy entranceway, if she'd been small enough. As it was, they ended up on her apartment floor—she'd folded her sofa-bed for company and they couldn't stop to unfold it.

Steve said, "Women are crazy, you know that?"

"Why?"

"They always want to shower first and then make love."

"In this town, you'd better."

"All women are like that."

251

"All women? Are you trying to tell me something?"

"I read it somewhere."

She got up, found her robe, and tugged it on. "Want something to drink?"

"Something alcoholic. I'll never be able to sleep after all that coffee."

"Who asked you to come, by the way?"

"To coffee? Di."

"To the meeting."

"Haven't you heard? Ninety-six percent of the population's codependent. Why should I be in the healthy four percent?"

He followed her in the kitchen, winced as roaches scattered. "I'll never get used to that."

"How about a Dixie?"

He accepted it and she made herself an iced tea, hoping it would counteract her returning weariness.

"That was the weirdest conversation with Alex. Did you hear it?"

Steve shook his head.

"He's figured out I'm a cop. He even knows I asked him out yesterday because I thought he was the Axeman. But he seems to think I don't have the backing of the department—that I'm just some dummy with a theory. And he pretty well let me know he wasn't even slightly nervous about me."

"That's creepy. Just how some super-arrogant psychotic would react."

"Yeah. Or some arrogant but innocent bystander."

"I'm serious. Maybe he was throwing down the gauntlet."

"Maybe. But he'd have to be really crazy to do that."

"The Axeman's not a well human."

"I wonder what Cindy Lou would say." The phone rang. "Maybe that's her calling. Has to be. If it's not Jimmy Dee."

At the mention of her landlord, Steve winced. She answered happily, a musical "Hellooo," and the next thing she said was "Oh, shit."

Steve mouthed. "What is it?" and she turned her face, finger in her ear.

When she hung up and turned around, he said, "Oh, my god."

"What?"

"You're white. Do you feel okay?"

He got up as if to steady her but she moved back. "I'm fine."

She hated this in herself. Some people blushed when they were in love, Skip lost her color when she'd had a shock. She'd gladly have traded. "There's been another."

"Someone you know?" She thought he asked because she seemed so upset, and it was almost true, almost someone she knew. Should she tell him? Hell, she'd have to interview him—might as well do it now and save time.

"I can't tell you yet. You're a witness."

"What do you mean? I didn't see anything."

"You're an alibi witness."

"Oh. I guess I am."

"What happened at PJ's after I left?"

"Sonny and Missy were gone by the time I got back from Bruno's. No problem about covering you, by the way. You're certainly welcome."

"Sorry. Thanks."

"Sonny came back in a few minutes. He said Missy'd lost her keys—he'd had to let her in with his. He didn't find them, but he stuck around. After a while Alex left with Peggy. Then Sonny left again. And finally Di and me and Cindy Lou. I'd say we were all out of there within half an hour."

"What about Abe and Nini?"

"Nini? Oh, the one with the red fingernails. I forgot about those two. They got into a conversation and probably never noticed we were gone. Come to think of it, it was a really intense conversation. Like when people are really attracted

253

to each other. You know, like they don't notice when they've finished their drinks and kind of just sit there running their mouths until closing time? And the next day can't remember a damn thing they said, but still can't wait to see the person again."

"Come on. How do you know he wasn't trying to recruit her as a client or something?"

"They kept leaning toward each other and touching. Making a lot of eye contact."

"What time would you say you left?"

"About ten-thirty, I guess." Abe and Nini had been gone when Skip returned after seeing Alex home. It was after midnight now.

"Do you mind telling me who's dead? I'm getting a little tense."

"Abe Morrison's baby-sitter."

Depression hovered like a black and smothering air mass, something like smog, but thicker, almost vaporous. Tendrils of it had wafted into Skip's car, and pillowy cushions of it that would engulf and swallow her seemed poised for ambush in the heavy night outside.

On the way to the scene she had to fight to stay centered, not to give in to despair and fall asleep or cry, maybe scream. She focused on the task ahead, tried not to blame herself for the murder of a teenager, not to wonder what she could have done to prevent it. Stayed at Alex's all night?

Asking herself the question, straight out like that, she realized that right now she didn't have much confidence in him as a suspect. If he knew she was a police officer and he was the Axeman, surely he wouldn't have confronted her about it; it just wasn't wily.

But who knew what a crazy person would do?

That wasn't the point. The point was whether she'd given it her best shot or not. She remembered going back to PJ's, how worried she'd been about the others—damn! She just hadn't felt she could baby-sit Alex when there were so many other suspects. And then she'd lost them all. They'd scattered before she could get to them.

The thing that bothered her most was that Abe had announced at the meeting that he had a baby-sitter that night—that a teenage girl was alone at his house. Should they have made their investigation public? Would that have made people more cautious? Maybe. Maybe someone like Nini, for instance, wouldn't have wanted to be alone with a man from the group. Maybe Abe would have worried more about his children, wouldn't have said that, would have gone home earlier.

But they hadn't really been sure. . . .

Anyway, it was Joe's decision, not hers.

She knew nothing could be done, that all the hindsight in the world wouldn't bring the girl back to life. But she couldn't shake this heartbroken feeling she had, this sense of inadequacy, as if for once she'd had something really important to protect and she'd blown it.

She wasn't normally squeamish, but she dreaded seeing the body.

Abe lived in an old-fashioned white-frame raised bungalow on Hampson Street in the Carrollton section. It wasn't a great house, probably a rental, but it had a small porch and a small yard, and it was a pretty good neighborhood. In fact, it was a gorgeous street. But plenty of middle-class white people—lawyers, professional people of Abe's ilk—thought nothing Uptown was safe anymore and would no sooner have their kids grow up here than send them to public school. Abe, being "from away" as New Orleanians said, might not know about that.

Joe and Cappello were at the scene. It was Cappello who had called, and she looked almost as pale as Skip. Joe wasn't much better.

The victim, Jerilyn Jordan, was lying on the couch, the scarlet *A* above her, written in lipstick this time, not blood, and it wasn't scarlet, it was a sort of bluish-pink.

She had been strangled, but not with hands. A striped cotton scarf, in shades of fuchsia and rose, had been wound about Jerilyn's thin neck.

The girl looked about sixteen. She had short brown hair and her limbs were honey-colored, though her face was engorged and purplish now, marred by darker purple hemorrhages. She was wearing a pair of white shorts, a blue T-shirt, and sandals. "Straight-A student," said Cappello, and that was all Skip needed. She was blinking back tears before she could stop herself, turning away so the others couldn't see. Never since she'd been in homicide had she experienced anything like this hopelessness, this feeling that she could have done better, she could have stopped it. This feeling of involvement.

The coroner hadn't yet arrived and they had no estimate of time of death.

Abe hadn't been able to give much of a statement so far, saying only that he came in, found her, panicked, ran straight to his kids' room, found them okay, hustled them out the back, and drove them to his wife's house before calling the police. Officers had been dispatched to both addresses and Abe had been taken to police headquarters for further questioning.

"Is anyone doing the neighbors?" asked Skip.

Cappello shook her head, looked grateful. "Not yet. You want to?"

Skip nodded.

"Jerilyn's parents live next door. They know. They came over when they saw the first car that got here—wouldn't you if you knew your kid was here and a police car drove up?"

"Oh, shit."

"It was grim. Anyway, they said she came over about six-thirty and they never heard a peep till they saw our guys.

They were watching television. They said she sat for Abe now and then, liked the kids, didn't mind him. That's about it. You can talk to them again if you like.''

Skip intended to. No matter how much it hurt to sit through an interview with two people who had just lost their daughter, she was going to do it. She was going to talk to everyone on the block, and do it now, even if they cursed her up and down and threatened to sue the city.

But when she had done it, and had interviewed the other neighbors, she was no further ahead than before. Everyone loved Jerilyn, most thought Abe was okay, and no one had seen or heard anything except one woman who heard a car door slam at around ten or ten-thirty, maybe eleven, and a ten-year-old boy who wasn't sure. He'd gotten up to go the bathroom and maybe had seen a car leave the Morrisons'. But maybe it had ''just been going down the street.'' He didn't know what time that was, but he'd gone to bed at ten-thirty, so it had to have been after that. He couldn't describe the car.

Everyone was scared shitless, and most of them, those who had known Jerilyn, were heartbroken as well, their faces drawn with the pain of a child's death and the urban-crime fear the city lived with. The bogeyman had come to their block in his nastiest, cruelest form.

Twenty-four

THE ENTIRE AXEMAN task force had been called in, Cindy Lou included, but they weren't yet all there. Those who were were drinking coffee, comparing notes, trying to reconstruct who sat where at the inner-child meeting, trying to remember every face, every name, to make sure no one slipped through the cracks. It had been a fairly large group, about forty people—though four of them were cops and one was Cindy Lou.

Abe was waiting for her, disheveled, pasty, and sweaty, hair standing on end as if he'd run his hands through it over and over.

"Skip. What are you doing here?"

"Didn't they tell you I'd be here?"

"Detective Langdon. They said Detective Langdon."

"Well, that's me."

"I didn't know." He seemed disoriented. "You're a cop."

She smiled sweetly, sat down across from him. "And you're the Axeman."

She wouldn't have thought he could lose more color, look any more distressed, but he seemed to shrink suddenly, a balloon stuck with a pin. "I could have lost my daughters," he said.

She was just thinking she'd never seen a lawyer act less like one when he rallied. "Did I hear you right?" he said. "Did you accuse me of being the Axeman?"

258

"Are you?"

"Am I in custody?" Skip gave up any thoughts of calling in the paramedics. He was going to be fine.

She shook her head. "What happened after I left PJ's?"

"Am I a suspect?"

"Not at the present time." She knew she sounded like an automaton, but a flat "no" would have been a lie.

He drew himself up, squared his shoulders, appeared to find some inner strength in becoming Abe the Lawyer. "I'm going to talk to you. I know and you know I could refuse or I could call a lawyer, but I also know you want to move fast on this. And this came too damn close to my girls for me to stand in the way. So I'm not going to make you wait while I wake up a lawyer. I'm innocent and I want to go home after I've talked. Fair enough?"

Skip shrugged. It depended on what he said.

"Okay," he said. "After you left PJ's, I got talking with Nini. Everyone else left and I asked her if she wanted to go to the Maple Leaf. They have Cajun dancing on Thursday nights. I taught her how."

"What band was there?"

"Band?"

"Who was playing?"

"I don't know. All Cajun bands sound the same."

"What time did you leave?"

"I guess about eleven, eleven-fifteen. She has to work tomorrow."

"Don't you?"

"Yes, but I wasn't ready to go home."

"Did you go to the Maple Leaf in separate cars?"

"Yes."

"So you didn't take her home?"

"No. I just walked her to her car."

"And then what?"

"And then I went home."

"Okay. Very carefully describe what happened then."

"I drove home. I parked. I went in and"—he thought about it a moment, apparently decided on a courtroom delivery—"saw Jerilyn lying on the couch with the *A* above her. And all I could think of was my kids. That they might be dead too."

"How did you know Jerilyn was dead?"

"I didn't. I just assumed it."

"Think back."

He took a minute. "I was nervous because the door was unlocked. I guess that was it. When I went in, I was already afraid. The light was off. I turned it on and I saw the *A* first. And then I smelled something. I didn't know what it was, but thinking back I guess it was urine. Did you see her?"

Skip nodded.

"She looked dead, didn't she? She looked so dead."

"Did you walk over and look carefully?"

"I didn't even pause. I was in the kids' room in about a half a second."

"Did anyone besides the members of the group know your kids would be alone with a sitter tonight?"

"My wife. Jerilyn's parents. And anyone they told, or Jerilyn told."

Skip had already asked the parents if they'd told anyone or if Jerilyn had. They hadn't and didn't think she had—not even her boyfriend, with whom she was currently fighting.

"Did you get Nini's phone number?"

He looked puzzled. "Why?"

"Did you get it?"

"She gave me her card." He pulled it out of his pocket.

Skip copied Nini's name and number. "What time did you get home?"

"I didn't look at my watch." He was testy.

Skip waited.

Finally he said, "I guess about ten minutes after I left the Maple Leaf."

"And when did you get to your ex-wife's?"

260

"About ten minutes after that."

"Excuse me a minute."

Skip hunted up Cappello. "Do we have an estimate yet on time of death?"

"The coroner came about midnight. He said no more than two hours earlier. So sometime after ten; that's going to be about the best we can do."

She went back and told Abe to go, but not to go home; there'd be a police seal on the door. She wondered if he'd go to his ex-wife's house and whether she'd take him in.

Cappello called Skip in. The members of the task force had, from Skip's pilfered phone list, identified nineteen people who'd been at the meeting the night before, and fanned out to talk to them. Alex, Di, Sonny, and Missy had been left to Skip.

"Nini?" said Skip.

"Hodges has already seen her. She verifies Abe's story. Says she got home about eleven thirty-five."

"Pretty damn precise."

"She was keeping a close watch on the time. Worried about getting enough sleep."

"What about Abe's ex-wife?"

"She had a blind date last night—perfect alibi because he never saw her before. Other than that, she seems okay, no criminal record. She didn't mention the baby-sitter to anyone."

"So it still looks as if it's in the group."

"Joe thinks it's pretty certain and so do I. You?"

"Yeah."

"You can forget that stupid undercover business. There's no reason to hide anything now. Go to Di's first, will you? Maybe she'll give you the phone list."

"Want to come?"

"No thanks." Cappello sighed and Skip knew she did want to, wanted to be out on the street. "I'm going to stay here and act as message central."

If Skip hadn't been in such a grim mood, she'd have found it comic, what she had to do next—change identities in front of people's very eyes. She was tempted to go home and put on a uniform—it would lend authority—but wasn't about to take the time.

To Di's intercom she said, "Police. Skip Langdon."

In a moment Di appeared on her balcony, flowing pink nightgown spilling boobs. "Skip, what is it? Why are the police here?"

"I'm a detective, Di." She held up the badge. "I need to talk to you."

"Now?"

Di was so sleepy (or such a good actress), it took a while to persuade her, but eventually Skip was seated in the incense-smelling living room, candles lit for illumination. She had thrown a T-shirt over her nightgown and looked almost as good with no makeup as she usually did. Skip wondered if that was the purpose of the candles.

"A couple of things, Di. I need you to tell me what you did after you left PJ's."

"Why?"

"Just tell me."

"But why? Something bad's happened, hasn't it? Why are you here in the middle of the night?"

"There's been a murder."

She shrank back, covering her heart with her hand. "Who?"

"For right now, I'm going to ask the questions, Di. Where did you go after you left PJ's?"

"I came home."

"Alone?"

"No. Steve came with me—the new guy from the group."

He hadn't mentioned that—only that he'd walked her to her car. "Steve Steinman?" she said.

Di looked blank. "I don't know. The big guy. Cute."

"How long did he stay?"

262

"An hour—two, maybe."

"Till midnight?"

"Maybe not. Maybe till about eleven."

"May I ask what you talked about?" *No, I may not. Did I?*

"What we talked about? I don't know. He told me about L.A. He used to live there."

"And he left around eleven?"

She shrugged. "About that, I guess."

"Did you go out again?"

"No."

"Talk to anyone on the phone?"

"No."

"A young girl was murdered tonight. A sixteen-year-old straight-A student. Do you know anything about it?"

"Do I? Why me?"

"Just answer the question."

"Of course not. But who? What girl?" She was getting upset, voice starting to give way, tears welling.

"It was Abe Morrison's baby-sitter."

"Oh, no!"

Skip didn't say anything.

"Sixteen?"

Skip nodded.

"Nooo! A little girl!" She got up and started throwing things, magazines she'd had stacked on the floor, a book from the coffee table. It was so sudden, Skip would have thought it an act if not for the anguish of her cry.

Skip stood. "Di, take it easy." She reached for Di, thinking to steady her, and caught her eye. A strange look passed between them. Skip couldn't have said what it looked like to Di, but to her it seemed like mother to child, herself being the mother.

Di's shoulders sagged. "I can't stand the thought of anyone hurting a child."

"I know. Nobody can." It wasn't the time to bring up

263

certain little unpleasantnesses—if Di was sticky about the phone list, she'd have to get a court order to get it. "I was wondering. Would you mind if I borrowed the phone list from tonight?"

"The phone list? I only have the one copy. Do you want someone's number?"

"I'll copy it and return it first thing tomorrow."

As if hypnotized, Di glided to the bedroom, came back with it. She looked puzzled, but at least didn't ask any more questions.

Skip counted twenty-eight names. She said, "Did you happen to notice how many people were at the meeting?"

"Forty-two." Di answered automatically, belatedly came alert. "What does that have to do with anything? Skip"— long pause—"could I see your badge up close?"

"Sure." Skip produced it.

"I'm sorry, I didn't mean to doubt you. I just don't see what the meeting has to do with a murder . . . and it's hard to see you as an authority figure."

Skip grabbed on to the last part, hoping to distract her. "I know; I should have worn my uniform." She flashed as much of a smile as she could muster. "I just thought you could help me with the names of people who aren't on the phone list."

"But if they aren't on the list, that means they don't want to be called."

"This is a murder case."

"Wait a minute." She finally seemed to get it. "You suspect someone in the group."

Skip shook her head. "We don't have a suspect yet. We just want to talk to everybody who was there. Ask them if they know anything." *Do I have to spell it out for you?*

She was caught between her innate cop's need not to tell one fact more than she had to and her need to be polite enough to get Di to help her. She couldn't come back tomorrow. Di was going to hate her before she left.

Di looked at the phone list. "I know all these people. The new black man is named Jim—he came to my party with one of the musicians. The man who delivered my flowers was there too—Adam. The cute one. That's two more."

"How about the short guy in the corner?"

"The one with the glasses? Oh, the other one. With the chipped tooth. I think his name's Bennett."

"You wouldn't know his last name, would you?"

Di shook her head.

Tediously, laboriously, Skip brought up every face she could remember, and most of them Di was able to connect with a name on the phone list. The others she knew only by first names.

But this is only a first shot, Skip thought. *We'll get them. Eventually, we'll get them all. If it matters.*

She had a feeling the Axeman was someone she already knew.

"You've been a big help, Di. Now I wonder if we could talk about your criminal record."

"I beg your pardon?"

"You're Jacqueline Breaux, aren't you?"

She looked alarmed. "How do you know that?"

"I know that, and I know you have a criminal record."

Tears came, but Di was quiet. She seemed to have spent her passion a moment ago. "I thought that was in the past," she said at last. "Excuse me a moment."

She found a box of tissues, plucked one, and sniffled. "You think I abused my own kids and now I've killed a child?"

"You choked a child, Di."

"I didn't!"

"You pleaded guilty to it."

"Could I ask you something? How do you think I live?" Her voice was alive with indignation, challenge. She was no

265

longer the victim, but her own champion, full of self-righteous fury.

Oh, boy, thought Skip. She said, "I don't know what you mean."

"I have no visible means of support. I was convicted of abusing my child. Do you really think that eighteen years later I'm still getting alimony from the husband who had every reason to divorce me? Don't you wonder how I can afford this apartment? Living like this? Do you think I knock over gas stations, or what?"

"Well? What?"

"I'm being paid off, that's what. If you don't believe me, look up the court records of our divorce. They'll show you something you won't believe. I got custody of the kids. Me. The supposed abuser. My husband didn't contest it. You know why? Because that was part of the deal too."

She picked up a candle and began to play with it. Skip had the feeling she was an ex-smoker, would have smoked a cigarette a decade or so ago. "I knew he was rough with the kids. I just didn't know how rough. Remember my share? I had a rough childhood too. I didn't know what was normal. I just didn't know." She blew the candle out, lit it again. "I did know he choked Donnie. I caught him, and I stopped it, but I didn't know it had gone so far. It was just one of the things he did that I didn't like. I was always stopping him and he was always telling me I was spoiling the kids, I was too soft on them, they were already 'rotten as mud.' That was his phrase, 'rotten as mud.' That's what he said about a couple of little kids who'd been beaten. Beaten and other things. I never saw the marks on Donnie. Not till the police got there. A neighbor noticed and called them."

Her voice was strong, getting stronger. "Do you know who I was married to? Walt Hindman. Do you know him?" She scanned Skip's face for a reaction.

"Everybody knows the Hindmans."

"Walt Hindman wasn't about to get hauled into court for

266 ·

child abuse. So it was all nicely hushed up. I pleaded guilty and it was the best deal I ever made. He got out of my life and out of my kids'—and in addition to everything else paid all our shrink bills for the next ten years. I got generous child support and an annuity for the rest of my life. And he put both the kids through college.'' For a moment her face grew soft. "He didn't mean to be a bad father.'' She caught herself. "Listen to me, making excuses for him. He was an animal, I know that now. I just thought that was pretty much the way everyone was. And I wasn't innocent, I know that too. I let him get away with it. But I faced that and I'm stronger for it.'' She sounded it. Or she was a very good liar.

Skip said, "Do you have anything on paper?''

"Lots of stuff. But nothing admitting he did anything.'' She turned up her palms, smiled her most ethereal smile. "All you've got is my word for that.''

Twenty-five

IT WAS NEARLY three when she banged on Alex's door. Lamar answered, wearing a pair of pajamas that were probably as old as she was. He looked wizened and sad in them.

"Hey, Lamar. Remember me?''

"Step in the light there. I think I do, I just can't call your name.''

"Margaret. But you can call me Skip this time.''

"Well, I know I've met you somewhere.''

"Is Alex home?''

"Elec? You want to see Elec?"

"Dad, what the hell's going on?" Alex had walked into the living room.

"Alex, it's Skip. I'm a police officer." Remembering he knew that, she said, "I mean I'm here on police business."

"Po-lice!" said Lamar. "Now I recognize you. You're the questionnaire lady."

"Dad, you know this woman?" Alex had on a pair of undershorts and one of the nastier scowls Skip ever hoped to see.

"Shore. This is that good-lookin' one I was tellin' you about. The one with the nice big bottom."

"What the *fuck* is going on?"

Skip held up her badge. "Could I come in, please?"

Lamar let her in while Alex went to find a pair of pants. "Lamar, I'm real sorry I woke you up. Why don't you go on back to bed?"

"Well, I'm up now. What's Elec done?"

"Were you awake when he came home?"

He thought a minute. "Nope. Didn't even know he *was* home."

"What time did you go to bed?"

"Oh, 'bout nine or ten."

Alex stomped back in. "Dad, for Christ's sake, go back to bed."

"I'm not doin' it."

"Sit over there, then. And be real quiet." He pointed to a Naugahyde recliner, probably hoping his dad would fall asleep in it.

Skip wasn't crazy about having an audience, but she decided not to argue. "Alex, where'd you go after we talked tonight?"

"Why do you want to know?"

"A girl got murdered tonight."

"What girl? What does this have to do with me?" His voice went up on the last word; it sounded slightly whiny.

"I need you to answer a few questions, please."

"Well, I need you to leave my house, please."

Damn these sophisticated witnesses.

He could make her leave and apparently he knew it.

"Alex, this is serious."

"I don't care. It's your problem. I don't have to cooperate with you and I'm not going to if you don't tell me what's going on."

Angrily, Skip fumbled in her purse for the picture of Linda Lee she had brought. "Did you know this girl?"

"This girl!" He looked at the picture and then back at Skip, upset for once, knocked off his pins. "What about this girl?"

"You knew her, didn't you?"

"This girl wasn't murdered tonight. What the hell's going on here?"

"Answer the question, Alex."

"This is the one who got the axe. I *thought* that was her. I saw her picture and I thought it was the same girl. But then I thought it couldn't be. Her hairdo was different or something. She came to our group once. The teddy-bear group. I asked her to go for a motorcycle ride. That's really her, isn't it? I never knew her name."

"She didn't mention it on the motorcycle?"

"She didn't go."

"How many times did you see her?"

"Skip, what the hell is this all about? It's three A.M. and this happened two weeks ago."

"I told you."

He put it together instantly; Di never had gotten it. "Another Axeman murder! Who?"

"A girl named Jerilyn Jordan. A high-school student."

He showed no emotion. "I never heard of her."

"What time did you get home tonight?"

"Why me, dammit? I don't know the girl."

269

She saw that he would just badger her until she told him. "She was Abe Morrison's baby-sitter."

"Abe Morrison? Oh, Abe from the group. Did he do it?"

She didn't answer, but his mind kept working. "Hold it a second. Wait a minute. That's two from the group. More or less from the group, connected with it. You think the Axeman's from the group, don't you?" He sounded excited.

"Alex, it's late. Could you just answer the questions, please?"

"Oh, man, wait till I tell my agent." His voice was positively gleeful. "This is great. This sheds a whole new light on things."

"Are you going to cooperate with the police or not?"

He put on a good-boy look. "I arrived home about ten-thirty. I watched television till eleven-thirty or twelve and then I went to bed. I was awakened from a good night's sleep by a police officer at approximately two fifty-two A.M."

Lamar said, "That's a bald-faced lie."

"What's a bald-faced lie?"

"You went out again. I heard you on your little scooter."

Alex turned back to Skip. "That's right, I did. I went out to get some beer about fifteen minutes after I got home. Say about ten forty-five."

"And you came right back?"

"Yes."

"No, you didn't."

"Dad, who's telling this story?"

"I never heard you come back."

"Well, I had to have come back sometime or I wouldn't be here now."

"Well, I didn't hear you."

"I can't help what you heard or didn't hear in that drunken haze of yours. I went out to get some beer and I came right back."

"I was still awake at eleven-thirty because I was watching television. You weren't home then."

270

"Dad, you weren't even awake when I got home the first time."

"I know, but you woke me up with that dadgum scooter of yours and I couldn't get back to sleep."

"Listen to him," said Alex. "Will you listen to him? You know what it's like to live with a seventy-five-year-old six-year-old?"

Rummaging quickly, Skip produced a picture of Tom Mabus. "Have you ever seen this man?"

"He's the other victim, isn't he? I only saw the woman."

"Often?"

"No. Just the once. A couple of weeks ago, maybe three."

"Try to remember."

"Well, it wasn't last week. You were there. The week before that. That's when it was. Three meetings ago."

The night she died? Either that or the night before. Skip's stomach felt slightly queasy. "Do you remember what she was wearing?"

He shrugged. "No. Pants maybe. Yeah. Not shorts or a dress. Because I noticed she could ride the motorcycle if she wanted to. One of those subliminal things."

"Do you remember what color?"

"Are you taking a fashion survey, or what?"

She summoned a smile. "I guess not. Good night, boys." She sincerely meant the last word.

Sonny met her in running shorts and T-shirt, apparently hastily pulled on, not stopping for undergarments. She could see the well-defined outline of his substantial equipment through the shorts. A puppy shot out the door when he opened it. But its legs were too short for the stairs—Skip caught it while Sonny blinked in the light.

"That's Zeke," he said.

He seemed so groggy she wondered if he'd taken a sleeping pill. When she got to the part about being a police officer, he said, "Missy! Something's happened to Missy."

271

"No, don't worry. Missy's fine. But we do have a problem and I need to ask you some questions."

"A problem?"

Skip decided to ignore the question. Sonny was so absurdly Southern-polite he wouldn't be so crude as to press her. "May I sit down?"

His apartment was a typical student's. Not much furniture and what there was was covered with debris. But top-of-the-line stereo equipment, hundreds of dollars' worth of compact discs. Some workout equipment, one painting that had be to a Rob Gerard.

"Sonny, I need to ask what you did tonight after you left PJ's."

"I took Missy home. And then I came home and tried to study. But I couldn't. I was just too tired. I fell asleep with the lights on."

"Did you call anyone? Or did anyone call you?"

"No. I was dead to the world. I woke up sometime and pulled my clothes off. That's all I remember." He patted Zeke and lifted him up to his lap. He was a golden puppy, a lab or a retriever, with the requisite cute floppy ears and nippy little teeth.

"Such a sweet puppy."

"I just got him. I think that's why I talked about my grandfather tonight. My first dog died right after my grandfather did."

"How sad, both things at once."

Sonny forced a smile. "But I have Zeke now."

"How did your other dog die?" *Did you strangle him, by any chance?*

He shrugged. "I'm not sure. I was so little . . ."

The shrug had been too nervous, the answer a little too quick. Skip sensed bravado rather than truth. She pulled out her photo of Tom Mabus. "Do you recognize this man?"

"No." But he suddenly looked very frightened.

"What's wrong?"

"I know who he is. He's one of the Axeman victims."

"Why would that scare you?"

"The other one. I think I might have known her. I mean I think I talked to her." It was a kind of croak. "I've got to get some water."

He left and came back wiping his mouth. Skip had laid Linda Lee's picture on his scratched-up Fifties coffee table. "This one?"

"Yeah." He looked very serious, a little boy sent to the principal's office. "I think she came to a meeting once. She spoke to me. I *think* she's the one."

"What did she say?"

"Missy and I weren't sitting together. She came over after the meeting and asked if I'd like to have coffee—just came out and said it. Said she'd seen me across the room and thought she'd like to meet me. I was real embarrassed. I said I had to go home and study. I didn't even tell her Di and everybody would probably go to PJ's. I just sort of stammered. I got a real bad feeling when I saw her picture in the paper. Like after I turned her down maybe she asked someone else." He paused a moment and tried to grin. "Is that what they mean by codependent? When you feel responsible for something like that?"

But Skip was more interested in something else—Linda Lee *had* been drinking coffee. "You mean you suspected someone else from the group?"

"The group? No. I just thought if she was in the habit of doing that . . . some guy got her."

"Did you see her ask anyone else?"

"No. I got out of there fast. Missy had her own car, so I didn't have to wait."

"Can you remember when it was?"

"Oh, yeah. It was the Thursday before I saw her picture in the paper. That's why I was so freaked."

"Why didn't you call the police?" She tried to keep the anger out of her voice.

"Well, I wasn't sure it was her. And you know; I didn't want to get involved."

"Do you know a Jerilyn Jordan?"

"No. Why?"

"She was murdered tonight."

He sat back and blinked at her, fighting the words off. Finally, he said, "I don't understand. What does it have to do with me?"

"She's Abe's baby-sitter."

"Abe?" Skip wondered what kind of doctor he'd make. His mind seemed fuzzy, he couldn't seem to wake up.

She decided she liked that. He was vulnerable. She made a decision; nodded as if she possessed superior wisdom.

"Yes, Abe. The man who shared about having to get a baby-sitter."

"Oh, yeah, I remember that. I know the guy. We had a meeting at his house once."

"Do you understand what this means?"

But he just sat there, looking more and more depressed, lips tight, eyes strained.

"Everyone at the meeting knew she was there. And I guess most regulars knew Abe usually went and had coffee afterward."

"Oh."

She said, "Three people have been killed, Sonny, and all of them are linked to that inner-child group. And now you tell me the group's actually been to Abe's house."

"So you think the Axeman's someone in the *group*?"

"Do you?"

"Missy! I've got to call Missy!" He shot out of his seat, dumping the puppy with a thunk, but Skip grabbed his wrist. If he got to Missy before she did, she'd lose the element of surprise.

"I'm going to see her right now. I'll have her call you." He sat down again, legs rubbery, not seeming to have much will of his own.

274

Skip was starting to think there was more to this than grogginess; he seemed a very depressed young man. But who wasn't, especially in this bunch? They didn't go to twelve-step programs because they were the picture of emotional health. Still, Sonny looked more like it than most.

He said, "She's going through a rough time—all that incest stuff." He shuddered. "Can you imagine? Your own father! What kind of father would do a thing like that?"

"How was she tonight? When you took her home?"

"A little shaky. Not too good, to tell you the truth. You know why?"

I can guess.

"She was worried about *me*."

Bingo.

"Because of what Di said about her doctor. He's my dad. I was really embarrassed when Di said it. For my dad, you know? But of course nobody but Missy knew who it was. Not even Di. I know *her* last name because—" He stopped, looking confused, but in a moment he brightened. "I saw it the night of the Axeman party. On her mailbox. But nobody knows my name. I never use it in there. Anyway, first I was embarrassed and then I was mad. I knew how it was going to affect Missy. I knew she'd be really worried about me." He leaned down, stroked the dog for comfort. "The girl wasn't raped, was she?"

Skip was so taken aback by the change of subject, she almost asked, "What girl?" "We don't know yet," she said.

"Poor Missy," said Sonny, as if she were the victim.

Missy's living room light was on and so was the porch one, ready for a visitor. Realizing Sonny had called her after all, Skip cursed herself for telling him about the Axeman. But at least it saved endless explanations and the tedious footwork of dodging questions.

Missy did an odd thing. As soon as she saw Skip, she let held-back tears come to her eyes and threw her arms around her, clung to her like a child needing a big sister. "Oh, Skip, I'm so glad you're here. Sonny's coming, but he said you'd want to see me first."

She looked about fifteen in her Lanz summer robe. "I'm so glad to have a friend in the police department."

She was so winning, this girl. Who wouldn't like her? And yet Skip knew that deep down Missy felt no one did, that she worked so hard at being liked to hide her imagined worthlessness. Skip had her problems with her own father, but for now she was just grateful she'd been spared Missy's ordeal.

"Sonny's told you what happened tonight?"

"Yes. And everything else—about the Axeman being someone in the group."

"I didn't say that. . . ."

"But he thought you thought that."

Well, he's right. "We don't have a suspect yet."

"It's so creepy."

"It is. It's horrible to think someone you know might be a murderer. Listen, Missy, I hate to do this, but I have to ask you what you did tonight after you left PJ's."

She shrugged. "Sonny brought me right home. That was all."

"Do you live alone?"

"I live with my aunt, but she left for Thailand this morning. That's why Sonny's so freaked out—because I'm all alone here. Oh, Skip, I'm so worried about him. And of course he's worried about me. But he's working through something really painful. Something he won't talk about."

"Is it something to do with the new puppy?"

She smiled. "Isn't he cute? I got him for him. I thought it might help because he's so sad about this grandfather stuff. It only started coming up the last few days. It's something about his whole family. I think he thinks they blame him for his grandfather's death."

"That's nothing. Knowing Sonny, he probably blames

himself." *The same way he thinks it's his fault Linda Lee got killed because he didn't have coffee with her.*

"Isn't that the truth? That's just what he's like. Maybe that's why he's more like that than most people. Because of his grandfather, I mean."

"I guess most little kids blame themselves when there's a death in the family."

"But Sonny's an extreme case. It's why he decided to become a doctor. He didn't do it because his father and grandfather were doctors. It's because he's still suffering guilt about someone dying that he couldn't save." She turned mournful blue eyes on Skip. "It's so sad, isn't it?"

Skip tried to smile. *Enough of this.* "He's worried about you too, kid."

Afterward, she went back to the office, but Cappello sent her home. Sent herself home as well, calling a task-force meeting at eight: "Last thing I want on my hands is a bunch of ornery cops who've been up all night."

Skip got two hours' sleep, but it was better than nothing.

By eight-thirty, they'd identified everyone at the meeting except two people and eliminated twenty-seven as suspects.

There were fifteen people who hadn't yet been interviewed or who had no alibis, among them Skip's four and the two they hadn't yet identified. All of them were possible suspects.

Of the thirteen who had been identified, four had criminal records, including Di and Alex. They decided to concentrate on these four, assigning full-time surveillance to all of them. Skip got Di.

O'Rourke was assigned to go over the phone list with various witnesses, and then to go over the many lists and diagrams composed over the past few hours by the task force—lists of people who'd been at the meeting, diagrams of the meeting room, each chair bearing the name of its

277

occupant. This way they hoped to identify the last two attendees and verify the others.

Out of the muck and mire had arisen several people who'd known Tom Mabus, one or two who could vaguely remember Linda Lee. And that was about it. Except for two things. One was the niggling feeling that, because of the scarf, this wasn't an Axeman murder after all. Maybe it was a copycat. The other was Cindy Lou's salty assessment of a few people she'd met the night before.

"That Di's a piece of work, man."

"I love it," said Abasolo, "when you throw around those scientific terms."

"She's got to have every man she can get, but my guess is she doesn't give them much in return. She's so far in denial about most things, she sounds like she's crazy half the time, but I don't think so."

"So she couldn't be the Axeman?"

"Sure she could. Good combination of organized and disorganized characteristics. But personally I like Abe, just because he's the biggest creep of all. Don't you love the way everything's always everybody else's fault?"

O'Rourke asked, "What does that have to do with anything?"

"Murderers justify their acts. That's easy to do if everybody else is in the wrong. Now Alex. He's a kind of mirror image of Di. She's got to have men, he's got to have women. He's emotionally about five years old, and anybody here who has kids knows I'm talking *seriously* dangerous. I'm tempted to say his attention span's probably too short to kill three people, but you never know—I once saw the damage after a five-year-old took a whole house apart.

"Sonny's so screwed up he's not even going to figure out how bad it is till he's forty-five or fifty, and by then he'll probably be a drunk. Killers don't usually look quite so nicey-nice, but trust me—there's some real turbulence under that bland facade. Skip's told me about her interview with his

278

brother—he had an early family life consistent with a killer's, but so did nearly all of them.

"Missy, for instance. History of abuse. On the surface she looks like a victim rather than a criminal, but you know how much rage you'd have if you'd been through what she has?"

"Is that fair?" said Cappello. "The average incest survivor isn't a killer."

"The average person who fits any of the profiles may not be a killer. A killer identifies with the aggressor and—oh, hell, who knows what turns them? That's what we *don't* know. Why two people can have parallel experiences and one's a serial murderer, the other's a psychologist."

"What," said O'Rourke, "are you getting at?"

"I'm just making a few observations, that's all. Just noticing that everybody who shared last night looks normal, looks good if you just know them casually, meet them on the street or something. Interview them in the course of an investigation. But every one of 'em's crazy as a bedbug."

"Oh, come on," said Hodges. "I saw 'em too, you know. We all did. They're no crazier than anybody else."

"I didn't say they were."

Twenty-six

SINCE DI LIVED near Skip, she figured she might as well have breakfast at home. And besides, if Steve had stayed, she had some unfinished business there.

He had. He was dressed and making coffee. "Hi, gorgeous. Catch him yet?"

"Don't gorgeous me. You're not just a witness anymore. You're an alibi."

"Whose?" He handed her a full mug.

"Don't pretend you don't even know."

"Well, I could sure take a guess. One of your suspects did happen to say she was really enjoying talking to me and even invited me home for a cup of herb tea. And I did happen to go."

"You didn't mention that last night."

"I just didn't get to it, that's all. I said I walked Di to her car. I didn't say what I did then."

"How long did you stay?"

"Twenty minutes max. I don't even know why I went except for maybe some crazy idea about getting closer to the whole scene. Anyway, it was coltsfoot tea or some damn thing that tasted like poison, and I found I couldn't hack more than fifty or sixty preposterous misstatements to the quarter-hour. I thought I was tough, but forget it. I've got a new respect for you girls in blue.

"I would say 'women in blue,' but you'd say if you've got 'boys in blue,' why not 'girls,' and the whole thing would just get stupid and predictable."

But Steve was warming up to full-tilt rant and couldn't be stopped: "What planet is that woman from? I didn't come all the way here from California just to meet someone dippier than my next-door neighbor, Rainbow Circle Melamed-Gutierrez, who is not, no matter what you're thinking, the unfortunate offspring of two unacquainted burnouts who got it on at Altamont and never saw each other again, but a plump, cheerful fifty-five-year-old with hair three feet out on all sides, talons from acrylic heaven, four inches of make-up, and crystals down to her knees. She's a 'personal effectiveness coach' who never eats anything with eyes and also happens to channel the entity Michael. Do you know what she told me?''

''Rainbow?''

''No, Di. I complimented her driving and she said she was a race-car driver in another life. So I mentioned that if she was, her career must have gone up in flames, so to speak, since she'd have to have died about the time cars were invented in order to have time to get reincarnated and live to whatever age she is now. You know what she said to that?''

''Something about linear time and real time, I bet.''

''You got it. She could be a race-car driver right *now*, as a matter of fact, and probably is. It's just in a parallel universe.'' He shook his head like a wet dog. ''So how long does she say I stayed?''

''She was having so much fun she lost track of time.''

''If she really meant to go out and murder that girl, why didn't she just go do it? She saw Abe staying with Nini, she knew the coast was clear then—why ask me over for tea?''

''How do I know? Maybe coltsfoot tea makes her homicidal. Maybe she only kills when she's sexually frustrated. Cindy Lou's the motive expert, not me.''

''Cindy Lou? The smart woman who came to coffee?''

''I love you. You know that?'' *Okay, I've done it. I've said the L word.*

''Huh? Isn't this a weird time to be getting romantic?''

''You didn't say 'the beautiful woman who came to coffee.' ''

''Oh, is that all. What about the multifaceted Cindy Lou?''

''I said she's the motive expert—she's a psychologist working on the case with us.''

''Hey, come to think of it, something weird happened— Cindy Lou's name just reminded me. I got to Di's house first. I had to wait for fifteen minutes, and when she did show up, she was driving like the proverbial bat. That's how the race-car thing came up. She said Cindy Lou yelled at her and asked directions, and they got to talking and she couldn't get away. I *thought* it sounded kind of thin.''

"Oh, brother. First she strangles a kid and then she makes herself a nice cup of tea."

"A revolting cup of tea."

"Well, we can't rule her out. She's got—"

"She's got what?"

Skip had almost said she had a criminal record, but remembered in time that it was none of Steve's business. "She's got my full attention, I'm afraid. Anyway, we can ask Cindy Lou if that happened."

First she canvassed Di's neighbors, in case there was someone nosy in the building. Sure enough, Rosemary Scariano upstairs had heard Di come home with someone, had heard that person leave a few minutes later (had even taken a peek to see if he was cute), and in another few minutes had heard Di leave. But she'd turned on her TV after that and had no idea when Di came back.

So Di had lied. She's said she hadn't gone out after she got back from PJ's.

Skip wondered how the killer had gotten in. It would have been easier for a woman. Much easier. What young girl would open the door to a man she didn't know? But how about if a pretty woman showed up and said, "I'm Abe's friend Wanda Jo and he's right behind me in his car''? Who wouldn't let her in?

Miraculously, there was a bar across the street from Di's apartment. Not that there weren't bars on every corner, but this one, in view of the stifling weather, had its door flung open so that a person inside could sit at a comfortable table nursing a Diet Coke and stare at Di's doorway till closing time. Which in New Orleans was never.

Di apparently had a rented parking space at the hotel next door to her building. She had to go there and wait for the attendant to bring her car, which would give Skip plenty of time to get hers. She came out shortly before noon and went to the Perrier Club. Then she had lunch alone, went shopping for T-shirts, and drove to Mercy Hospital.

Skip consulted her twelve-step schedules and noted there was a meeting there, which meant Di wouldn't be out for a good hour. She phoned Cindy Lou.

"Di told Steve she was late getting home last night because you asked for directions."

"Di lied," said Cindy Lou.

Di lied and Di was late. Possibly just late enough.

When the meeting was over Di went home, stayed there about half an hour, and came out wearing white pants and the peacock-blue T-shirt she'd just bought. She had on canvas shoes that matched the T-shirt. Dressed for a casual dinner perhaps, maybe even a date.

Di couldn't understand why she hadn't heard from him; why he hadn't shown up, hadn't answered his phone. She couldn't stand it. She had to see him, make sure he was all right, that they were all right. If Missy was there, so be it.

In answer to her ring, he came out on his balcony. "Di! What's up?"

"Can I come in?"

"Sure." Shrugging. Not overjoyed.

She had been to his place only once before, and was taken aback once again at how spartan it was. Again she remembered similar apartments from her own children's student days and felt momentarily disoriented. But he's not a *student* student, she told herself. He's a medical student.

Sonny answered his door wearing pants with the belt unbuckled and a half-buttoned white Oxford cloth shirt. "What is it, Di?"

He really didn't know, he'd completely forgotten.

He stood aside for her, closed the door when she stepped in, and turned immediately on his heel, buckling his belt as

283

he went, heading back to the bedroom, his new puppy at his heels. She stared after him a moment, then decided he meant her to heel as well.

He was putting on a tie.

"Isn't it hot for that?"

He shrugged.

"You must be going someplace special."

"Dinner with my parents."

"I just wanted to make sure you're all right. I mean, you're usually so reliable. It's so unusual for you to say you'll do something you don't."

He wasn't himself at all, the sunny Sonny she knew, who loved to be with her, whom she inspired; she knew it. He was cold, rejecting, seemed to want her to leave. But his eye lit on something on his dresser, a piece of paper, and his face cleared like the sky after a storm. "Di, remember when you thought I was a poet? Well, I'm doing it. I'm writing a poem."

"Sonny, did you remember we had a date last night?"

"Last night was the inner-child meeting."

"You were going to come over afterward."

He started, jumped as if icy fingers had touched him or she had shouted, "Boo!"

"Don't you know why I didn't come, Di? Couldn't you guess?"

Sure. You forgot.

"I had to take care of Missy! Didn't you see the way she was at that meeting? Do you think I could just leave her off at home?" He turned to face her, his face red, his voice furious.

"But you came back."

"What?"

"You came back to PJ's after you dropped her off."

"Well, I went right back when I didn't find her keys."

Had she had some kind of giant failure of compassion? Missy had seemed okay at PJ's.

284

"Sonny, I'm sorry," she said. "I didn't realize."

"And then I came home and worked on the poem. I'd think you'd be glad about that. It was your idea."

His face was still red, his voice still angry. He couldn't seem to shake whatever was bothering him.

Idly, she picked up the piece of paper. The poem was titled "The Physician."

> Smooth cuts the knife
> and a life is ruined. He is at the end
> of his path:
> His path of destruction.
> The metaphor is complete now;
> He has a lump he can palpate,
> a scar he can fondle.
> The healer as evil twin:
> Nelag, Galen backward.
> He lives on the edge, on the precipice,
> (though some would say on the cutting edge
> and perhaps he would say it himself).
> But she is destroyed.
> So smooth cuts the knife.

Di said, "It's about me!"

"No it's not. Look at the title."

"Well, it's still about me."

"Di, do you know who I am?"

Was he losing his marbles? What was she supposed to say to that? "You don't seem yourself, that's for sure."

"You know, don't you?"

She'd never seen him like this, his beautiful, bland face distorted with anger and pain.

Pain.

She hadn't seen that before, but suddenly she knew it had always been there, only slightly below the surface. It was there if you looked hard enough, and she never had; probably nobody ever did. She was sorry she'd seen it.

She hated him like this, wanted the old Sonny back. She tried for levity: "You look like the Axeman right now."

She came closer to him, dared, despite the psychic shield around him, to reach out and stroke his hair. Childlike frustration, utter unbelieving misery replaced his anger. "What are you trying to do to me?"

What was wrong with this woman? It was getting to be like *Play Misty for Me*, except that in the movie, the crazy woman had been in love.

How dare she come to his house? And why? Did she know who he was? Maybe she was playing out some kind of drama with him, watching him dangle.

I could ask her.

But he knew he wouldn't. Because maybe she didn't know, and if she didn't, he didn't want her to find out. He hadn't yet gotten over the shock of hearing his father described as a butcher, wouldn't have given it the slightest credence if he hadn't seen her body himself.

It was such an odd turn of fate, his meeting her, making love to her, and then her saying all that. Publicly. So that he would be sure to hear it, to feel the knife twisting.

It was too odd. Had she somehow found out his last name, had Missy told it perhaps? Had he slipped up, phoning about one of those group parties? "This is Sonny Gerard and I'd love to come on Saturday." Forgetting he meant to be anonymous.

At first he had taken the anonymity so seriously simply because he was embarrassed. Embarrassed to be going to some stupid meeting where adults played with teddy bears. Embarrassed to be pushed around by his girlfriend. Embarrassed that he didn't have the balls to say no. And really, really deeply embarrassed that he actually liked the meetings, felt purged when he'd been to one, the way church was supposed to make you feel.

That was the original reason he'd so guarded his identity. But now he saw how vulnerable he was. And he still didn't know what had happened. Had she singled him out to toy with as some sort of bizarre revenge on his father, or had the whole thing been coincidental? And if it was a revenge, was this all? Or was there more?

He was afraid of her. She looked like some mythical beast to him now, half snake and half woman, some creature who came in the night to steal splinters of his soul. Look at her, reading his poem. "It's about me!"

Could she possibly be so narcissistic?

Could and was. The universe centered around her.

The laugh he had thought so charming seemed now a cackle, the frivolous wrongheadedness that had so delighted him now seemed her attempt to twist the laws of nature to Di's Law.

Nothing about her behavior made sense. What was she doing here? Either she was evil and she was continuing her plan to hurt him because his father had hurt her, or she was forming an obsession with him like the woman in the movie. But he was still nagged by the fundamental difference—the woman in the movie believed she was in love. With Di it was nothing like that.

If she formed an obsession with a man, it would be no different from one she might form with a red fox coat or a ruby bracelet—when she saw something she wanted, she was ruthless. He knew that. When she seduced him, she cared nothing for Missy, didn't even pretend, just took what she wanted. He had a feeling there'd be trouble if it was withheld from her.

There was already trouble. She was right here in his house, uninvited, and saying he'd stood her up.

But he hadn't stood her up. He had absolutely no recollection of making a date with her for last night.

Perhaps she was crazy. Maybe it was just that simple.

He heard his own voice ask, "What are you trying to do to me?"

She said, "Sonny? Sonny, are you all right?"

Now what? What did she mean, was he all right? Was this some kind of *Gaslight* scheme?

The longer she stayed, the more confused he got; therefore there could be but one solution. He had to get rid of her.

He used a line he had learned from Missy, who had gotten it from her therapist: "This isn't a good time." He turned away from her and begin tying his tie, feeling her presence, her body heat, more than seeing what she was doing. It was like staring someone down, only the object was the opposite—to avoid eye contact. She stayed awhile, and then she left.

Missy arrived almost immediately. Thinking she might have seen Di leaving, he told her Di had been there.

"What did she want?"

"Me. I think."

"What! She's probably over forty!"

More likely over fifty. "Maybe it wasn't that," he said. "She was acting weird. Like she was here to help me with something. Like there was something wrong with me."

"She says she used to be a shrink, you know."

"Does she?"

"Should we tell Skip about her? Is she acting that weird?"

"I don't know." He didn't know if she'd really been out of line or if his growing revulsion for her only made it seem so.

Missy had often been to his parents' house, and though she knew perfectly well what to expect, he noticed she had deliberately dressed down. She was wearing linen pants, a silk T-shirt, and sandals. Passable, but definitely not standing on ceremony. She thought it was nuts to put on a coat and tie to go to dinner at your parents' house on a Friday night, and had said so. Sonny did it because it was his ritual. Because he tried to anticipate what anyone could possibly find wrong with him and plug up all the holes before they started burrowing in them; be better than the best little boy in the world. He wouldn't have said it to Missy, but the formal clothes felt like armor to him.

His dad met them in shirtsleeves and tie, as if he'd just come home from work and taken off his coat. He was in his mid-fifties, prematurely gray, and might have been handsome if not for the odd redness of his face and the way his brows knit; there were deep creases at the bridge of his nose, as if he'd worn them there, frowning. "Look at this girl, she's gorgeous." He kissed Missy on the mouth.

Sonny could see her struggling not to wince. She hated to be addressed in the third person.

His dad shook hands with Sonny, ushered them in, gave them drinks. His mother was in the kitchen.

The house was on St. Charles Avenue, a mansion; a showplace. The furnishings had been lovingly selected over the years by his mother and a decorator she seemed to employ practically full-time. Missy had actually gasped the first time she saw the Chinese rug in the living room.

His dad had made money and so had his dad's dad; every girl at McGehee's and Country Day who didn't like her nose had had it snipped by one of the Gerards; their mothers had been tucked and lifted as well. It all added up, and the Gerards liked to spend their money. But his mother still did her own cooking. She stewed and sweated over it too—they probably wouldn't see her for ten or fifteen minutes.

Sonny was melancholy, thinking of the interval, but didn't quite know why. His dad said, "How's classes?"

"Great. Great." His armpits were getting clammy.

"Haven't seen you in church lately."

"Well, I haven't had that much time."

His father raised an eyebrow. "Oh?"

"Studying."

289

No answer. The expression on his face said, "In bed with your little girlfriend."

Missy said, "Sonny and I . . ."

Oh no. He knew what she was going to say. His dad, of course, had seated her near him, so that Sonny didn't have her close for comfort—and for cueing. He couldn't squeeze her hand, make her shut up before it was too late.

"We've been exploring a different spiritual path."

"Oh?" Again the raised eyebrow. "Y'all Buddhists or something?"

Her laugh was a little too high-pitched; nervous. "Nothing like that. It's real mainstream. It's kind of a philosophy that talks about 'God as we understand him.' That's very nice, don't you think? All faiths are welcome."

She was so sweet, so naive; wanting so much to help him, rescue him. She had no idea how much trouble she was making.

His mother came in with stuffed mushrooms, and in the ensuing greetings he hoped it would all be forgotten. She was a short woman who'd gotten slightly dumpy. She hadn't had a facelift, hadn't even had her eyes or chin done, and wore her hair in a short style that emphasized the plumpness of her face. Sonny wondered why she'd eschewed the requisite nips and tucks, had even asked her. She'd said she liked herself the way the good Lord had made her.

"Jere, Missy here tells me she's converted Sonny to a new religion."

"Now, Dad, that wasn't exactly what she said."

His mother settled herself on the sofa next to him. "Sonny, you've always been such a strong Christian."

Sonny's tie felt suddenly tight. "Well, I still am, Mama. No fear about that."

His dad said again, "Haven't seen you in church lately. Y'all been going to this other church?"

"It's not a church, Dad."

"I thought you said you were still a Christian."

Missy said, "I think you can be on a spiritual path without going to a church, don't you?"

"Well, I thought you *were* going somewhere."

"Tell you what. I'll come to church this Sunday."

"Well, I hope you'll do that." His dad sounded angry, but Sonny couldn't figure out why. It had always been that way. When he was a kid, he'd say, "Daddy, why are you mad at me?" and his dad would say he wasn't, would sometimes shout it. But he seemed mad all the time.

I wonder why? He's got everything he ever wanted. What on earth could be bothering him?

His father got up and brought a new coaster for Missy's drink, carefully wiping the one he took away. She had drunk more slowly than the others and the glass had sweated.

In years past, his mother would have said, "Bull, why are you doing that? There's no way the moisture could possibly touch the table. That's the point of a coaster."

He never answered and she no longer asked. Everyone accepted his dad's little habits, said that's what made him such a good doctor—his perfectionism.

Seeing him take the coaster gave Sonny a feeling like a stab in his side. If his dad was such a perfectionist, how had he managed to mess Di up?

Thinks he's God. If you asked him, he'd say it was er fault. Weak abdominal wall.

He hated thinking that, hated the way it came unbidden to his consciousness. He tried not to think about what made his dad tick, tried to just accept him as he was, laugh at the little compulsions, ignore his superiority; but this thing with Di had him going. Whatever people said about Bull Gerard, they didn't say he was incompetent.

They're too scared of him.

They went in to dinner, to the shrimp remoulade his mother had made. Sonny complimented her lavishly.

"Shrimp are a little overdone," said Bull.

Sonny felt light pressure on his thigh—Missy being supportive, saying, "He's difficult, but not impossible. You'll get through it. I'm here."

It didn't help, it made things worse. He always felt so incompetent around his dad. Kind of melancholy and alone, the way he'd felt when he'd been sent to his room for some transgression or other. There was something under the melancholy, something else, but he didn't know what to call it. It made him not want to be touched, made him reject his mother when she came to comfort him then, made him now want to slap Missy's hand away.

Roast duck followed the shrimp. By now his father had had two Scotches and a couple of glasses of wine. Sometimes a few drinks mellowed him out.

"January's a quiet month," he said. "Be a good time to get married."

Missy froze; dismay filled his mother's eyes, and then compassion. She trained them on Sonny, silently telling him she was sorry, there was nothing she could do.

"Gee, Dad, I don't think so. Missy and I struck a deal, you know—we're not getting married till I get out of med school."

"No sense paying for two apartments when you could live in one."

Missy said, "Oh, no problem, Dr. Gerard. I live with my aunt, rent-free, in a gorgeous apartment."

"I'm gonna buy y'all a little house."

"Dad, I don't think we're quite ready to get married; to tell you the truth, I've got my hands full with medical school."

"I got married before medical school. And January's a good month. Christmas is over, Carnival's just starting."

Sonny made a great show of chewing. "Great duck, Mama."

"It's about time you grew up, accepted the responsibilities of a man. Isn't that right, Missy?"

Missy was tight-lipped, white. Sonny realized this was

292

what the evening was about. His dad had somehow gotten it into his head to marry him off this January and had invited him over to announce it.

The same way he'd announced which schools Sonny would be attending and what subjects he'd take.

Missy said, "I don't think I'm ready, Dr. Gerard. I don't have enough recovery yet."

"Sonny didn't tell me you'd been ill. Why didn't you come to me?"

"Listen, Dad, neither one of us wants to get married this January."

"What's this about Missy being sick?"

"I didn't mean I'm sick. I meant recovery from my co-dependency."

"Codependency? Isn't that something to do with being married to an alcoholic? I didn't think you'd been married, girl."

For almost the first time the whole evening, Sonny's mother spoke up. "You don't have to be married to be codependent. You don't even have to be around an alcoholic." To Missy she said, "Are you in Al-Anon, Missy? I've never seen you there."

"I don't want to get into that!" Bull Gerard's customary ruddy glow had deepened to a florid mask, his brows had come together in the Jehovah-like fury Sonny recognized from drawings in Bible story books.

All he needs is a long white beard.

Bull turned placatingly to Missy. "Girl, tell me what I'm going to do. I got one son who won't do a damn thing anybody tells him, can't even make an honest living, got the hardest goddamn red head anybody's ever seen on a human being. I got another that just can't accept responsibility. You know, Sonny's mother and I were delighted he picked you, couldn't have been more delighted. You're good for him, keep him on the straight and narrow. Sobered you right up, didn't she, Sonny boy?"

Missy was clearly puzzled. "He never seemed very—"

"Oh, he sowed a few wild oats. Ran us a merry chase all through high school. Didn't you, Sonny?"

"If you say so, Dad." *There was the time I got a B in trig.*

"You know what your problem is, Sonny? I really don't think you have much self-esteem. Missy, did Sonny ever tell you about his grandfather? Sonny was only a kid, didn't mean to do anything wrong. But you know, he's never been the same since?" Bull took a long swallow of his wine. "You've got to quit blaming yourself, Sonny. It's over and done now." He spread his arms, the pictures of expansiveness. " 'Course nothing will ever bring my daddy back, but the Lord forgives you. You've got to forgive yourself, go on with your life."

Sonny felt a steel band closing around his middle, knew he wasn't going to be able to manage dessert.

Missy massaged her forehead.

Bull said, "What is it, honey?"

"It's nothing. I get these migraines now and then."

"Shouldn't be drinking wine. You got a good neurologist?"

She smiled. "I have all the right stuff. I just forgot my pills."

"We'll give you some coffee. That'll knock it out."

She shook her head. "I think it's too late for that. It's already too far gone."

"I guess we'd better go." Sonny did his best to try to sound reluctant. He didn't think he'd ever loved her so much.

Safe in the car, he hugged her to him, laughing to release the tension. "Maybe I will marry you in January."

"Let's go somewhere and get praline parfaits."

"That's probably what Mama was going to serve for dessert."

"You're crazy if you think I'm going back in there. I may not marry into this family at all." She pulled her head away from his neck. Her eyes were very round. "Sonny! Maybe

294

that's what he's trying to do. Turn me off so badly I'll dump you.''

Sonny started the car, didn't answer.

She brushed his one lock of hair back. "Do you think he hates you that much?"

"I don't think he hates me at all. Why do you say that?"

"He's all over you all the time. He can't leave you alone."

"I get off easy. You should see him with Robbie."

"He probably hates him too. There's so much hate in that man!"

Sonny shrugged. "I don't really think so. He's just old-fashioned, I guess. He does the best he can, like anybody else.''

Twenty-seven

DI CERTAINLY HADN'T been exaggerating that time at the Napoleon House when she'd told Skip she went to three meetings a day. She was "healing herself," if Skip remembered correctly; recovering from "dis-ease." She'd gone straight from Sonny's to an Al-Anon meeting.

It was a popular gathering. Alex was also there, along with Adam Abasolo—a curious way, to Skip's mind, of tailing someone, but Abasolo was so cocky it probably wouldn't occur to him he couldn't pull it off. Skip's mother was there too.

So Elizabeth went to Al-Anon as well as OA. This was a whole other side of her. She might have been going to OA just to lose weight, but you didn't go to Al-Anon unless you were in pain. *Or else wanted to make new friends.*

But somehow it was nearly impossible to see her mother as an adulteress. Not because Skip had illusions, simply because Elizabeth didn't seem to have much sexual energy. She could have been the prototype for the jokes about women who won't make love because they've just had their hair done.

Still, it did give Skip a turn to see her walking out with Alex. Was he going to whisk her someplace on his hog? She had to laugh at the idea.

Her other door opened.

"Langdon! Made you." Abasolo slipped in beside her, scrunched down beside her.

"Hi, Adam. Aren't you afraid you'll lose your guy?"

"Naah. This is good cover for me. He's waiting for your lady."

"Glad to be of service, but you've got to pay for it. What went on at the meeting?"

"Oh, nothing much. The subject was rage. Alex said he gets so mad at someone in his life he wants to kill."

"Did he say he just needed to put that out there?"

"Said his higher power ordered him to strangle people."

"Right. How about Di?"

"Oh, Di. Model of sanity. She *never* has any problem with rage. Talked about how she used to help people control it when she was a therapist."

"An inspiration to all of us."

"Here they come. Did you hear about the new letter?"

"What new letter?"

"Gotta run."

Elizabeth had gone and Di had caught up. She and Alex stood and chatted a few minutes; then he took her to her car. Skip followed her home and stayed till the lights went out.

She couldn't wait to get home and call Cappello.

"What's this about a letter?"

296

"Postcard—this time to us, not the press. Axeman likes to keep in touch."

"Mailed after he killed Jerilyn?"

"Had to be, I guess. It was delivered today."

"I wonder if he mailed it before—if he knew he was going to kill her."

"Well, here's what it says. 'Esteemed Mortal—Couldn't sleep, so I thought I'd drop you a note. Don't be put off by the scarf. It was me, all right. By the way, the scarlet *A* was Fiesta.' "

"Fiesta?"

"Jerilyn's lipstick color. Had to be after he did her, unless he knew her well enough to know her lipstick color."

"I don't even know my own lipstick color."

"Me neither. I guess he looked at it so he could write the note."

"Or planted it."

"Why bother?"

"I don't know. What else about the postcard? Was it typed?"

"Yep. Same typewriter as before. Ordinary card you could get anywhere. No prints."

She thought of calling Steve, but it was nearly midnight. She lit some incense and a candle, took them in the bathroom and soaked for a while in the soft light. Baths weren't usually her style—she was too tall for the tub—but she was too tired to stand up in the shower.

Di had been surprised when Alex asked for her help. After what he said at the Coda group on Thursday, she'd imagined he was still angry, taking rejection like a petulant child. But when she thought about it, his attention span was so short he couldn't even sustain anger, much less the gentler emotions. He claimed to be a writer but she doubted seriously if he'd ever written anything—how on earth would he keep his mind on it long enough to finish?

297

He was probably just one of those people who bumbled through life going from one crummy little job to another, living off their relatives when things got tough. Still, somewhere or other he'd gotten together enough money to buy a fancy motorcycle. For the first time it occurred to her to wonder how.

He'd asked her to meet him at his father's house in Lakeview. So where did Alex live, she wondered? Who the hell was he? She wondered if what she was doing was wise, and immediately shook off the notion.

I'm not like that. I'm going to do what life offers and not be afraid.

Alex had seemed shaken the night before. In the meeting, when he talked about his rage, he had sounded coldly furious, yet conjured for Di an instant vision of a different Alex, red-faced and bulge-veined, near-apoplectic, cold only in the recollection.

Afterward, he had seemed very different indeed. Almost frightened. He had spoken to her with humility, a new deference: "Why didn't you tell me you were a therapist?"

"I guess it never seemed important."

"Di, I've got a problem. Have you ever worked with old people?"

"Sure."

"Well, I never have."

"I beg your pardon?"

"I mean, I haven't read much about them. What do you know about Alzheimer's?"

"A little."

"Could you recognize it?"

"Probably. Why?"

"My dad's started to worry me. I used to think he was just an old poot. But I swear to God he's getting worse." She could have sworn she saw worry in his face, but it was only a flicker and might have been her imagination. If Alex had emotions, he hid them well.

He said, "Could you—I don't know—look at him or something?"

"Well, I don't have an office or anything. I'm only practicing a little right now."

"Come to lunch tomorrow. At his house."

"His house? Why not yours?"

"I've been staying there. I'm too worried to leave him alone."

"Alex, if it's that bad, you already know the answer."

He took her hand as if he needed something to hold on to. "Di, please. I really need another opinion."

"Someone's already seen him?"

"I mean another besides mine, which doesn't count."

He had told her he'd say she was his girlfriend, which was part of the reason she'd agreed to do it. It would be fun to see Alex pretend to act solicitous. Aside from that, of course, she was glad to help. She'd seen plenty of Alzheimer's—ought to damn well be able to recognize it.

The old coot who answered the door smelled like he'd already had a beer or two, but not necessarily a bath. "You the girlfriend?"

She gave him her hand. "I'm Di."

"Lamar. Hot, idn't it?"

"Unseasonably."

"They gotta get those rocks back on the moon."

She heard Alex's voice: "Okay, Dad, it's all yours."

He appeared behind his father, in jeans as usual, hair still wet from the shower.

"Too late, son. She's already here."

"Hi, Di." To his father, "I'll entertain her till you're ready."

"Ready now. If she don't take me like I am right now, she ain't gonna take me."

"Well, I wouldn't take you. Not as far as the corner grocery store."

Di was tired of standing out in the heat. "Maybe I'd better leave and come back."

"Elec, you lamebrain. See what you're doing?" He gestured Di into the house. "Come on, come on, come on, come on."

The house was dark and mildewy. The furniture looked ancient; the place probably hadn't been cleaned all summer. A putrid smell from the kitchen said nobody'd taken out the garbage lately.

"I thought we'd eat in the backyard," Alex said.

"You crazy, boy?" He kicked his son in the shin. "It's a hundred degrees out there."

"Ow." Alex held his leg and hopped around the room. "What the hell do you think you're doing, you old bastard?"

"Who you talking to like that?"

Di resisted the urge to hold her ears.

Skip, parked just down the block, wondered if they always yelled at each other, these two, routinely shattered the quiet of this most domestic of streets.

A man who was setting his sprinkler looked toward the Bignell house in surprise. As soon as he'd gone back inside, Skip got out and slipped to the side of the house. The windows were closed for the air conditioning, but she could see in. The three of them were standing in the living room, Di looking a little awkward, the other two conscious of nothing but each other, faces full of fury, bodies wary, poised against attack.

"You talking to your dad? You got the fuckin' nerve to talk to your dad like that?"

Di said, "Fellows, don't you think—"

"Who the hell do you think you are, toots?"

Di smiled. "Now, Lamar, I'm just—"

"Who the fuck are you?"

She was suddenly very solicitous, voice very phony,

pseudo-soothing. "I'm Di, Lamar. Alex's girlfriend. Remember now?"

"Why the fuck would I forget whose goddamn girlfriend you are. *I* wouldn't want you. No way would I take you whether you was lamebrain's pick of the week or not. You're skinny and you haven't got a brain in your head. Why the fuck would I want you?"

"Language, Dad. This is Lakeview."

"Language, my ass!" A look passed between Di and Alex. Skip didn't know what to call it exactly, but thought it wasn't conspiratorial. There was something excited about it. "I don't give a shit what kind of fucking language I use. I don't give a fuck!"

He picked up a pillow from the sofa and threw it at Alex. His son started toward him, but Lamar was gone. Out the door. Beating it down the street, hollering, "Fuuuuuuck! Does everybody hear me? Fuck you, you shitheads!"

Skip fell into step behind him. "Hey, Lamar, whereyat?"

He stopped and turned around. "Hey, Margaret. Margaret, zat you? What you doin' here, you pretty little thing?"

"Came to see Alex, but I saw you first."

"No, I saw you first, before lamebrain did, so I get to flirt with you." He seemed to have forgotten his mission. "Now you come on in and I'll fix you some iced coffee or somethin'. Sho' is hot out here, ain't it?"

"Sure is," said Skip. "Wonder why that is?"

"We gotta get those rocks back on the moon."

She led Lamar up the walk to his house, walking past Alex and Di, who had started to give chase, but stopped when they saw Skip. Following Lamar's lead, she ignored them, giving him her full attention and wondering why he'd taken a fancy to her.

But there were more important things to figure out—like what she was going to tell Alex she was doing here, and how to extricate herself in time to keep Di in sight.

As she chatted aimlessly with Lamar, an idea came to her: a plan that made losing Di for a bit worthwhile.

"You know what?" said Lamar. "You remind me of my ex-wife."

Di and Alex stared speechless after Skip and Lamar.

Finally Di said, "What's she doing here?"

"Who cares? What did she do to him? Hit him with a nice stick?"

"Nightstick?"

"Forget it. Listen, what do you think?"

"I think your dad's a case and a half."

"Yeah, well, so do the neighbors. The question is, is he demented or just mean as hell?"

"Does he get depressed?"

"Depressed! How would I know? Think the old fart's going to come complaining to me?"

She shook her head in bewilderment. "He's really a case."

"Well, you're a lot of help."

"I'm sorry, Alex, I can't do miracles. Why don't you take him to see somebody?"

"I brought you to see him."

She started to get into her car. "Is he eating a lot of animal fat?"

"Animal fat!"

"Maybe you should try him on raw vegetables."

When Alex joined them, Lamar and Skip were sipping iced coffee at the yellow vinyl table, oblivious of the pernicious garbage smell.

" 'Bout time, lamebrain. I gotta clean up. Don't know what Margaret'll think of me." To Skip he said, "Kid hogs the bathroom, what you gonna do?"

And he left, docile as a doe.

"Why does he like you so much?"

"Probably thinks I'm going to arrest you. What was Di doing here, anyway?"

"None of your business. What are you doing here?"

"Well, uh . . . it's not exactly police business. I mean, you still have the right to remain silent and everything, but you could also yell at me, I guess. It's my mom."

"Your mom?"

"Yeah. Her name's Elizabeth and she's a compulsive overeater. She's in Al-Anon too."

"Elizabeth! Well, well, well. I feel you and I are getting to know each other better and better." He didn't sit, but hovered over her.

"You know her?"

"Oh, yes." He said it as if he'd been sleeping with her—at the very least fending her off. He'd probably make his own mother sound like a slut.

"Well, she certainly knows you. She was a fan of yours before I was."

"Oh, shit."

"Don't worry, she won't blow your cover. She takes anonymity very seriously—as you might imagine, considering what a social climber she is. But maybe you don't know about that."

"It figures."

"Anyway, she doesn't know I know you, of course. And she was bragging about how she'd met you through the program—in fact had seen you around for a while and then finally connected your face with the one on your book jacket. Now I'm getting to the embarrassing part."

"Will I like it?"

"Well, you'll like seeing me squirm, anyway. See, she's the original woman who has everything and her birthday's coming up."

"You want me to sign a book? That's all this is about?"

"Uh . . . not exactly. She's already got all your books. I was hoping you might sell me some silly memento."

"A torn T-shirt or something? I'm flattered, but I'm not Mick Jagger. I don't exactly have a stash of souvenirs for fans. What did you have in mind?"

Skip was so genuinely embarrassed by what she was doing that she felt herself flush. So much the better. No pain, no gain. "I don't know. I thought maybe an old manuscript page or something. Maybe you could write a note on it."

"You'd pay *money* for that?"

"Sure."

"I don't know what kind of jerk you think I am. . . ."

"And you don't want to."

"For God's sake, I'll give you a whole chapter. Whatever you want."

"Great."

"Something from *Fake It Till You Make It*?"

"Actually, she likes the earlier books better, if it's not too much trouble."

"Big deal. None of them are trouble. They're all on the hard disk."

He left her alone while he went to print something out, and came back with a sheaf of still-untorn computer pages. "How about this one, on 'Unconditional Love'? That ought to get her, huh? Oh, brother: I was the turd of turds when I wrote this."

"Don't be so hard on yourself."

"Do you think my father has Alzheimer's?"

"No." But she considered. "I mean, how would I know? You're the psychologist."

"Yeah, but I'm his son."

He chatted her up a little more, wrote a sweet note on the chapter, and saw her out with a pat on the shoulder. *Funny what a little flattery'll do for a person's personality.*

It was gratifying to watch Alex behave like a normal human being for a change, but she hadn't accomplished her mission. She still didn't know whether he owned a manual typewriter.

Twenty-eight

SINCE THERE WAS no way to tell from the outside whether Di was in, she phoned. When the machine answered, she was annoyed with herself, felt at loose ends. And so when she saw someone else going into Di's building, she simply slipped in behind, saying, 'Hi,' as if she belonged. Not for any special reason, simply for lack of anything else to do. And that was why, she told herself, she happened to try the door. Yet when it opened she panicked.

Oh, well. If Di was home, she could make up some excuse.

"Di?" she called.

No answer. Oh, well again. A quick look and who would know?

Skip, this is breaking and entering.

Not really. We're friends. I didn't find her home and came in to leave her a note.

Liar.

Well, the door was ajar. I had a weird feeling—had to look in and make sure everything was okay.

No matter what games she played with herself, she couldn't find a way to justify what she was doing.

Neither could she stop herself.

But she did leave the door ajar, thinking she'd use the last explanation if it should prove necessary. And with her first step in the door her attention was so riveted she couldn't have left if her conscience had attacked her with a cattle prod. Thrown casually on the back of the sofa, as if it had annoyed the wearer, prompting hasty removal, was a scarf almost identical to the one that had killed Jerilyn Jordan. It was a cheap rectangle of Indian cotton, a long neck scarf fringed on the ends. Like the one around Jerilyn's neck, it was striped, but in shades of taupe and aqua rather than fuchsia and rose. It was the sort of inexpensive accessory women sometimes bought two or three of, in different colors. As soon as Skip saw it, she realized she'd seen it earlier—Di had been wearing it as a belt.

Skip took a quick survey of the living room, and one other thing caught her attention. There was a famous collection of Louisiana stories, some of them folktales, some historical. It was the most accessible source of information about the original Axeman. Funny she hadn't noticed it before, when she'd perused Di's books for the sort a hypnotherapist would have. Had Di had it in her bedroom, copying the Axeman's give-me-jazz letter?

Since the light was on in the bathroom, she looked there next. On the counter were the usual perfumes and toiletries and some other things, apparently just pulled from one of the vanity drawers—hair color and discolored vinyl gloves, used at least once before in the rejuvenation ritual. Gloves like those the Axeman probably used.

Putting them on to avoid leaving prints of her own, Skip opened the drawers and found more gloves, a whole box of them. She took a clean pair and replaced the used ones.

Di's bed was made, her bedroom in perfect order except for the outfit she'd worn that morning, which had been tossed on a chair. An armoire held clothes, but there was also a closet. Skip looked first through an antique bureau, finding a drawer containing a pile of scarves, at least two being different-colored twins of the two she'd already seen.

Jesus, she thought, *if I could find a typewriter, I could get a warrant.*

And in the bottom of the closet was a Smith-Corona portable, thirty years old if it was a day. Skip's heart threatened to crash through her sternum in a percussive frenzy, fall out on the floor, and hop around the room. She covered her chest with her hand to quiet it, like some sixth-grader pledging allegiance.

Did she dare to type something out, something to compare with the Axeman's notes?

No. That was inviting permanent nerve damage. And anyway, she heard someone on the stairs now. Pulling off the gloves, she called, "Di? Oh, Di? Di, are you home?"

She had safely reached the living room and was standing tentatively like a person who'd just arrived by the time Di came in.

She put a hand to her throat. "Oh, Di. There you are. I saw your door open and I got worried."

Di had changed to shorts and a worn white T-shirt with a faded French Quarter scene on it, obviously a knockabout rather than formal one. She had a white paper bag in her hand. "My door was open? But I remember locking it."

Skip shrugged. "It was like this. Shall we look to make sure no one's here?"

Soberly, Di nodded. They looked in the closet, in the armoire, even under the bed, Skip doing the work, Di hovering nervously. Skip said, "Do you have jewelry? Why don't we check it?"

Di opened a bureau drawer, pulled out a box, pronounced everything safe. "I guess I forgot to lock up. I was going to color my hair, but I thought I didn't have enough stuff for more than a touch-up." She opened her paper bag, pulled out hair color and conditioner. "I guess I got in too big a hurry."

"Are you sure? Who else has a key?"

"No one. Not even a neighbor."

"Let's look at the lock."

There were no scratches, no signs of forcing. The door

had two locks—an ordinary button one and a deadbolt. Without the deadbolt, a credit card could have done the honors.

"Think back," said Skip. "Did you put the bolt on?"

"I thought I did. But I was starving—Alex was supposed to feed me, but he didn't, the rat. And I was pissed because I had to go out to the drugstore. So I *guess* I could have forgotten. But I think I'd at least have remembered to close the door."

There were windows open too—in almost every room. Someone could have come in that way and left through the door. But maybe they hadn't. And Skip knew something Di didn't—that the door hadn't actually been open.

She said, "I guess you're okay, then. I'll get out of your hair. I just felt bad about interrupting your visit with Alex and I wanted to apologize."

"Oh, no problem. I was done there, anyway. Listen, I'm still starving. Want a cheese-and-tomato sandwich? I usually don't eat cheese, but every now and then I've got to have protein or I feel like I'll faint."

Skip hadn't eaten either, and she was so glad not to be offered a scrumptious plate of celery and carrot sticks, she accepted instantly. As Di sliced seven-grain bread, lite cheddar (no salt, no fat), and tomatoes, Skip set the table and poured iced tea.

"I'm glad you came over," said her hostess. "You know, I always knew there was something about you you weren't telling. I wouldn't have picked you as a detective, exactly, but maybe as a writer or something like that. I never believed that civil-service stuff."

"But I do have a civil-service job."

Di set down the sandwiches, motioned for Skip to sit. "Only technically. There was something special about you, something exotic. I always saw it." She chewed. "How's the case coming?"

Skip nearly choked.

"You know what you should be doing? I have a feeling

308

you should be looking in the inner-child group. Everybody in there knew that poor girl was alone at Abe's last night. And Tom Mabus came now and then. There's a connection there—do you see it?''

''Yes. Now that you mention it, I think I do. But you know, I'm really starting to feel close to those people. It's hard to see anyone in there as a killer.''

''Well, you just have to be objective about it. Have you noticed how angry Alex can get?''

''Do you think he did it?''

''Alex? He's a narcissist, but I don't see him killing. Only in the heat of passion. Not like this.''

''How do you know these murders weren't crimes of passion?''

''I just know.''

''How?''

''It just doesn't feel that way to me. They're premeditated.''

''What do you think the motive is?''

''You really want to know?''

''Sure.''

''You know I'm a therapist. I'm just not practicing now.''

''I thought you were a hypnotherapist.''

''Oh, well, I am, but you have to be a therapist first; then you learn hypnosis. It's a specialty, not like being a paralegal or something.''

''I see.''

''Well, speaking as a therapist, I think he's showing off. I think he's just trying to get attention.''

''Um. Three people dead? Couldn't he just join Toastmasters or something?''

''Oh, Skip, you're the funniest thing.''

''What makes you think it's a man?''

''A man?''

''You keep saying 'he.' ''

''Oh, I know it is.''

"How do you know?"

"Once again speaking as a therapist, it's not a woman's crime."

"How's that?"

"Well, for one thing, he calls himself the Axeman. What woman would do that?"

A clever one. One trying to fool somebody. Or a crazy one. You, maybe. Skip took a bite to avoid having to answer.

"For another, he strangles. A woman wouldn't be strong enough."

Goose bumps broke out on Skip's arms. Her scalp prickled. "Who do you think is doing it, then?"

"Abe." Di's eyes were bland, her voice matter of fact.

"Why Abe?"

"Intuition."

"Wait a minute. That was a pretty strong statement. It must be more than intuition."

"No. Just a feeling." She smiled without showing teeth and Skip knew why—they probably had canary feathers stuck between them.

"Tell me something. I never get feelings like that. Would I if I knew hypnosis?"

"Oh, sure. It can really put you in touch with your inner self."

"Not to be confused with my higher power." She was sorry the instant she said it. But Di seemed barely to notice. "Same difference."

"How would I go about learning? Could I do self-hypnosis?"

"Not only could but should—it's the only way to go. You could learn from books. And there's lots of good tapes available."

"How about a hypnotherapist? Wouldn't that be the best way?"

"That would be good." But she didn't seem entirely convinced. In fact, Skip got the idea she was a little uncomfortable.

"Can you recommend one?"

"Gosh, I really can't. But you could try the phone book. I'm sure there must be lots of good ones still practicing."

"Well, who trained you?"

"That was so long ago. . . ." She let the thought trail off and her face went vague, but Skip kept intense eyes on her. It did no good. She only smiled the toothless smile again.

"Gosh, Di, you've never told me about that part of your life." She knew she was being transparent, but she was getting the idea that Di was so self-involved, she didn't take in information like other people.

"Oh, well, I was very successful. I had patients standing in line, practically. And I made a lot of money too."

"I thought Walt supported you."

This time she gave Skip a smile with some teeth in it. "He does. I spent it all—all the work money. Going to Europe and things."

"Where did you work?"

"Oh, out of my home mostly. Most therapists do."

"You never had a job-type job?"

"Oh, sure. I worked at a little place out on Airline Highway. I don't even know if it's still there." She shuddered. "Worst experience of my life."

"Why?"

"I hate authority. Don't you?"

Skip left feeling disoriented, even a little battered. Di had certainly come up with some innovative ideas, at least in her own mind. Not exactly clever, but transparently self-serving. Skip rubbed her head.

What makes a person so dim?

But she knew the answer—utter self-absorption. And if Di was the Axeman, the self-absorption might work to Skip's advantage. Know-it-alls had to tell people how much they knew; and in doing it, they gave things away. By claiming to

311

be a voodoo priestess, when in fact she'd probably simply read a book about voodoo, she had given away something important—that she was a liar.

Probably she's no hypnotherapist either. In a way it's a shame about that annuity—it's probably kept her from doing anything with her life.

But it certainly hadn't kept her from having fantasies.

If Di was the Axeman, what was her motive? Was it the one she suggested—to get attention? Surely not. Even if that was part of it, there had to be more. Maybe it was something from childhood—she'd been hurt and now she liked to hurt other people. Shrinks were always coming up with that one. Skip sighed.

It's probably right most of the time.

She went back to her office and turned to "Clinics" in the Yellow Pages. There were pages and pages of them. She tried hospitals, then mental health. And sure enough there was a place on Airline Highway: The New Resources Pavilion. She dialed, asked for personnel, and got no answer. Well, it was a Saturday. She asked for administration, and still got nowhere. Finally, in desperation, she said to the operator, "I'm trying to find out about someone who used to work there. Who could I ask on a Saturday?"

"Well, I been here forever. Who was it?"

"Jackie Breaux."

"Lord, yes. Jackie Breaux. Haven't thought about her in ten years."

"What did she do there?"

"She was a nurse."

"Is there anyone there today who might remember her?"

"Let me look." The friendly voice was back in a minute. It was funny, Skip reflected. Some people were wildly suspicious when you weren't up to anything and others were incautiously helpful when they ought to keep their mouths shut. "I'm going to connect you with Suzanne LeHardy. She's been here for umpteen years."

312

LeHardy was the charge nurse on the third floor and she'd worked with Jackie Breaux for two years. Jackie had been a psychiatric nurse.

Skip said, "I've got a job application from her and I'm trying to make a decision over the weekend. Hope you don't mind my calling."

"What can I do for you?"

"Well, there seems to be some confusion. She's applying for a job as a therapist, specializing in hypnotherapy. I thought she worked there in that capacity."

"Did she say that?"

"Maybe I misunderstood. Did she ever assist in hypnosis sessions or anything like that?"

"Not to my knowledge. Well, let me rephrase that: No. Not in any legitimate way."

"Oh, gosh, that sounds ominous."

"Well, Jackie's a good worker, she just . . . doesn't go by the rules."

"Were you her supervisor?"

"For part of the time, yes."

"Do you mind if I ask why she left."

"Oh, gosh, should I tell you? I have a feeling personnel might have its own policy on that. I think you'd better call back Monday."

Skip said she would. If there had been patient abuse, it would certainly help her case.

She went in to see Cappello. The way she told it, Di's door had been not only ajar, but nearly wide open. Skip had seen the scarf in the living room and about that time Di had come home. They'd had lunch, she'd gone to the bathroom and seen the gloves there. She'd seen a typed grocery list on Di's refrigerator, leading to the speculation that maybe she owned a typewriter. She had a criminal record (though she glibly explained it away) and she'd lied about other things. There was the possibility of patient abuse at her job.

Cappello said, "Did you actually see a typewriter?"

313

If Skip said yes, Cappello would want to try for a warrant and that would mean lying to a judge. She wasn't about to do that. "Just the note," she said.

Cappello shrugged. "I hate to take a chance on a warrant at this point, but bring her in and talk to her. See if she'll admit to having a typewriter and let us compare it with the Axeman's notes."

Skip thought she should have been exultant on the way back to Di's, but she wasn't. She wondered what was wrong. Had she gotten too close to Di? Did she like her? Well, yes, she did. Even though Di was a perpetual bullshit machine who thought the world revolved around her, there was something likable about the woman, some sense of meaning no harm. Could you murder three people and still exude that? Maybe, if you were a sociopath. People liked sociopaths, even juries. Why shouldn't Skip?

Di wasn't alone. She was with two uniformed officers.

"Skip. I know you're in homicide," she said. "I didn't want to bother you with this—you know these officers?"

Introductions were made and then Di explained: "After you left, I went through the house one more time, just to make sure nothing was missing. But guess what?" She sounded genuinely puzzled. "I found something that isn't mine. I mean, somebody *was* in here, but they brought something rather than took anything. What kind of burglar is that?"

"What did you find?"

"A typewriter. An old portable typewriter."

Skip felt sweat on her neck, at her waist, her armpits. *Oh, shit.*

"I guess we'd better confiscate it," she said. "We'll get the crime lab to dust it. You wouldn't have any gloves I could borrow, would you?"

"Skip, could I ask you something? What kind of burglar would do this?"

"Are you sure it isn't yours? Maybe you lent it to someone and they returned it."

"I've never even owned a typewriter. And I certainly wouldn't have one now. If I needed something like that, I'd get a computer."

There were no prints on the typewriter. But that was of minor interest considering the real news—it was the one on which the Axeman had written his notes.

I wonder, thought Skip, *if there's a suicide hot line I can call.*

Cappello was as close to losing it as Skip had ever seen her. "Did you actually step into Di's apartment?"

"That's about all I did—stepped in to call Di."

"And that's when Di came home? She actually found you in her apartment?"

"Oh, shit, Sylvia. I've been kicking myself around the block about this. I know what a lawyer could make of it—I planted the evidence, but miscalculated; Di came home too soon."

"Di's thought of that too. Count on it." Cappello spoke through clenched teeth. "Listen, I'm sending someone else to watch Di tonight. You take the night off, okay?"

If Di's the Axeman and she gets off because I screwed up, I'm going to die. I'm just not going to be able to get through it.

In fact, I might die anyway.

She was so depressed she didn't even phone Steve. She went and got a joint from Jimmy Dee, and tried to think of a way out.

Twenty-nine

SUNDAYS WERE GREAT as far as Sonny was concerned. Casualties from the Saturday-Night Knife and Gun Club were more or less taken care of—oh, there might be one or two still lying on gurneys if there was a bed shortage, which there usually was, but they were going to make it. And if they didn't, it wasn't Sonny's fault.

There could be an auto accident, but there probably wouldn't be. Some amateur handyman might cut his hand or something. Maybe a kid would fall and break a leg. An old lady could be sitting in church and notice her ankles were swollen. Everybody'd be too hung over to commit violent crimes.

If every day were like Sunday, he wouldn't have to worry about getting through the damn rotation. He strode in the back door of the hospital, whistling, in a hell of a mood. Hardly a soul stirred in the waiting room. A tired-looking black woman with a toddler at her heels was shaking an old man sitting in a wheelchair near the wall. He had fallen forward in sleep—no telling how long he'd been waiting. "Daddy? *Daddy!* Oh, my Lord, he's in a coma!"

She was hysterical, or maybe nuts, but Sonny was in a great mood. He was supposed to be a healer and this morning he felt like one. He walked over to the woman, thinking to help, and as he did, the old man fell to the floor. Sonny dropped and felt for a pulse. There wasn't one. The man's wrist was cold.

The woman was wailing, "I had to go back home, be with my baby. I couldn't stay; I just couldn't stay. Now my daddy's done gone into a coma and I couldn't be here to do nothin' about it."

Sonny felt as cold as the man on the floor. Woodenly, his arms heavy and mechanical, those of a toy soldier, he started doing chest compressions, knowing there was no use. The triage nurse rushed by, came back with help.

When they had him on a roller, Sonny leaped aboard, straddled him, and kept working, looking into a pair of fixed and dilated pupils. Futilely they went through the motions—the shock, the IV, the tube; when he saw the flat line on the monitor, he didn't even wait for the charge resident to say the phrase "DOA." He stopped working, and left, his own chest constricted. He had thought of going out again, to get out in the air, but he'd forgotten the man's daughter would still be in the waiting room.

"My daddy? My daddy?" she said, unable to ask the question.

"I'm sorry."

"I couldn't stay with him; I wanted to, I just couldn't."

"It's not your fault, there was nothing you could do. It was just your daddy's time."

"My daddy ain't dead. He ain't dead! He just in a coma."

He probably shouldn't be dead. Probably wouldn't be if he'd gone to a private clinic, if he hadn't been a poor man who'd had to sit for hours in a waiting room, silently slipping through the cracks, dying with no one even noticing.

He left her without another word, went back outside, stood on the ramp, and took deep breaths.

It shouldn't have happened, it shouldn't have happened.

Blood pounded in his ears along with the refrain. *It wasn't my fault; didn't happen on my shift.*

Why couldn't he convince himself?

He went in with a black cloud over his head, engulfing him. Before, he had been quick of step, senses alert, a healer. Now he felt as dead as the man on the floor, as depressed and guilty as his daughter. About as much like a healer as the bewildered kid hanging on to her.

The thing wouldn't lift. All morning he went through the motions—asking questions, comforting, helping out where he could—and it was all empty action, all performed by a robot. Sonny was hovering somewhere above himself, not the one doing the work at all.

Missy brought sandwiches at mid-afternoon, and he was surprised to see her, had forgotten she was coming. He wasn't hungry at all.

She said, "Want to go up on the roof?"

"Sure." He was surprised to find that he did, that once more he longed for air, for relief from these yellowish tile walls, from this suffering. He was surprised to find he had any preferences at all.

Knowing he hadn't eaten before he left home, she had brought egg salad on whole wheat, a sort of delayed breakfast. She'd found potato chips without salt (she disapproved strongly of salt), had sliced carrot sticks, and had even somehow dug up some peanut butter cookies, his favorite.

He was annoyed by her solicitude. By her relentlessness, by her neediness, by her inability simply to let him be.

She flapped her T-shirt against her skin. "Whoo. A breeze, finally. You have to go this far up to find one. Honestly, I think we'll have to shave that poor little dog of yours—he gets so hot, he just sits and pants. He was so cute after you left this morning. You know what he did? He tried to get up in my lap, but he couldn't reach, so he figured out how to get up on the coffee table and jump on the sofa from there. Wasn't that smart?"

He didn't answer.

"Sonny? Sonny, what is it? You're not even eating your sandwich."

"Missy, you're not my mom."

"I didn't say I was your mom. I'm your girlfriend and I want to know what's going on."

"Nothing's going on."

"Oh, Sonny." She rubbed his thigh, looked pleadingly into his eyes. He could have thrown up. "Don't be like that."

"Missy, would you leave me alone for once? I get so damn tired of your everlasting *loving care*, I could jump off this roof."

"I just want to help." Her voice was low, almost a whisper, and she looked down as she spoke as if in shame, a little girl chastised.

"Well, back off."

"You don't know how bad I feel for you when you're this way. It's as if your pain is my pain—don't you understand that?"

"You know what, Missy? All this helpful mothering you're always doing is really just a bid for attention. You want to feel okay about yourself, so you find somebody to *help*. Well, guess what? It's not very goddamn helpful!"

"Sonny, you're yelling!"

"The more I know you, the more I don't see you growing up. You're stuck in childhood, always looking for that nice daddy you never had—you can't stand to see me sad or moody or anything else for a minute because then I'm not being your damn daddy."

He was starting to gibber, but he couldn't stop himself, couldn't seem to get back on a logical train of thought. He knew he was mad at Missy, even though he might not be too clear about the reasons, and that was good enough. He just wanted to yell, spit out whatever came into his mind, at high volume.

"You think you're the only one in the world who was ever molested? You're making a goddamn career out of it, Missy. When are you going to get over it? It's time!"

"Sonny! Oh, Sonny!"

"I'm sick and tired of having to be so fucking understanding all the time. Oh, Missy's like this because her life's been so hard. She doesn't know when to quit because there weren't any boundaries in her family. Boundaries! Goddamn shrinky word! You taught me to say it yourself. Well, when are you going to get some goddamn boundaries, Missy? When are you going to learn that I'm me and you're you, and to fucking leave me alone once in a while?"

Her fist came down in the middle of his chest. "You fucker!" It was a meaningless insult, two syllables of nothingness, but her tone was as jagged and dangerous as a bread knife.

Sonny! Oh, Sonny! He remembered the desperate look in her eyes as she had said it, realized he hadn't taken it in, and should have.

Her open hand connected with his ear, with the whole side of his head, knocking him sideways. He wouldn't have thought she had that much force in her, couldn't understand what he had unleashed.

Now both hands were fists, pounding him on the shoulders, in the face, hard, harder than was reasonable for a woman her size. "Fucker! Dickhead! Fuckface!"

He was getting creamed. He had his arms up to protect himself, he was trying to grab her flying fists, but she was fast, driven by an unsuspected fury.

"Missy. My God! Oh, Missy—what have I done?"

He thought later that it was the despair in his voice that stopped her. "Missy, I'm so sorry." He held her by her elbows and watched her face turn from furious to frightened. Terrified. She looked at him as if he were Jack the Ripper and broke away.

He reached for her, afraid that something in her had snapped, that she'd run to the edge and jump; but instead she climbed through the window that led back inside, clambering clumsily, bruising her bare legs in her panic. His impulse was to try to follow her, to soothe her, talk her down, but he

320

resisted, knowing she was too far gone, that she hated him right now, that she was afraid of him.

She has good reason.

Sonny thought that he should be the one to jump off the building, that Missy had trusted him and he had betrayed her.

Like what happened with Gan-Gan.

But that wasn't what happened with Gan-Gan.

"You know it was, son. You killed your own grandfather."

I didn't mean to!

"You didn't mean to upset Missy either. But you turned her from the sweetest girl in the world into a violent, cursing harpy."

He hadn't realized how much his father's voice echoed in his own brain.

Later, when the call came, it didn't seem real, it seemed like some crazy part of his mind that had somehow broken out and spilled over into life. His father had never phoned him at work before.

"Sonny, you feeling okay? Missy called, said she's worried about you."

"Missy called *you?*" How dare she! How dare she break the trust between them. They were two against the world, two against a lot of things, firm allies against his father.

Okay. Okay, so she did it out of revenge. I betrayed her, so now she'd betrayed me. Now we're even.

But it didn't feel even. He felt controlled, Missy's marionette, Papa's puppet—pull its strings or push its buttons, no matter, either way it'll fall apart.

"She said you seem awful depressed lately. She on the rag or something?"

"I don't understand why she called you." He did, he just wanted to know what story she'd given him.

"She said you were under terrific pressure from med school, from your rotation—which rotation, son? I don't even know."

"What did she want you to do about it?"

"I don't know. She said she just needed to put it out there."

"Well, now she has."

"I got somethin' to tell you, boy. Get rid of her."

"What?" He had heard it, but he couldn't comprehend. "Get rid of her? Friday night you had our wedding all planned."

"She doesn't want to marry you. She said that Friday night."

"She said what?"

"You gotta face it, boy. For once in your life you gotta act like a grown-up and look at what's happenin' right before your eyes. The girl is not gonna marry you. She's pretty, don't get me wrong. Real pretty thing. Sweet thing. But she's just not wife material. Into that weird religion and all. You've gotta forget her, son."

Even for his father, this was pretty strong stuff. Sonny said, "Dad, I want to ask you a question. I hope you won't take it wrong, but this is pretty weird, what you're saying."

"What do you mean, weird? You're my son, I'm telling you what I know."

"Dad, are you drinking too much?" His face went hot the minute the words were out. He'd never spoken to his father that way.

"What did you say to me?" Furious.

"Well, Mama said she was in Al-Anon. I was just wondering."

"You leave your mother out of this!" He was yelling so loud Sonny had to hold the phone away from his ear.

Sonny said he'd have to call back, his beeper had just gone off. He was shaking when he hung up; the conversation had upset him more than he realized.

He had recognized words from his childhood, a phrase he'd heard a lot after he'd mouthed off, "talked back," his father called it—"What did you say to me?"

It was always shouted, always with eyes narrowed, face

suffused, belt in hand, buckle out "so it'll really hurt." It had to be answered. If Sonny didn't answer, his father would beat him until he said the words again, and then would beat him for saying them. If he did answer, they could skip the preliminaries.

Missy hadn't even called first, had driven to Di's without even thinking about it. She had to talk to her; of course Di would be there for her.

And Di was. Of course she was.

She greeted Missy from her balcony, fresh in a pair of pink shorts, holding a glass of something that looked like lemonade. Missy felt a twinge of jealousy. *All she needs is a picture hat.*

Di would probably look as if she'd just come back from a pedicure and facial if bombs were falling on the city. Missy was suddenly aware that she hadn't washed her hair since yesterday, and she was getting a pimple on her chin. She had chosen Di to be her sponsor in Coda because she admired her so much it was like hero worship—and she felt concomitantly intimidated. Like she couldn't measure up in a million years.

Even with all that was on her mind, she said almost involuntarily, "You look terrific, Di! How do you do it?"

"Really? I've spent the whole day down in the dumps about feeling so ugly." Absently, she poured Missy a lemonade and handed it to her, not offering first, behaving like a mother whose kid has come in hot and sweaty. "You remember that new guy who came to the meeting Thursday? Steve? He was at the meeting I went to last night, but I just couldn't get him interested. I feel about a million years old."

"He must be crazy. You look like a million dollars." But even as she spoke, she felt a twinge of resentment. *What about me?*

"Really?" said Di. "Do you honestly think that?"

"You're gorgeous. Everybody says so."

"Yes, but you. Right now. Do you really think so?" She held up a hand. "Look closely before you speak. Look at my neck and under my eyes."

What the hell's wrong with her? Missy thought. And then it dawned on her that something was. Di wasn't herself. Without thinking, she went into helper mode; this was what she did best and often she did it unconsciously. "What's the matter, Di? You seem really down."

"I don't know what's wrong. I eat nothing but live food. I never cook anything. I don't know why it's not working."

"You're on a diet? You haven't lost as much weight as you wanted?" She looked doubtfully at Di's perfect proportions.

"Oh, Missy. Oh, Missy." They hadn't left the kitchen—had been standing companionably, lemonades in hand—so there wasn't a box of tissues handy and Di had to grab for a paper towel. Before she applied it to her features, Missy saw them twist in misery. Di turned away and sobbed, probably, Missy realized, so she couldn't see her looking ugly. "Missy, I'm getting old."

"Old?" Missy didn't get it.

"I found this guy really attractive, but when I talked to him, I gave him my best smile, flirted, and everything, I realized he was just being polite. I might as well have been his mother."

Missy couldn't suppress a giggle. "His mother? Oh, Di, I don't think so."

"I have something to say to you, Missy. It's the sort of thing I don't say because I don't talk about age, I don't think it's important. But today I think it's important."

"What is it, Di?"

"I have a feeling that young man is twenty years younger than I am."

Twenty years! What was with Di? She couldn't possibly be twenty years older than anyone, that was ridiculous. And Missy guessed the new guy was quite a bit older than she herself was—he could be thirty, maybe.

She laughed. "Di, you must have found the Fountain of Youth."

"Missy." She looked terrified. "Missy, what if there isn't one?"

Thirty

SKIP KNEW THAT if she had too many Diet Cokes, she'd have to go to the bathroom and maybe miss Di if she came out. But it was hard to pace yourself when you had all day. And she had to face the fact that the day was quickly dwindling. So far she had had exactly one glimpse of her quarry— when Di had come out on the balcony to speak to Missy. Now Missy had gone, and she was Di's only visitor of the day. It made for a boring Sunday.

And the thing that happened when you were bored was that you thought about things. You couldn't stop thinking about things. You couldn't make your mind stop because your butt was sore and you didn't want to think about that. As long as your suspect stayed inside, there wasn't anything to watch, so you couldn't think about what was actually happening. You'd already thought about sex until the subject had all the vitality of a discarded condom. And thoughts of food only made you hungrier. So things were what was left. Meaning the case.

Which was starting to be a sore subject because Skip was so angry at herself. What had seemed so obvious yesterday now seemed as phony as your corner S&L. What had seemed utterly damning evidence now seemed fraudulent. What had seemed a diabolically clever move on Di's part—calling the cops about the typewriter—now had another possible explanation. She had almost completely switched over to the theory that Di was being set up.

There were a few delicate little questions she needed to ask, but now that Di knew she was a cop, she didn't think she'd get any answers. The microscopic inquiries would seem so threatening, she'd clam up and call a lawyer. But sitting there sipping her long-running and ever-warming Diet Coke, she conceived a brilliant plan. Well, perhaps not brilliant, but she gave herself points for creativity.

It was simple. First of all, Di obviously had a crush on Steve. And Steve, often to her regret and inconvenience, had out-of-control detective fantasies. Why not put both these situations to perfect use? Why not, in fact, have Steve go in as her proxy? Ask the questions she couldn't?

Maybe it's sensory deprivation. Maybe I'm just desperate to talk to him.

She tried, but she couldn't talk herself out of it. She phoned and asked him to meet her at the bar, and when he walked in wearing khaki shorts and a magenta T-shirt, her stomach flopped over the way it had when Bo Chantlan had shot a rubber band at her at Sunday school in the fifth grade. How did she stand it when he wasn't here? How the hell had her vacation gotten so screwed up?

"Hi, handsome."

"From you that's a compliment."

"What's that supposed to mean?"

"I get the feeling you really don't say that to all the guys."

"Yeah, you right, as we say down here."

"I know I'm right. Compliments aren't your strong suit."

Weren't they? But she couldn't let herself get distracted now. "Steve, I need your help."

"Anything."

She explained what she wanted.

To her surprise, he balked. "I don't know. I just don't know."

"What! You usually have to be physically restrained from playing detective."

"I love the way you restrain me."

"Next time I'm using handcuffs." Flirting sure beat the hell out of staring into space. She pulled herself together. "Wait a minute. What's wrong? I thought you were going to jump at this."

"That woman gives me the willies."

"Oh, come on. If I can sit here all day looking at her door, you can take a half-hour of astro-chat."

"I didn't really tell you the whole story. She got pretty physical."

Skip settled back in a pout. "Oh, great."

"Hey. You're jealous."

"Don't be ridiculous." She meant it. And she was shocked at the realization. She was actually very secure about Steve, really believed he loved her. When had that happened?

Anyway, jealousy wasn't the reason she was pouting. It was because this news bolstered her theory all the more. "Look," she said, "the way you told the story before, it looked as if she was using you as an alibi. But this way's different—if she really thought she was going to seduce you after the meeting, she wasn't going to have time to kill anybody."

"You said yourself maybe she kills when she's sexually frustrated."

"Yes, but I never had a lot of faith in it. Tell me the truth. Do you honestly see Di as a killer?" This was unfair because he didn't know about her rap sheet.

He thought about it. "On the surface she seems too flaky, but a lot of flakes can get it together when they need to."

"Oh, hell. Well, let me appeal to your sense of justice. I think she's innocent. I think someone's trying to set her up,

327

that someone being someone who's already killed three people.''

''All right, all right.''

''You'll do it?''

''Yes, but here's what I'll expect in return. . . .'' When he had told her, and she had fought down the urge to simper like an Ole Miss girl, they went over his cover story.

Di looked great when she came out on the balcony. She was wearing shorts that showed off smooth thighs, slim ankles, gorgeous legs. The combination of dark, dark hair and white, white skin gave her an indescribably delicate look, like a porcelain figure, endlessly fascinating in its fragility. Shadows seemed to form on white expanses of neck and chin, faint blue ones that were probably illusions caused by the outlines of veins.

If only she wouldn't open her mouth.

''Hey, gorgeous,'' he said, and congratulated himself on remembering the Southern ''hey'' for ''hi.'' ''You want to be in a movie?''

When she had let him in to discuss the situation, he said, ''Did I ever tell you I'm a filmmaker?''

''A producer?''

She had sat him on her Victorian settee and he felt large and awkward, beset by pillows. She sat next to him, with a decent amount of air between the two of them, but not so much that he couldn't smell her perfume. Why would she be wearing perfume on a quiet Sunday at home?

She wasn't. She put it on while I was coming upstairs.

That should have heartened him, made him sure of his success, but he felt uneasy about what he was doing. Fraudulent.

And I was once a reporter. How times change.

''Not a producer,'' he said. ''That's far too grandiose a title for the kind of films I do—small ones. Twenty-minute, thirty-minute masterpieces that make the rounds of the festivals and even win occasionally."

One will win sometime. He had made only three.

"I've decided to do an Axeman film—if I can get the money for it. Anyway, that's what I meant about being in movies: I'd love to interview you when the time comes."

"Is that really why you're here, Steve?" There was no mistaking her tone. It was that of a woman who was used to being appreciated. He ignored it.

"Not really. I'm here because I heard about your typewriter."

"My typewriter? But I don't have a typewriter."

"The one you called the police about. I started talking to some cops for the film, and they told me the Axeman's letters were typed on it."

She gasped. "Oh, my God. He was in here."

"How did he get in, Di?"

"I must have left the door unlocked."

"And if you didn't? Does anyone else have a key?"

"No! Well . . . I don't know."

"What do you mean?"

"Oh, nothing. I don't know." She was starting to fall apart.

"Know what else they told me? He didn't strangle Jerilyn with his hands—he used a scarf."

She gasped again, and this time he could see she was frightened. The scarf meant something to her.

"It was a cotton scarf made in India, a long striped one they said, in reds and pinks."

"Oh, my God. Oh, my God. Oh, my God."

"What is it?"

"I have one like that."

"Di, are you okay? Do you want me to get you some water or something?"

"Oh, my God."

"Hold it. Are you afraid you're a suspect? Listen, if you've got a scarf like that, you can't be the Axeman, right? Because his scarf's around Jerilyn's neck.''

"I lost it. I left it somewhere." Her voice dropped to a whisper. "With my lipstick."

"With your lipstick? You left your scarf and lipstick somewhere?''

She nodded.

"Where?''

But Di didn't answer, just sat there as if in shock. He had to hand it to Skip, she was definitely on to something. He got up, as if pacing, went straight to the book Skip had mentioned, and plucked it from the shelf. "I have this too,'' he said. "I got it because it has the Axeman story in it.''

"What is it?'' she said.

He handed it over to her.

"This isn't my book.''

"Whose is it?''

"I don't know. I don't know how it got here.''

He made his voice very concerned, nauseatingly sanctimonious: "Have you been having blackouts, Di?''

"No! Listen, you have to go now." She rose to emphasize the point.

But he had an odd feeling that if he did, she would phone the person she was protecting, give him a chance to wriggle out, and probably endanger herself. He stood, but instead of going, he walked to the French doors, the ones that led to the balcony.

"Steve? Steve, what are you doing?'' There was fear in her voice. Perhaps she thought he meant to close them, had decided he was the Axeman.

He stepped onto the balcony and signaled Skip in the bar across the street. She stepped into the light.

"There's Skip,'' he said. "Were you expecting her?''

"Skip? Oh, my God. Skip?'' Di joined him on the balcony.

"Skip!'' called Steve. "Come up.''

330

Di rushed to let her in, apparently having decided her presence wasn't the worst idea in the world—perhaps she was still afraid of him. Or perhaps she just wasn't thinking clearly.

Steve didn't give her a chance to gather her wits. "Skip, whereyat?" he said as if he hadn't seen her in a week or two. He didn't give Di a chance to wedge a word in. "Skip, Di says she lost her scarf and her lipstick."

"Lipstick," said Skip. "Fiesta, right? He wrote the *A* in Fiesta."

"Oh, Jesus." She had scrunched her hands into semi-fists and wedged them up against her mouth, maybe trying to get it to stay shut. "Oh, Jesus, Mary, and Joseph. What's going on? What's going on here?"

Skip said, calm as a Valium addict: "Someone's setting you up, Di. He strangled Jerilyn with your scarf, and then he wrote the *A* with your lipstick. Or did you do it yourself?"

"No!"

"Then he planted the typewriter."

"And the book," said Steve.

"And the book. You think he's a friend of yours, but he's trying to get me to arrest you. You probably gave him the keys yourself."

"No!" She had crossed her arms under her breasts, her hands holding her elbows so tightly they looked like claws. "I left my extra set on the table." She indicated a dark, carved one. "I keep it there and when someone comes, I throw it to them from the balcony. It's gone, though. I wondered if he forgot to give it back."

"Who, Di? Who? Alex?"

"Alex?" She wrinkled her brow as if trying to remember who on earth Alex was. "Not Alex. Sonny. I was at his house. I forgot some things—I put on fresh lipstick—" She interrupted herself. "That's why he didn't come Thursday! I went by his house twice, once after I left PJ's and then when Steve left. He was going to follow me home, but he didn't. He just left me at PJ's. Oh! Steve, I didn't mean—"

331

Steve said, "Missy didn't lose her keys. He came back to make sure Abe was still there."

"I've got to go," said Skip.

What she needed were Di's keys. But she needed a search warrant to get them. Okay, okay. She'd get one. But first Sonny. He wasn't under surveillance. Somehow, she felt desperate to find him, just to pin him down, to know where he was before she called Cappello.

She went back to the bar and called the hospital. He'd been there, but he'd gone home sick. She said she was Missy and asked how long ago he'd left. An hour.

Then he ought to be home. But he wasn't. At least he didn't answer his doorbell. She tried phoning and got no answer.

Missy's?

As she was standing on the porch, about to ring the bell, the door burst open and Skip found herself face to face with Alex.

"I wouldn't go up if I were you. I came to return a book I borrowed. Sonny just got there and he's in an awful mood."

A book. Sure. You hoped to find Missy alone. She smiled. "Probably because of me. I asked him to meet me here, and he sounded like he had better things to do."

Alex held the door for her. Skip went up the stairs and stood for a moment outside Missy's aunt's apartment, not wanting to knock, hoping to hear what was going on, to make sure it wasn't violence. She felt her hand going to her purse, snapping it open just in case.

Missy was talking. "Oh, Sonny, I feel so awful. I've never done anything like that in my entire life. I don't know if I'm losing my mind or what. I'm out of control. I called my therapist, but he wasn't in, and then I went to see Di—"

"No, Missy, I'm the one who should be apologizing." It was Sonny's voice. "I was like that, like the way I was,

332

because somebody else died this morning and I felt really horrible about it.''

"At the hospital? You mean you lost a patient?''

"I didn't exactly lose him, I made him die. I make a lot of people die, there's something about me.''

"Sonny!''

"But I can make it right. I can stop it. I have to get the atonement right, that's all. I'm still fine-tuning the atonement. See, it happens when I try to help them. If I try to help them, they die.''

"Sonny, don't be ridiculous. Every doctor loses patients. You make it sound as if you never save anybody, as if that's not what being a doctor's all about. I don't see why you're so down on yourself.''

"It's that way for other people. It's different for me. It's getting so all I have to do is touch them, like that old man this morning. I thought it was a fluke the first time it happened. I thought all I had to do was atone with a blood sacrifice, like I had to do that other time. And I tried to be kind. I know I was kind. I deliberately chose someone unimportant. Anyway, it was meant to work like that. She asked me to go for coffee at the right time—just after the first one died. You had your car and so I could take her. The only thing I didn't have was gloves; I had to drop by the hospital and get some, but she didn't mind. She thought she had a new boyfriend.

"No harm was done that time. Nobody knew her, she didn't know anybody. And it was a life for a life. You know it had to be that way. It's the only way to stop the killing.''

"Sonny. Sonny, we have to get you some help.''

"But it wasn't to be, it didn't work. I mean, it didn't work permanently. Before, it worked for twenty-two years. I don't know what went wrong, but I knew when it happened again, it had to be done again. But this time it wasn't happenstance. I planned it. I called Tom from the phone list—just called and asked him to meet me for coffee. I knew nobody knew him and he didn't know anybody. But he was more important than she was. He didn't have friends, but at least he had a daughter. I thought he was the one.''

''Sonny, stop!''

''And then I had a really good idea. I thought I could make the sacrifice first, and then my patients would be safe. I thought if I killed a lot of chickens, it would be the same as one person. But you can't do it that way. The sacrifice has to be second. You can't atone if you haven't done a crime yet. I should have known that.'' He was talking very fast, getting something off his chest that had been sitting there squeezing his lungs.

''And then I realized it couldn't be someone unimportant; it had to be someone very important. Someone who'd really be missed. Someone young, someone very, very innocent who'd never done anything wrong in her life, someone a lot of people loved. So when Abe said he had a baby-sitter, I knew she was the one. See, there wasn't anybody in the group who was young enough, who matched up right; it had to be somebody outside the group. Yet the group was the sacrifice pool. I already knew that. Because it was anonymous. It was there. All past events had shown that was correct.

''And so the baby-sitter was the one. I thought for a minute it might be one of his children, but that couldn't be. Because you'd have to kill the baby-sitter to get to the kid. Do you see that? Only one sacrifice was required. You understand that, don't you?''

Missy was making wheezing noises, as if she had asthma.

''It's not numbers you need. You need the right sacrifice. But it happened again today, so I know it can't just be a young person, it has to be someone even more precious than that. It has to be someone you love.''

''Sonny, this is just too silly for words. You're so over-tired, you're so freaked out by that crazy father of yours—''

''Don't say anything against my father!''

334

"Sonny, all doctors lose patients."

"Oh, no. They save people. And I will too after this, Missy. I can't tell you how sorry I am about this, but it's got to be done."

"You can't mean . . ."

"Oh, Missy, I'm so sorry."

". . . what I think . . ."

"I love you, Missy."

". . . you mean."

Skip was paralyzed. Should she try to get help? Yes, by all the rules. But she didn't dare leave, even for a second. She was Missy's only lifeline and she knew it.

Was the door locked? Bound to be. If she tried to kick it in and it didn't give right away, Sonny would be warned. He'd have a little time before she got in. Too much time.

"Sonny, no! No!"

He must have attacked her. Skip kicked, the door gave.

Sonny was standing close to Missy, but not holding her, apparently having let her go.

"Freeze or I'll blow your fuckin' head off!"

He stared at Skip, but only for a second. He ran into the bedroom and his leg was just going over the sill, out the already-open window, by the time she'd followed. He had a lead of only a second or two but it was enough. She watched him land on a bush, jump off, and start running. "Stop, goddammit! Freeze or I'll shoot!"

But she was bluffing. He was unarmed. Which meant there was only one thing to do—follow him out the window.

"Missy!" she yelled. "Call for back-up. Ask for Sylvia Cappello!"

She was still debating what to yell next—Geronimo or bombs away—when she realized she'd already landed; she was sliding off the shrubbery, and nothing seemed to be broken. She was in a narrow space between houses. She turned toward the street as Sonny had done.

She had help! Sonny was running down the street, was

already halfway down the block, but someone was giving chase. Alex. Oh, great. Just what she needed.

"Alex, get out of the way!" she yelled as she pounded after them.

But Alex was gaining on him, was almost upon him. He wasn't about to stop.

Skip yelled, "Sonny, freeze!" but she was pissing in the wind and she knew it.

And then to her amazement he did freeze. He simply stopped and turned around, seemingly calm as a cat. The problem was, Alex was still in the way.

Suddenly, things looked different. Alex had been about to jump Sonny, but he stopped and sidestepped, like there was a wire stretched across the road at neck level. Sonny struck at him. Alex backed away. Sonny ran at him with his fist at chest level. Alex turned his back on him, obviously rethinking the whole thing, intending to run the other way, but Sonny grabbed him around the neck, jumped on his back.

"Let me go!"

What the hell was happening? Skip couldn't tell.

Sonny said, "Come one step closer and I kill him."

She stopped so fast she practically skidded, painfully aware of the comic aspect of it, but trying desperately to keep her balance; if she went down, she was out of control. If she wasn't already.

And she saw, as she focused on Alex, that she was. Sonny's hand, tight around his neck, was holding a small blade at his jugular.

"It's a scalpel," Sonny said. "Do you know how sharp these things are?"

Thirty-one

THE SIRENS OF the first black-and-whites sounded in the distance, and when they had arrived, and the officers had come to take her place for a moment, she literally limped back to the car, feeling the weight of her now-drenched hair and clothes.

She had stood for only a few minutes with her gun pointed at Sonny, while neighbors came out and went back in, but she could truthfully say they were the worst few minutes of her life. It was bad enough trying to focus on Sonny, putting everything into keeping him from making a move, trying to be damn sure she didn't let him hurt Alex. But in addition there had been the neighbors, of whom she could get only glances out of the corners of her eyes. She'd had to hope none of them had a gun and none of them took it into their heads to shoot her. She'd had to keep shouting that she was a police officer, to "go back inside *now*!" knowing that her outfit—baggy khaki pants, sandals, and tank top—didn't help her image.

Her butt fell to the seat of the black-and-white, with no help from the rest of her body. She had to fight to keep from leaning over, resting her head on the dashboard. But she couldn't; it would give away how close to collapse she was. She was reaching for the radio as Cappello pulled up.

"Joe's on the way," she said. "I've already ordered the block closed off."

Skip rubbed her forehead. "Hostage negotiators?"

"I didn't know we needed them."

Skip gestured. "He's got Alex; how's that for irony?"

Quickly, she ran down what had happened, then went to see about Missy and call Cindy Lou. Missy was staring out the window, pale, unmoving. Skip thought she was a good candidate for Cindy Lou's ministrations, but she wasn't ready yet to start picking up the pieces. There was still hard work to do.

"He didn't mean it," Missy said. "He's just overtired. He didn't really mean it."

"Missy, listen to me. You've had a bad shock, but you can't let yourself pretend it didn't happen. You have to be strong for a little while longer."

Missy seemed to draw strength from the notion that some-one wanted something from her. "Is there something I can do?" she said, and there was hope in her voice.

"Maybe. But first I want you to drink something."

Skip went and got her some juice. When Missy had drunk it and some of her color had returned, Skip said. "I heard a lot of what he said."

"About killing his patients?"

"Yes."

"You know, his family blames him for his grandfather's death. He was . . ." Her face started to go, her voice caught in a sob, but she stopped till she could untwist her muscles, speak normally. "He was four years old at the time."

"Jesus." Skip was all too familiar with the principle of blame. She'd seen families where the father was so wasted on crack he was barely recognizable as a human being and he'd say it was all his wife and kids' fault for nagging and crying. She knew a girl at McGehee's who hadn't been out a single afternoon or evening since the ninth grade, when she'd "disgraced the family" by cutting school one day and getting caught. As it happened, her father had been simul-taneously involved in a public bribery scandal, but the girl was the one who got blamed for "disgrace." Skip had grown up herself with a father who never made a mistake that wasn't followed by "Look what you made me do!"

Finding someone else to blame was part of being a Southerner, as Cindy Lou had so rudely remarked.

And so was cruelty. The crack dad had beaten his wife and kids. The McGehee's girl had been deprived of an adolescence. Skip's own nice doctor dad usually took a swing at whoever had made him make a mistake. (More interesting, multi-layered punishments were reserved for more serious crimes.)

So she knew that if Sonny had been blamed for something as large as a death, there was probably cruelty attached to it, cruelty on a scale that would make a war criminal wince. Di's story had said plenty about his father, about his arrogance, his lack of feeling—in fact, how he'd tried to make it her fault he'd screwed up her surgery. Maybe the whole family was like that.

After all, they're all doctors.

But she banished the unworthy thought.

The horror of the whole thing, the thing she couldn't get past, was that whatever had happened, it had happened when he was four years old. She knew Sonny'd killed three people, including a teenager, and had heard him threaten to kill his own girlfriend, but thinking about what he'd been through, her heart went out to him. Not to the real Sonny, the monster he'd become, but to the former Sonny, the toddler who'd been accused of killing—and now was trying to wipe the slate clean by killing a few more people.

Crazy.

She saw Cindy Lou pull up. "Come on," she said to Missy. "Let's go down. Are you afraid?"

Missy shook her head.

She needed Missy to tell Cindy Lou what she knew, but she had a feeling Missy might be able to help—might be one of the few Sonny would talk to. He'd thought he had to kill her, had meant to and tried to, but the irony (and possibly the saving grace) was that he thought he had to kill her because he loved her.

You always hurt the one you love.

Yeah, but the point is he does love her.

By now, the entire block was sealed off, neighbors having been escorted out of their homes in case there was gunfire. Joe had arrived and wore a worried look. He was wiping perspiration from his face. A hostage negotiator with a megaphone was trying to talk to Sonny. Alex looked as if he'd dipped his face in white powder. As for Sonny, his own face was distorted, ugly—fearful, Skip thought, and that wasn't good. His hand still held the scalpel, steady as any surgeon's.

A man at the end of the block was creating a disturbance, trying to get across police lines. As she and Missy talked to Cindy Lou, she tried to ignore him, but his voice was getting louder and louder. When she heard him say, "That's my son, dammit!" her stomach did one of its flips. How had Lamar found out?

But it wasn't Lamar. Missy heard it too, and without another word ran to him. "Damn you!" she shouted. "Damn you, Robson Gerard! Damn you and your stupid fundamentalist meanness. Damn you for what you did to him!"

She had her hands raised as if to fight, to scratch at his eyes, perhaps, but she couldn't get past the policeman he was talking to and ended up flailing at air.

Skip, walking toward them, heard Robson say, "Young lady, I am not a fundamentalist," and would have laughed if she'd had any sense of humor left.

She said, "Missy, this isn't helping things." As if word had come down from Mount Sinai, Missy lowered her hands and shut up.

To the cop Skip said, "Let him in." And to Robson, "We need to talk."

Skip sent word to the hostage negotiator, who asked if

340

there was anyone Sonny wanted to talk to—Missy was there; his dad was there.

Sonny said no. And that was all he said. He didn't want to talk, didn't want to leave, it looked like, just seemed to want an excuse to cut Alex's throat.

Cindy Lou, who after all had a couple of graduate degrees in psychology, pulled out all the stops to put Robson at his ease—or relative ease, under the circumstances—and said a powwow was called for, up at Missy's. Would that work for Missy?

Missy nodded as if hypnotized. Robson also nodded. Skip was ready to try anything.

But as they turned and started to leave, Sonny spoke for the first time except to say no. "Missy! Missy, I want to talk to you!"

Stunned, Missy turned toward him. "Sonny!"

Not the most brilliant comeback of the century, but Skip winced at the raw emotion of it. It was in her eyes too. She loved him. Even knowing what she knew, she loved him.

"I want to tell you what happened. Nobody ever believed me. I want to tell you. I want to tell everybody here. Is everybody listening?"

Missy said, "I'm listening, Sonny."

Other than that, the quiet was impenetrable.

"Gan-Gan told me I was the only one who could save him. He said he was going to die if he didn't get the medicine. He said all the doctors were wrong—he was the only one who knew what could save him and they wouldn't give him enough of the medicine. But if I gave it to him, he'd get well."

At Skip's ear, his dad said, "Bullshit!"

She said, "What really happened?"

"The boy was just careless, that's all. He gave his grand-dad his medication—that was one of his jobs. It was how we got him to learn how to tell time. He'd wait for the time for the medicine, and get it, and give the dose, and then take it back."

"Pretty big responsibility for a little kid."

"He comes from a medical family, Officer."

"Well, I still don't understand what happened."

"It's obvious, isn't it? He forgot to put it back; the next time my father was in pain, he got confused and took too many. That's why we never left it near him."

"He was in very bad pain?"

"Terrible. Nobody should ever have to see their father suffer the way I saw mine suffer."

"How do you know he didn't say that to the boy? That he'd be cured if he took it all?"

Robson answered angrily, a doctor snapping at a stupid nurse, "Because he wouldn't, that's why."

Skip's guts twisted. *If I feel like this, how could Missy feel?*

Uneasily, she looked to see how she was, and was later grateful for the instinct that made her do it. "Sonny! Oh, Sonny!" Missy started to run toward him.

Skip grabbed her around the waist. "No, Missy."

Sonny shouted, "Stay where you are, Missy! You can't help me and you can't help Alex. I just wanted you to know. I know what my father told you."

Skip still held her, and she was shaking now, her body about to crumple. "Missy, try to hold it together, okay? Can you stand up by yourself? Try."

Obediently, Missy pulled her body up. "Shall I let you go?" Missy nodded.

"Cindy Lou, what if she talks to him, tells him to let Alex go, that we'll give him some help—stuff like that?"

She shrugged. "It's worth a try."

"Lieutenant?"

"Sure," said Joe.

"Missy, are you willing?"

Missy looked unhappy. "But you won't get him help, will you? You'll send him to the electric chair."

"The law's not going to change for him. He'll have to stand trial and he may or may not be convicted, but that'll happen in any case—whether he kills Alex or not. Do you really want him to have another death on his conscience?" She felt a little twinge for manipulating her, but decided to ignore it. She could worry about that later; the point now was to save Alex's life.

Missy nodded, not in answer to the question but in assent. "You're right."

"Sonny!" she yelled. "Sonny, I love you and I want to help you."

Sonny didn't answer.

"Sonny, you have to let Alex go. It won't solve anything to hurt Alex."

Alex jumped and emitted a little cry. A trickle of blood ran down his neck.

Skip hadn't seen Sonny move. From the gasps around her, she gathered no one else had either.

"Oh, God!" said Missy.

"Let's go in," said Cindy Lou. "Let's go in right now. We've got to talk."

As Skip and Missy turned to join her, she said to Robson, "You too."

Missy, even in her despair, went automatically to get them some iced tea, and Skip was glad to have her out of the room. She had a feeling Cindy Lou wanted to get into some things with Robson that wouldn't hurt Missy not to know about.

She said what was plaguing Skip as well. "Dr. Gerard, somehow I don't think Sonny's told us the whole story, because I don't think he knows it. Or at least he doesn't know why it's important. What I'm wondering is what happened after his grandfather died."

"What happened? We buried him, what do you think?"

Skip found it hard to believe he could be so unpleasant even with his son surrounded by cops with guns.

"I mean, what happened to Sonny? Surely you didn't let him get away with what he did."

"Of course I didn't. What kind of parent do you think I

am? The boy was punished, of course. Do I honestly seem like a neglectful father?''

''Not at all.'' Cindy Lou showed him a mouthful of teeth you could have used for piano keys. ''I just wondered.'' She paused. ''Something that serious . . . how do you make the punishment fit the crime?''

''Fit the crime is right. I said to him, 'When I get done with you, you're going to know what a serious thing you did; I'm going to teach you what death is all about.' And when I got through with him, he did.''

''How did you do that?''

''Well, first I whaled the living tar out of him, of course. And then I made him go with me to take his dog to the pound. Had this old dog named Zeke we'd had since right after Sonny was born. I said to Sonny, 'Dead means they don't come back. When they're gone, they're gone. And I'm going to show you what I mean.' So we got old Zeke, and on the way there I explained how they kill the dogs—you know how they do it, right?''

''Right,'' said Cindy Lou hastily. ''It's not pretty.''

''Damn betcha it's not pretty, and I wanted that kid to know about it. We got there and I made him take that dog up to the attendant and say, 'I made a mistake that killed my grandfather and I want you to kill my dog, please.' ''

Skip gripped the edges of her chair, her palms wet, a knot of despair lodged in her belly, her throat tight with misery. In a way this was almost worse than listening at the door had been as Sonny confessed to three murders. She hoped Missy didn't come back before Cindy Lou was done, half-wanted to join her herself.

''Was that all?''

''Hell, no. I wanted him to feel it, see it, touch it, smell it. I wanted 'dead' to be more than a word to that kid. I wanted to make sure he'd never forget for one minute what he could do if he wasn't careful. I knew he'd be a doctor one day and how important it was going to be to know that relaxing his vigilance for one second, even one instant, could mean somebody's life. I just wanted him to know what 'dead' meant.

"So what I did was I went out and got a live chicken; I got two, just in case. And don't think it was easy finding them, either. Then I took him out in the back yard and I made him strangle one. Well, it didn't work. Kid went squeamish on me, nearly killed the first chicken, but didn't manage to twist its neck quite enough. I don't know what happened— he paralyzed it, I guess. Just lay there with its eyes open, making terrible noises. I finally had to make him step on its head."

Skip put her hand firmly over her mouth. *What I say three times is true: Police officers do not puke in public.* She said the last part two more times, like a mantra.

"Flat? I mean road kill. Kid started screaming like there was no tomorrow and running around the yard like—you know—a chicken with its head cut off. I thought, 'Good; kid's getting the idea.' Finally had to beat him to get him to shut up."

Missy came in with a tray of drinks.

"You know what?" said Cindy Lou. "I know it sounds crazy, but I drink milk in iced tea. Would you mind . . . ?"

"Of course not." She set the tray down and was gone, the perfect little hostess. "Threatened to beat him some more if he didn't get the second one right."

"The second chicken?"

"Oh yeah, the second chicken. He got it right. Screamed the whole time he was doing it, but he did it." Robson's face was set in a thin, grim line: *It hurt me more than it hurt him.*

"Then when those chickens were stiff, I made him go feel 'em, see what that was like. Then I let 'em stay there a couple days till they started to smell, so he'd get that part too. Then I made him bury 'em."

Skip went into the bathroom and washed her face in cold water. It helped some with the nausea, but her throat remained tight as a lock. She realized she wanted to cry even more than she wanted to vomit, and that that would be even less helpful. She took in a deep breath, then another, sat on the floor, and kept breathing. Finally Cindy Lou came and banged on the door.

Thirty-two

"YOU OKAY?"

Skip opened the door. "I'm great."

"Sure you are. You're the color of that sink. Well, listen, I'd turn pale too if I could. Black's a really good color for a police shrink."

Skip knew Cindy Lou was trying to distract her with banter, but she was too depressed. "I hope to God if I'm a cop for the next nine thousand years, I never hear anything like that again."

Cindy Lou whistled. "This from a woman who sees dead bodies all the time."

"What are we going to do, Cindy Lou?"

"You think the SWAT team'll let me talk to him?"

"Are you kidding? They'll try anything at this point."

Missy and Robson had gone back downstairs. "Damn," said Cindy Lou. "I don't want that animal anywhere near him."

"Sonny probably doesn't remember half that stuff."

"The hell he doesn't! And anyway, it doesn't matter. His unconscious knows, and what do you think's been going around killing people? Not sunny Sonny the cute WASP medical student.''

"Are you saying he's a multiple personality?''

"Nothing that weird, although it's a miracle he didn't shatter into a thousand pieces after what that child went through.'' Cindy Lou shook her head in disapproval. "People are so damn mean down here.''

"Like you don't come from Detroit.''

"I swear I think you people are meaner.''

Under the circumstances Skip couldn't come up with a rebuttal. Cindy Lou said, "I'll tell you something about that kid. I think he got the message right from the start—that it wasn't his grandfather who should have died, it was Sonny all along. If he'd killed Missy, I think he'd have been his own next victim.''

"Well, why the hell is he holding Alex, then? He can't expect to get out of this, and if what you're saying's right, he doesn't even want to.''

"You can be homicidal and suicidal at the same time. And you can be ambivalent even if you're crazy and a murderer. My guess is he doesn't even know himself why he's doing it. It's a safe bet he's terrified and not thinking clearly—after all, when he grabbed Alex, a six-foot cop with a gun was chasing him. But there's a thread of rationality here too—you have to admit it's his only bargaining chip.''

"He can't expect to get anything. How can he bargain?''

"I'll bet he's trying to figure that out right now.''

"Wait a minute, let me make sure I get this. Could you possibly be saying what I think you're saying—that Alex really isn't in much danger?''

"*Au contraire.*'' Cindy Lou's voice rose for emphasis. "I think he's in a hell of a lot of danger. Especially if anything changes, messes up the status quo. Sonny might just panic and start slashing.''

"Oh, shit.''

"Well, let's try to talk to him. There's a couple of pieces

347

of this that don't make any sense at all. Maybe he'll talk about those."

"The *A*'s and the letters, you mean."

"Yeah."

Skip fixed it for Cindy Lou to take over from the hostage negotiator (who seemed delighted with the break), and took the megaphone first. "Sonny, this is a good friend of mine— Cindy Lou Wootten. She's a psychologist and she wants to help you."

"Tell her to stick it where the sun don't shine." Skip almost smiled, it was so Sonny-like—anyone else would have said "up her ass."

Cindy Lou whispered, "He hasn't been answering most stuff, right? We got a sign of life here."

"Oh, terrific."

"I think he's ready to talk. No shit. If we can just keep his goddamn dad quiet."

"So why's he talking now when he wouldn't talk before?"

"You know what I think? Know what I really think? He likes you. Ask him if he'll talk to you."

"Sonny! How about talking to me?"

"I've got nothing to say."

Cindy Lou said, "Okay, good. You've got a great rapport going. Go to it."

Skip took a deep breath, aware of lepidoptera in the intestines. "Sonny, you know what I don't get? You did everything perfectly. We'd have never narrowed it down to the twelve-step programs if you hadn't sent that letter to the TV stations. Why on earth did you do that?"

Sonny said, "You know, Skip, I'm getting pretty damn tired of this."

She could have sworn that Alex, even held as tightly as he was, winced slightly. Perhaps Sonny had gripped him harder, or nicked him. She was getting ready to continue when Robson shouted, "Sonny, don't say anything! They can use it against you later."

"They can't touch me. I'm a doctor."

Oh, brother. "Cindy Lou, what's going on? That doesn't sound like Sonny at all. Are you sure he isn't a multiple?"

"He's starting to break."

"What makes you say that? He sounds like some other person—like . . . "

"His dad."

It dawned on her that that was right. "Yeah."

Cindy Lou shrugged. "Well, why not. His dad's an asshole. Come to think of it, all doctors are assholes. Now that you mention it, we've all got a little asshole in us. Why not Sonny? Damn right it's not like him. That's what he keeps under that golden-boy routine of his. If he'd let it out more . . ."

"Oh, don't say it." She was getting cross.

Into the megaphone she said, "Sonny, I feel like you need to talk. I promise I'll get all the help I can for you when this is over."

"Skip, you know this is no way to treat a doctor. Get me out of here now. Get me a limousine to the airport and a ticket out of here." He paused, thinking. "To the Bahamas."

"Let Alex go."

"You know I can't let Alex go."

"Sonny, why'd you write the letter?"

"I wish to God I'd never written the damn letter! Jesus, I wish I'd never done it!" The arrogant Sonny was gone.

"Why'd you do it, Sonny?"

"I don't know."

Cindy Lou pinched Skip. "Don't answer. Let him think about it a little bit."

The quiet was killing. The air was thick enough to squeeze.

Finally Sonny said, "I thought I ought to."

"Okay, okay," said Cindy Lou. "Let him think about what *that* means."

Skip didn't know much about Cindy Lou's fancy theories

349

of "splits" in non-split personalities, but this was familiar ground, this she had seen before. And it did seem like something split, every time she saw it. It was a more elaborate version of that weird thing that made experienced criminals forget to wear gloves, brag in bars about wasting somebody, tell you they didn't mean to do it before you ever accused them. And half the time the thing they didn't mean to do, the crime they described in detail, wasn't the one they were being questioned about.

It was the mechanism that makes a man park his car outside his girlfriend's house on a day he knows his wife's going to be in the neighborhood. It was the urge to confess, the part of not just every criminal, but every human being, that wants to be caught.

In a few minutes, Cindy Lou said, "Ask him about the Axeman."

Skip said, "Why the Axeman, Sonny? You could have written some other kind of letter."

"I grew up with the Axeman." His voice was very soft. "My grandfather told me about him. It was like the bogeyman. He'd say, 'If you don't be good, the Axeman'll get you.' And sometimes . . . sometimes when I wouldn't go to bed he'd put a sheet over his head and say, 'The Axeman cometh!' "

"And then what?"

"Then we'd roughhouse. He'd tickle me and I'd laugh a lot."

"It was true, wasn't it, Sonny?"

"What?"

"The Axeman got you."

Sonny didn't answer. They waited about ten minutes. Finally Skip said, "Did the *A* stand for Axeman?"

He said something she couldn't hear, that no one could hear.

"What?"

"I didn't mean to do it that way. That wasn't what I wanted.

350

But it happened the first time and I had no choice. Do you see that? After that the Axeman existed. I had to let—''

''You had to what?''

Once again he didn't answer.

''Why did it happen that way the first time? If you didn't want to do it, why did you?''

''The goddamn lipstick broke!'' He sounded furious, and once again Alex made some kind of involuntary movement.

''The lipstick broke? You meant to write something else?''

''I already told you.'' This time he spoke in a conversational tone, not trying to be heard; sounding sullen.

''No you didn't.''

''I told Missy.''

Skip looked at Missy. She shrugged, obviously had no idea what he meant.

''She doesn't remember.''

''I told her.''

''Tell her again.''

He shouted the word as if to be heard in Baton Rouge, and the anguish in it seemed that of every lost soul since the dawn of madness. ''Atonement!''

The sound was like a diamond rubbing against a diamond, harder on the soft evening than anything else on Earth is hard; primitive and ugly and inevitable. Yet the feeling of that tiny terrified child so many years ago was so naked in the shout, it had an underlying innocence, almost a bewildered sweetness, so much did it express about the wish to undo what is done.

It was answered by an answering shout, every bit as hard and ten times as ugly, for it had no anguish in it, nothing resembling innocence, but hatred instead. Evil. It was more a toxin than a sound; spewed slime. ''Asshole!''

Robson spewed it. ''The *A* was for asshole, you asshole. You've always been an asshole, ever since the day you came naked into this world! And you're *still* an asshole! No father deserves an asshole like you!''

351

A sound like a sob came out of Sonny. Slowly, gradually, he lowered the arm around Alex's neck, and then he let Alex's hand go, the one he had held behind his back. As if on eggs, Alex started to walk. Sonny's sobs did not tear the air as his shout had done, as Robson's had. They were like a bass beat that lodged in Skip's body, permeated to her toes. It was the deepest misery she had ever heard or felt.

But Cindy Lou was deep in what she would probably have called denial if she'd had her wits about her. "That's ironic as hell," she said, and walked away.

Skip had burned her uniform once, when she had felt overwhelmed at corruption she couldn't attack; helpless. But that seemed a matter of petty bureaucracy now. This wasn't the city or the state or the department, this was the race. The human animal; the beast. What was she supposed to do now, burn her skin?

The answer came to her almost as quickly as the question. Yes, burn it. Burn it with passion. With love. If it's human beings who disgust you, get as close as you can to one of them. Let the slime pour out of you as your head fills, your body fills, with life and hope. And starting over. And love.

How could she think of love at a time like this? And yet she saw that it was the only sane thing she could think of. She phoned Steve and told him to come get her key, to wait for her. She told him she loved him.

She still had a long night ahead.

By the time she joined him, she knew one more thing she didn't want to: why Sonny had framed Di, had found it so necessary to write the Axeman note that named her lipstick color, arrived so promptly because it was mailed so promptly; was written and mailed after strangling Jerilyn. Who had been carefully killed with Di's scarf, after which the typewriter had been carefully planted.

Such elaborate plans.

Di was the only one of his victims for whom he had no

compassion, whom he truly wanted to destroy. He had planned the frame in the half-hour between the time he realized he hated her and the time he killed Jerilyn. He had to go home for the scarf and lipstick, but the lost time was worth it. Di had committed an unpardonable sin. She had blown the whistle on his father.

Rebecca Schwartz and her friend Chris are asked to auction off a baking family's legendary sourdough starter that has been inherited by Chris's boyfriend. The event attracts national attention, and all the bakers are prepared to bid. But then a series of threatening phone calls and a brutal murder begin to scare off the bidders. Rebecca finds herself racing to catch a killer—and save the sourdough—as she sifts through the tangled relationships of the tightly knit baking community in the never-ending sourdough wars.

THE SOURDOUGH WARS

by Edgar Award–winning

Julie Smith

Finally available in paperback.
Published by Ivy Books.

Be sure to read these
bestselling mysteries by

JULIE SMITH